W9-CJY-948

Date: 7/16/18

J GRA 741.5 TIN
Baltazar, Art.
Tiny Titans. Aw yeah Titans!

tiny titans

AW YEAH TITANS!

Art Baltazar & Franco
writers

Art Baltazar
artist & letterer

TINY TITANS: AW YEAH TITANS!

Published by DC Comics. Compilation Copyright © 2013 DC Comics.
All Rights Reserved.

Originally published by DC Comics in single magazine form in
TINY TITANS 45-50 Copyright © 2011, 2012 DC Comics. All Rights
Reserved. All characters, their distinctive likenesses and related
elements featured in this publication are trademarks of DC Comics.
The stories, characters and incidents featured in this publication are
entirely fictional. DC Comics does not read or accept unsolicited
ideas, stories or artwork.

DC Comics, 2900 W. Alameda Avenue, Burbank, CA 91505
Printed by Transcontinental Interglobe Beauceville, QC, Canada.
6/23/16. Third Printing.
ISBN: 978-1-4012-3812-4

PEFC Certified
Printed on paper from
sustainably managed
forests and controlled
sources
PEFC/01-31-106   www.pefc.org

Library of Congress Cataloging-in-Publication Data

Baltazar, Art.
  Aw yeah Titans! / Art Baltazar ; Franco.
    pages cm. -- (Tiny Titans ; volume 8)
  ISBN 978-1-4012-3812-4 (pbk.)
  1. Graphic novels. I. Aureliani, Franco, illustrator. II. Title.
  PZ7.7.B33Aw 2013
  741.5'973-dc23
                                    2012048789

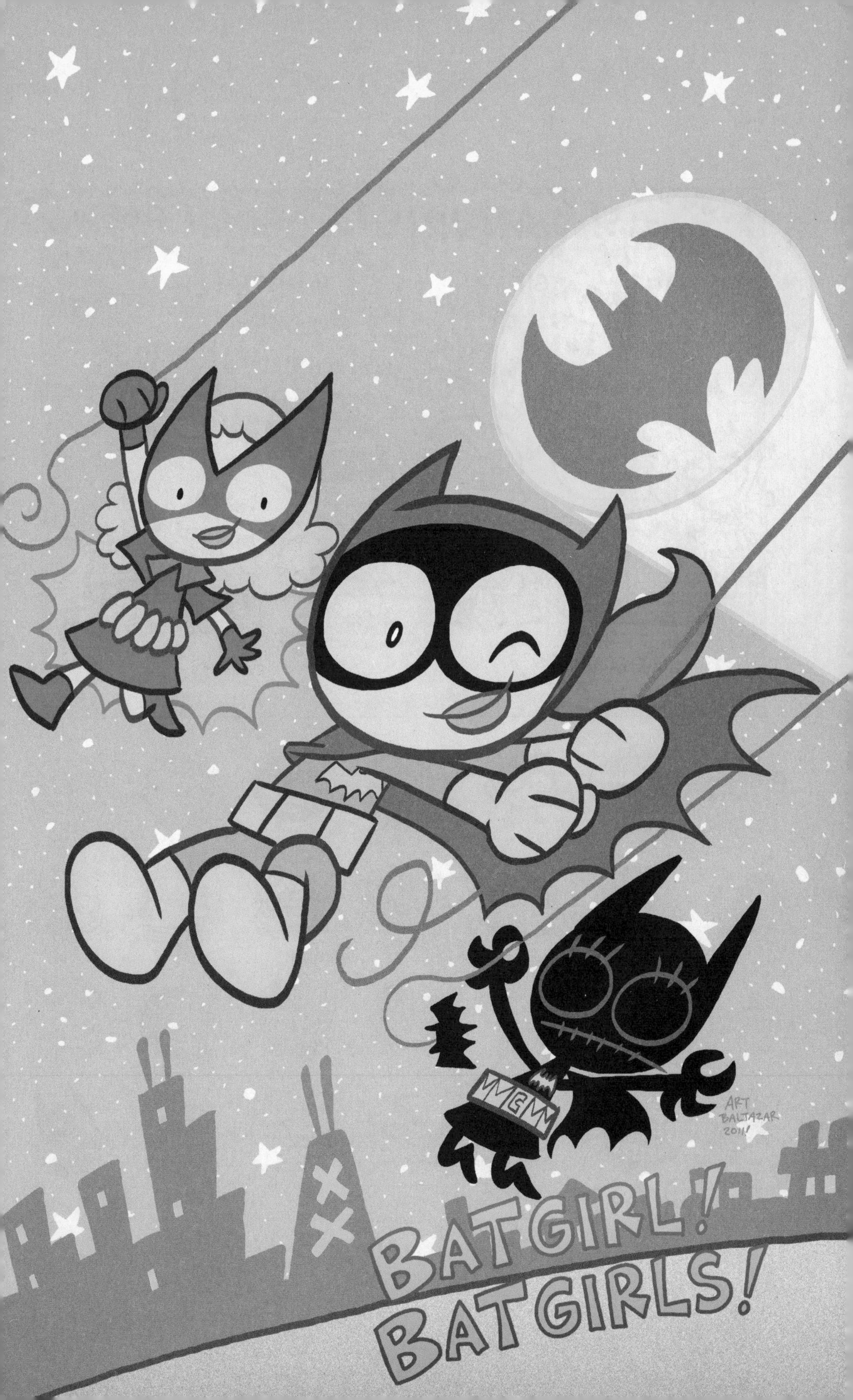

BATGIRL!
BATGIRLS!
ART BALTAZAR 2011!

tiny titans

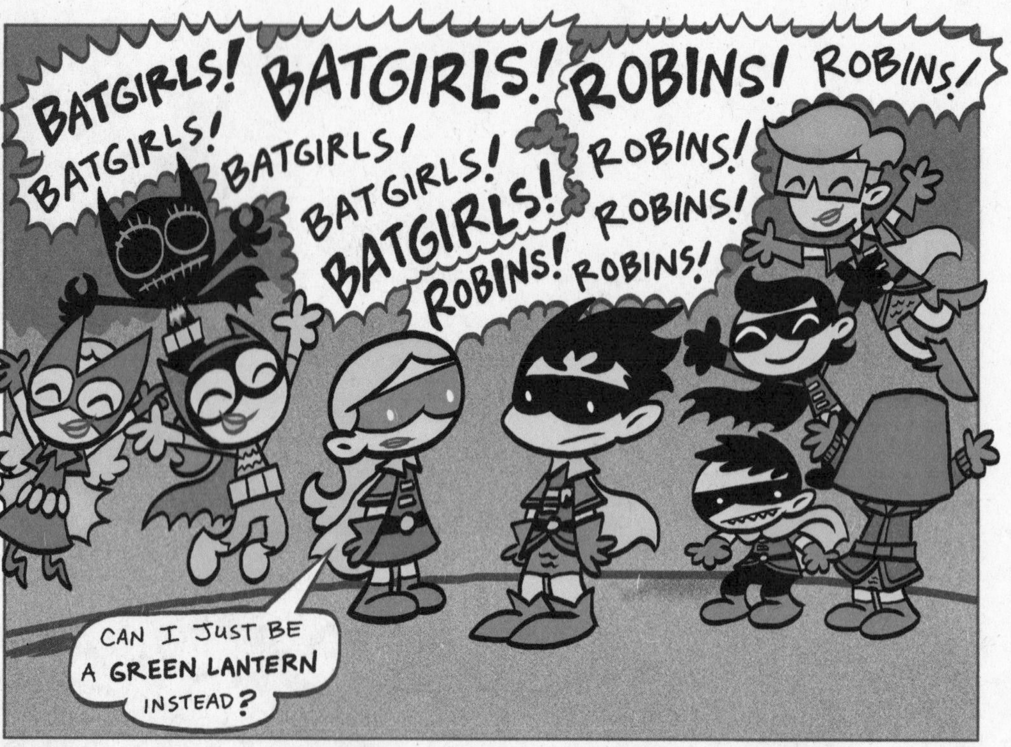
BATGIRLS! BATGIRLS! BATGIRLS! BATGIRLS! BATGIRLS! BATGIRLS! BATGIRLS!
ROBINS! ROBINS! ROBINS! ROBINS! ROBINS! ROBINS!
CAN I JUST BE A GREEN LANTERN INSTEAD?

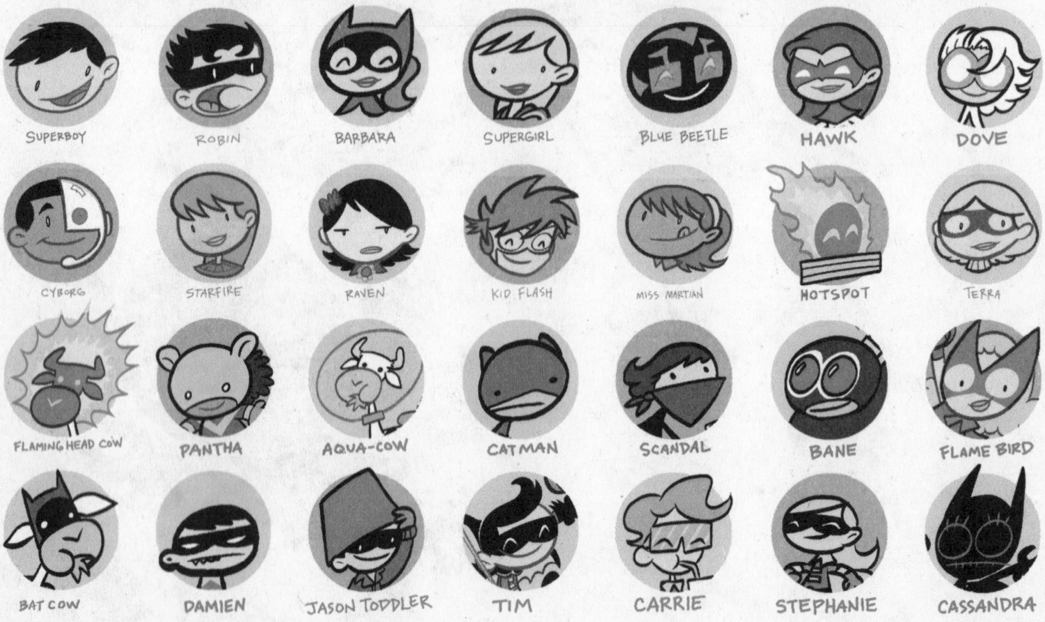
SUPERBOY
ROBIN
BARBARA
SUPERGIRL
BLUE BEETLE
HAWK
DOVE
CYBORG
STARFIRE
RAVEN
KID FLASH
MISS MARTIAN
HOTSPOT
TERRA
FLAMING HEAD COW
PANTHA
AQUA-COW
CATMAN
SCANDAL
BANE
FLAME BIRD
BAT COW
DAMIEN
JASON TODDLER
TIM
CARRIE
STEPHANIE
CASSANDRA

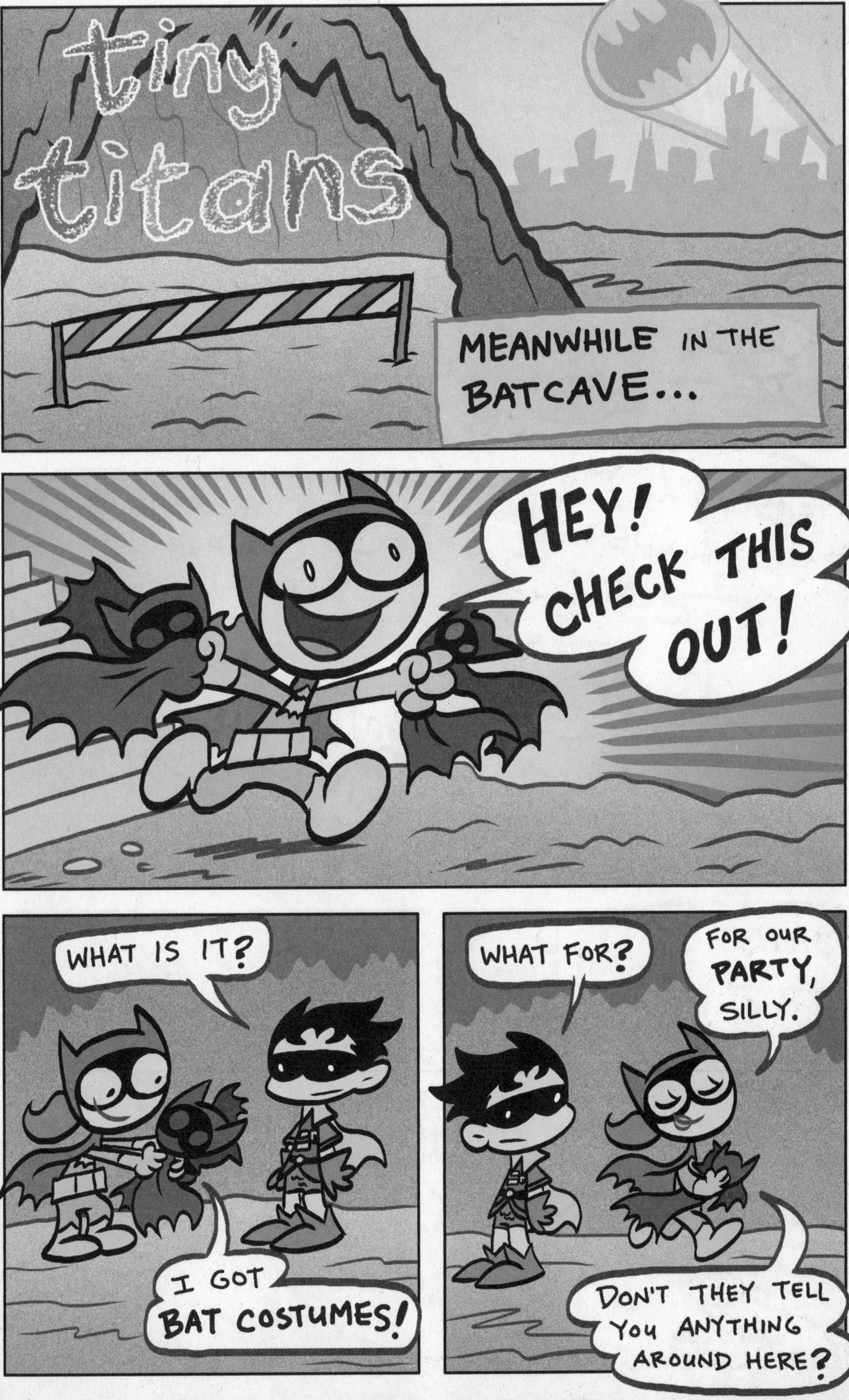
tiny titans
MEANWHILE IN THE BATCAVE...
HEY! CHECK THIS OUT!
WHAT IS IT?
I GOT BAT COSTUMES!
WHAT FOR?
FOR OUR PARTY, SILLY.
DON'T THEY TELL YOU ANYTHING AROUND HERE?

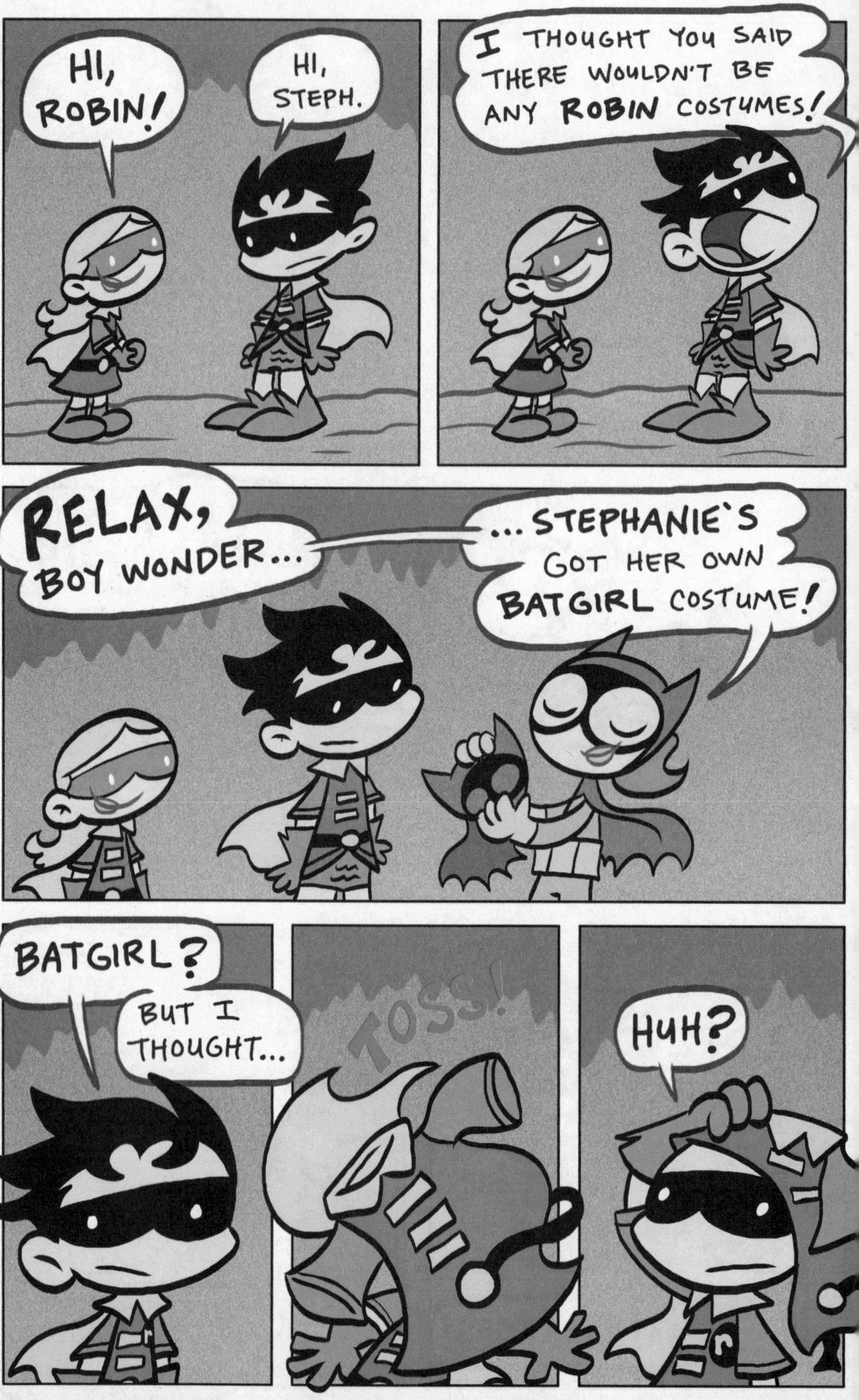
HI, ROBIN!
HI, STEPH.
I THOUGHT YOU SAID THERE WOULDN'T BE ANY ROBIN COSTUMES!
RELAX, BOY WONDER...
...STEPHANIE'S GOT HER OWN BATGIRL COSTUME!
BATGIRL?
BUT I THOUGHT...
TOSS!
HUH?

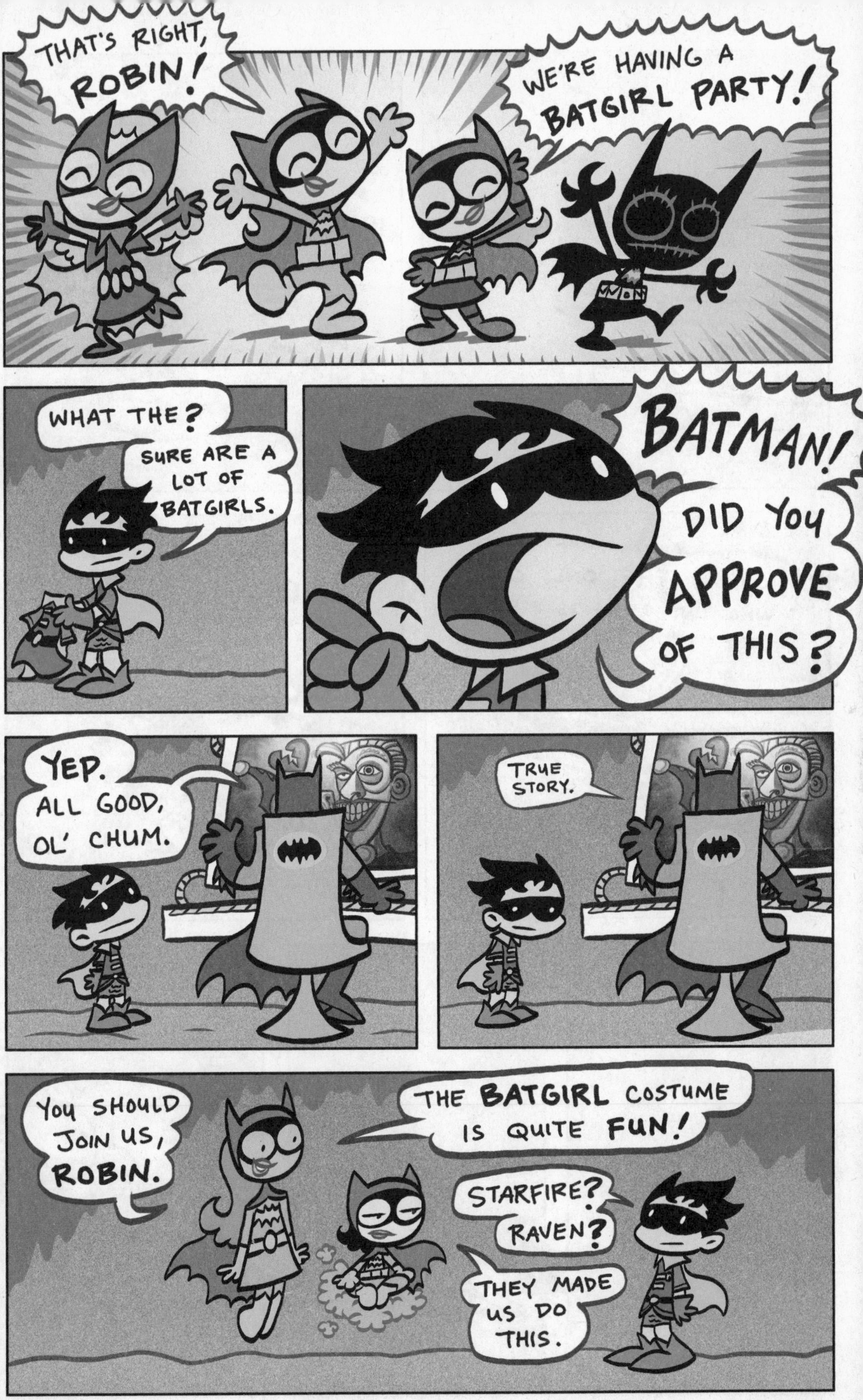
THAT'S RIGHT, ROBIN!
WE'RE HAVING A BATGIRL PARTY!
WHAT THE?
SURE ARE A LOT OF BATGIRLS.
BATMAN!
DID YOU APPROVE OF THIS?
YEP. ALL GOOD, OL' CHUM.
TRUE STORY.
YOU SHOULD JOIN US, ROBIN.
THE BATGIRL COSTUME IS QUITE FUN!
STARFIRE?
RAVEN?
THEY MADE US DO THIS.

-DRESSIN' IT UP.

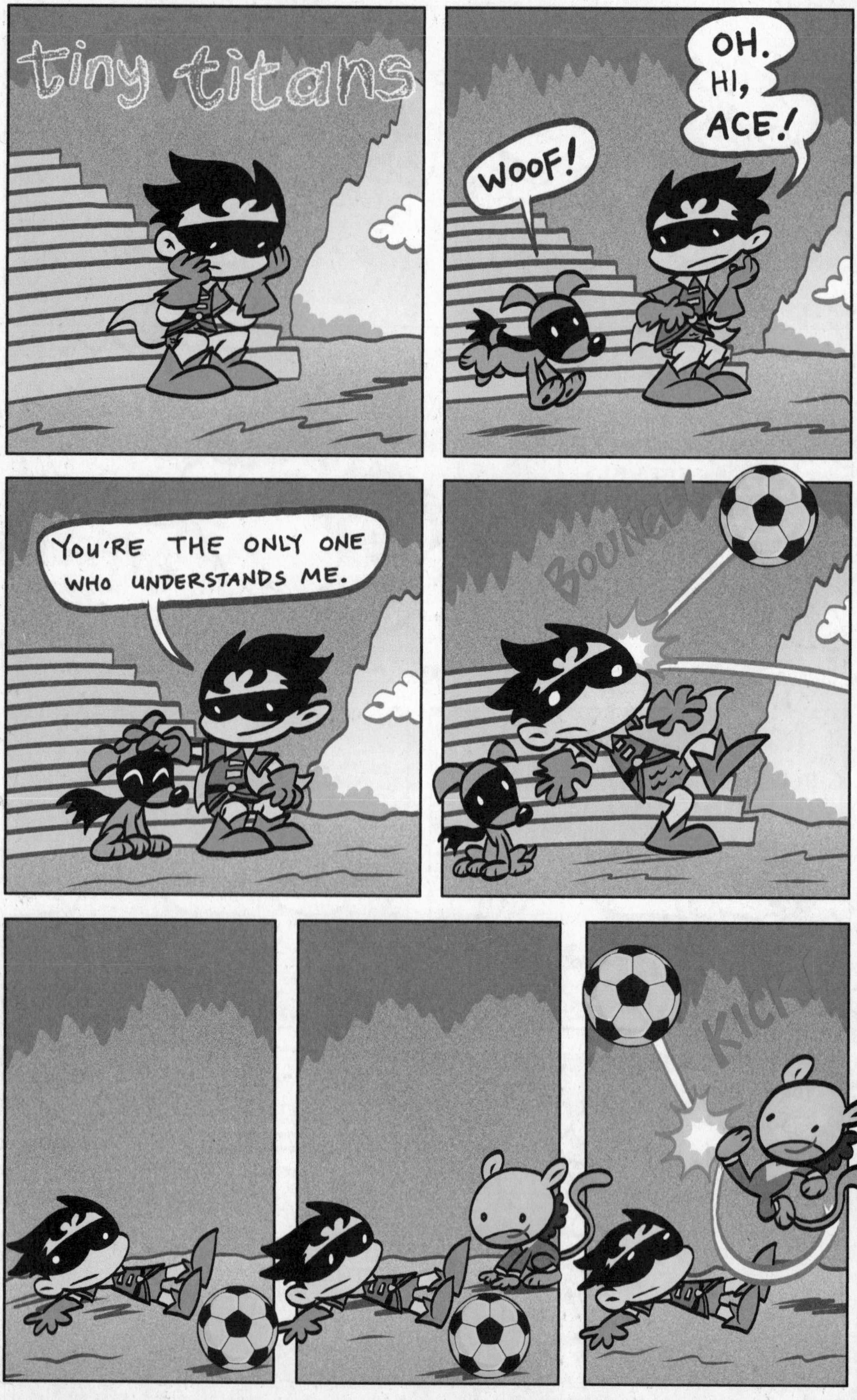
tiny titans
WOOF!
OH. HI, ACE!
YOU'RE THE ONLY ONE WHO UNDERSTANDS ME.
BOUNCE!
KICK

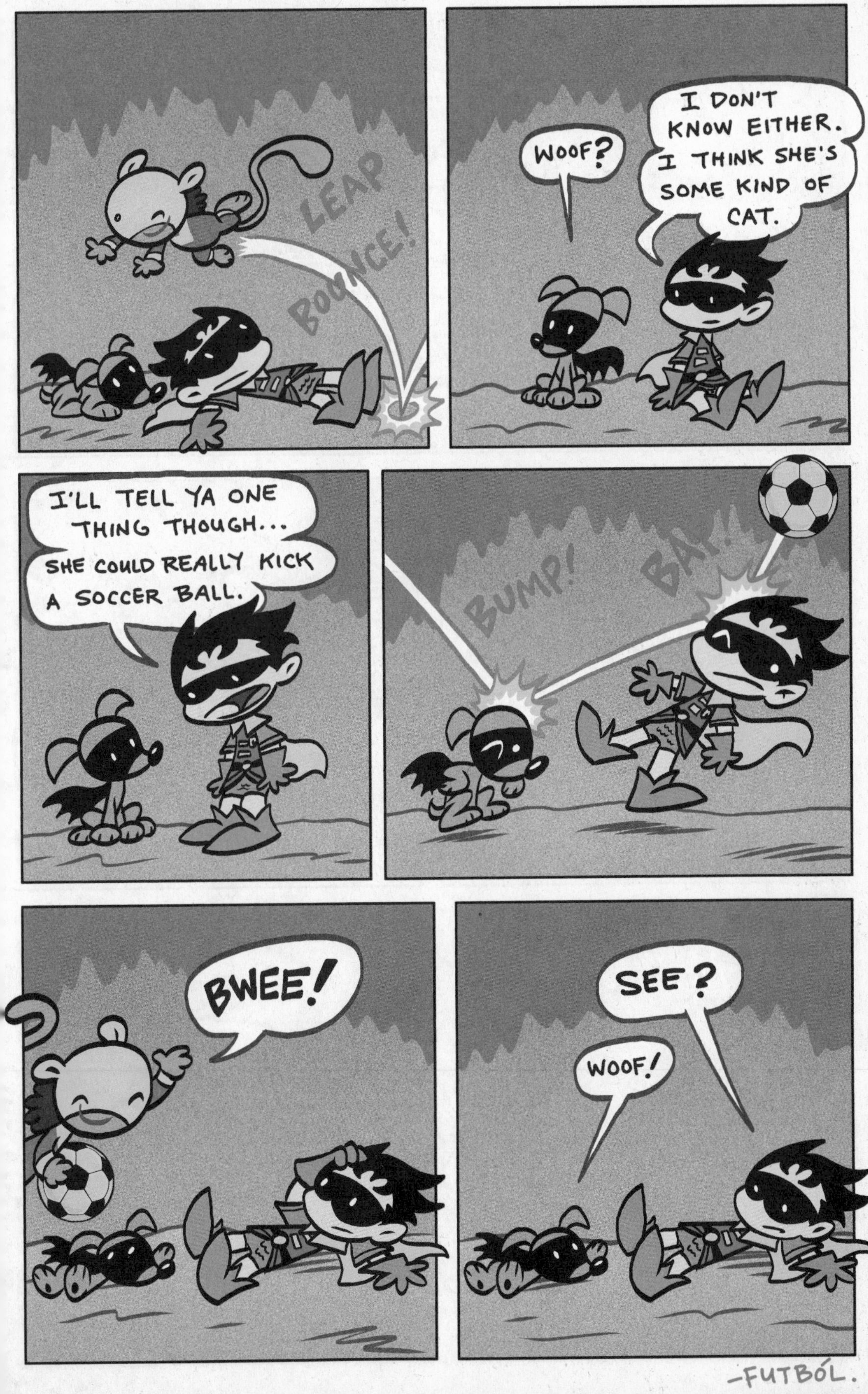
LEAP
BOUNCE!
WOOF?
I DON'T KNOW EITHER. I THINK SHE'S SOME KIND OF CAT.
I'LL TELL YA ONE THING THOUGH...
SHE COULD REALLY KICK A SOCCER BALL.
BUMP!
BWEE!
SEE?
WOOF!
-FUTBÓL.

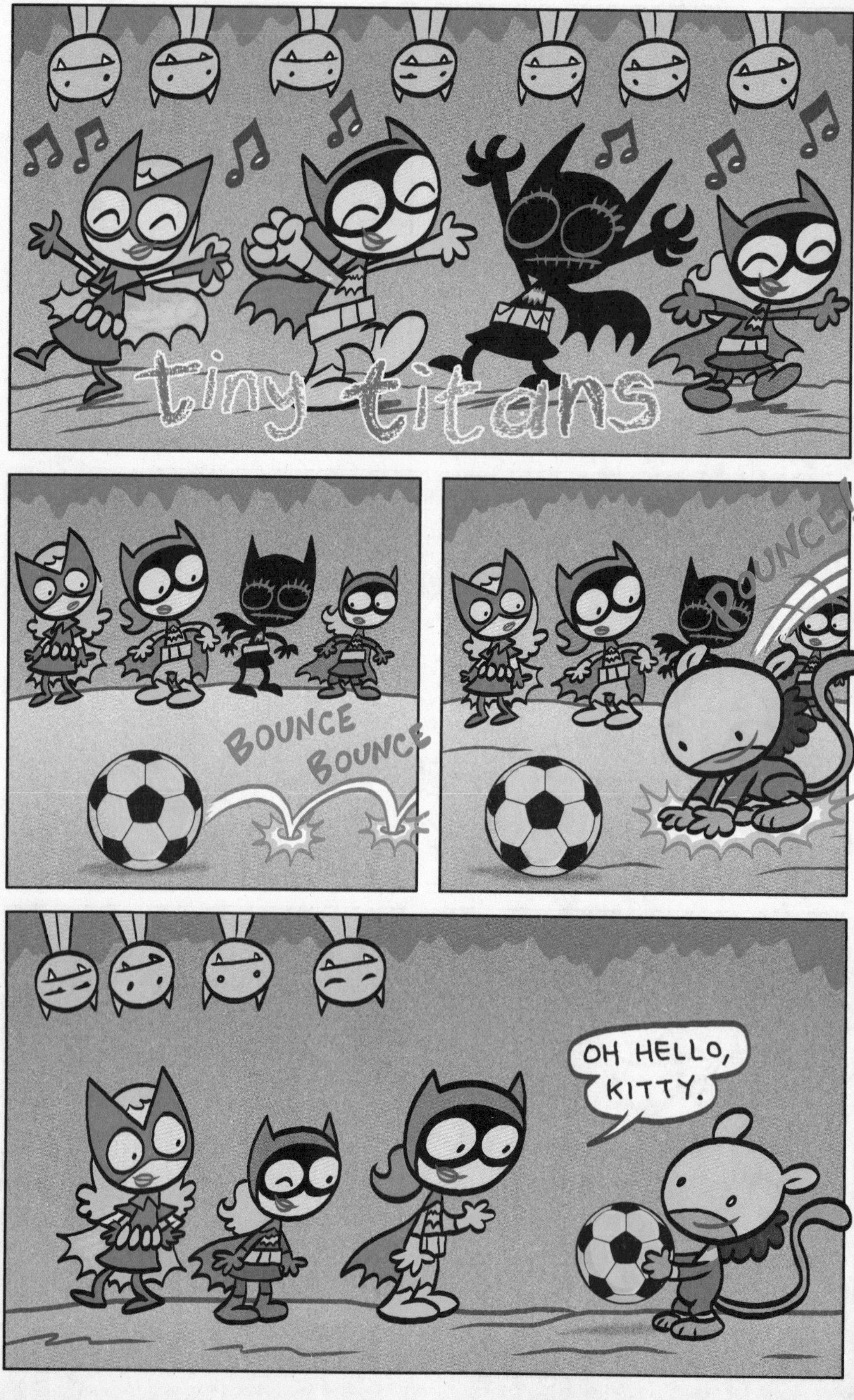
tiny titans
BOUNCE
BOUNCE
POUNCE!
OH HELLO,
KITTY.

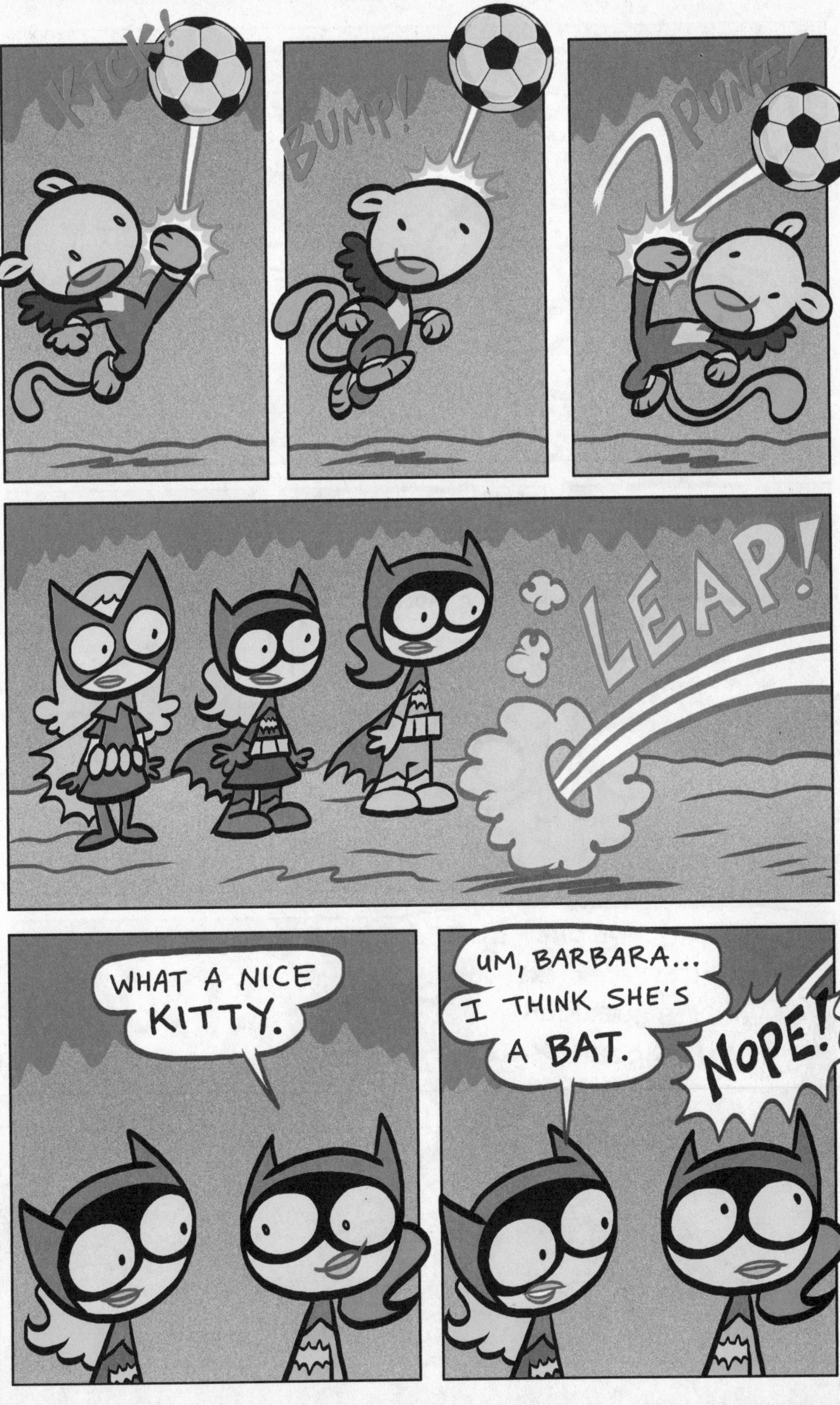
KICK!
BUMP!
PUNT!
LEAP!
WHAT A NICE KITTY.
UM, BARBARA... I THINK SHE'S A BAT.
NOPE!

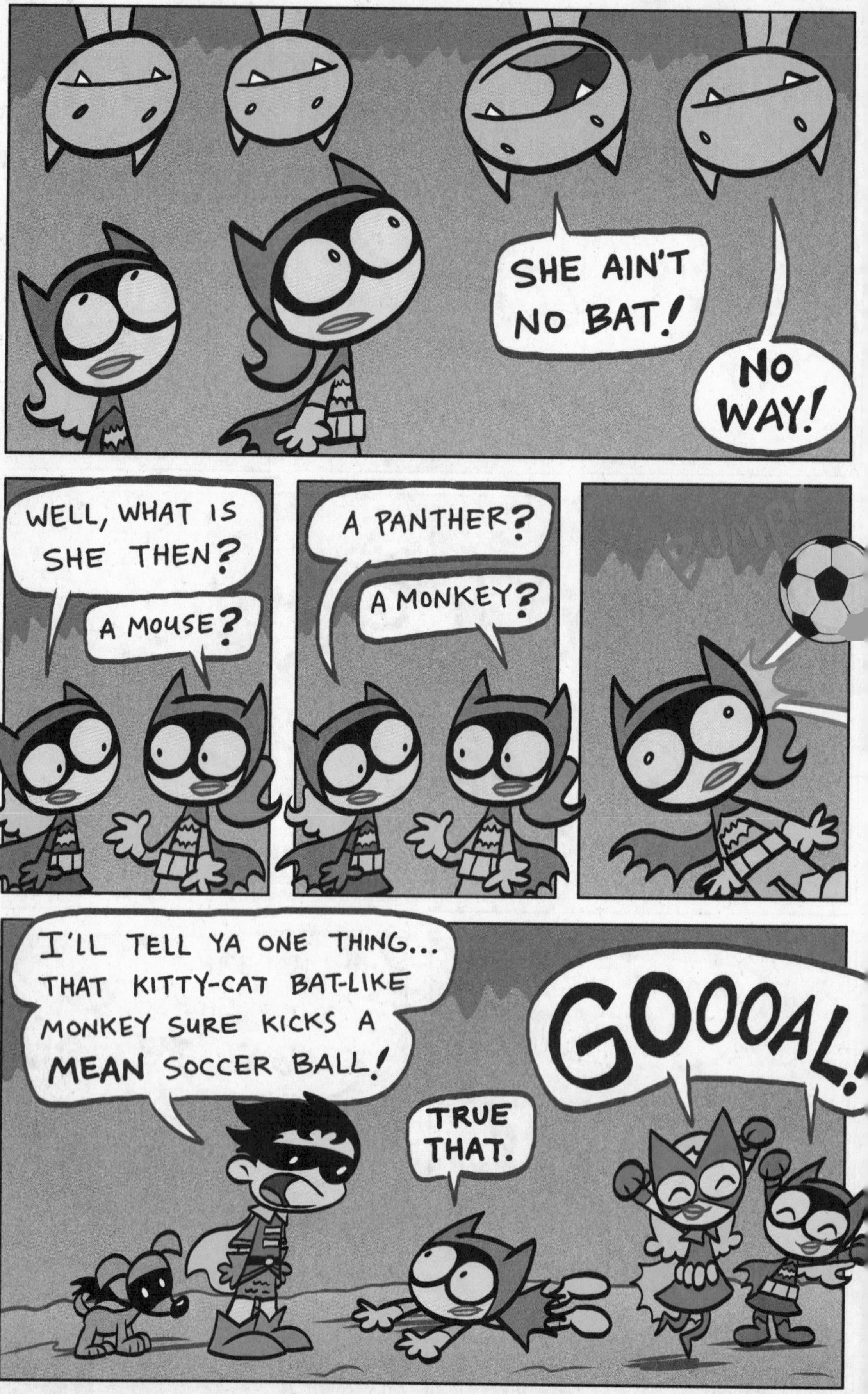
SHE AIN'T NO BAT!
NO WAY!
WELL, WHAT IS SHE THEN?
A MOUSE?
A PANTHER?
A MONKEY?
BUMP!
I'LL TELL YA ONE THING... THAT KITTY-CAT BAT-LIKE MONKEY SURE KICKS A MEAN SOCCER BALL!
TRUE THAT.
GOOOAL!

–GAME ON!

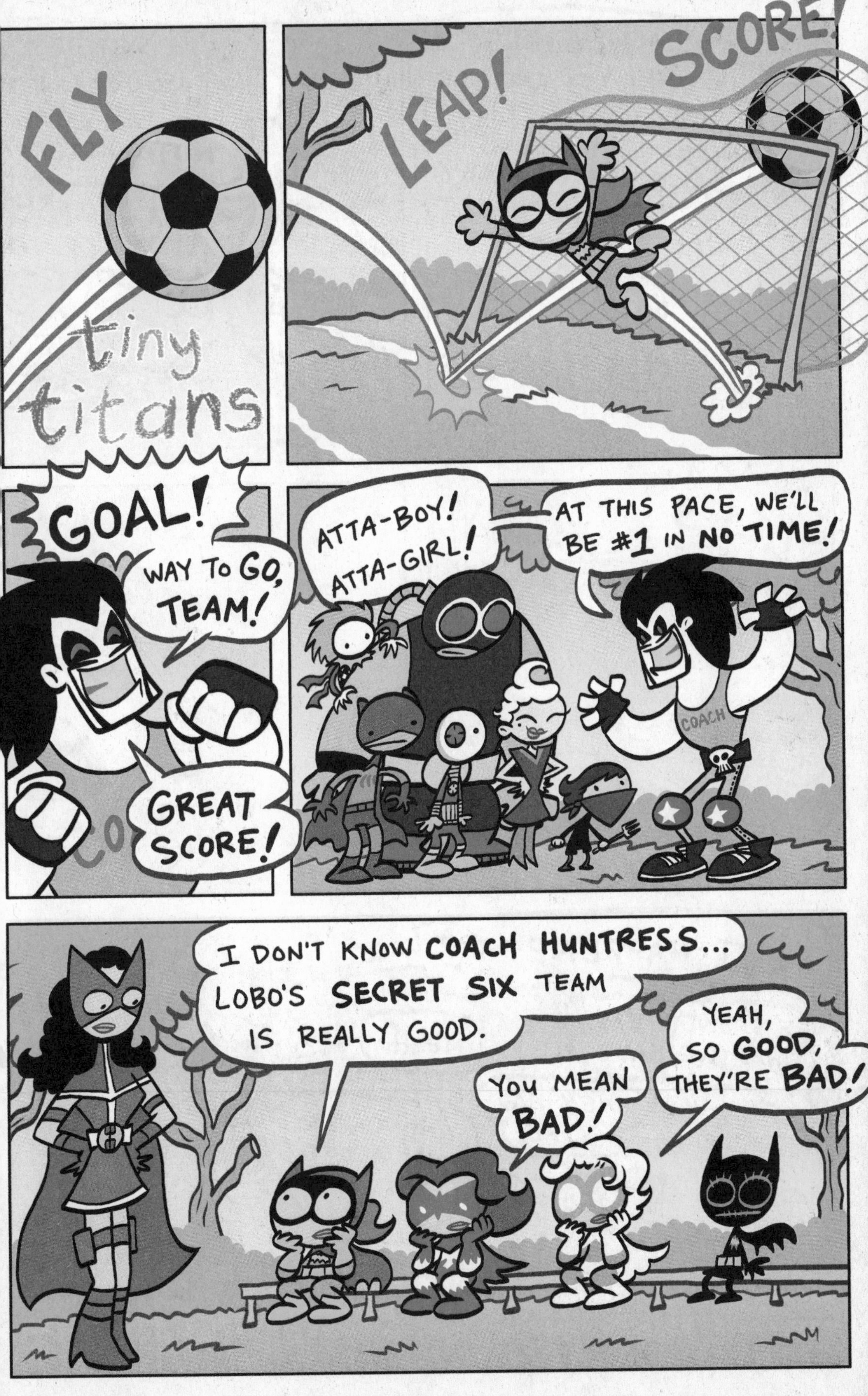

FLY
tiny titans
LEAP!
SCORE!
GOAL!
WAY TO GO, TEAM!
GREAT SCORE!
ATTA-BOY! ATTA-GIRL!
AT THIS PACE, WE'LL BE #1 IN NO TIME!
COACH
I DON'T KNOW COACH HUNTRESS... LOBO'S SECRET SIX TEAM IS REALLY GOOD.
YOU MEAN BAD!
YEAH, SO GOOD, THEY'RE BAD!

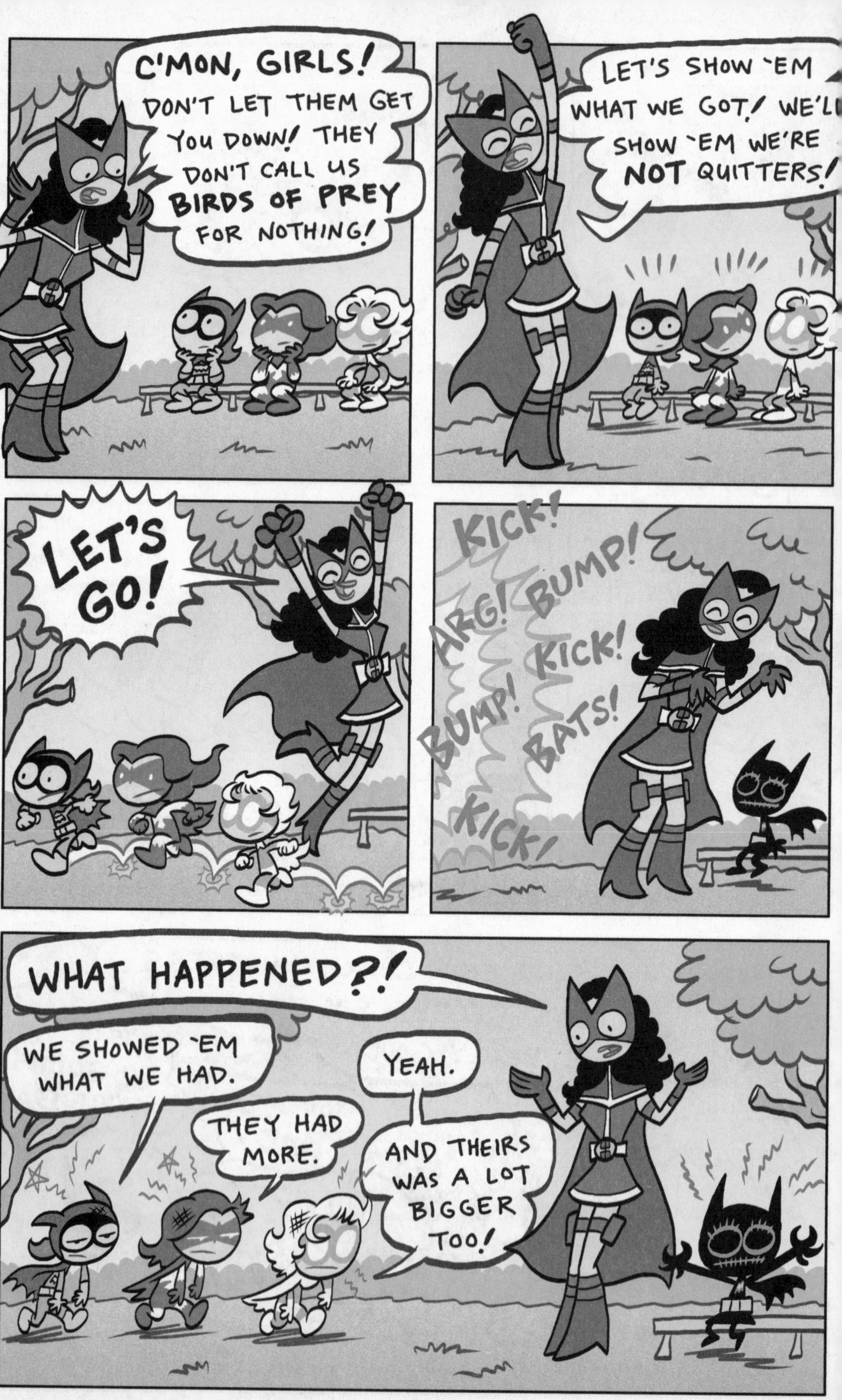
C'MON, GIRLS! DON'T LET THEM GET YOU DOWN! THEY DON'T CALL US BIRDS OF PREY FOR NOTHING!
LET'S SHOW 'EM WHAT WE GOT! WE'LL SHOW 'EM WE'RE NOT QUITTERS!
LET'S GO!
KICK!
BUMP!
ARG!
KICK!
BUMP!
BATS!
KICK!
WHAT HAPPENED?!
WE SHOWED 'EM WHAT WE HAD.
THEY HAD MORE.
YEAH.
AND THEIRS WAS A LOT BIGGER TOO!

–SIXTH SENSE.

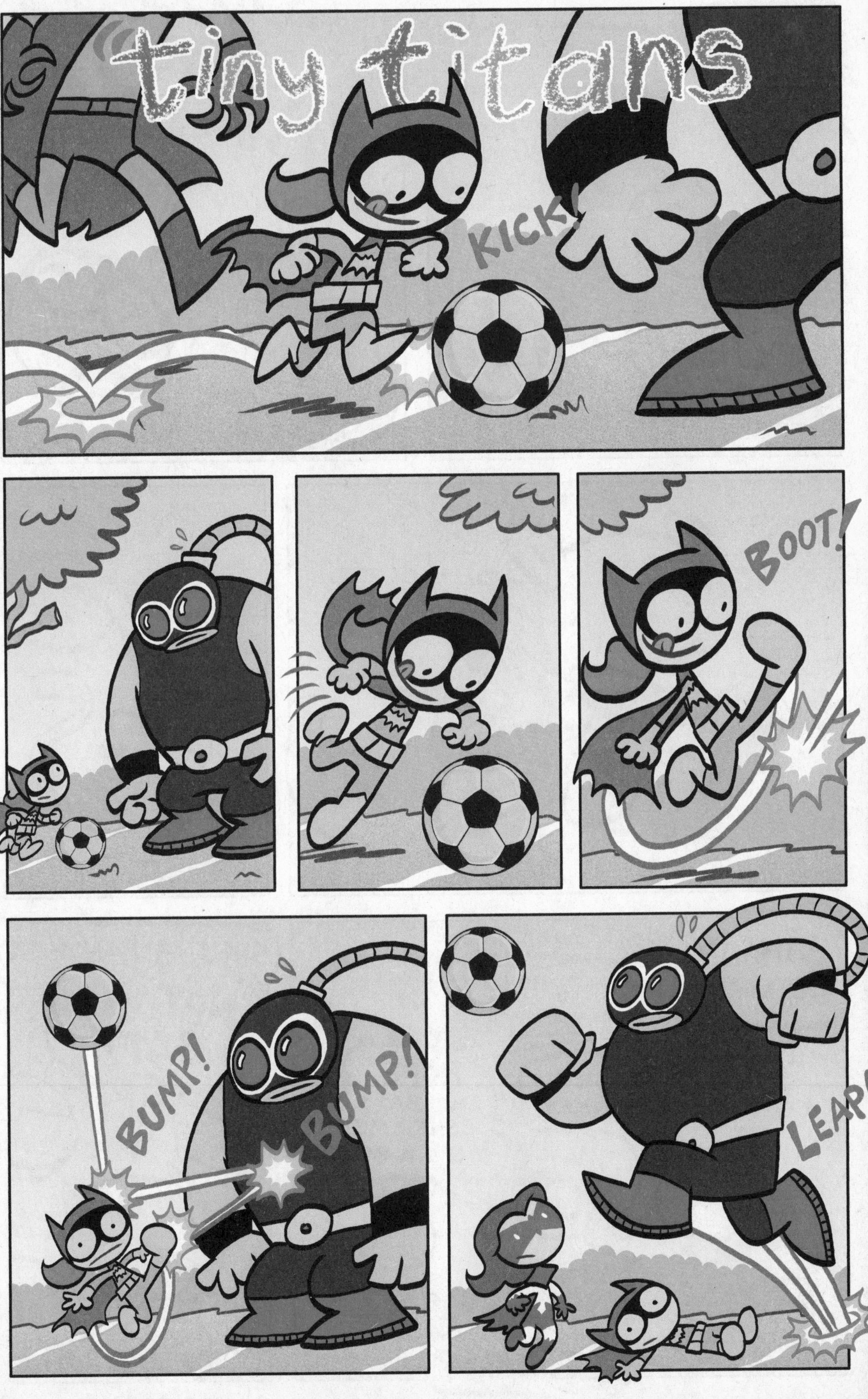
tiny titans
KICK!
BOOT!
BUMP!
BUMP!
LEAP!

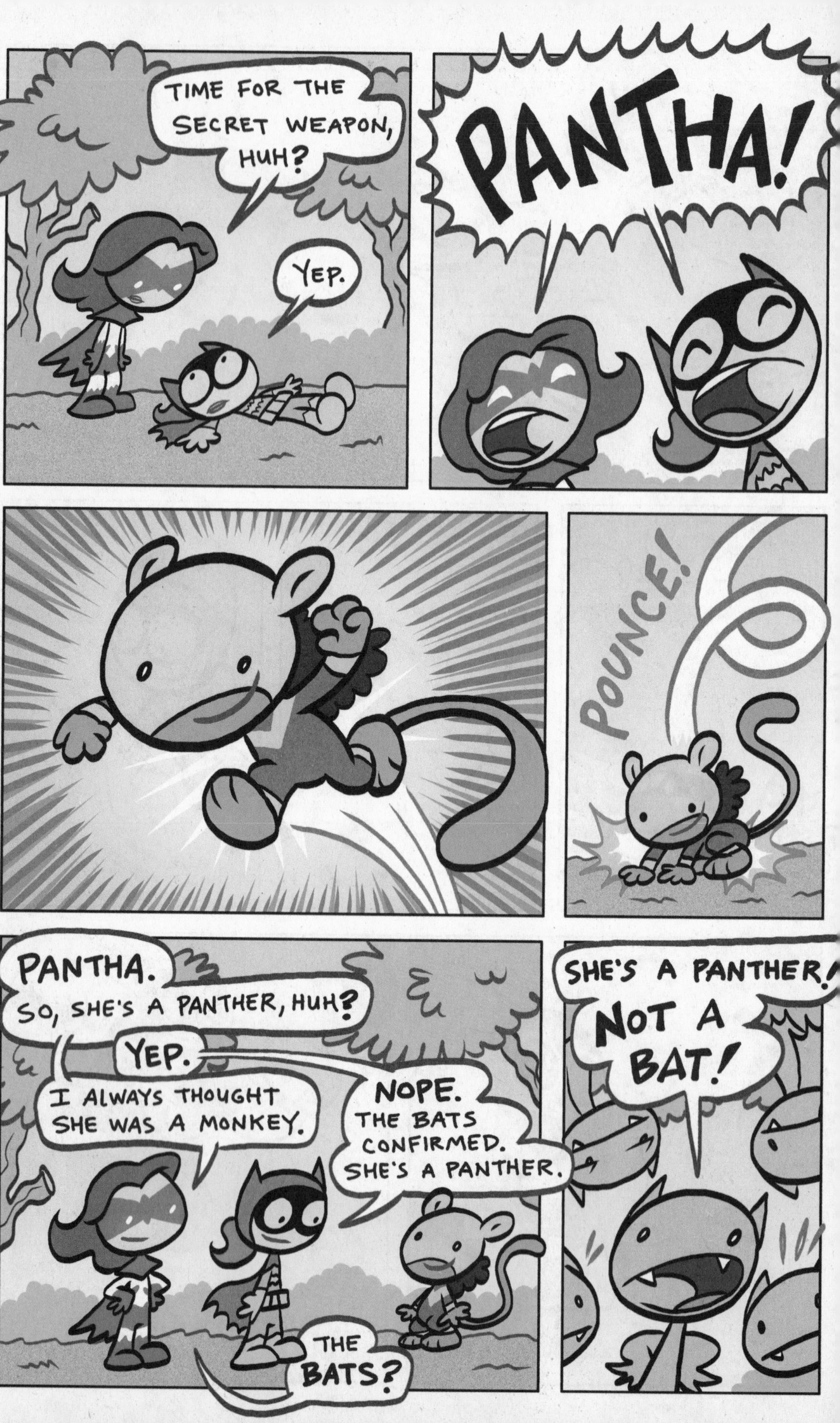
TIME FOR THE SECRET WEAPON, HUH?
YEP.
PANTHA!
POUNCE!
PANTHA.
SO, SHE'S A PANTHER, HUH?
YEP.
I ALWAYS THOUGHT SHE WAS A MONKEY.
NOPE. THE BATS CONFIRMED. SHE'S A PANTHER.
THE BATS?
SHE'S A PANTHER!
NOT A BAT!

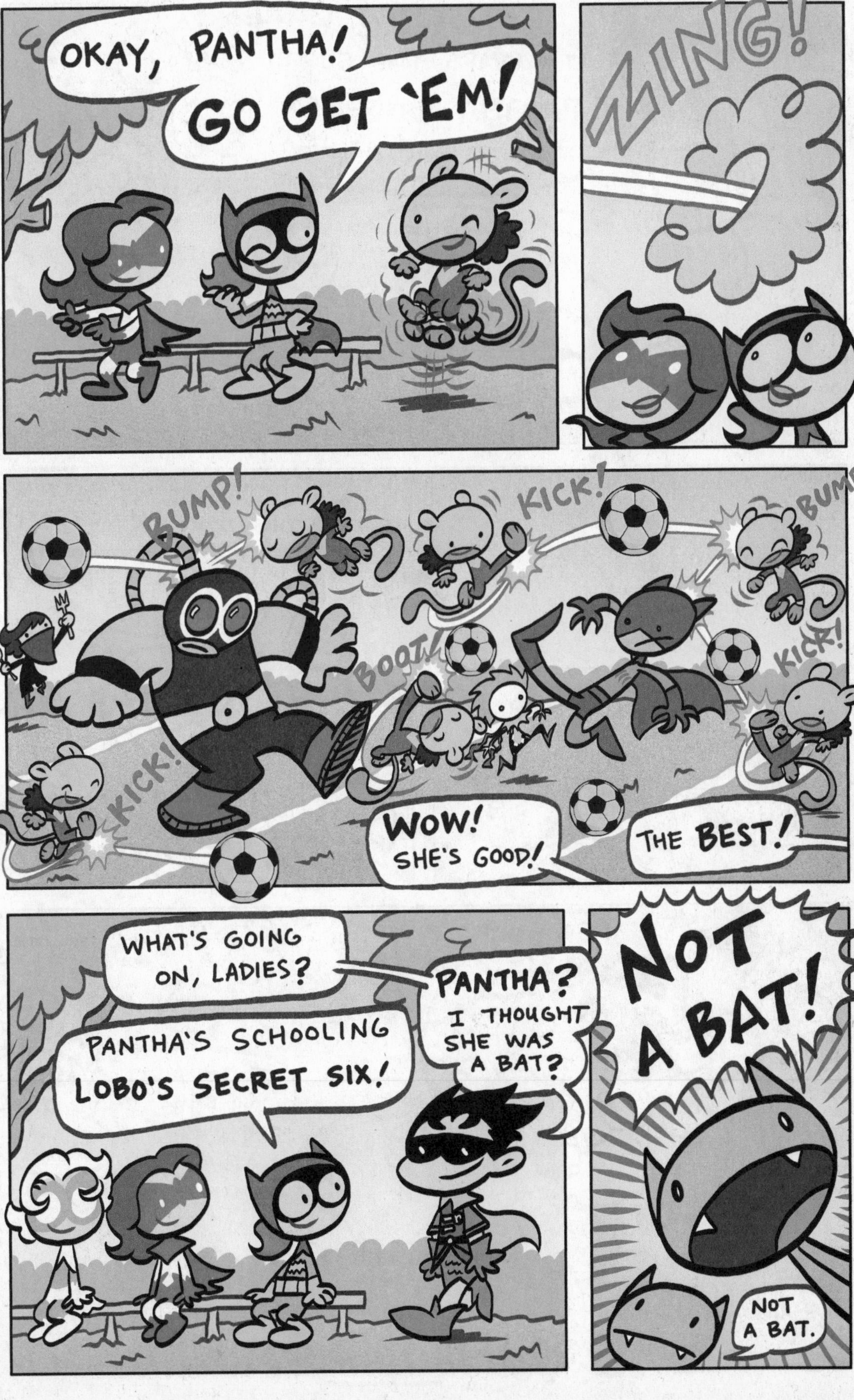
OKAY, PANTHA! GO GET 'EM!
ZING!
BUMP!
KICK!
BUMP
BOOT!
KICK!
KICK!
WOW! SHE'S GOOD!
THE BEST!
WHAT'S GOING ON, LADIES?
PANTHA'S SCHOOLING LOBO'S SECRET SIX!
PANTHA? I THOUGHT SHE WAS A BAT?
NOT A BAT!
NOT A BAT.

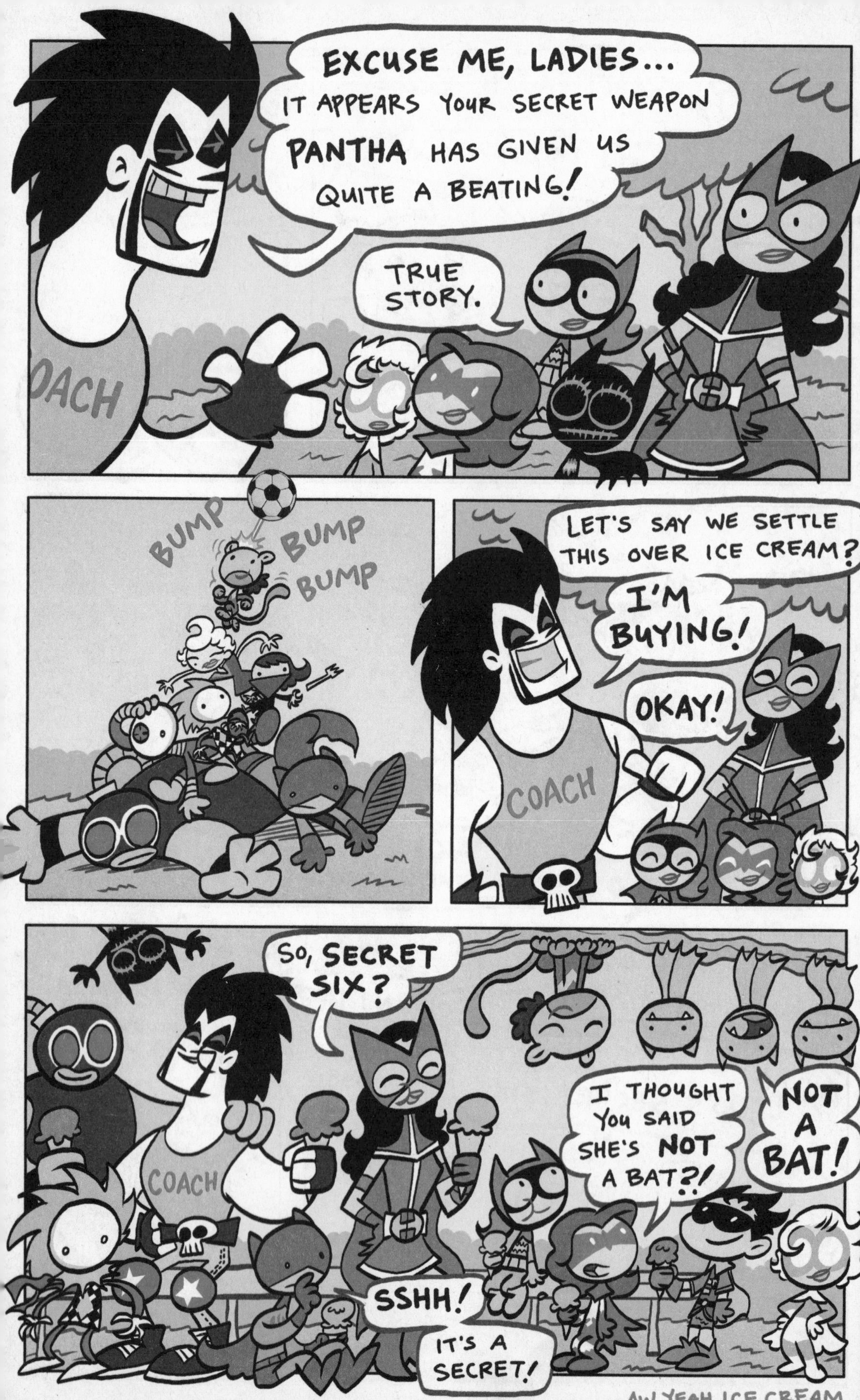
EXCUSE ME, LADIES...
IT APPEARS YOUR SECRET WEAPON PANTHA HAS GIVEN US QUITE A BEATING!
TRUE STORY.
COACH
BUMP
BUMP
BUMP
LET'S SAY WE SETTLE THIS OVER ICE CREAM?
I'M BUYING!
OKAY!
COACH
SO, SECRET SIX?
COACH
I THOUGHT YOU SAID SHE'S NOT A BAT?!
NOT A BAT!
SSHH!
IT'S A SECRET!

—AW YEAH ICE CREAM.

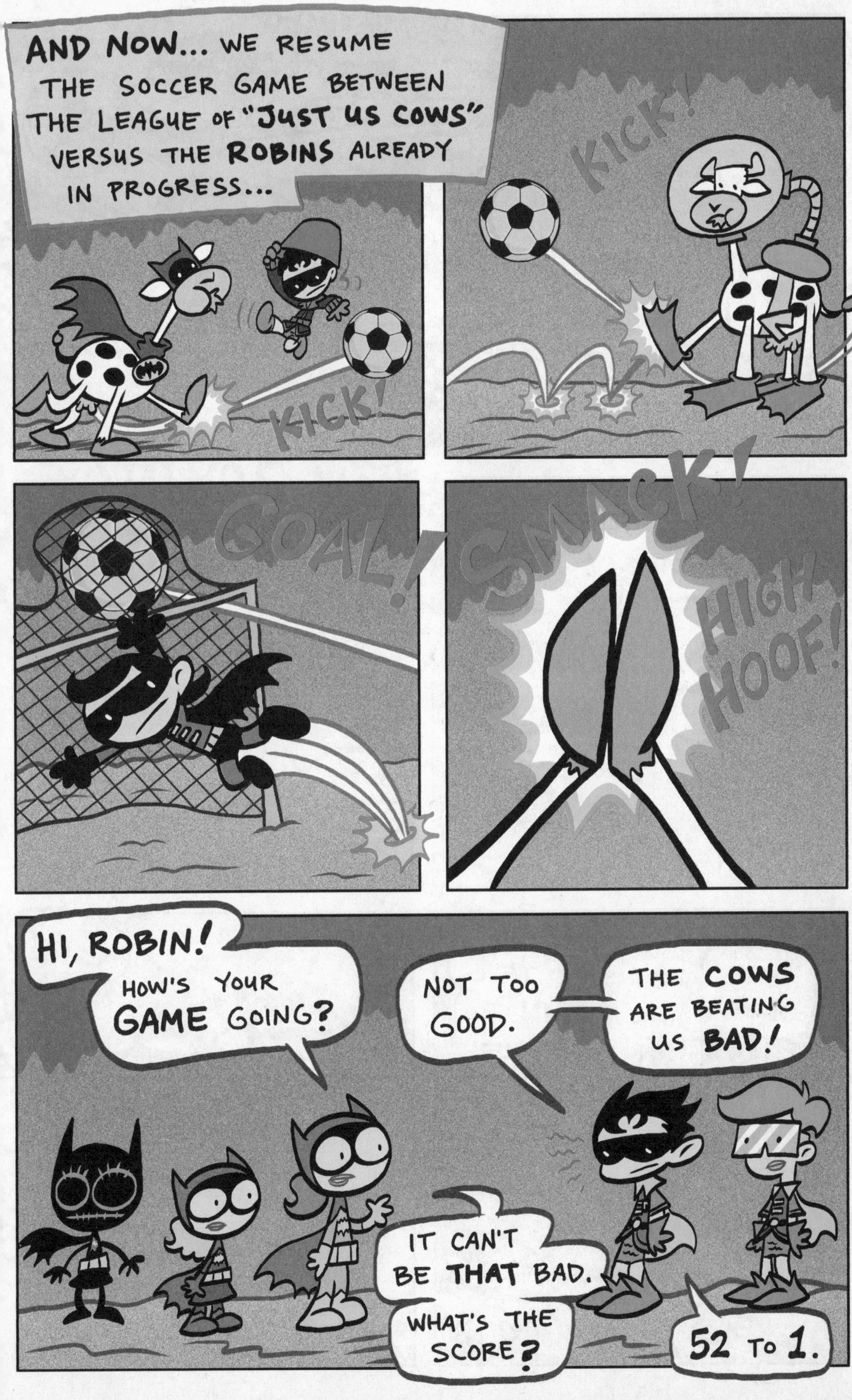
AND NOW... WE RESUME THE SOCCER GAME BETWEEN THE LEAGUE OF "JUST US COWS" VERSUS THE ROBINS ALREADY IN PROGRESS...
KICK!
KICK!
GOAL!
SMACK!
HIGH HOOF!
HI, ROBIN! HOW'S YOUR GAME GOING?
NOT TOO GOOD.
THE COWS ARE BEATING US BAD!
IT CAN'T BE THAT BAD. WHAT'S THE SCORE?
52 TO 1.

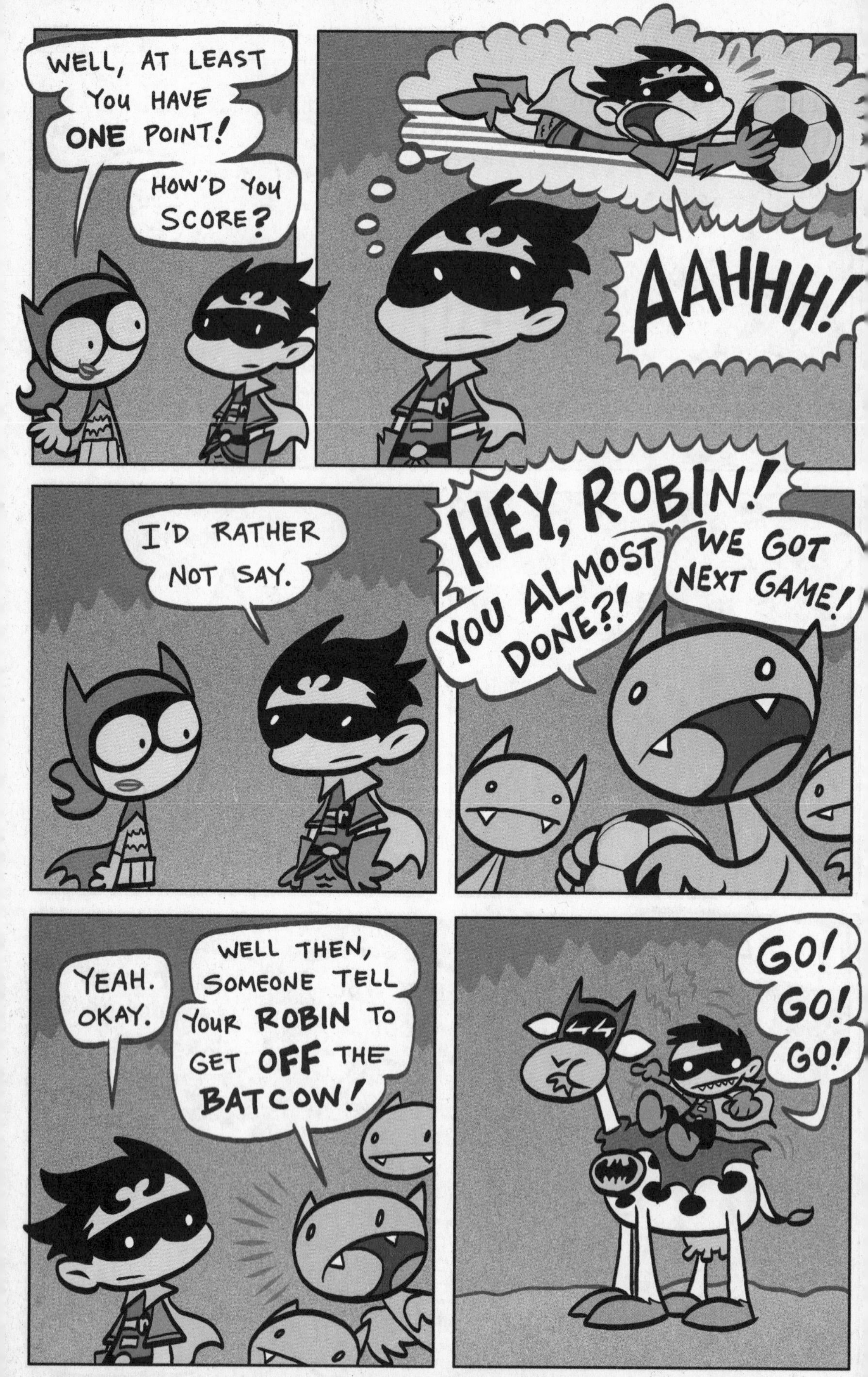
WELL, AT LEAST YOU HAVE ONE POINT!
HOW'D YOU SCORE?
AAHHH!
I'D RATHER NOT SAY.
HEY, ROBIN!
YOU ALMOST DONE?!
WE GOT NEXT GAME!
YEAH. OKAY.
WELL THEN, SOMEONE TELL YOUR ROBIN TO GET OFF THE BATCOW!
GO! GO! GO!

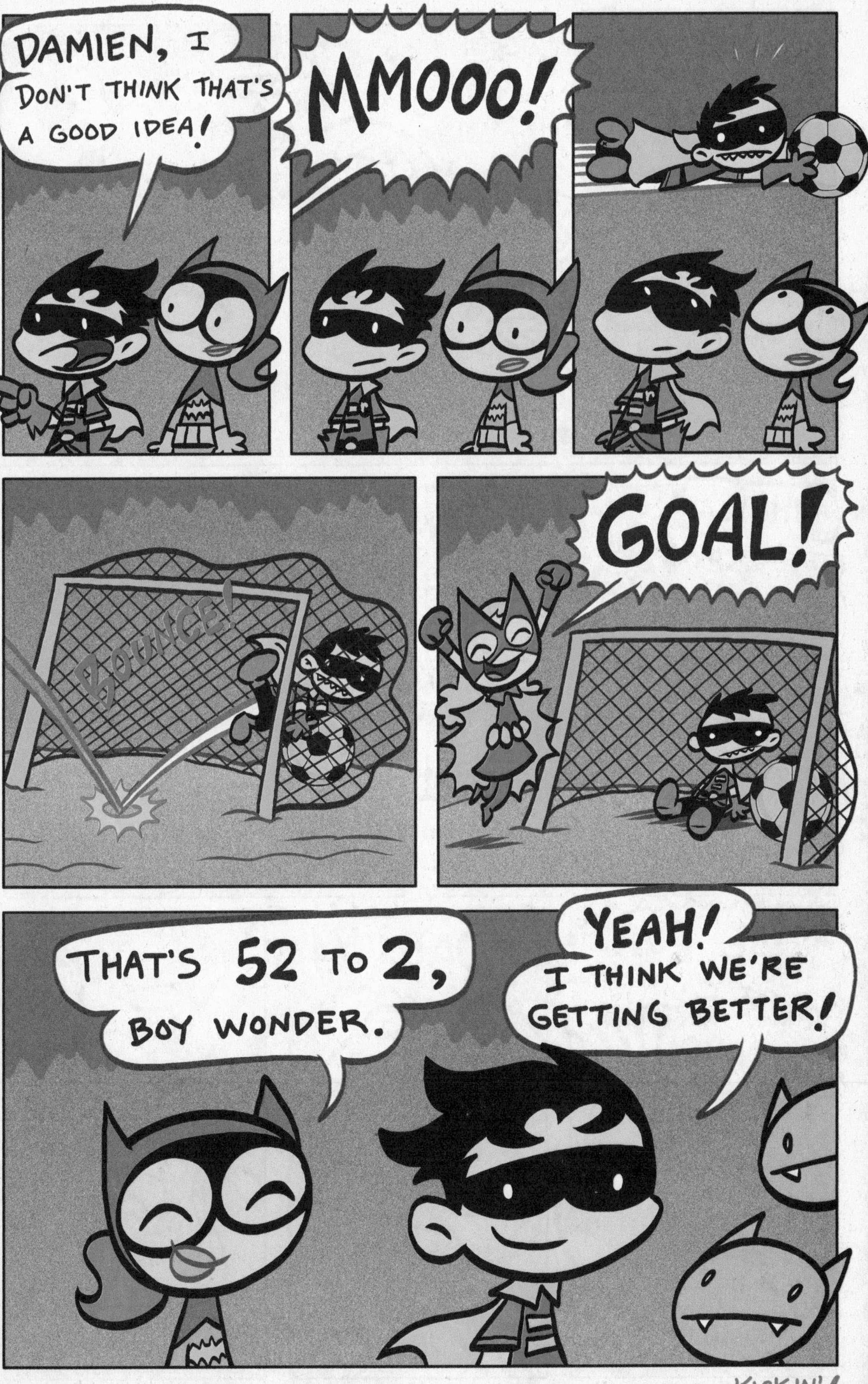
DAMIEN, I DON'T THINK THAT'S A GOOD IDEA!
MMOOO!
BOUNCE!
GOAL!
THAT'S 52 TO 2, BOY WONDER.
YEAH! I THINK WE'RE GETTING BETTER!

—KICKIN'!

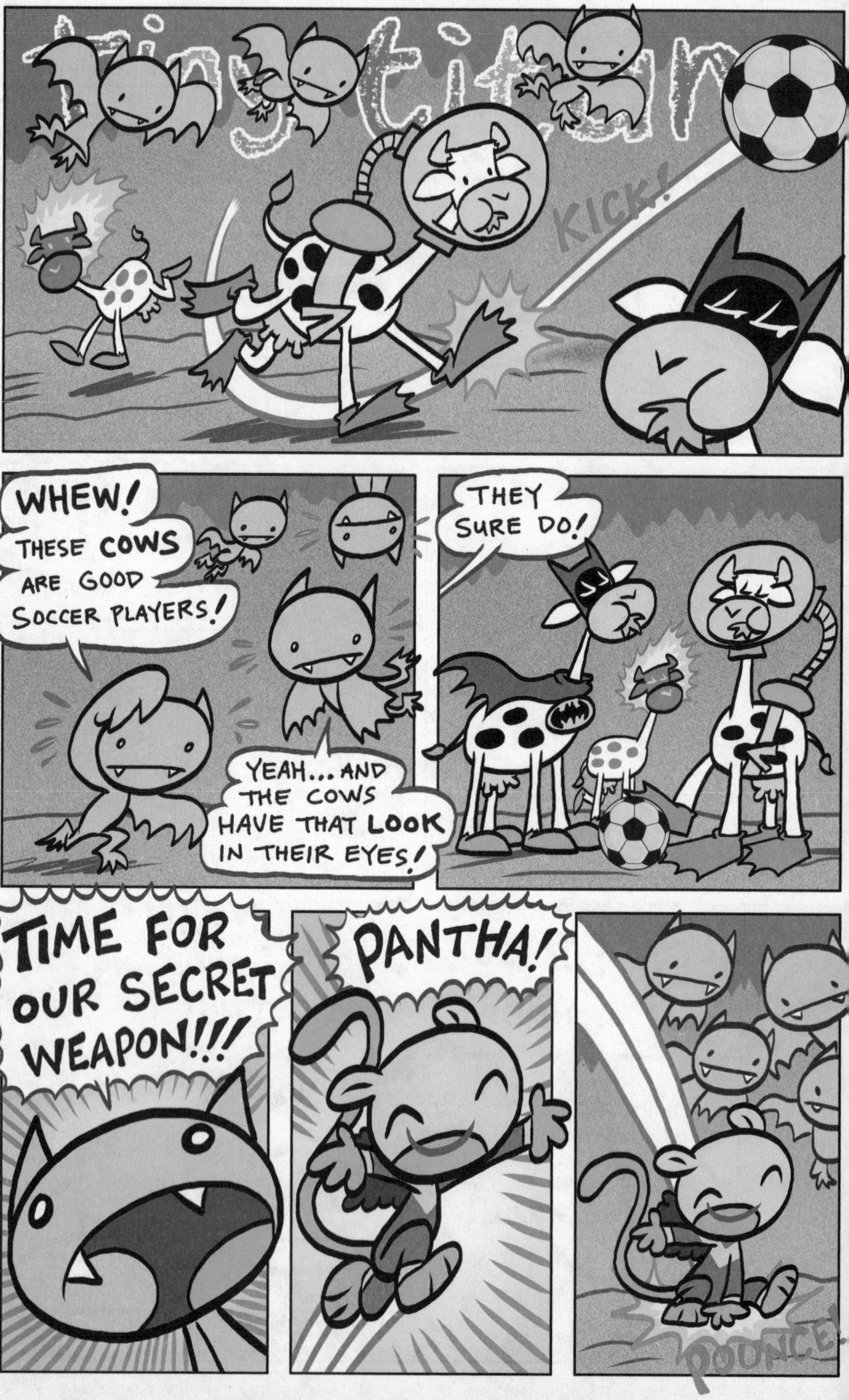
tiny titans
KICK!
WHEW! THESE COWS ARE GOOD SOCCER PLAYERS!
YEAH... AND THE COWS HAVE THAT LOOK IN THEIR EYES!
THEY SURE DO!
TIME FOR OUR SECRET WEAPON!!!
PANTHA!
POUNCE!

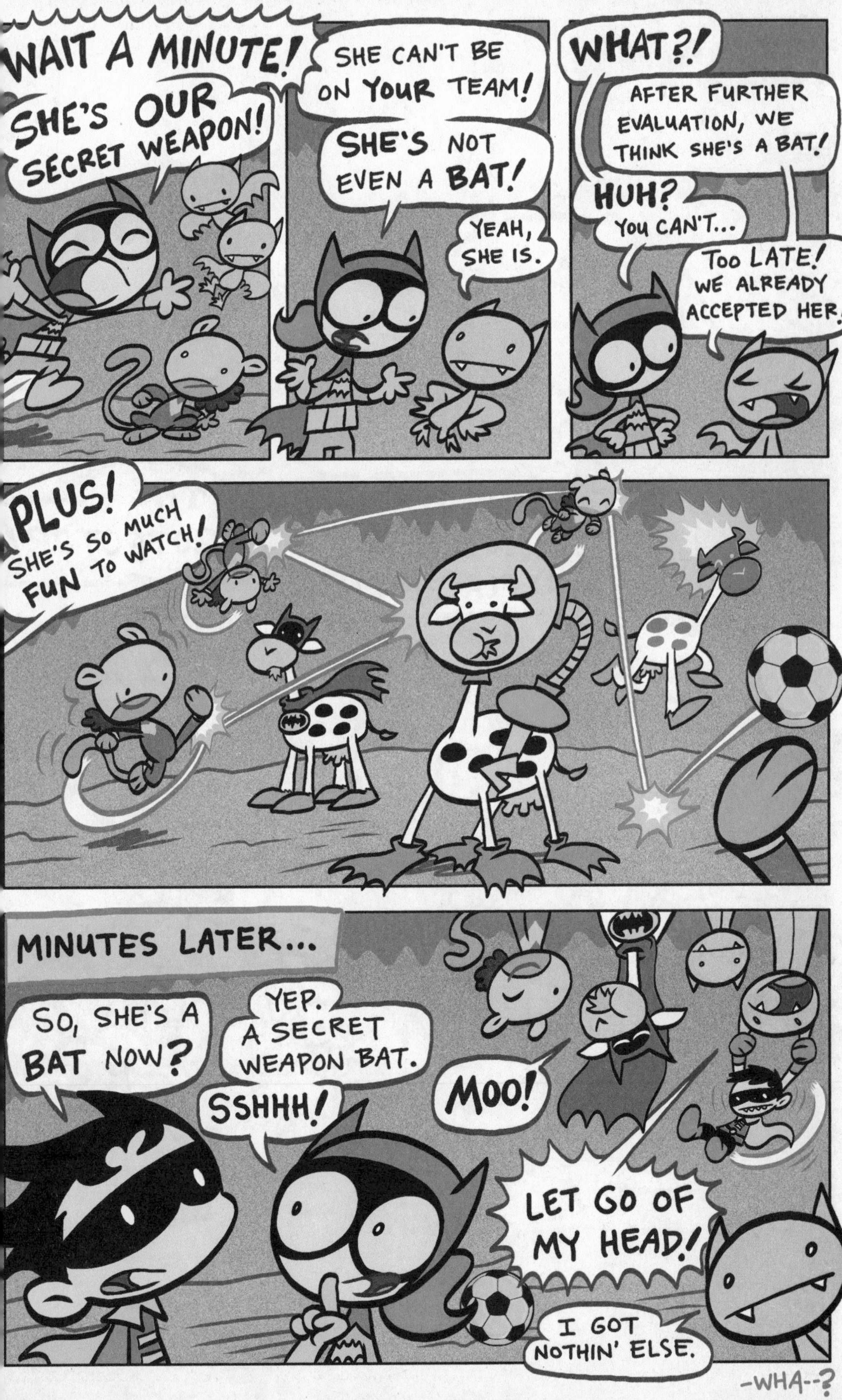

WAIT A MINUTE!
SHE'S OUR SECRET WEAPON!
SHE CAN'T BE ON YOUR TEAM!
SHE'S NOT EVEN A BAT!
YEAH, SHE IS.
WHAT?!
AFTER FURTHER EVALUATION, WE THINK SHE'S A BAT!
HUH?
YOU CAN'T...
TOO LATE! WE ALREADY ACCEPTED HER!
PLUS! SHE'S SO MUCH FUN TO WATCH!
MINUTES LATER...
SO, SHE'S A BAT NOW?
YEP. A SECRET WEAPON BAT.
SSHHH!
MOO!
LET GO OF MY HEAD!
I GOT NOTHIN' ELSE.
-WHA--?

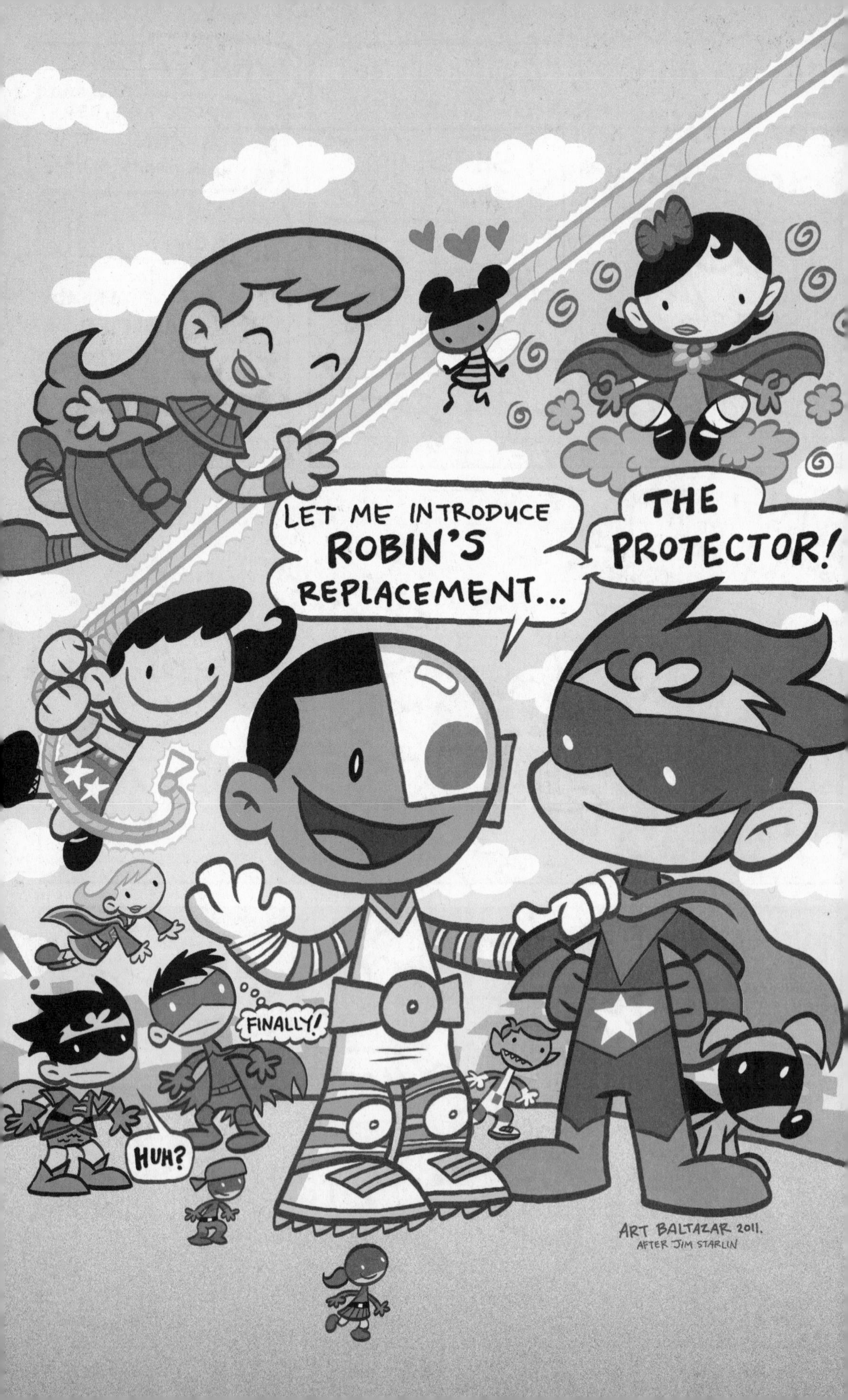
LET ME INTRODUCE ROBIN'S REPLACEMENT...
THE PROTECTOR!
FINALLY!
HUH?
ART BALTAZAR 2011.
AFTER JIM STARLIN

tiny titans

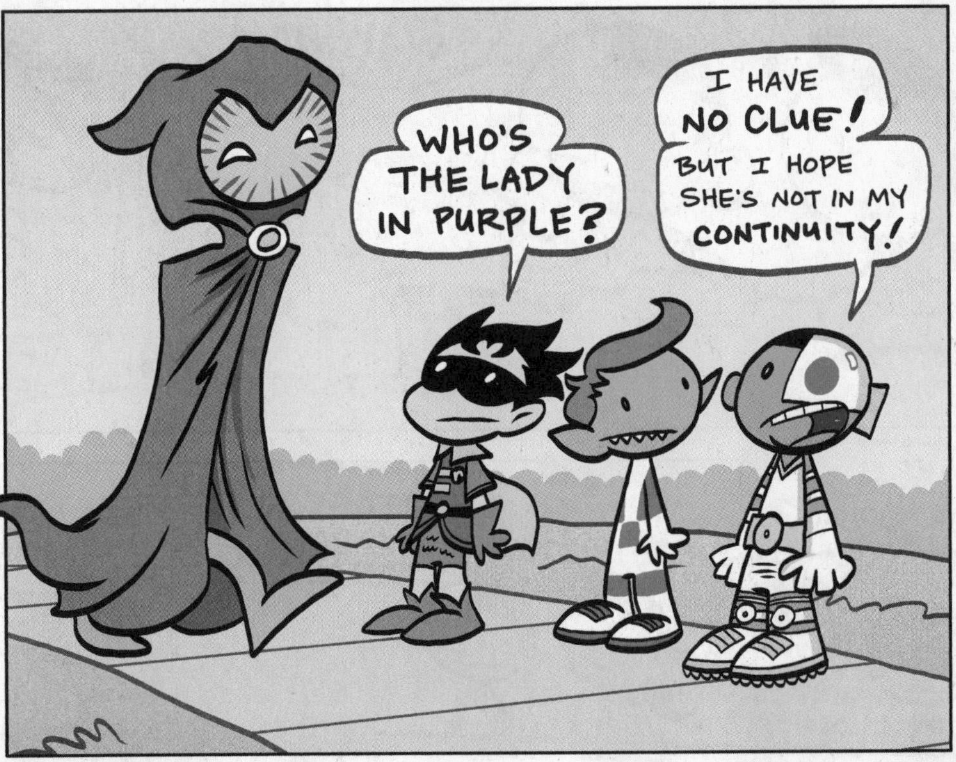
WHO'S THE LADY IN PURPLE?
I HAVE NO CLUE! BUT I HOPE SHE'S NOT IN MY CONTINUITY!

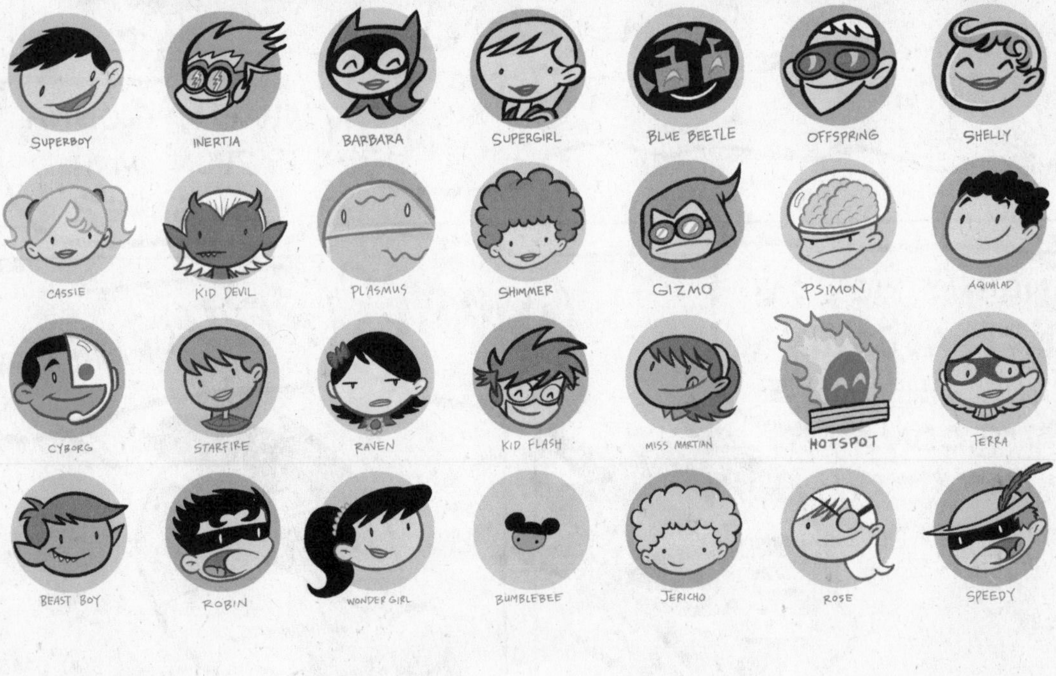
SUPERBOY
INERTIA
BARBARA
SUPERGIRL
BLUE BEETLE
OFFSPRING
SHELLY
CASSIE
KID DEVIL
PLASMUS
SHIMMER
GIZMO
PSIMON
AQUALAD
CYBORG
STARFIRE
RAVEN
KID FLASH
MISS MARTIAN
HOTSPOT
TERRA
BEAST BOY
ROBIN
WONDER GIRL
BUMBLEBEE
JERICHO
ROSE
SPEEDY

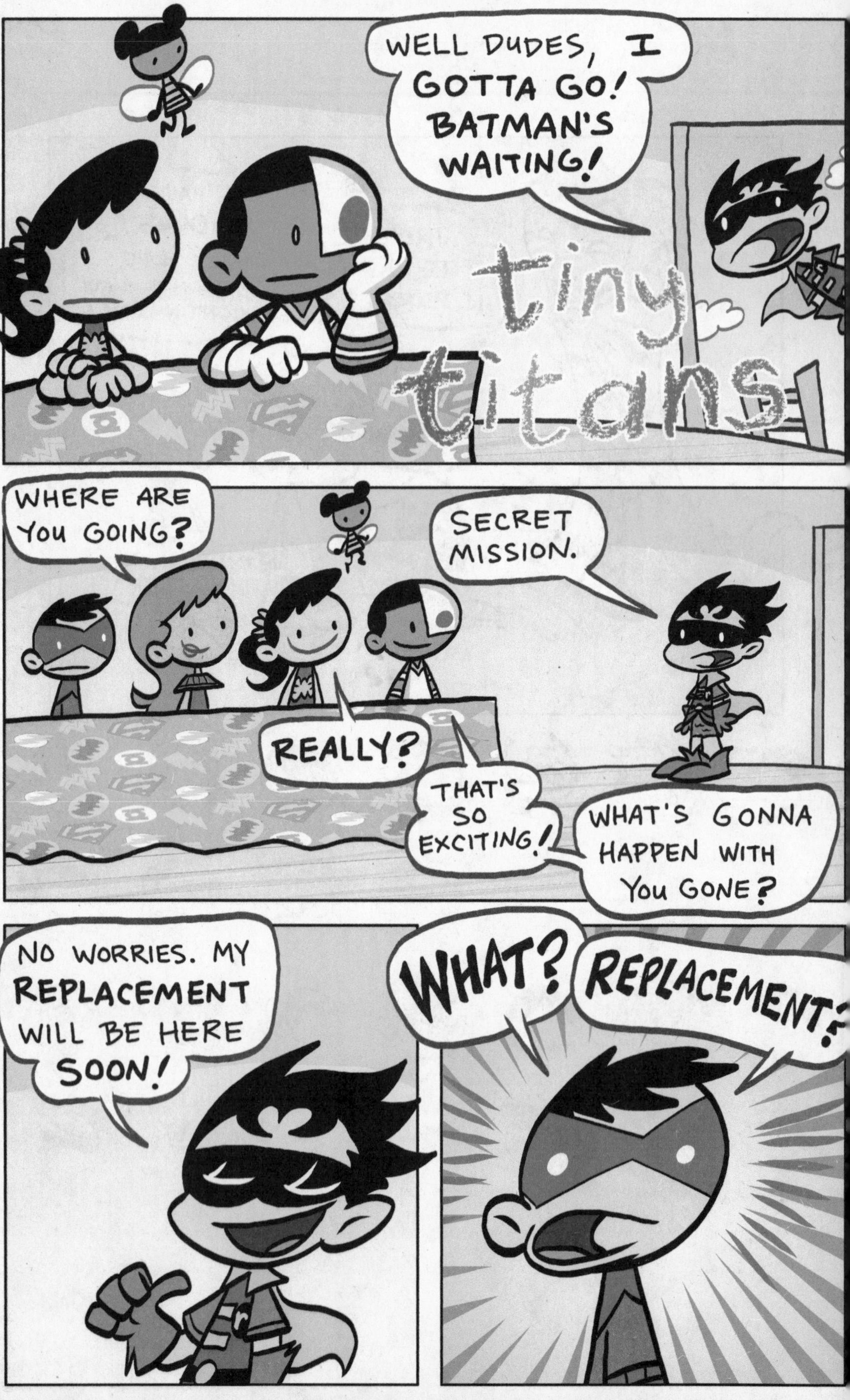
WELL DUDES, I GOTTA GO! BATMAN'S WAITING!
tiny titans
WHERE ARE YOU GOING?
SECRET MISSION.
REALLY?
THAT'S SO EXCITING!
WHAT'S GONNA HAPPEN WITH YOU GONE?
NO WORRIES. MY REPLACEMENT WILL BE HERE SOON!
WHAT?
REPLACEMENT?

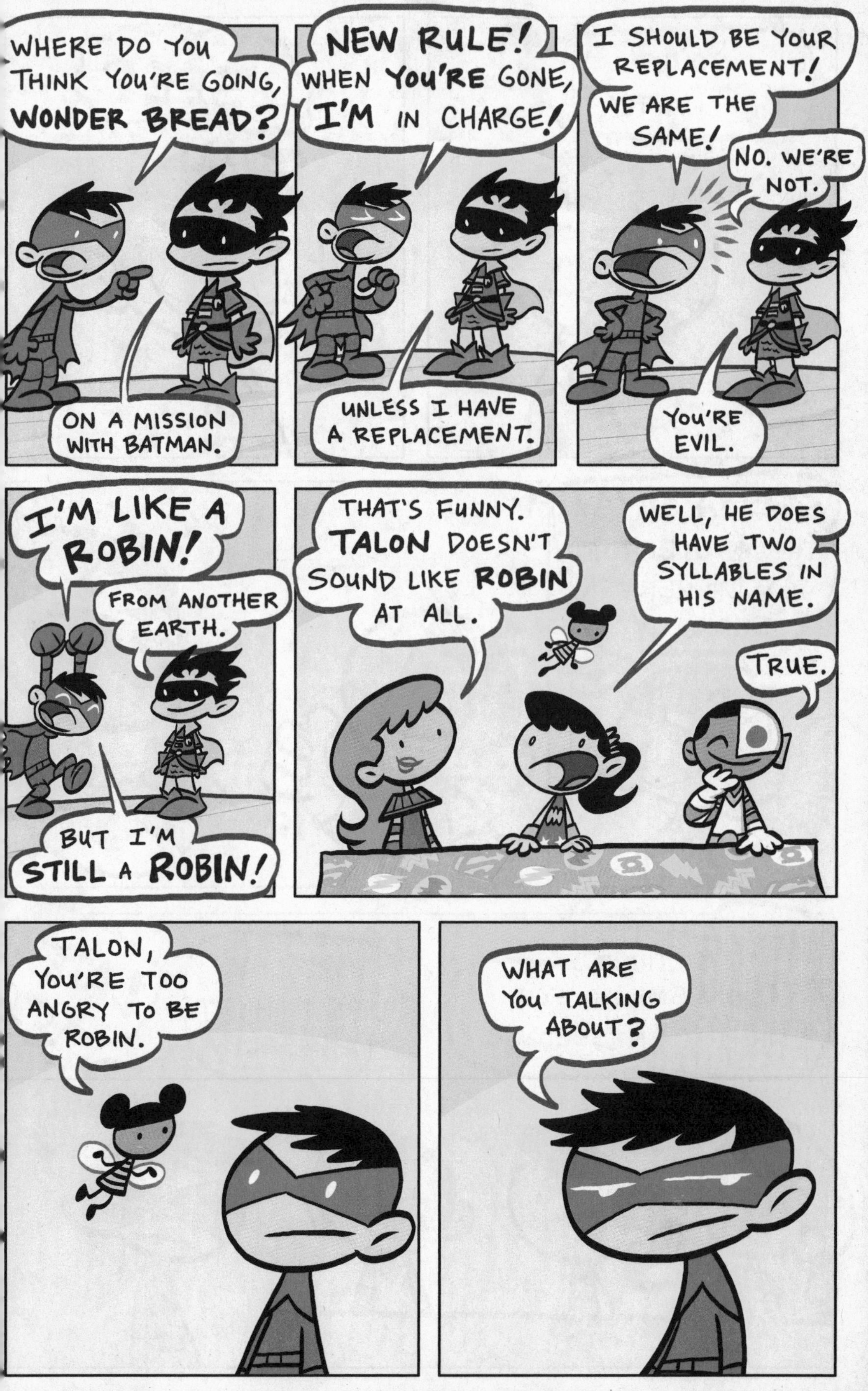
WHERE DO YOU THINK YOU'RE GOING, WONDER BREAD?
ON A MISSION WITH BATMAN.
NEW RULE! WHEN YOU'RE GONE, I'M IN CHARGE!
UNLESS I HAVE A REPLACEMENT.
I SHOULD BE YOUR REPLACEMENT!
WE ARE THE SAME!
NO. WE'RE NOT.
YOU'RE EVIL.
I'M LIKE A ROBIN!
FROM ANOTHER EARTH.
BUT I'M STILL A ROBIN!
THAT'S FUNNY. TALON DOESN'T SOUND LIKE ROBIN AT ALL.
WELL, HE DOES HAVE TWO SYLLABLES IN HIS NAME.
TRUE.
TALON, YOU'RE TOO ANGRY TO BE ROBIN.
WHAT ARE YOU TALKING ABOUT?

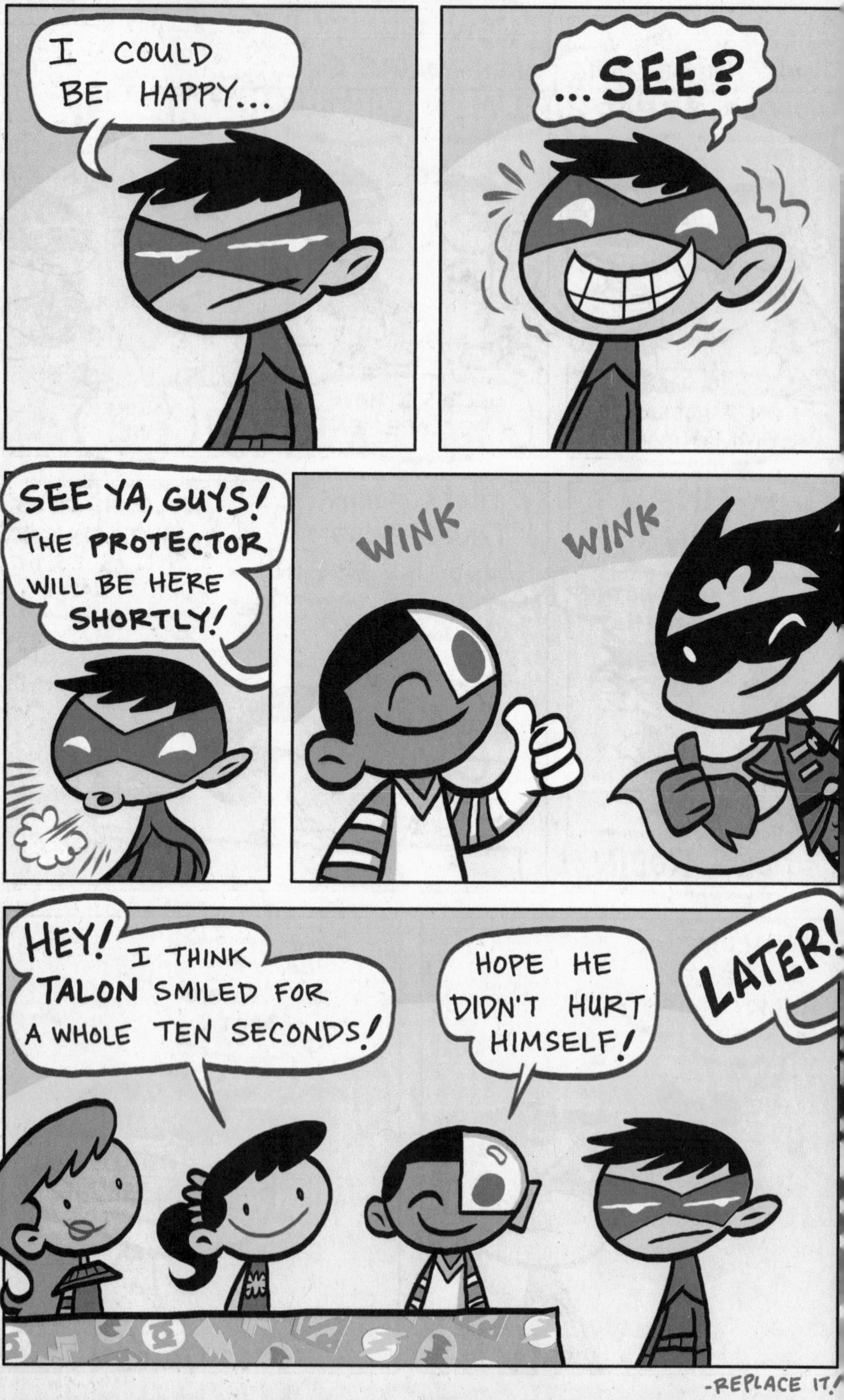
I COULD BE HAPPY...
...SEE?
SEE YA, GUYS! THE PROTECTOR WILL BE HERE SHORTLY!
WINK
WINK
HEY! I THINK TALON SMILED FOR A WHOLE TEN SECONDS!
HOPE HE DIDN'T HURT HIMSELF!
LATER!
-REPLACE IT!

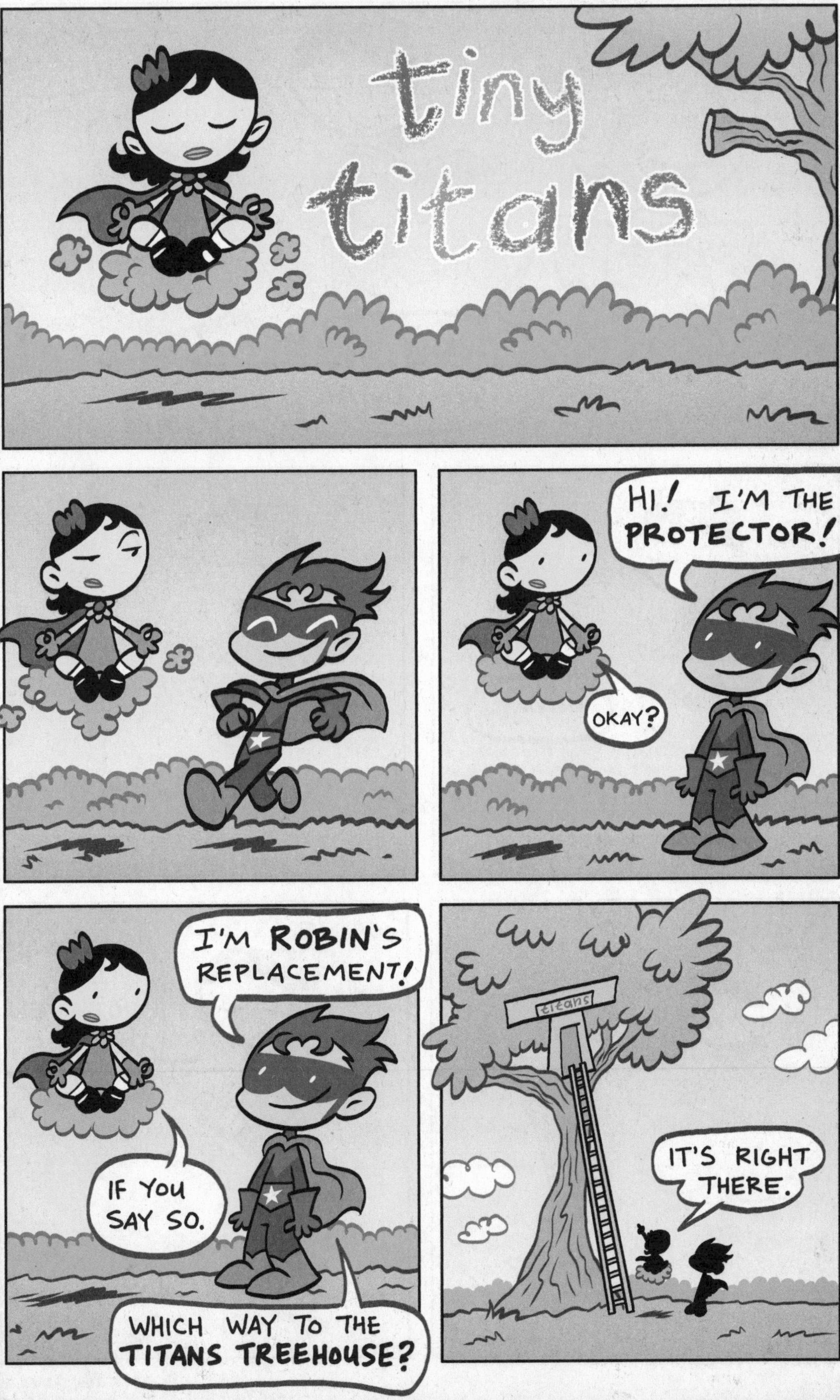
tiny titans
HI! I'M THE PROTECTOR!
OKAY?
I'M ROBIN'S REPLACEMENT!
IF YOU SAY SO.
WHICH WAY TO THE TITANS TREEHOUSE?
titans
IT'S RIGHT THERE.

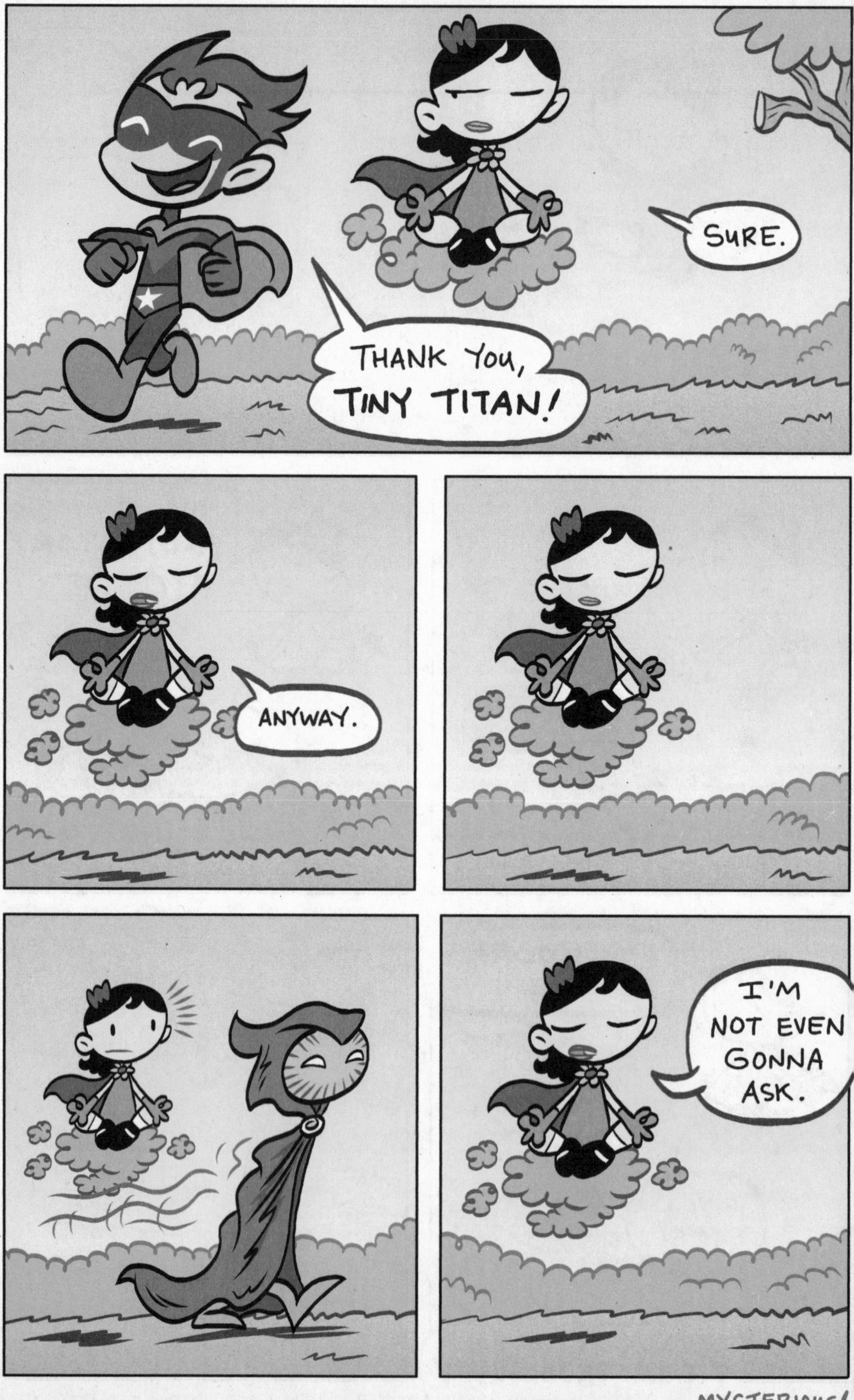
SURE.
THANK YOU, TINY TITAN!
ANYWAY.
I'M NOT EVEN GONNA ASK.

–MYSTERIOUS!

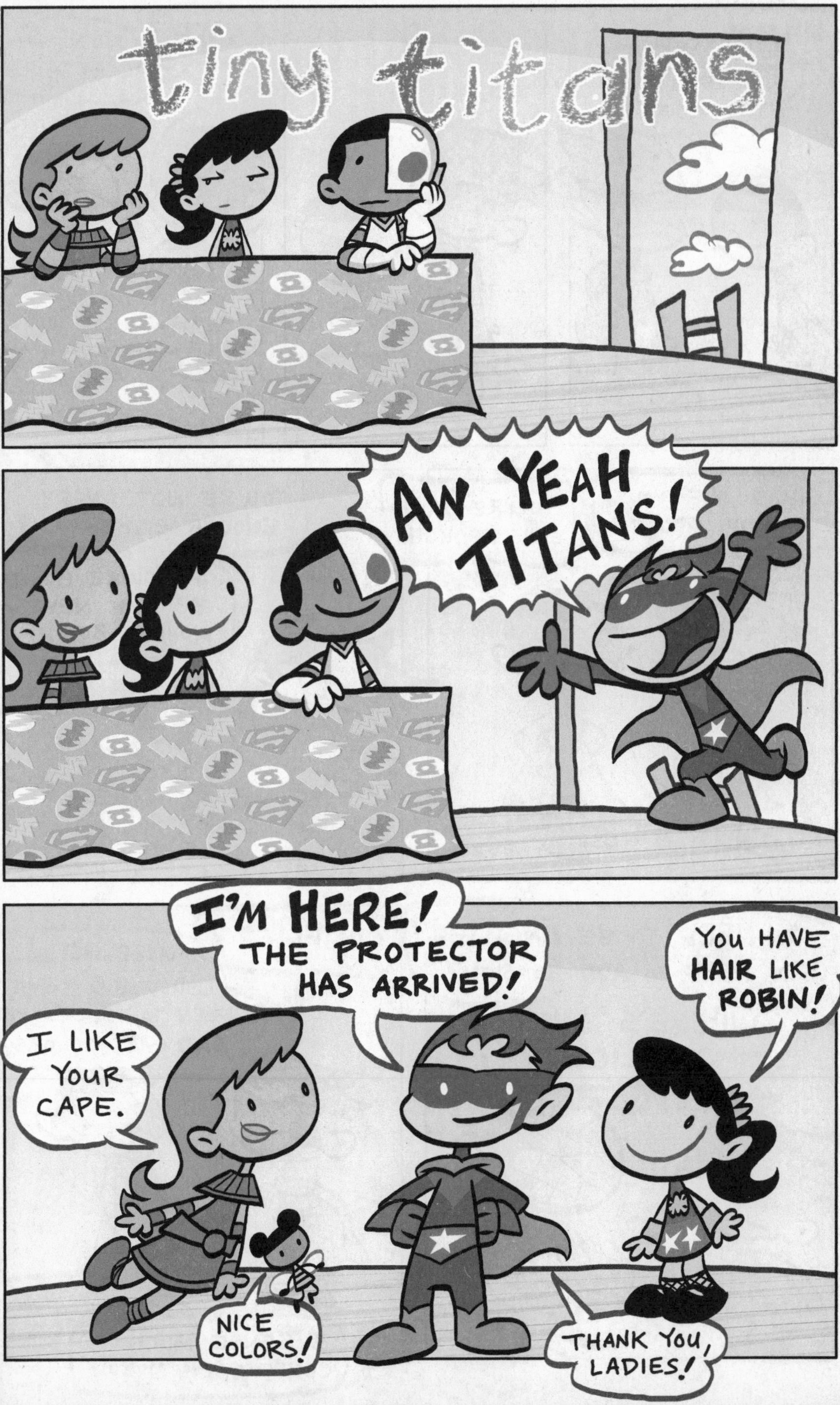
tiny titans
AW YEAH TITANS!
I'M HERE! THE PROTECTOR HAS ARRIVED!
You HAVE HAIR LIKE ROBIN!
I LIKE YOUR CAPE.
NICE COLORS!
THANK YOU, LADIES!

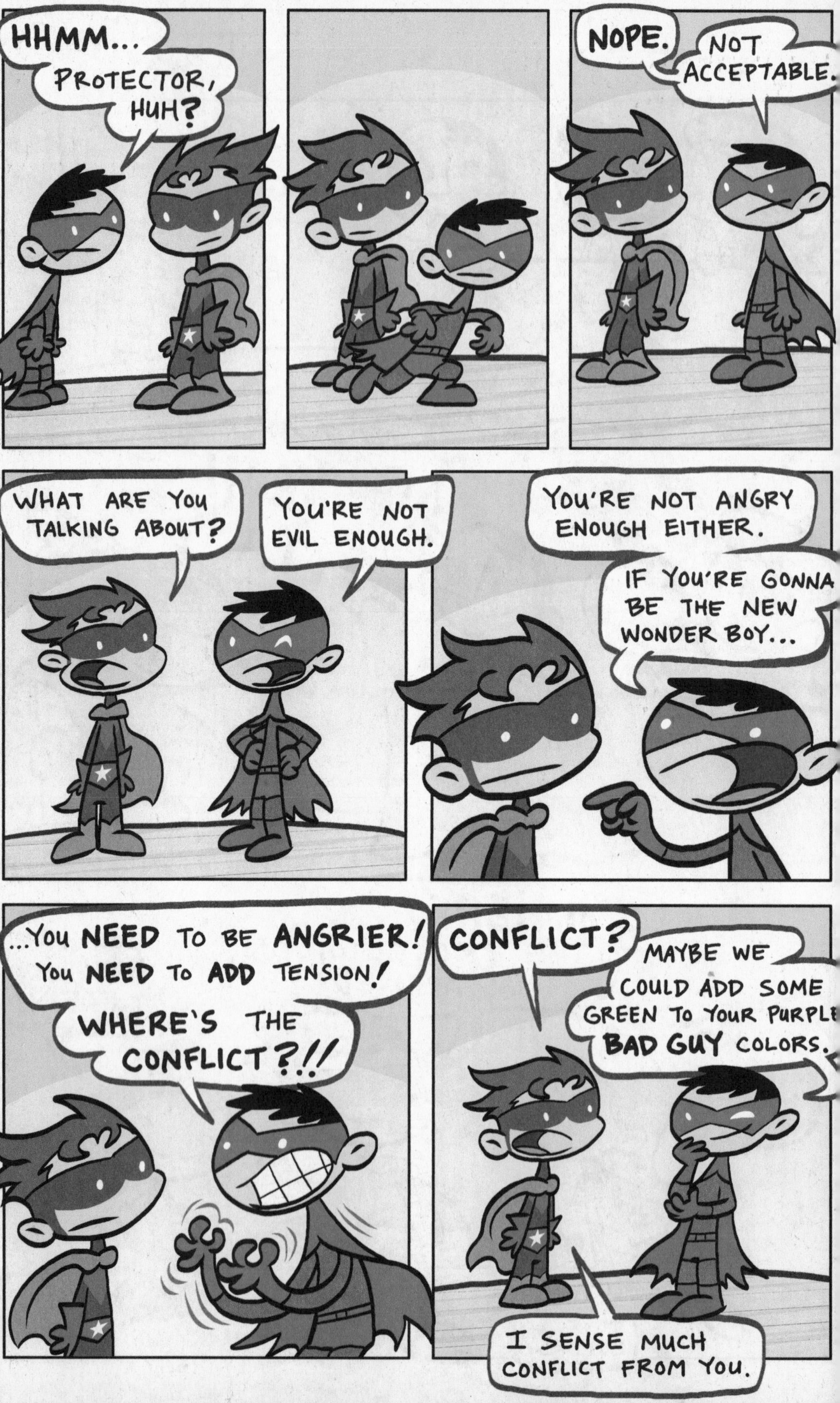
HHMM...
PROTECTOR, HUH?
NOPE.
NOT ACCEPTABLE.
WHAT ARE YOU TALKING ABOUT?
YOU'RE NOT EVIL ENOUGH.
YOU'RE NOT ANGRY ENOUGH EITHER.
IF YOU'RE GONNA BE THE NEW WONDER BOY...
...YOU NEED TO BE ANGRIER! YOU NEED TO ADD TENSION!
WHERE'S THE CONFLICT?!!
CONFLICT?
MAYBE WE COULD ADD SOME GREEN TO YOUR PURPLE BAD GUY COLORS.
I SENSE MUCH CONFLICT FROM YOU.

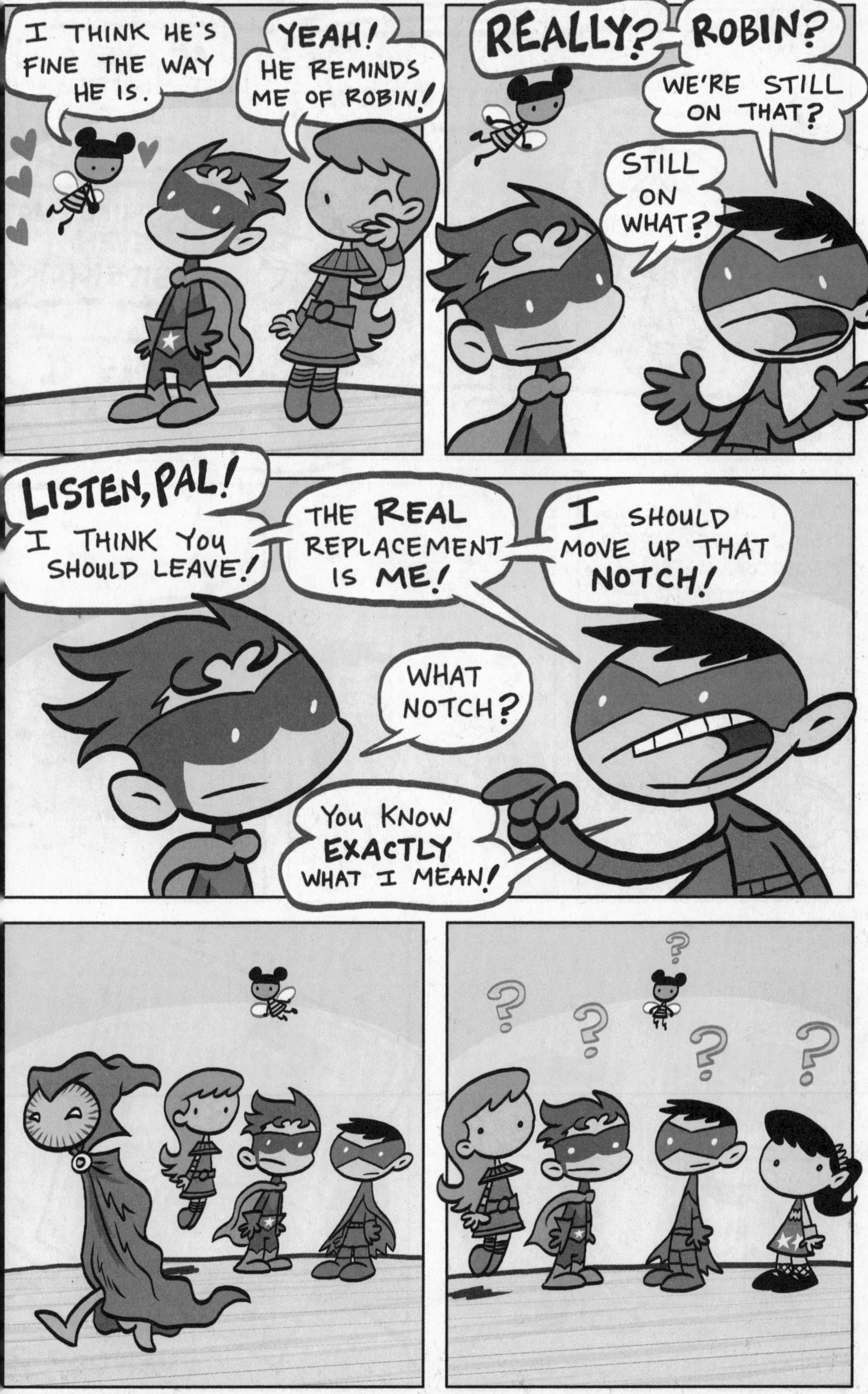
I THINK HE'S FINE THE WAY HE IS.
YEAH! HE REMINDS ME OF ROBIN!
REALLY?
ROBIN?
WE'RE STILL ON THAT?
STILL ON WHAT?
LISTEN, PAL! I THINK YOU SHOULD LEAVE!
THE REAL REPLACEMENT IS ME!
I SHOULD MOVE UP THAT NOTCH!
WHAT NOTCH?
YOU KNOW EXACTLY WHAT I MEAN!

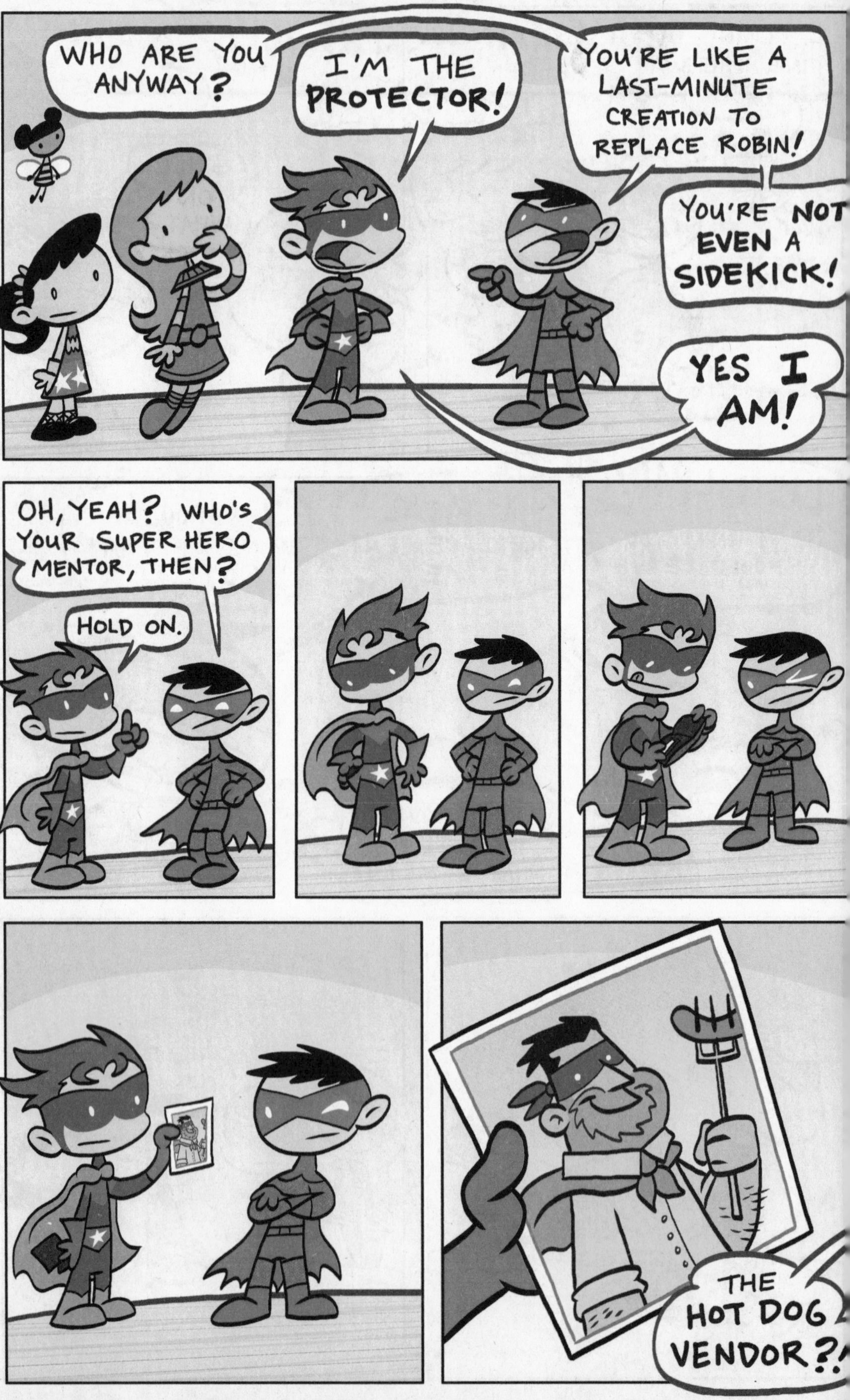
WHO ARE YOU ANYWAY?
I'M THE PROTECTOR!
YOU'RE LIKE A LAST-MINUTE CREATION TO REPLACE ROBIN!
YOU'RE NOT EVEN A SIDEKICK!
YES I AM!
OH, YEAH? WHO'S YOUR SUPER HERO MENTOR, THEN?
HOLD ON.
THE HOT DOG VENDOR?!

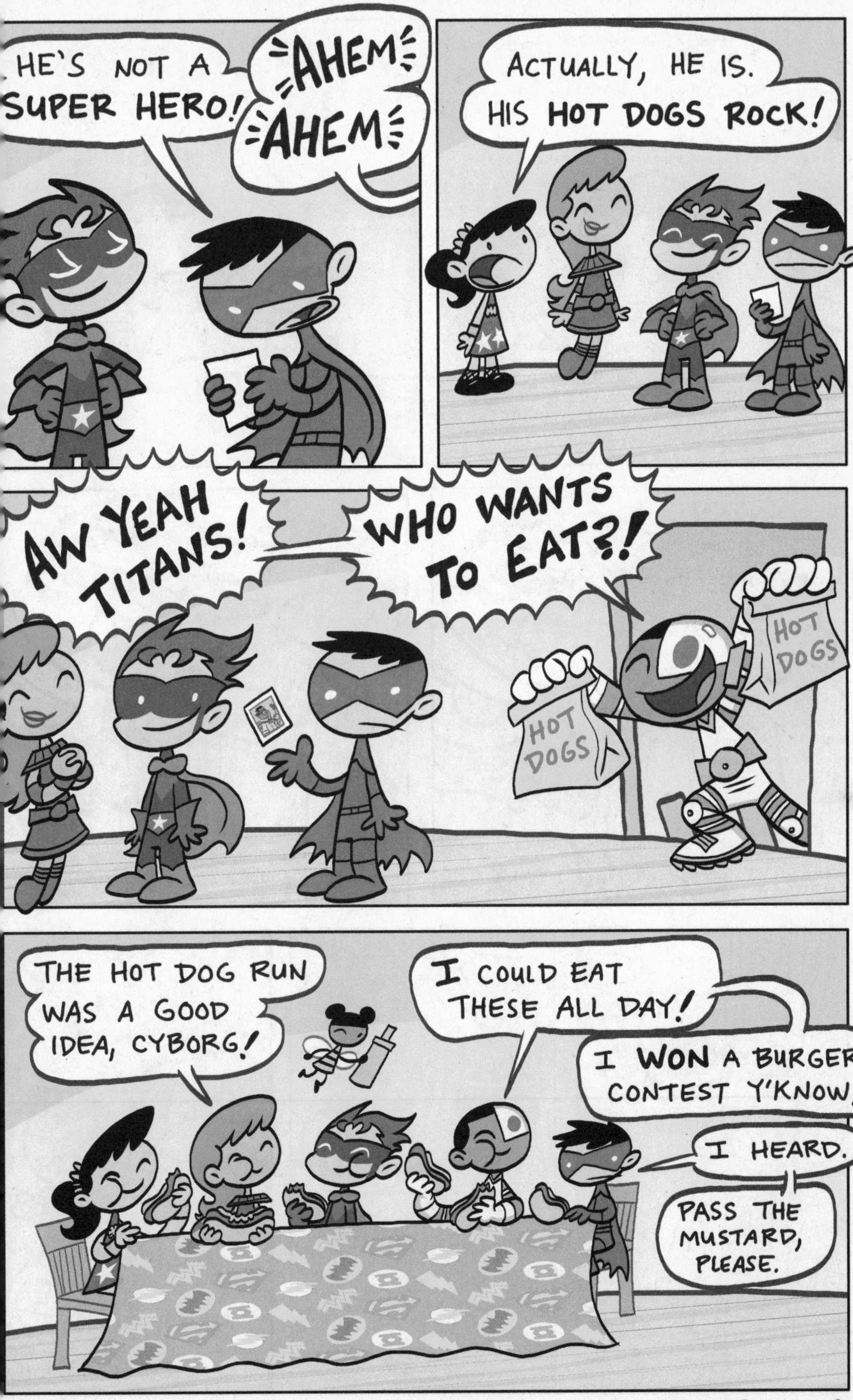
HE'S NOT A SUPER HERO!
AHEM AHEM
ACTUALLY, HE IS. HIS HOT DOGS ROCK!
AW YEAH TITANS!
WHO WANTS TO EAT?!
HOT DOGS
HOT DOGS
THE HOT DOG RUN WAS A GOOD IDEA, CYBORG!
I COULD EAT THESE ALL DAY!
I WON A BURGER CONTEST Y'KNOW!
I HEARD.
PASS THE MUSTARD, PLEASE.
-MENTORLICIOUS.

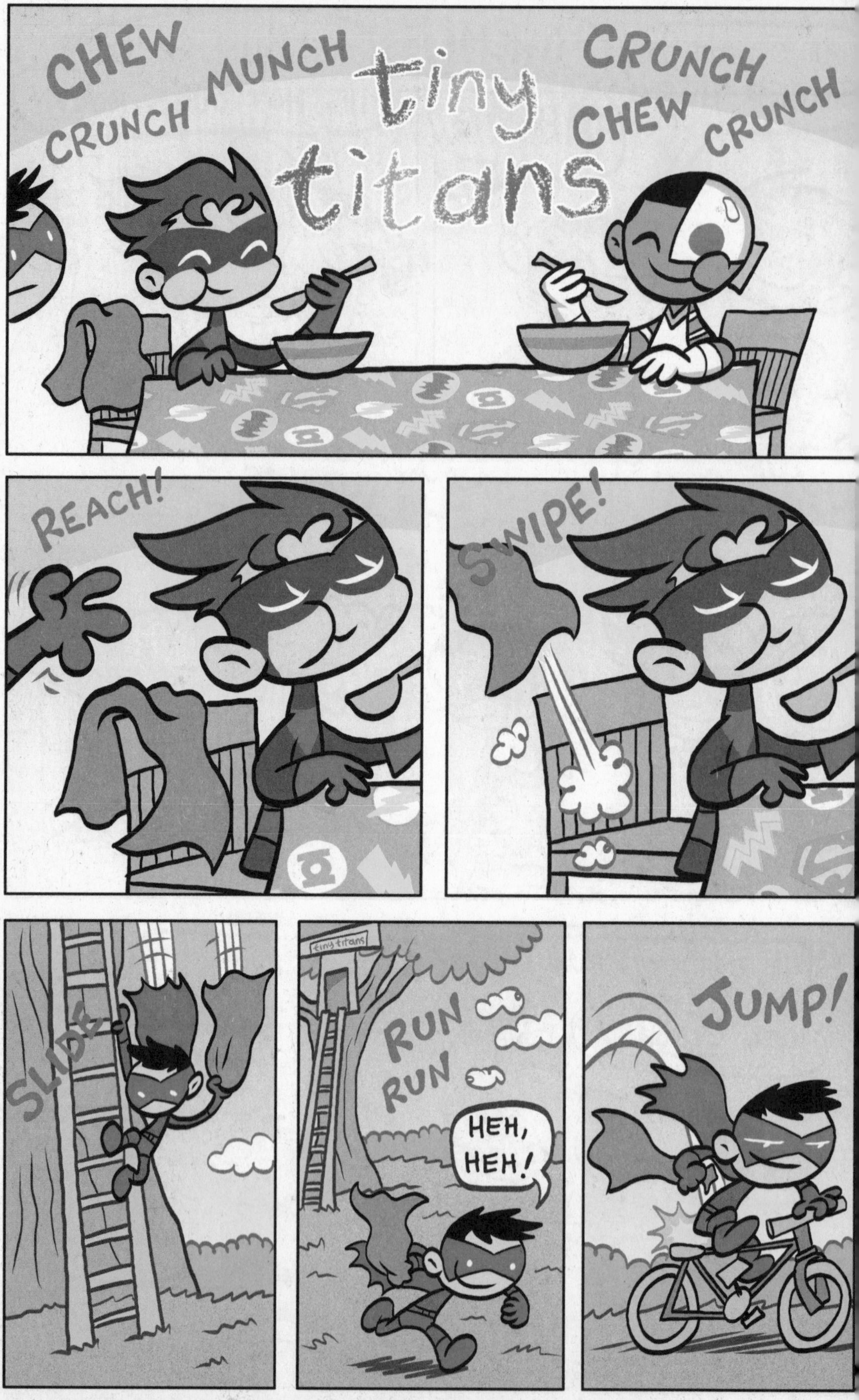
CHEW
CRUNCH
MUNCH
tiny titans
CRUNCH
CHEW
CRUNCH
REACH!
SWIPE!
SLIDE
tiny titans
RUN
RUN
HEH, HEH!
JUMP!

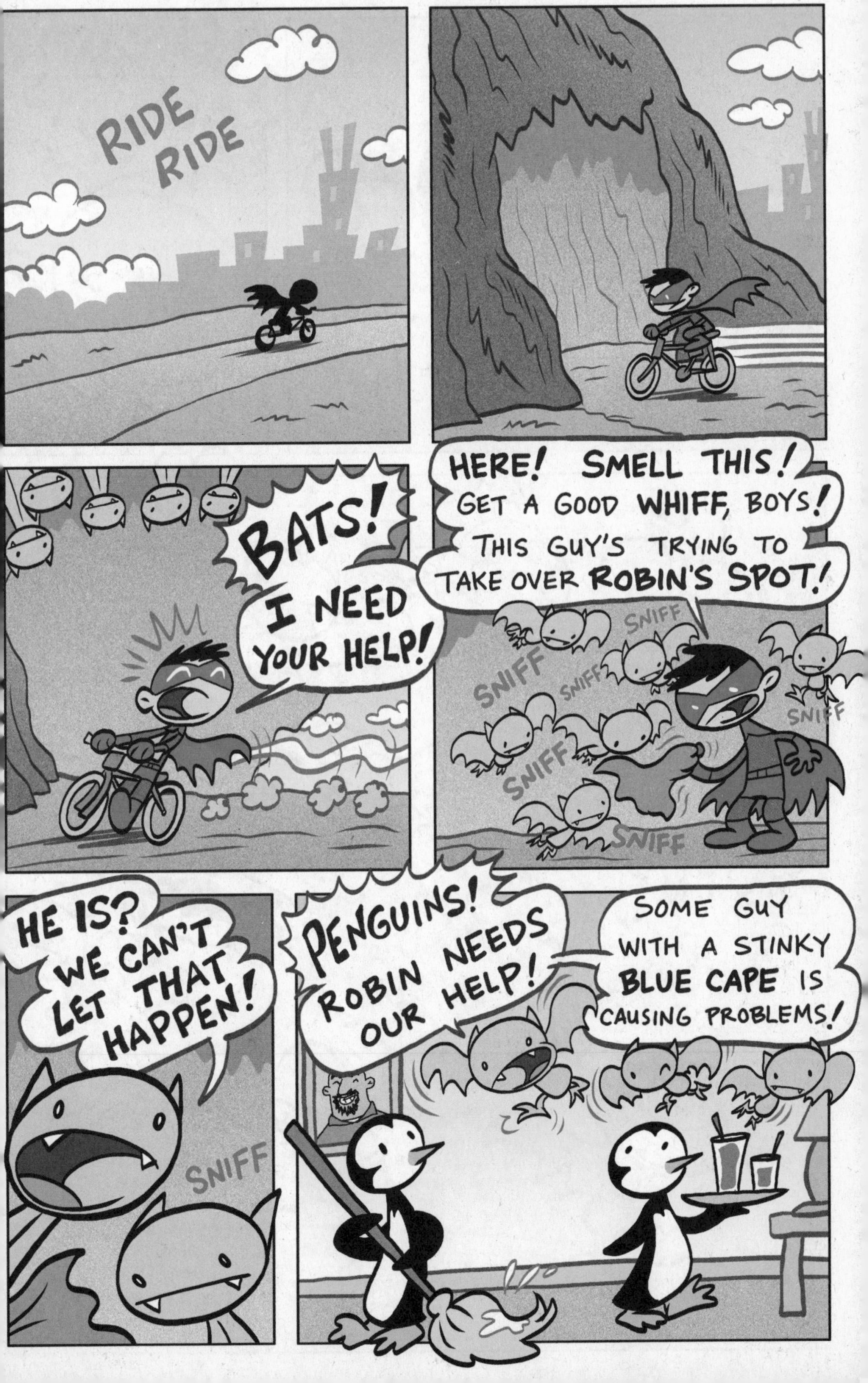
RIDE
RIDE
BATS!
I NEED YOUR HELP!
HERE! SMELL THIS! GET A GOOD WHIFF, BOYS! THIS GUY'S TRYING TO TAKE OVER ROBIN'S SPOT!
SNIFF
SNIFF
SNIFF
SNIFF
SNIFF
SNIFF
SNIFF
HE IS? WE CAN'T LET THAT HAPPEN!
SNIFF
PENGUINS! ROBIN NEEDS OUR HELP!
SOME GUY WITH A STINKY BLUE CAPE IS CAUSING PROBLEMS!

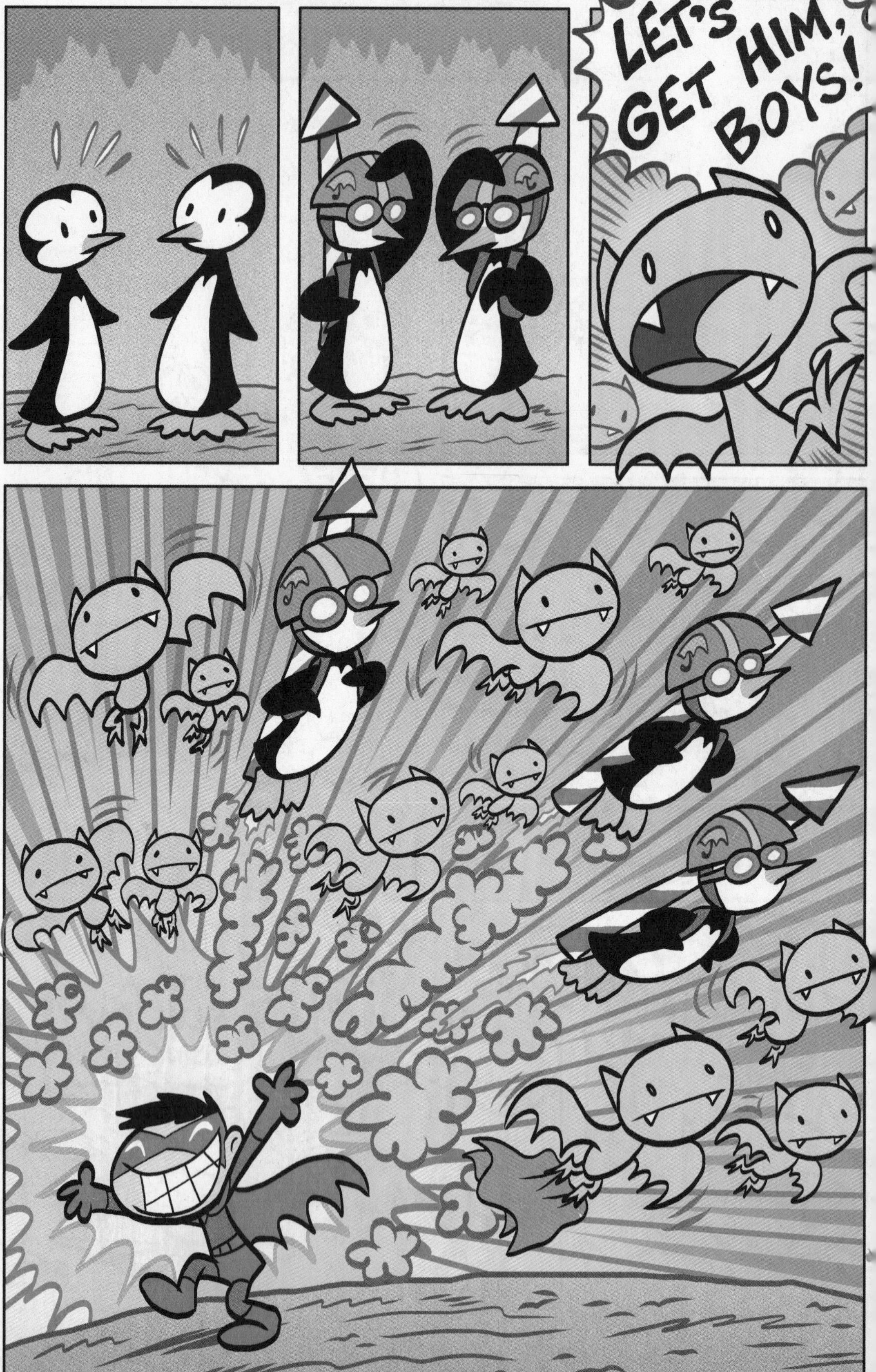
LET'S GET HIM, BOYS!

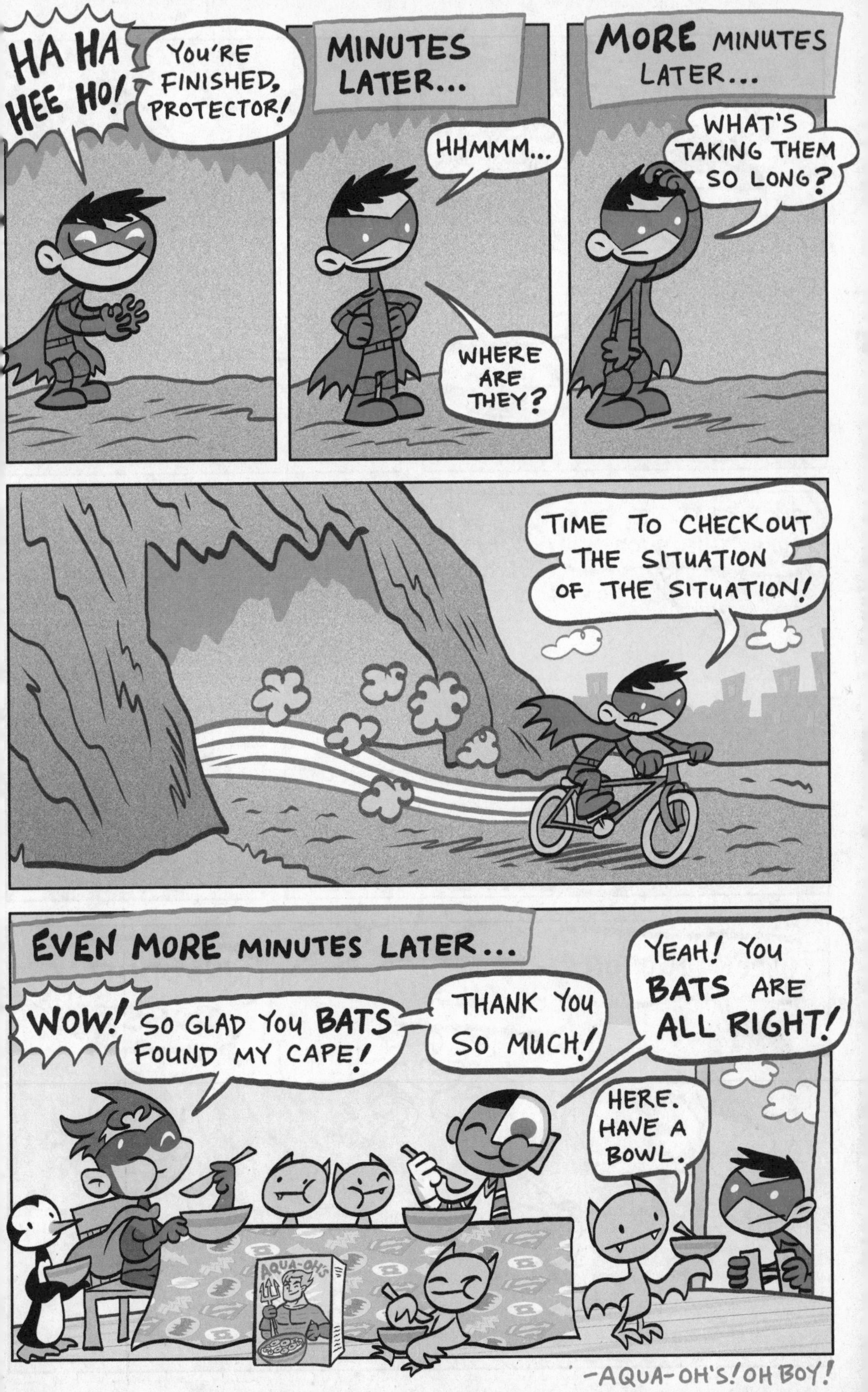
HA HA HEE HO!
You're FINISHED, PROTECTOR!
MINUTES LATER...
HHMMM...
WHERE ARE THEY?
MORE MINUTES LATER...
WHAT'S TAKING THEM SO LONG?
TIME TO CHECKOUT THE SITUATION OF THE SITUATION!
EVEN MORE MINUTES LATER...
WOW!
SO GLAD YOU BATS FOUND MY CAPE!
THANK YOU SO MUCH!
YEAH! YOU BATS ARE ALL RIGHT!
HERE. HAVE A BOWL.
AQUA-OH'S
-AQUA-OH'S! OH BOY!

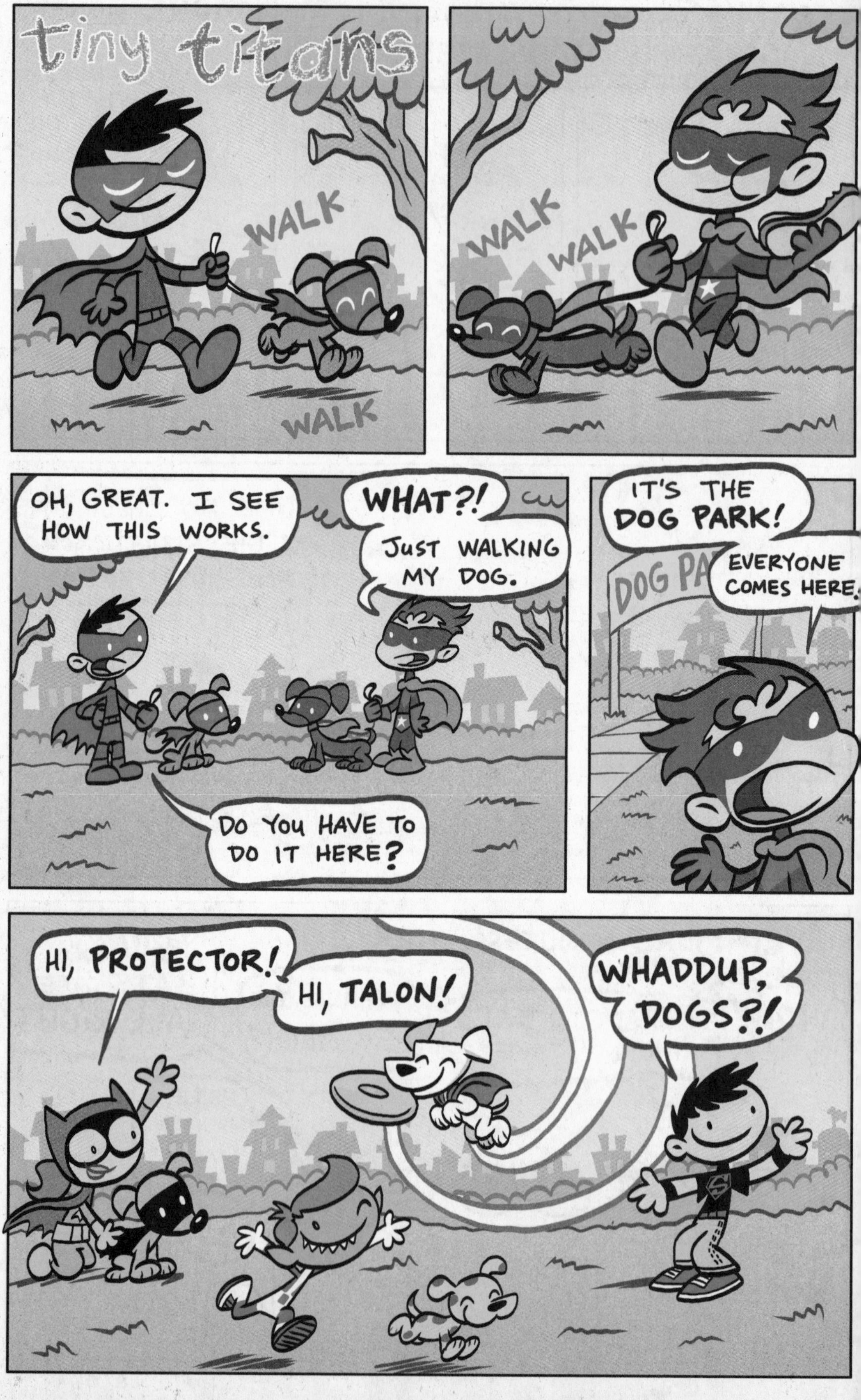
tiny titans
WALK
WALK
WALK
WALK
OH, GREAT. I SEE HOW THIS WORKS.
WHAT?!
JUST WALKING MY DOG.
DO YOU HAVE TO DO IT HERE?
IT'S THE DOG PARK!
EVERYONE COMES HERE.
HI, PROTECTOR!
HI, TALON!
WHADDUP, DOGS?!

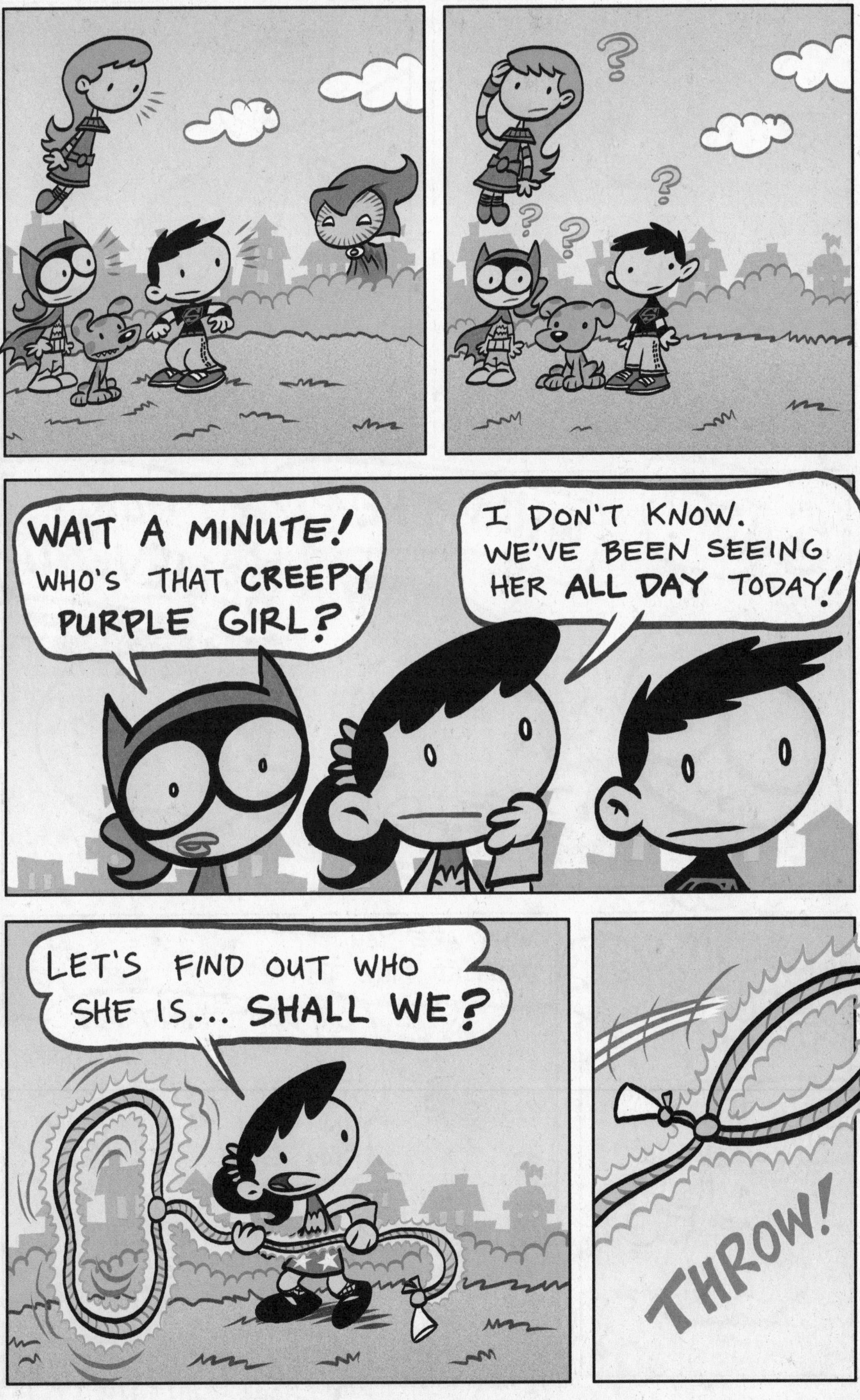
WAIT A MINUTE! WHO'S THAT CREEPY PURPLE GIRL?
I DON'T KNOW. WE'VE BEEN SEEING HER ALL DAY TODAY!
LET'S FIND OUT WHO SHE IS... SHALL WE?
THROW!

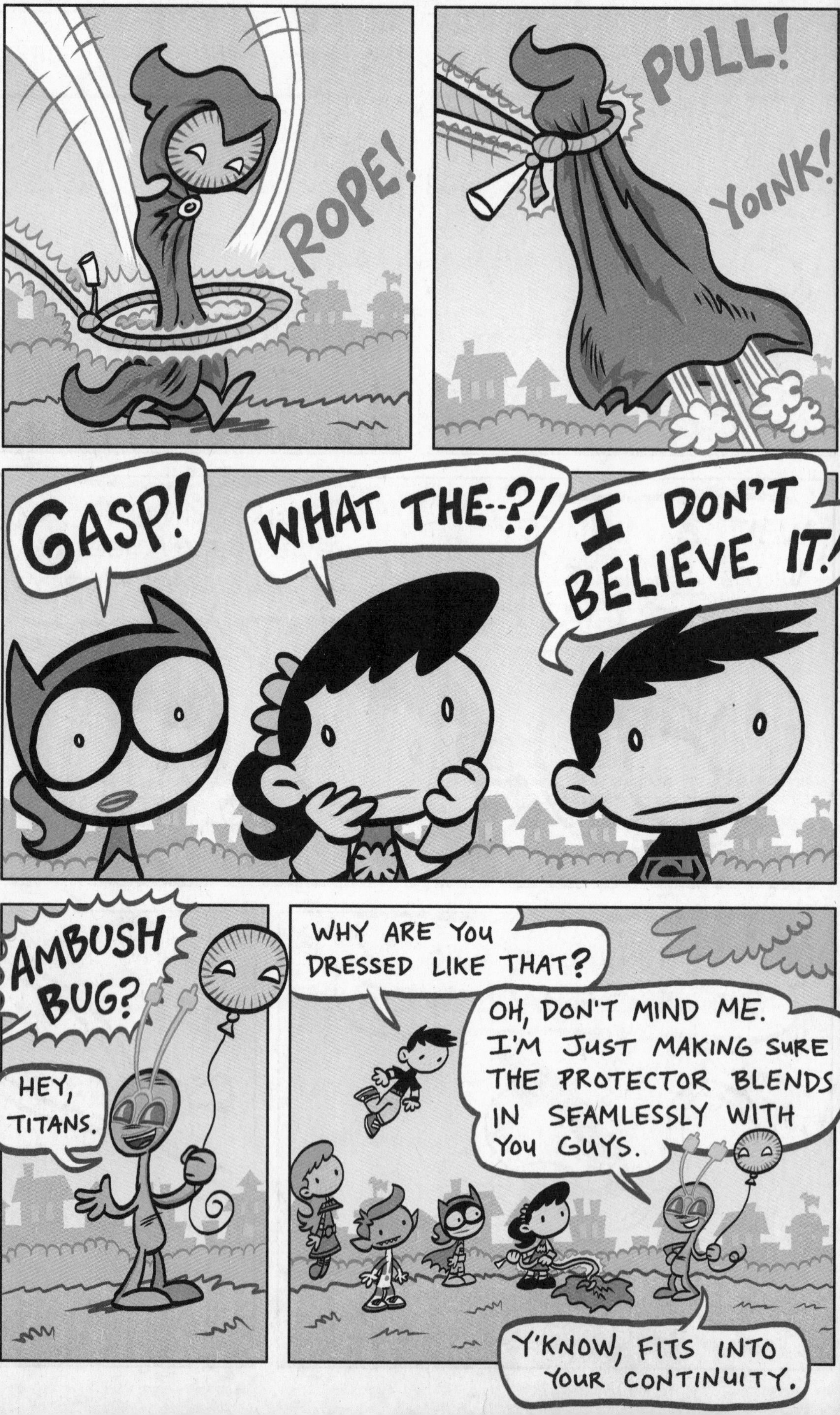
ROPE!
PULL!
YOINK!
GASP!
WHAT THE--?!
I DON'T BELIEVE IT!
AMBUSH BUG?
HEY, TITANS.
WHY ARE YOU DRESSED LIKE THAT?
OH, DON'T MIND ME. I'M JUST MAKING SURE THE PROTECTOR BLENDS IN SEAMLESSLY WITH YOU GUYS.
Y'KNOW, FITS INTO YOUR CONTINUITY.

CONTINUITY?

WHAT'S CONTINUITY?

WAIT, I GOT THIS.

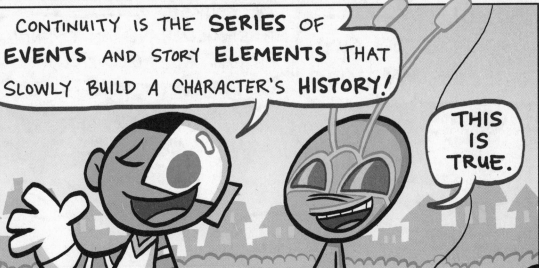

CONTINUITY IS THE **SERIES** OF **EVENTS** AND STORY **ELEMENTS** THAT SLOWLY BUILD A CHARACTER'S **HISTORY!**

THIS IS TRUE.

DIG?

WE DIG.

OH, THAT MAKES SENSE.

HOW WAS THAT?

VERY GOOD. I THINK YOU GOT IT NOW.

AFTER ALL, **I AM A SUPER HERO!**

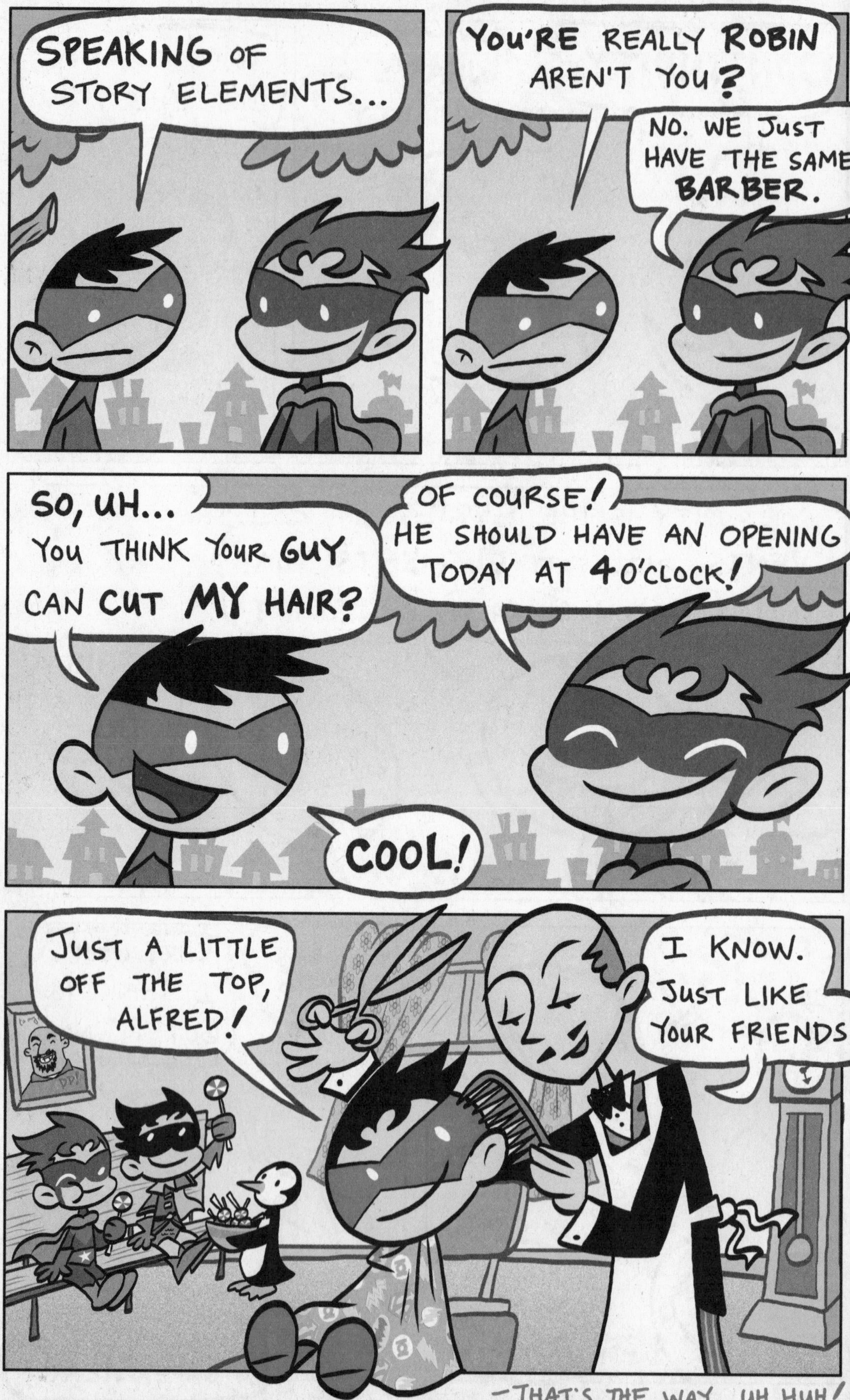
SPEAKING OF STORY ELEMENTS...
YOU'RE REALLY ROBIN AREN'T YOU?
NO. WE JUST HAVE THE SAME BARBER.
SO, UH... YOU THINK YOUR GUY CAN CUT MY HAIR?
OF COURSE! HE SHOULD HAVE AN OPENING TODAY AT 4 O'CLOCK!
COOL!
JUST A LITTLE OFF THE TOP, ALFRED!
I KNOW. JUST LIKE YOUR FRIENDS

—THAT'S THE WAY...UH, HUH!

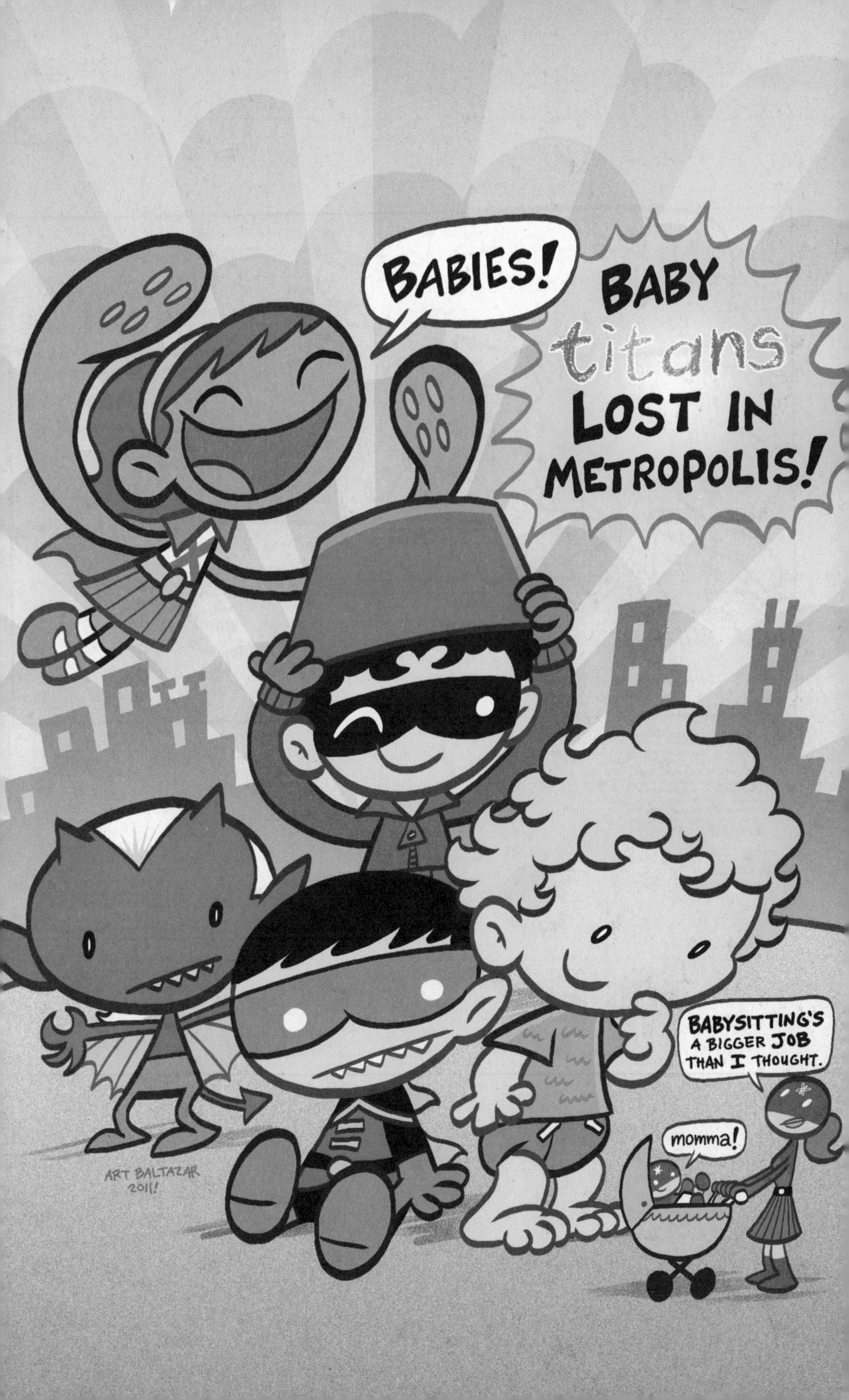

BABIES!
BABY titans LOST IN METROPOLIS!
BABYSITTING'S A BIGGER JOB THAN I THOUGHT.
momma!
ART BALTAZAR 2011!

tiny titans

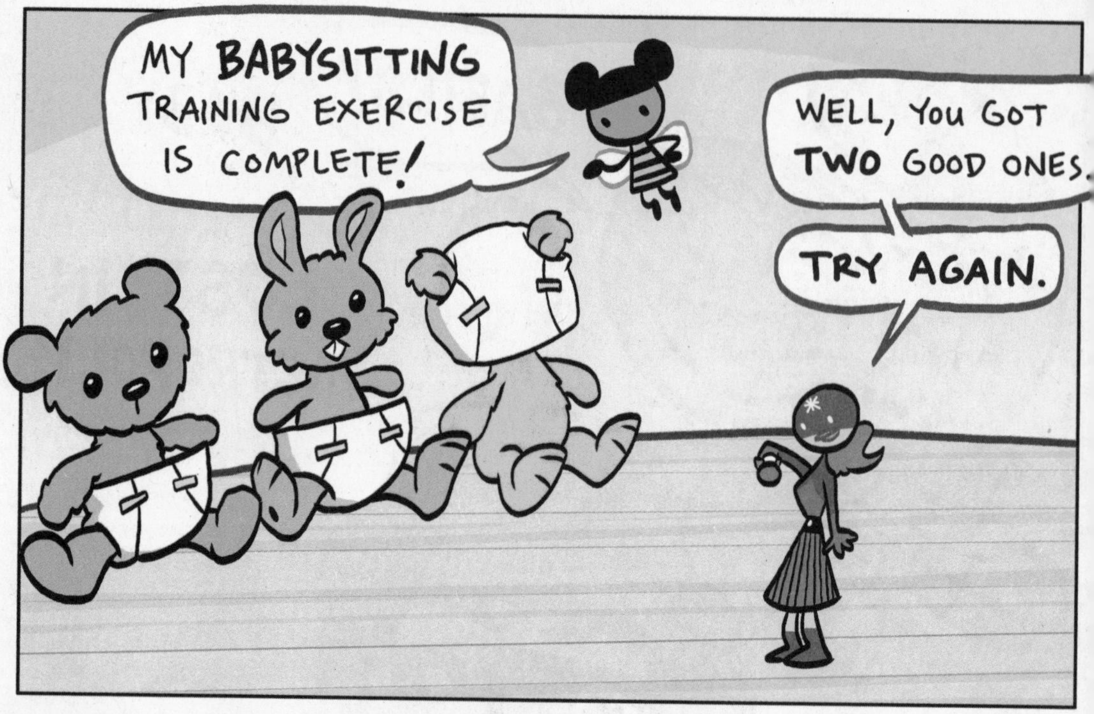
MY BABYSITTING TRAINING EXERCISE IS COMPLETE!
WELL, YOU GOT TWO GOOD ONES.
TRY AGAIN.

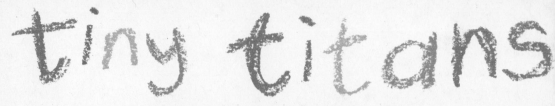

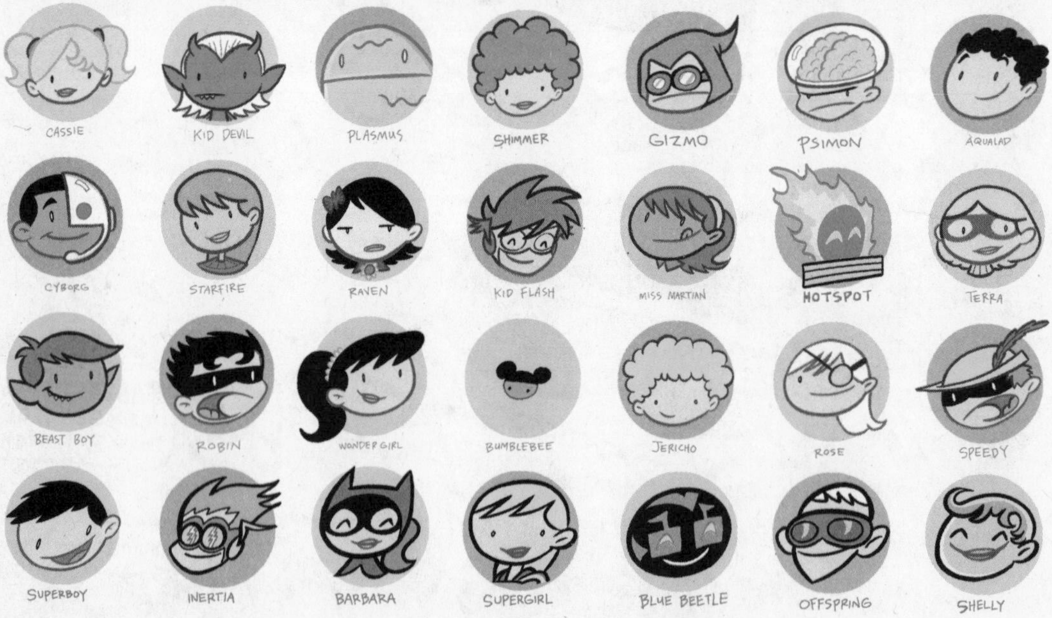
CASSIE
KID DEVIL
PLASMUS
SHIMMER
GIZMO
PSIMON
AQUALAD
CYBORG
STARFIRE
RAVEN
KID FLASH
MISS MARTIAN
HOTSPOT
TERRA
BEAST BOY
ROBIN
WONDER GIRL
BUMBLEBEE
JERICHO
ROSE
SPEEDY
SUPERBOY
INERTIA
BARBARA
SUPERGIRL
BLUE BEETLE
OFFSPRING
SHELLY

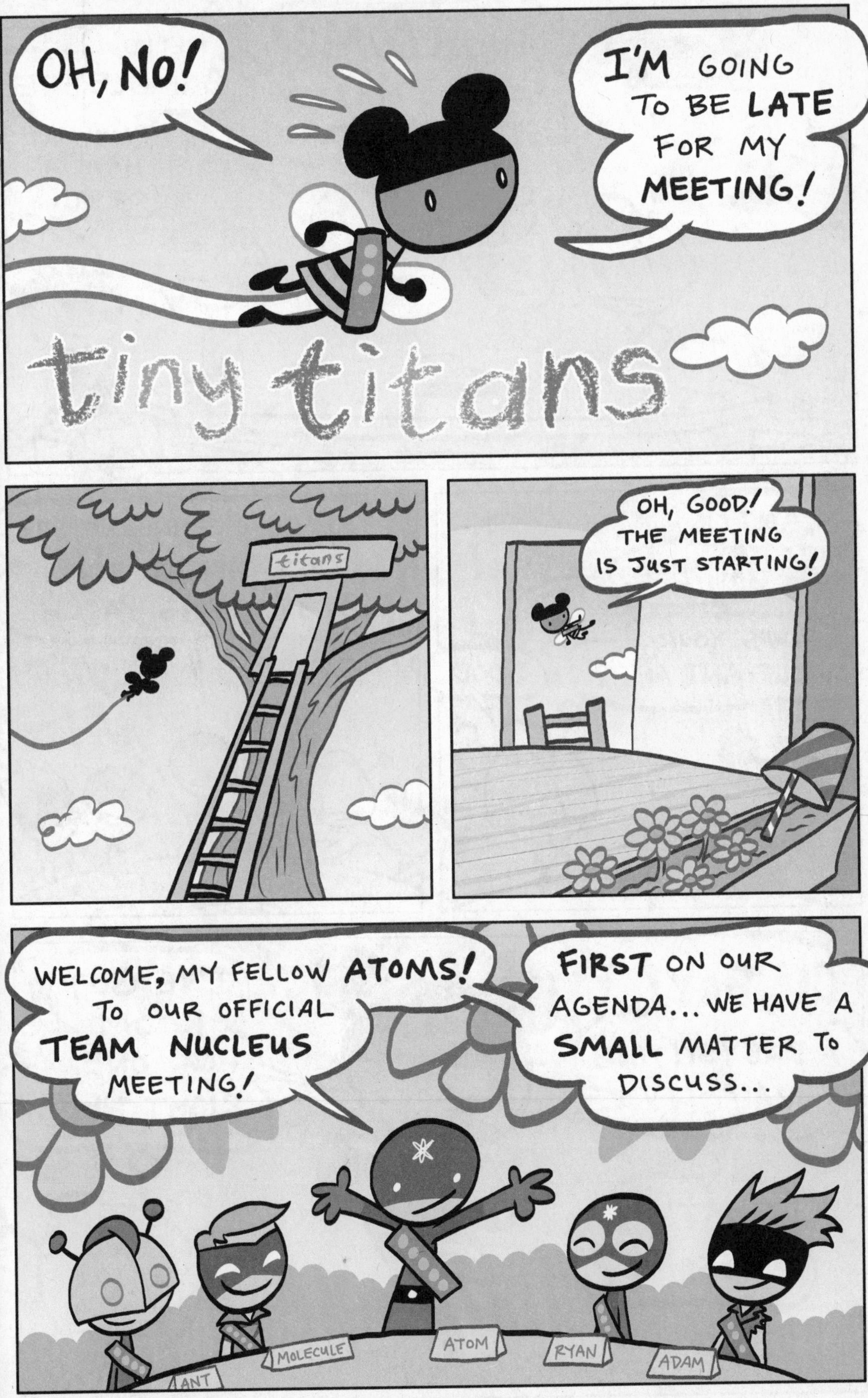
OH, NO!
I'M GOING TO BE LATE FOR MY MEETING!
tiny titans
titans
OH, GOOD! THE MEETING IS JUST STARTING!
WELCOME, MY FELLOW ATOMS! TO OUR OFFICIAL TEAM NUCLEUS MEETING!
FIRST ON OUR AGENDA... WE HAVE A SMALL MATTER TO DISCUSS...
ANT
MOLECULE
ATOM
RYAN
ADAM

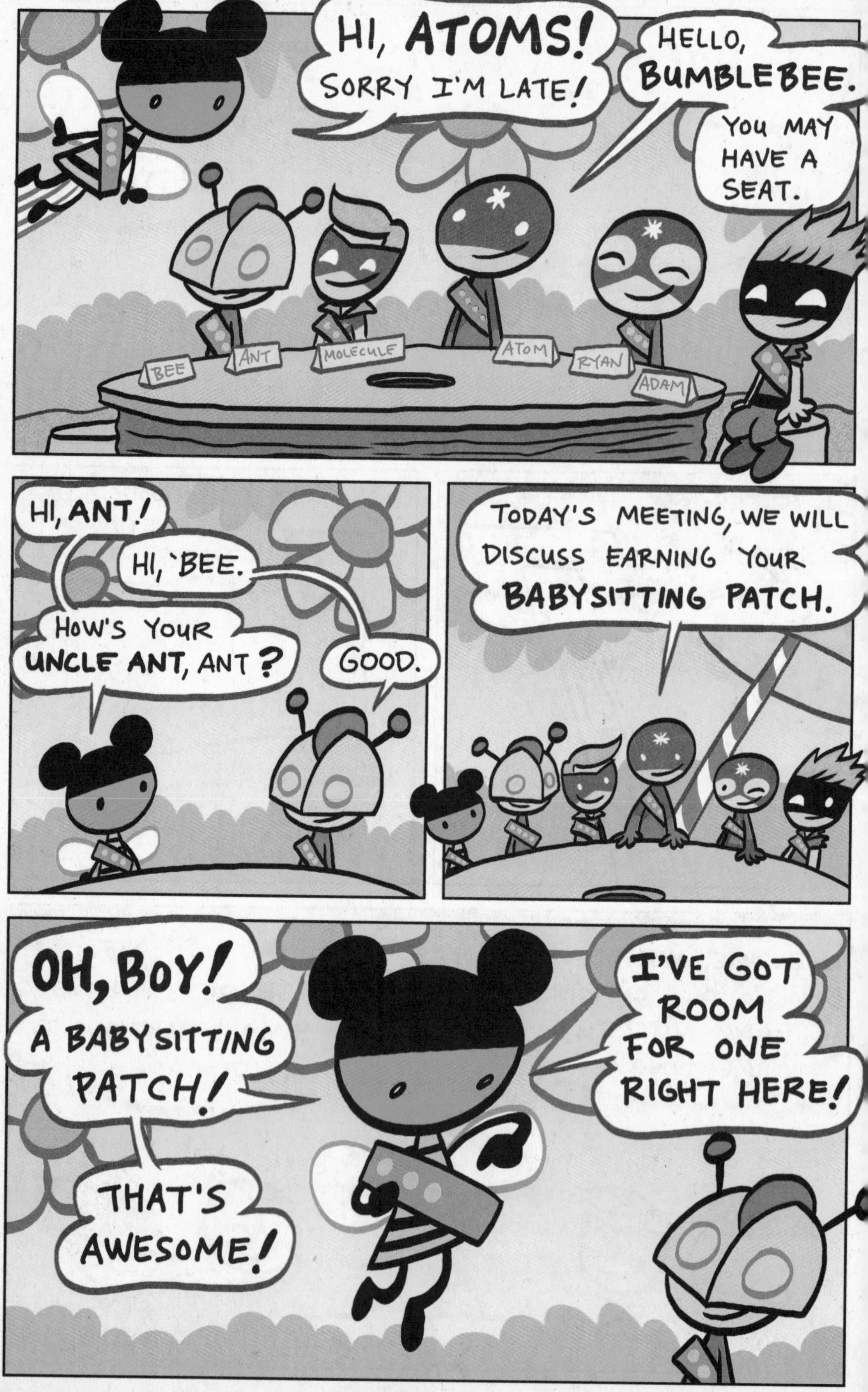
HI, ATOMS! SORRY I'M LATE!
HELLO, BUMBLEBEE.
YOU MAY HAVE A SEAT.
BEE
ANT
MOLECULE
ATOM
RYAN
ADAM
HI, ANT!
HI, `BEE.
HOW'S YOUR UNCLE ANT, ANT?
GOOD.
TODAY'S MEETING, WE WILL DISCUSS EARNING YOUR BABYSITTING PATCH.
OH, BOY! A BABYSITTING PATCH!
THAT'S AWESOME!
I'VE GOT ROOM FOR ONE RIGHT HERE!

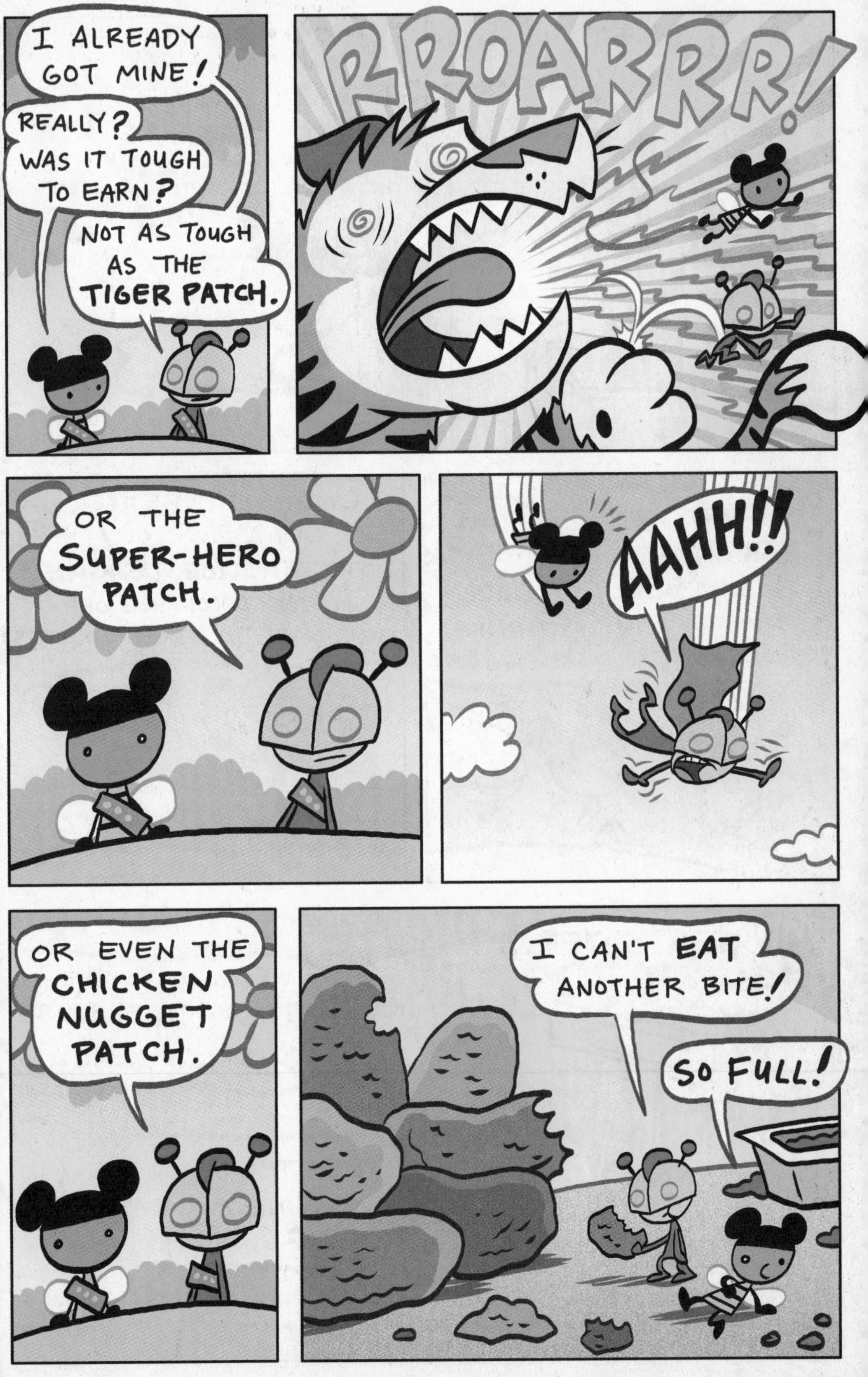
I ALREADY GOT MINE!
REALLY? WAS IT TOUGH TO EARN?
NOT AS TOUGH AS THE TIGER PATCH.
RROARRRR!
OR THE SUPER-HERO PATCH.
AAHH!!
OR EVEN THE CHICKEN NUGGET PATCH.
I CAN'T EAT ANOTHER BITE!
SO FULL!

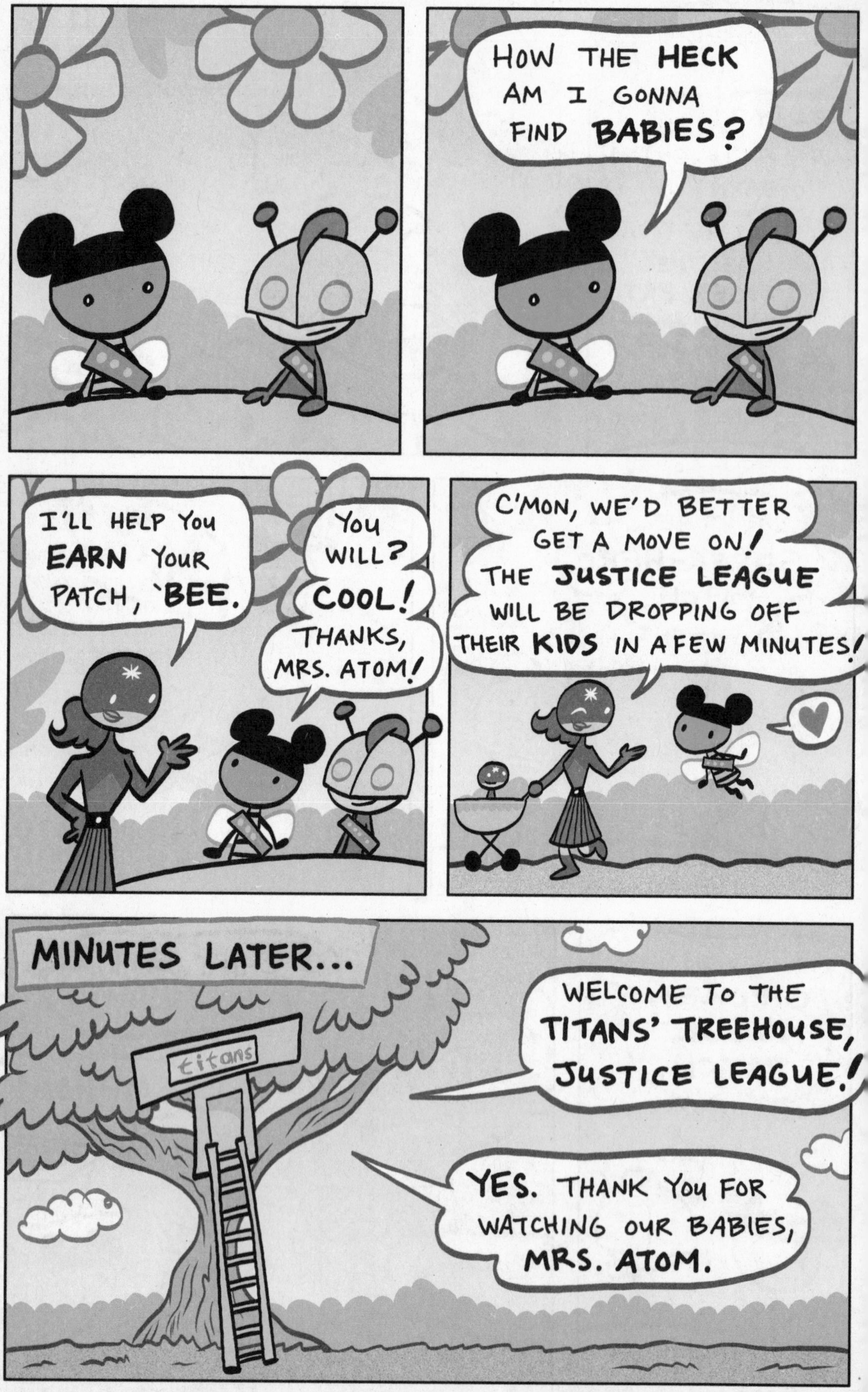
HOW THE HECK AM I GONNA FIND BABIES?
I'LL HELP YOU EARN YOUR PATCH, 'BEE.
YOU WILL? COOL! THANKS, MRS. ATOM!
C'MON, WE'D BETTER GET A MOVE ON! THE JUSTICE LEAGUE WILL BE DROPPING OFF THEIR KIDS IN A FEW MINUTES!
MINUTES LATER...
titans
WELCOME TO THE TITANS' TREEHOUSE, JUSTICE LEAGUE!
YES. THANK YOU FOR WATCHING OUR BABIES, MRS. ATOM.

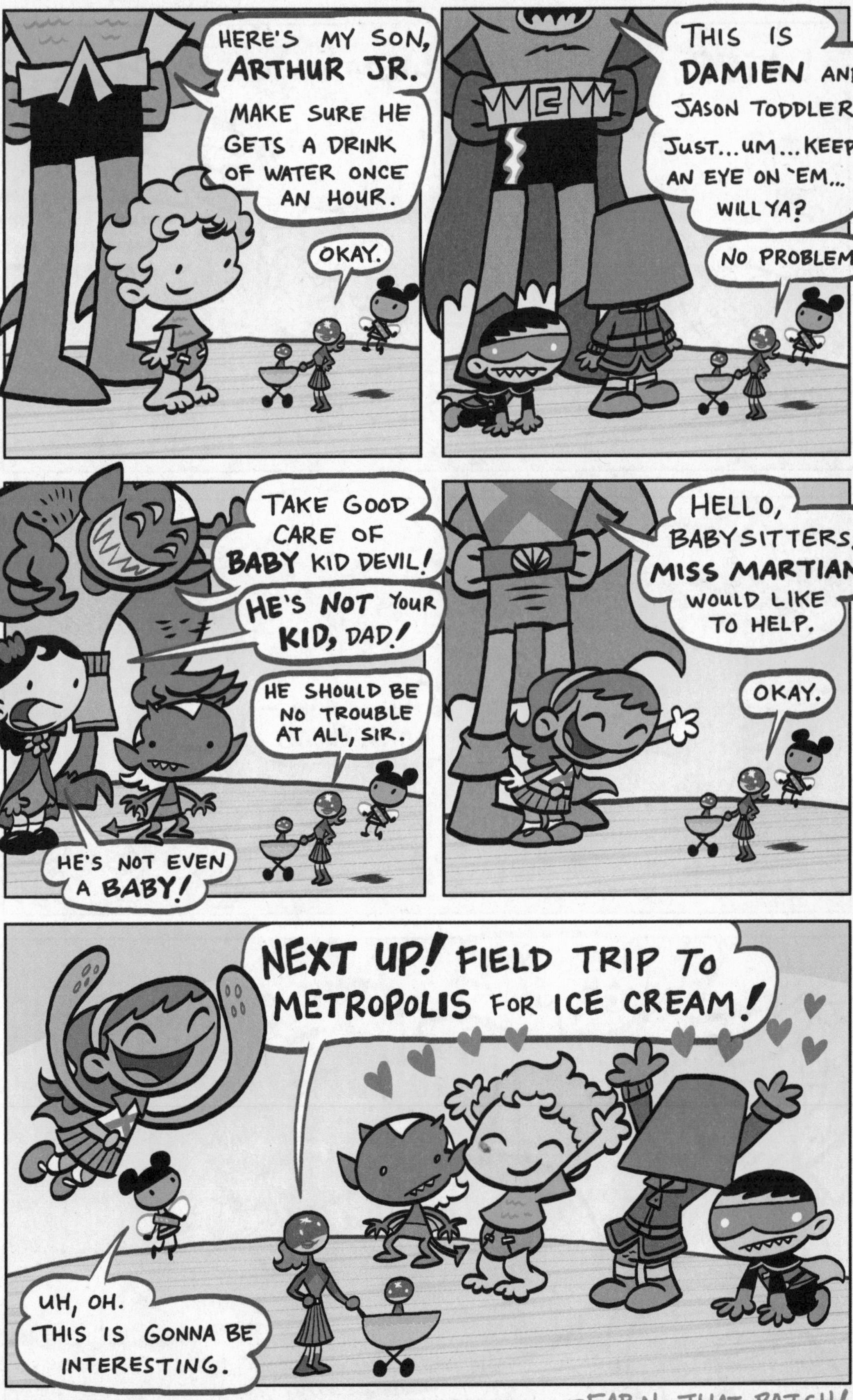
HERE'S MY SON, ARTHUR JR.
MAKE SURE HE GETS A DRINK OF WATER ONCE AN HOUR.
OKAY.
THIS IS DAMIEN AND JASON TODDLER.
JUST...UM...KEEP AN EYE ON 'EM... WILLYA?
NO PROBLEM.
TAKE GOOD CARE OF BABY KID DEVIL!
HE'S NOT YOUR KID, DAD!
HE SHOULD BE NO TROUBLE AT ALL, SIR.
HE'S NOT EVEN A BABY!
HELLO, BABYSITTERS! MISS MARTIAN WOULD LIKE TO HELP.
OKAY.
NEXT UP! FIELD TRIP TO METROPOLIS FOR ICE CREAM!
UH, OH. THIS IS GONNA BE INTERESTING.

-EARN THAT PATCH!

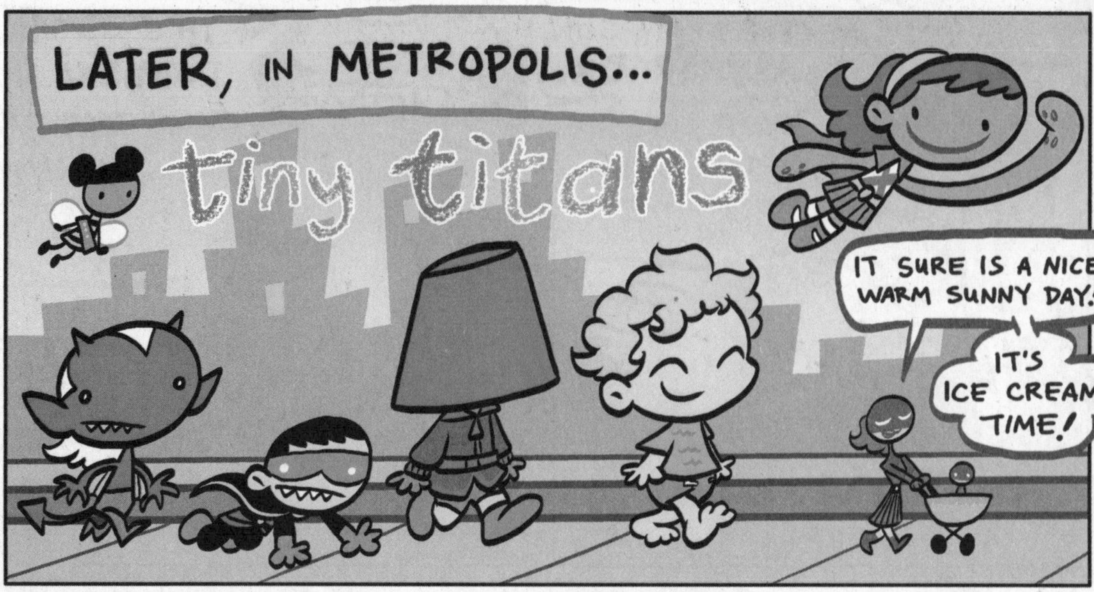
LATER, IN METROPOLIS...
tiny titans
IT SURE IS A NICE WARM SUNNY DAY!
IT'S ICE CREAM TIME!

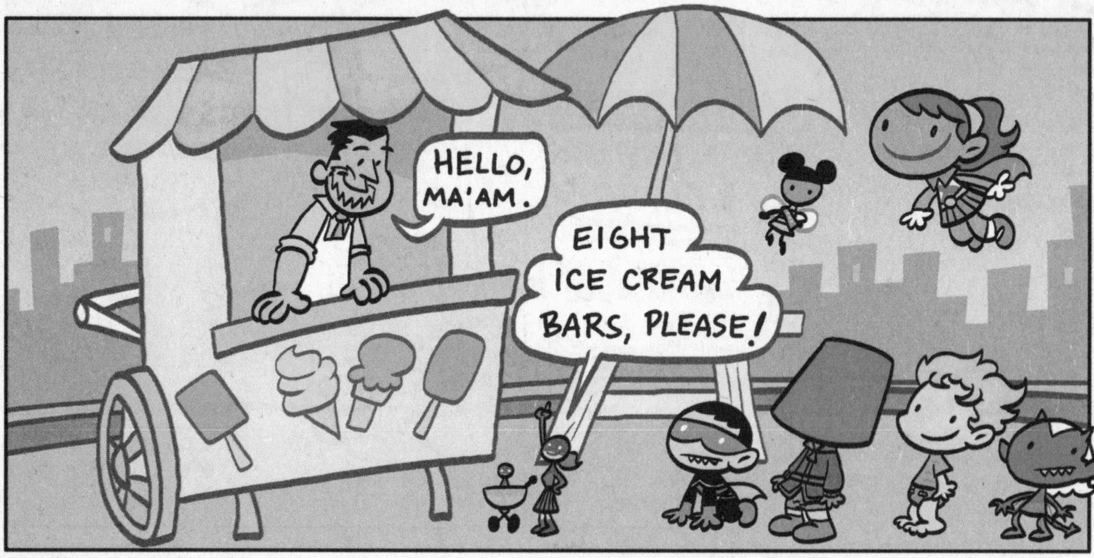
HELLO, MA'AM.
EIGHT ICE CREAM BARS, PLEASE!

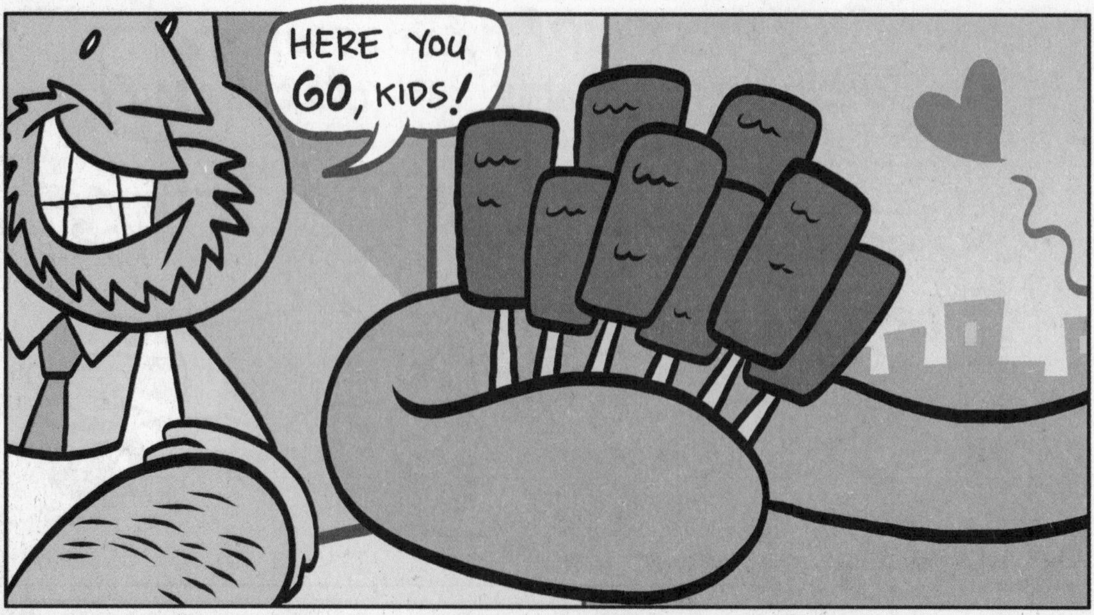
HERE YOU GO, KIDS!

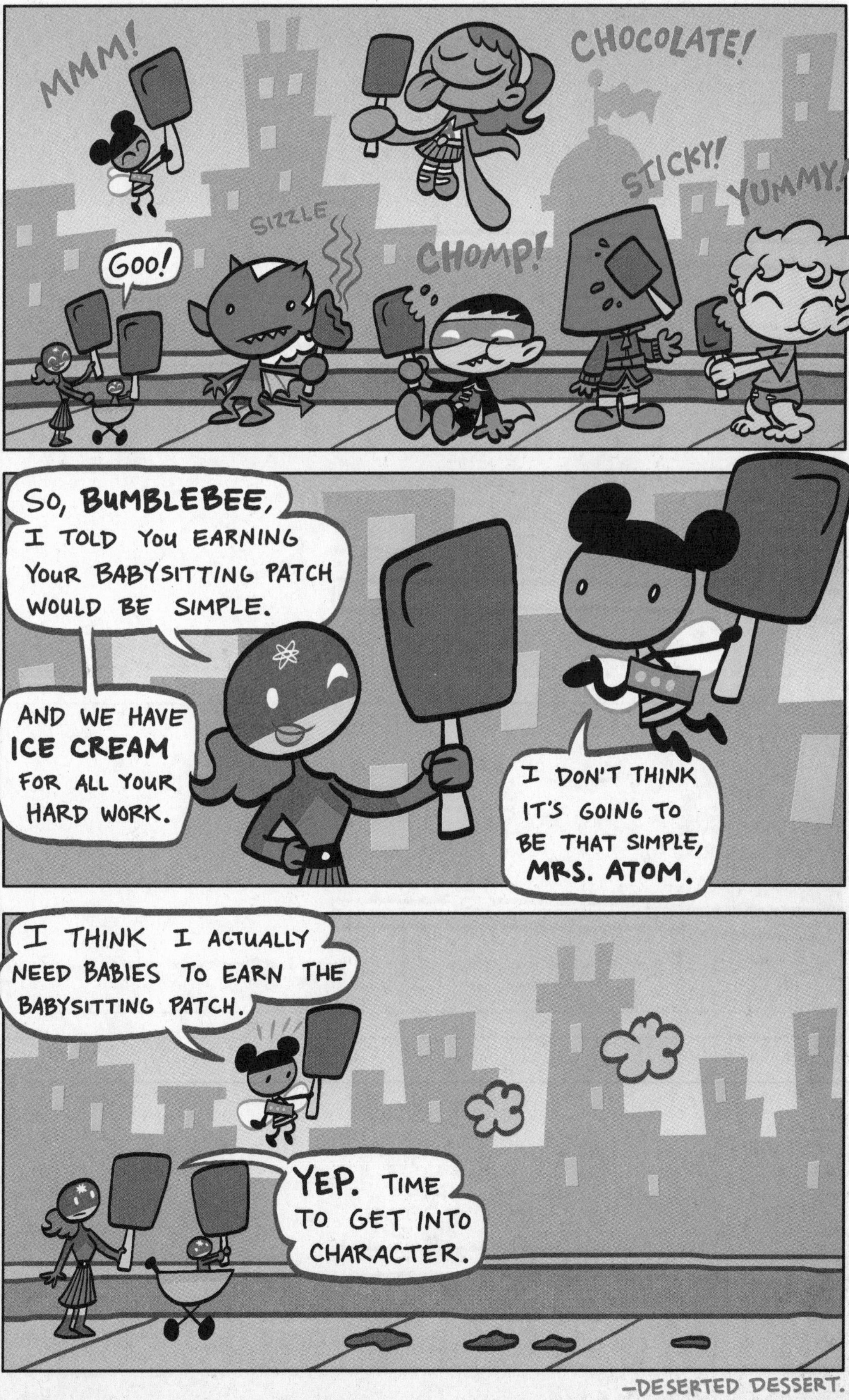
MMM!
CHOCOLATE!
GOO!
SIZZLE
CHOMP!
STICKY!
YUMMY!
SO, BUMBLEBEE, I TOLD YOU EARNING YOUR BABYSITTING PATCH WOULD BE SIMPLE.
AND WE HAVE ICE CREAM FOR ALL YOUR HARD WORK.
I DON'T THINK IT'S GOING TO BE THAT SIMPLE, MRS. ATOM.
I THINK I ACTUALLY NEED BABIES TO EARN THE BABYSITTING PATCH.
YEP. TIME TO GET INTO CHARACTER.

—DESERTED DESSERT.

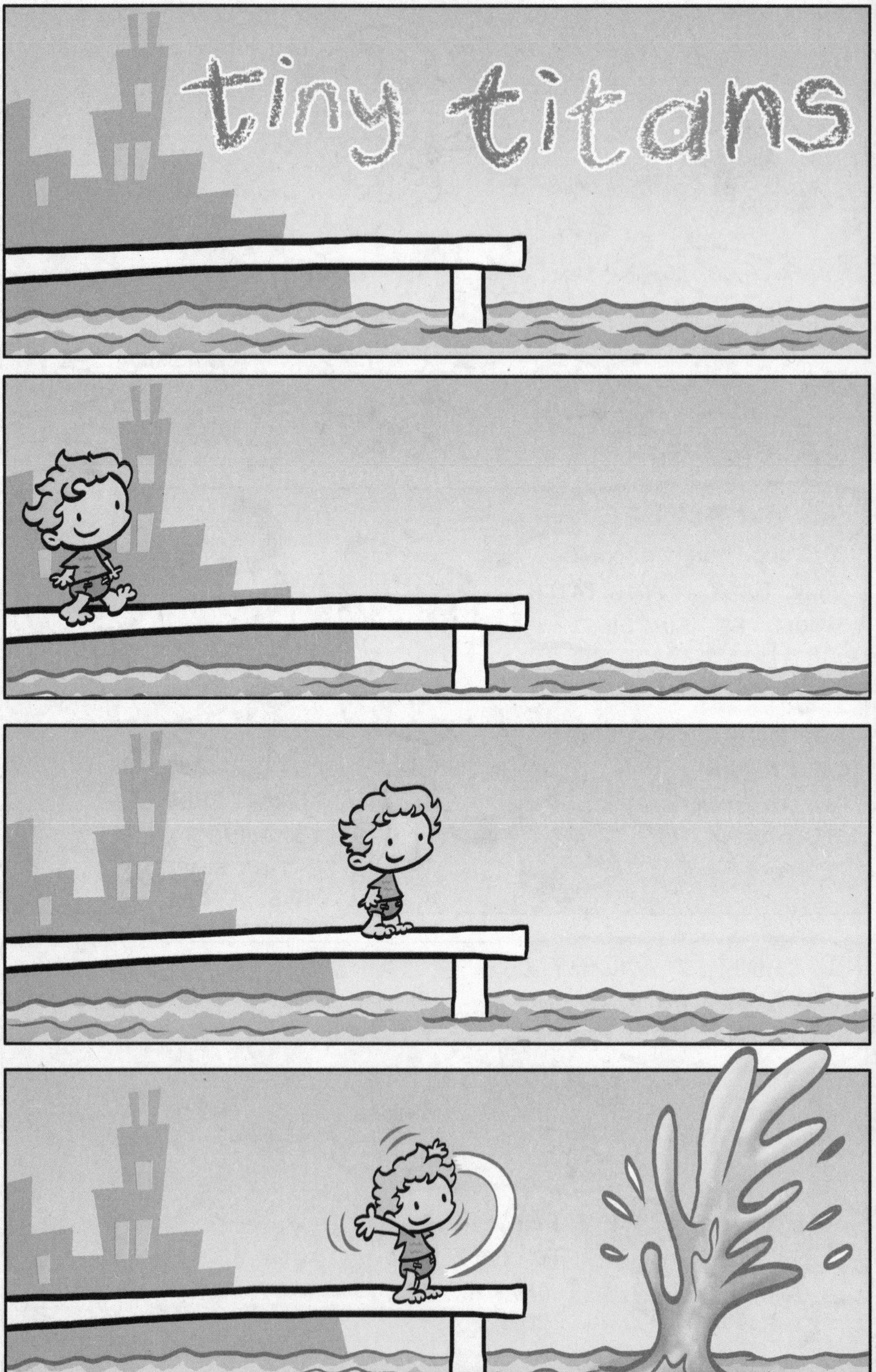
tiny titans

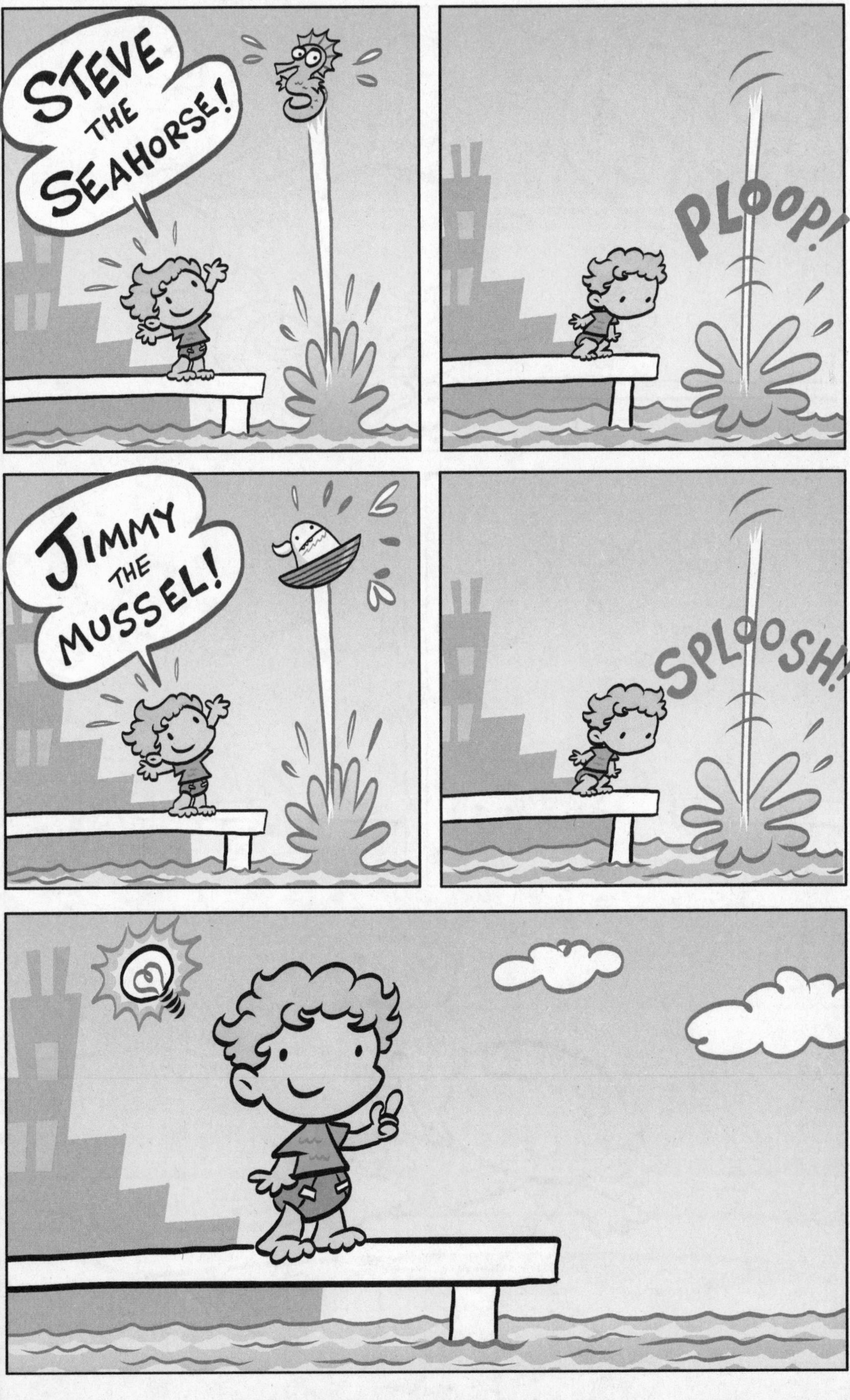
STEVE THE SEAHORSE!
PLOOP!
JIMMY THE MUSSEL!
SPLOOSH!

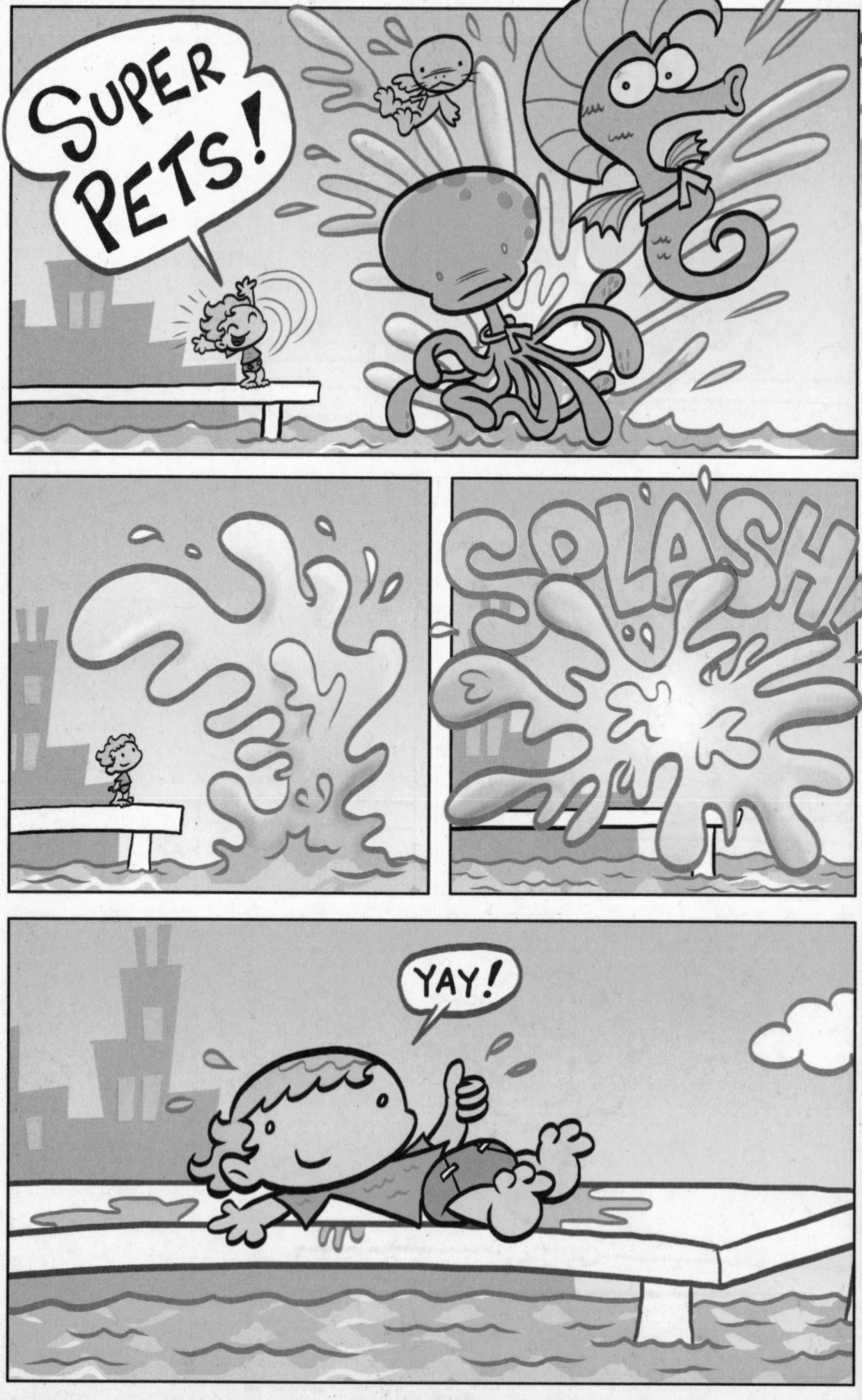
SUPER PETS!
SPLASH!
YAY!

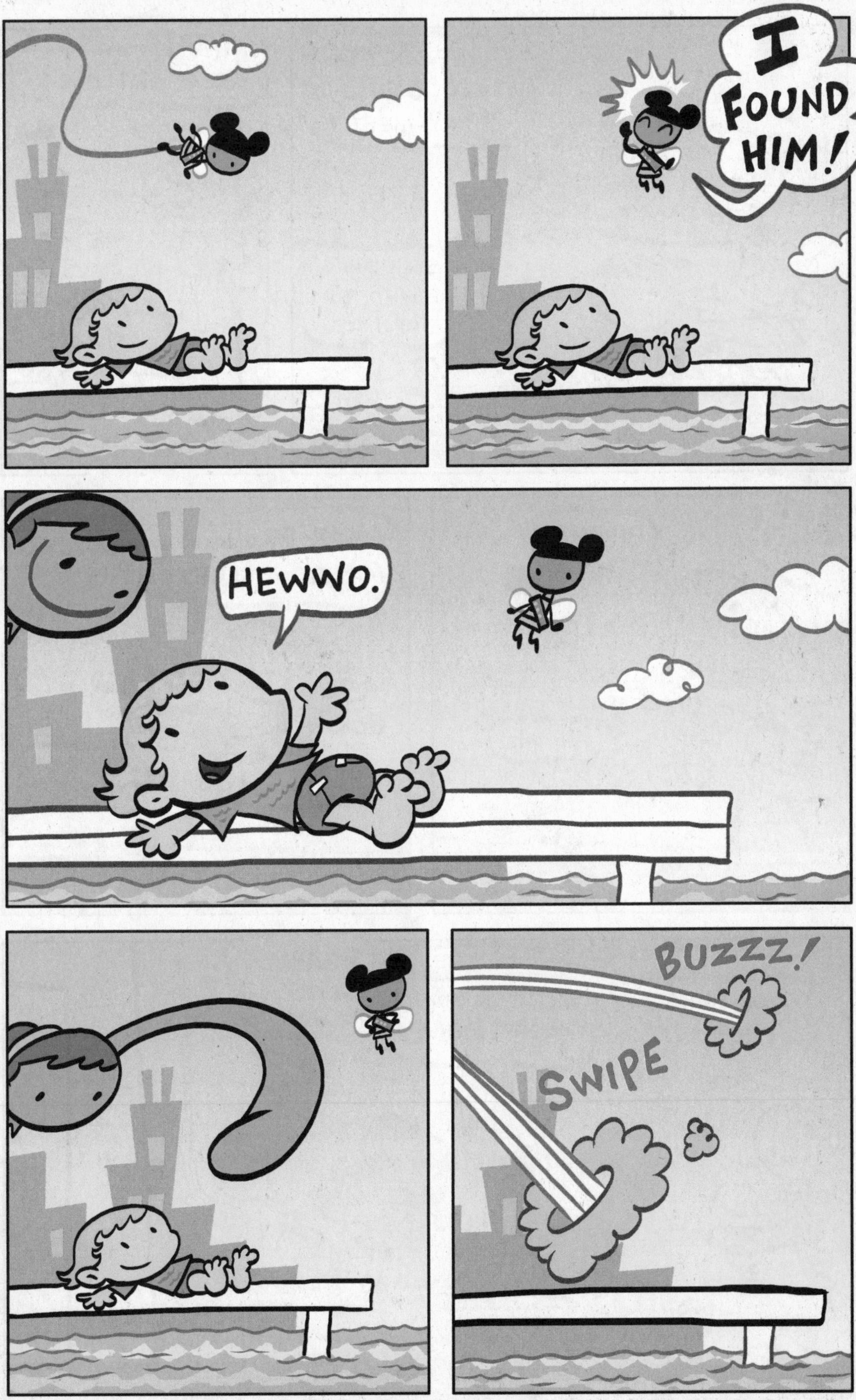
I FOUND HIM!
HEWWO.
BUZZZ!
SWIPE

-WATER.

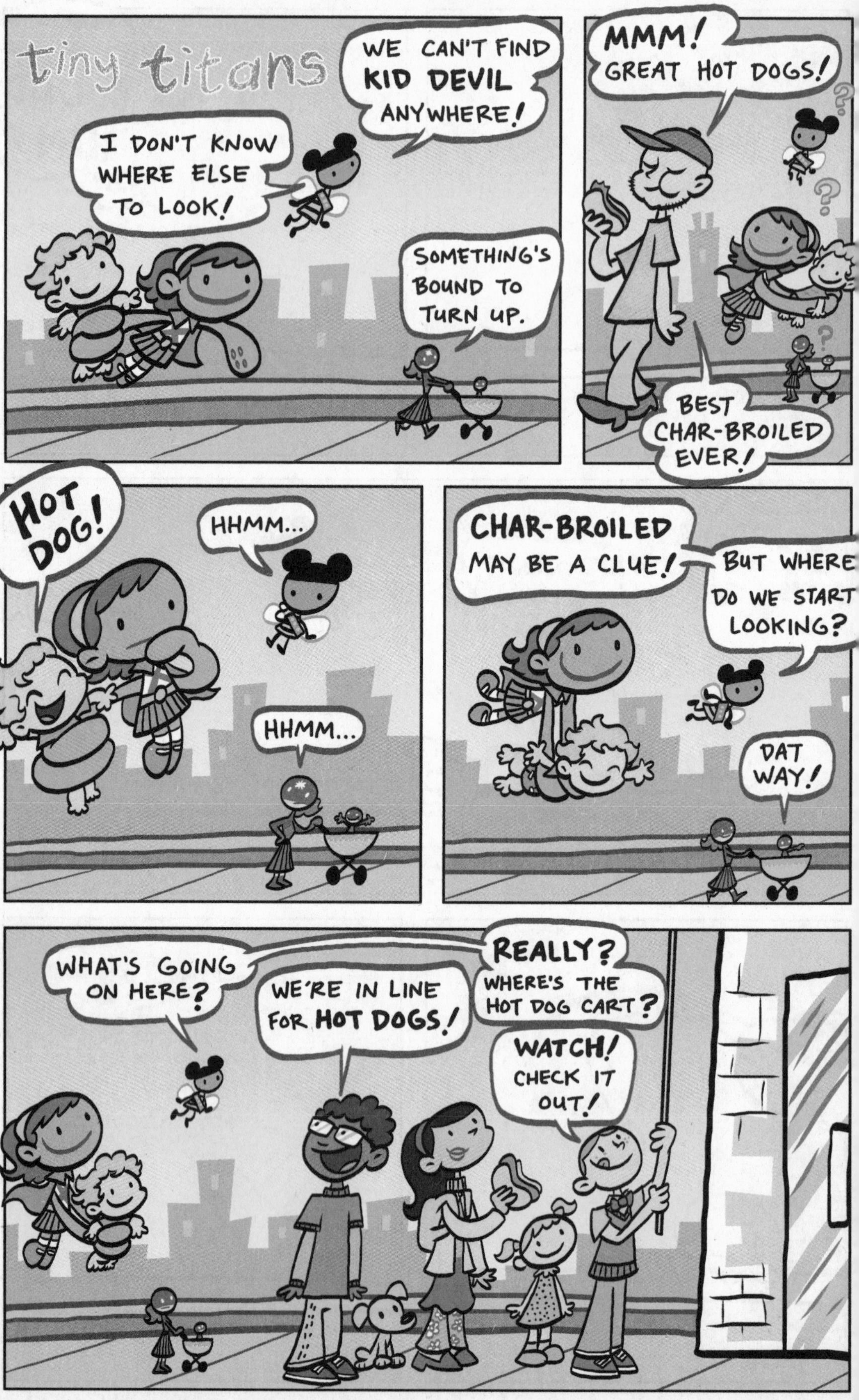
tiny titans
WE CAN'T FIND KID DEVIL ANYWHERE!
I DON'T KNOW WHERE ELSE TO LOOK!
SOMETHING'S BOUND TO TURN UP.
MMM! GREAT HOT DOGS!
BEST CHAR-BROILED EVER!
HOT DOG!
HHMM...
HHMM...
CHAR-BROILED MAY BE A CLUE!
BUT WHERE DO WE START LOOKING?
DAT WAY!
WHAT'S GOING ON HERE?
WE'RE IN LINE FOR HOT DOGS!
REALLY? WHERE'S THE HOT DOG CART?
WATCH! CHECK IT OUT!

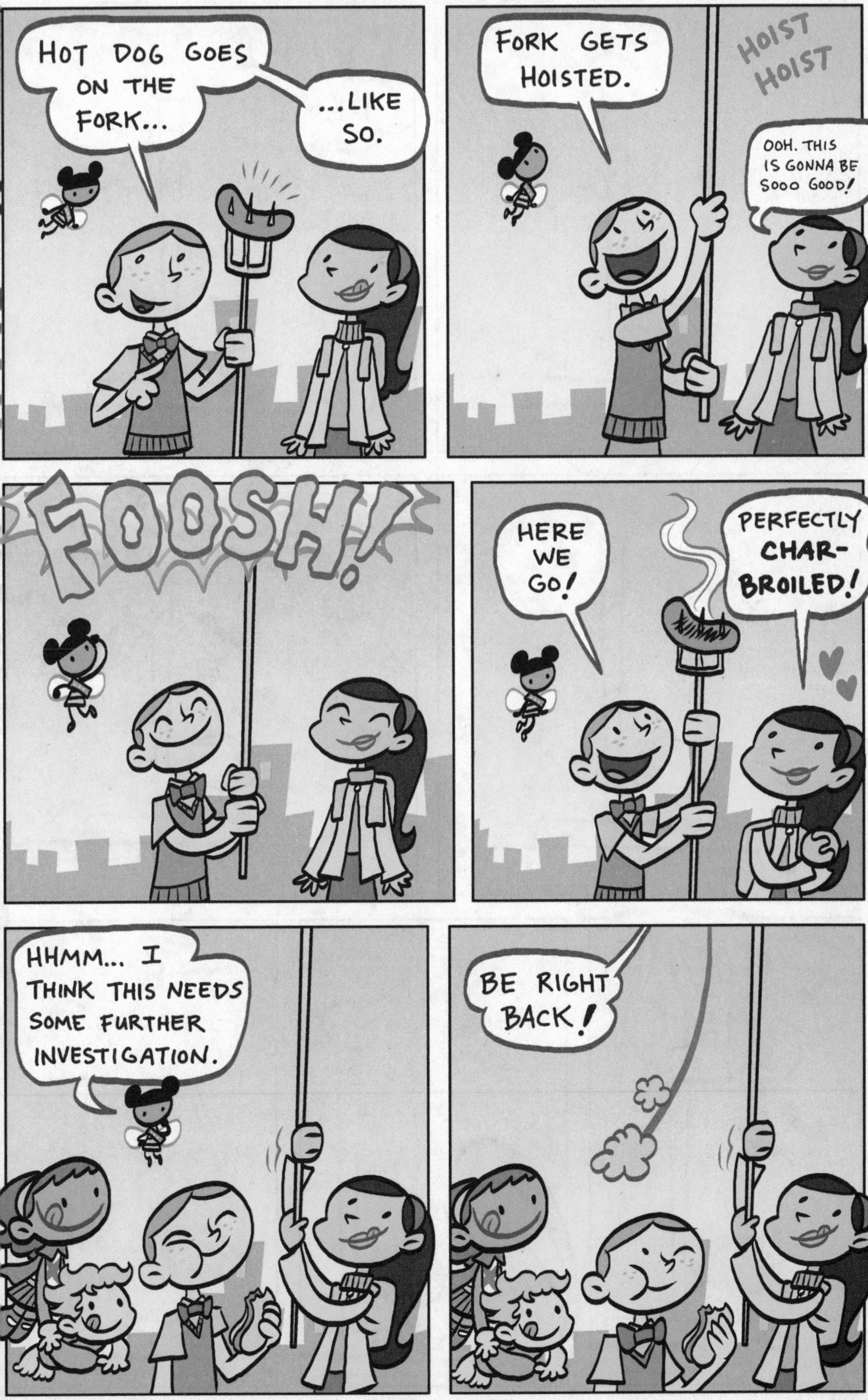
HOT DOG GOES ON THE FORK...
...LIKE SO.
FORK GETS HOISTED.
HOIST HOIST
OOH. THIS IS GONNA BE SOOO GOOD!
FOOSH!
HERE WE GO!
PERFECTLY CHAR-BROILED!
HHMM... I THINK THIS NEEDS SOME FURTHER INVESTIGATION.
BE RIGHT BACK!

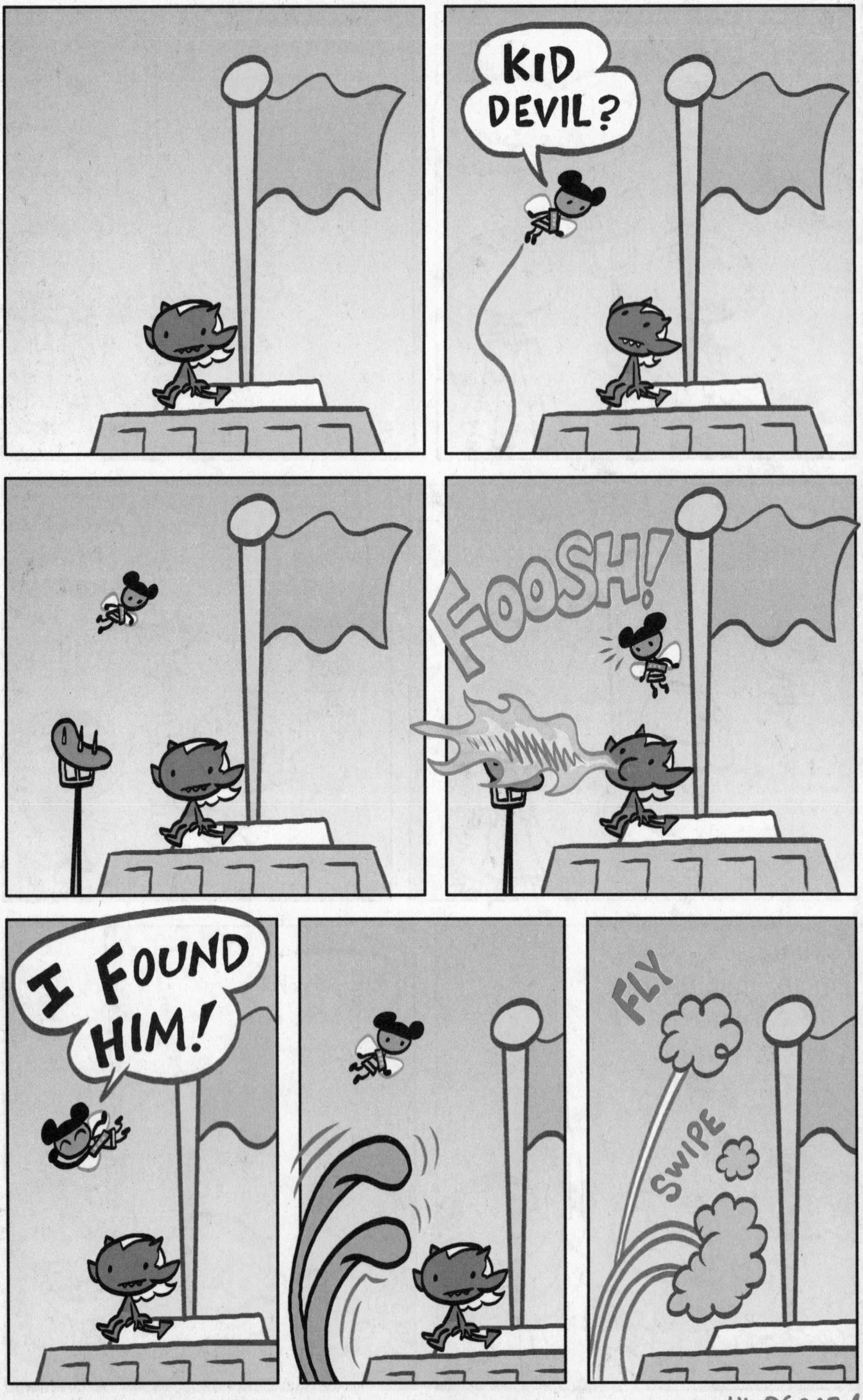
KID DEVIL?
FOOSH!
I FOUND HIM!
FLY
SWIPE

-HI, OSCAR!

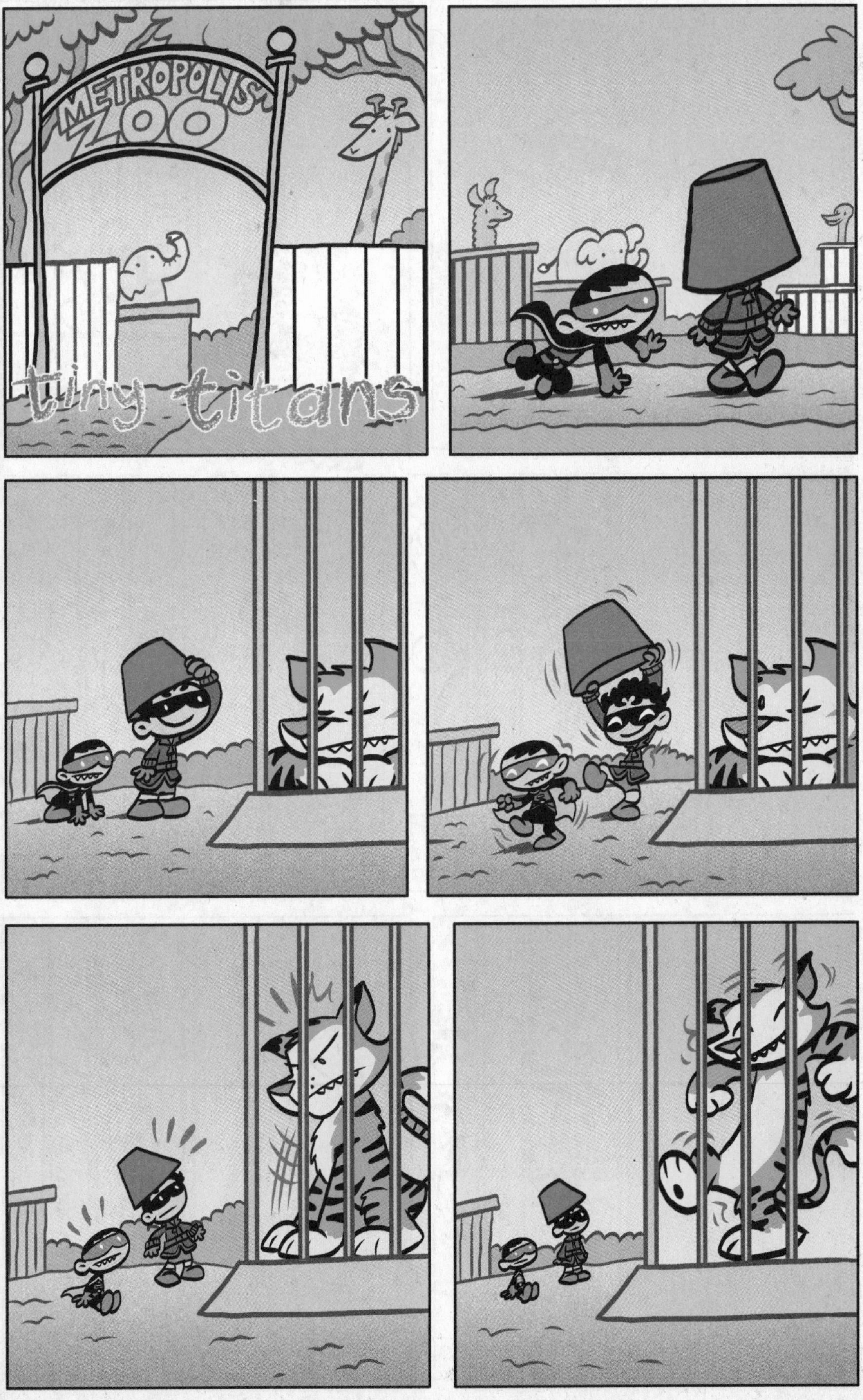
METROPOLIS ZOO
tiny titans

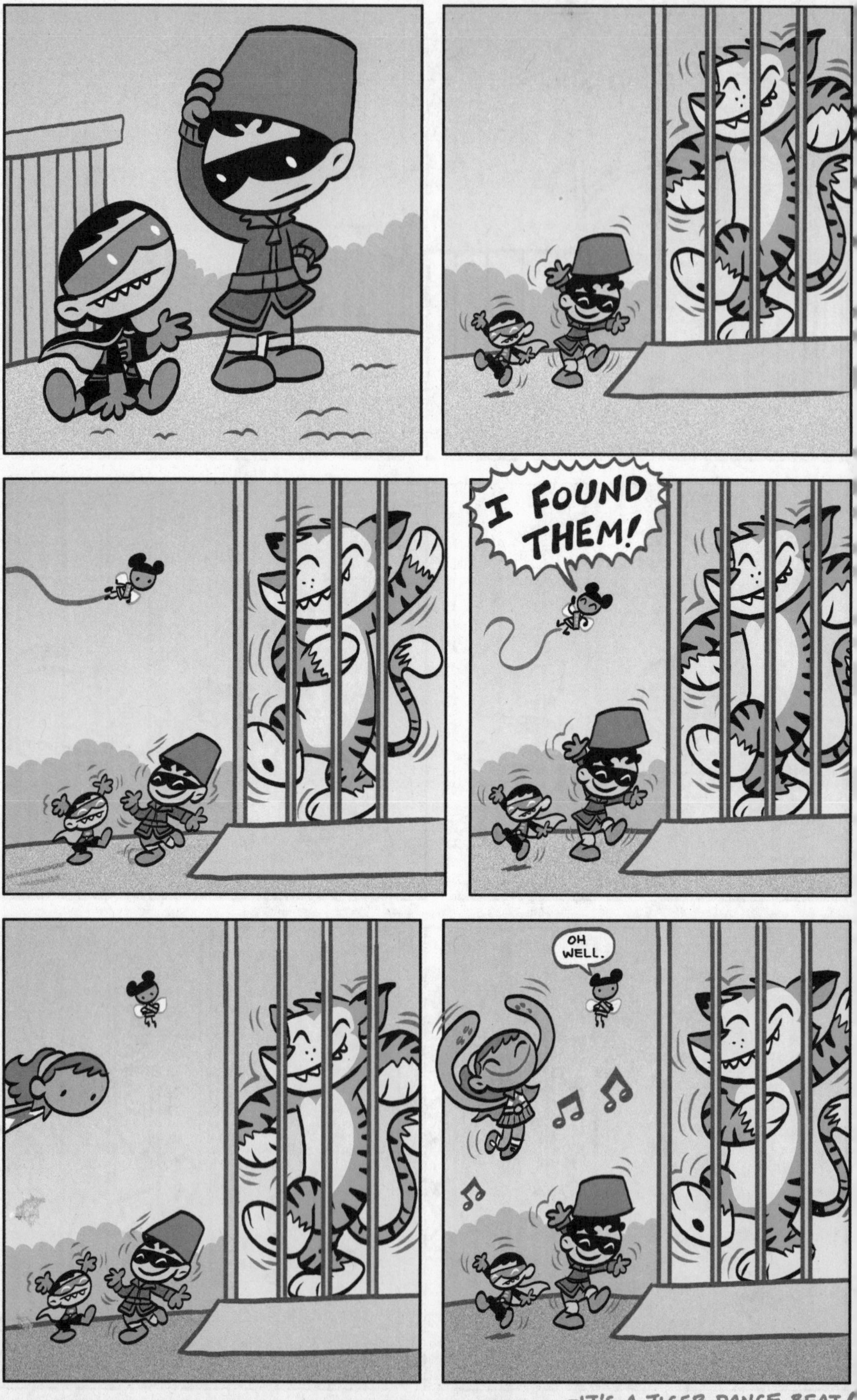
I FOUND THEM!
OH WELL.

-IT'S A TIGER DANCE BEAT!

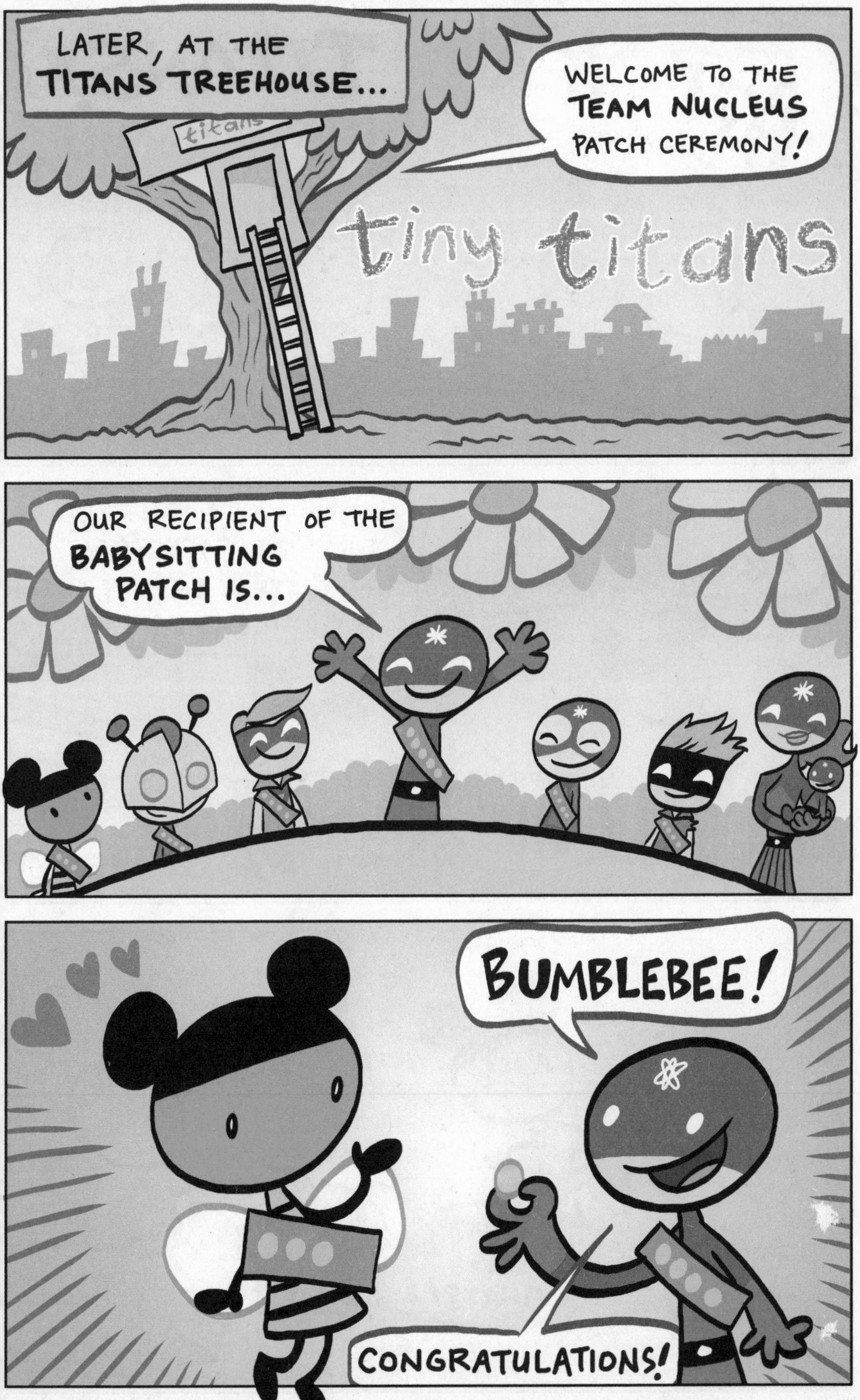
LATER, AT THE TITANS TREEHOUSE...
titans
WELCOME TO THE TEAM NUCLEUS PATCH CEREMONY!
tiny titans
OUR RECIPIENT OF THE BABYSITTING PATCH IS...
BUMBLEBEE!
CONGRATULATIONS!

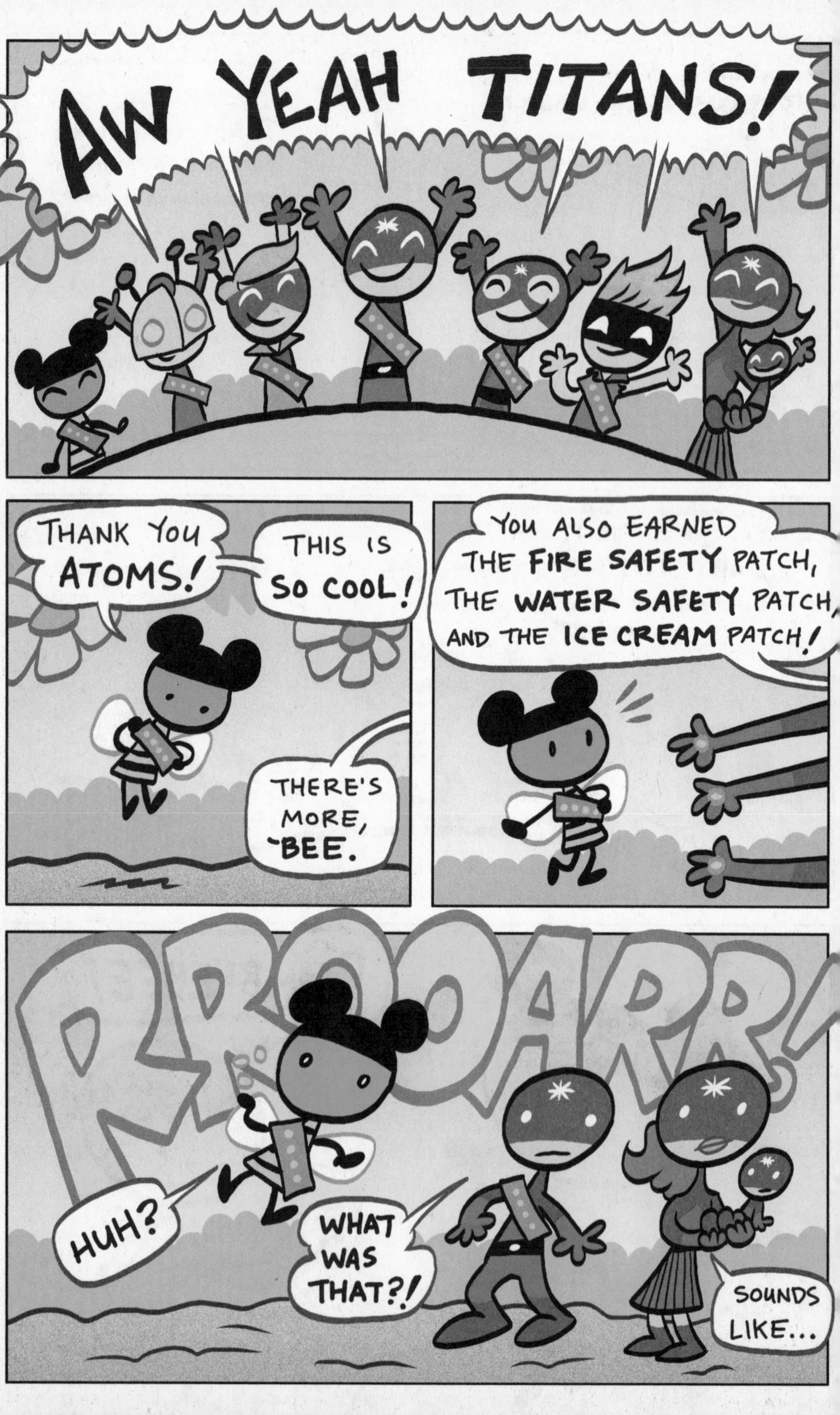
AW YEAH TITANS!
THANK YOU ATOMS!
THIS IS SO COOL!
THERE'S MORE, BEE.
YOU ALSO EARNED THE FIRE SAFETY PATCH, THE WATER SAFETY PATCH, AND THE ICE CREAM PATCH!
RROOARR!
HUH?
WHAT WAS THAT?!
SOUNDS LIKE...

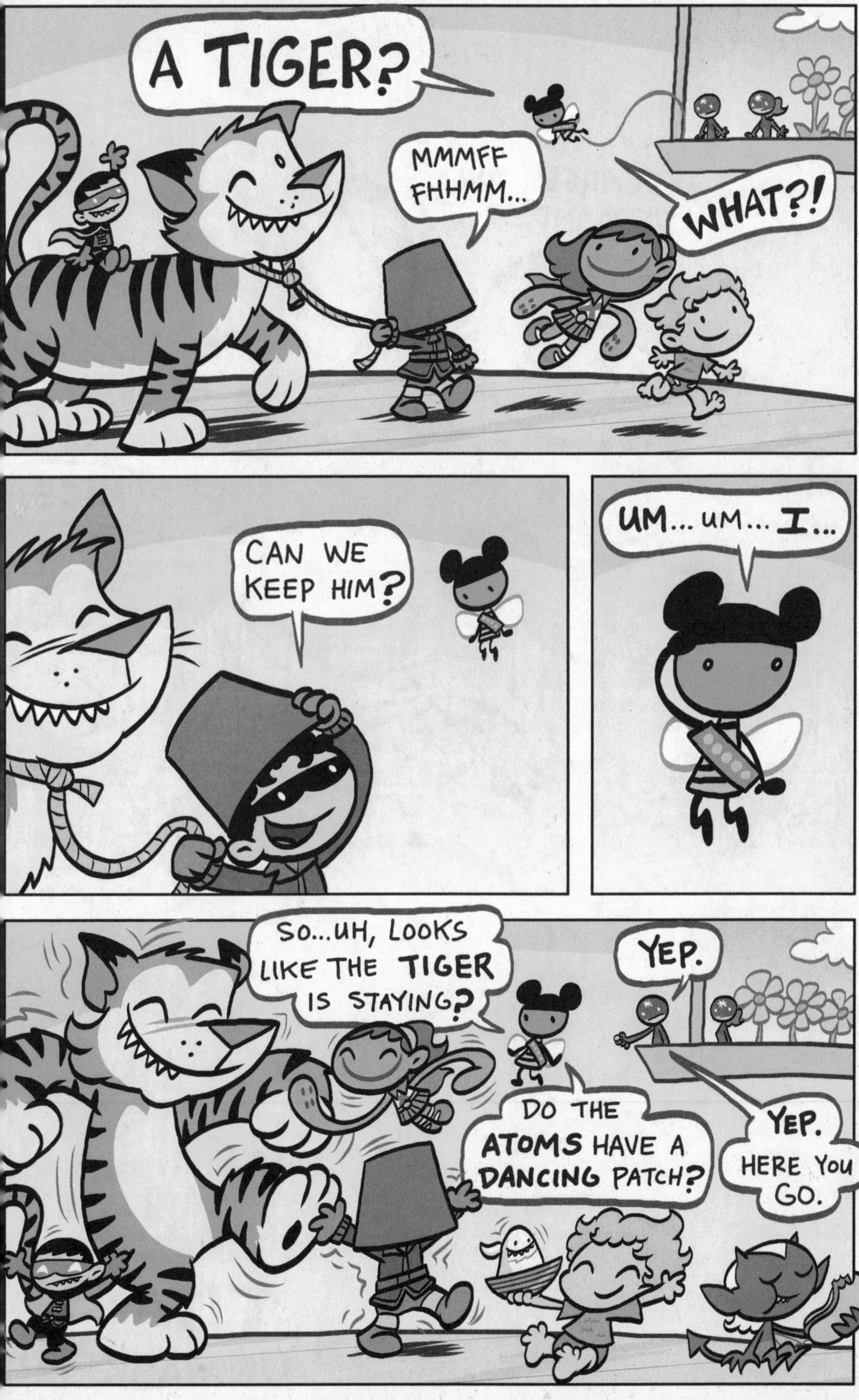
A TIGER?
MMMFF FHHMM...
WHAT?!
CAN WE KEEP HIM?
UM... UM... I...
SO...UH, LOOKS LIKE THE TIGER IS STAYING?
YEP.
DO THE ATOMS HAVE A DANCING PATCH?
YEP. HERE YOU GO.

—WELL EARNED!

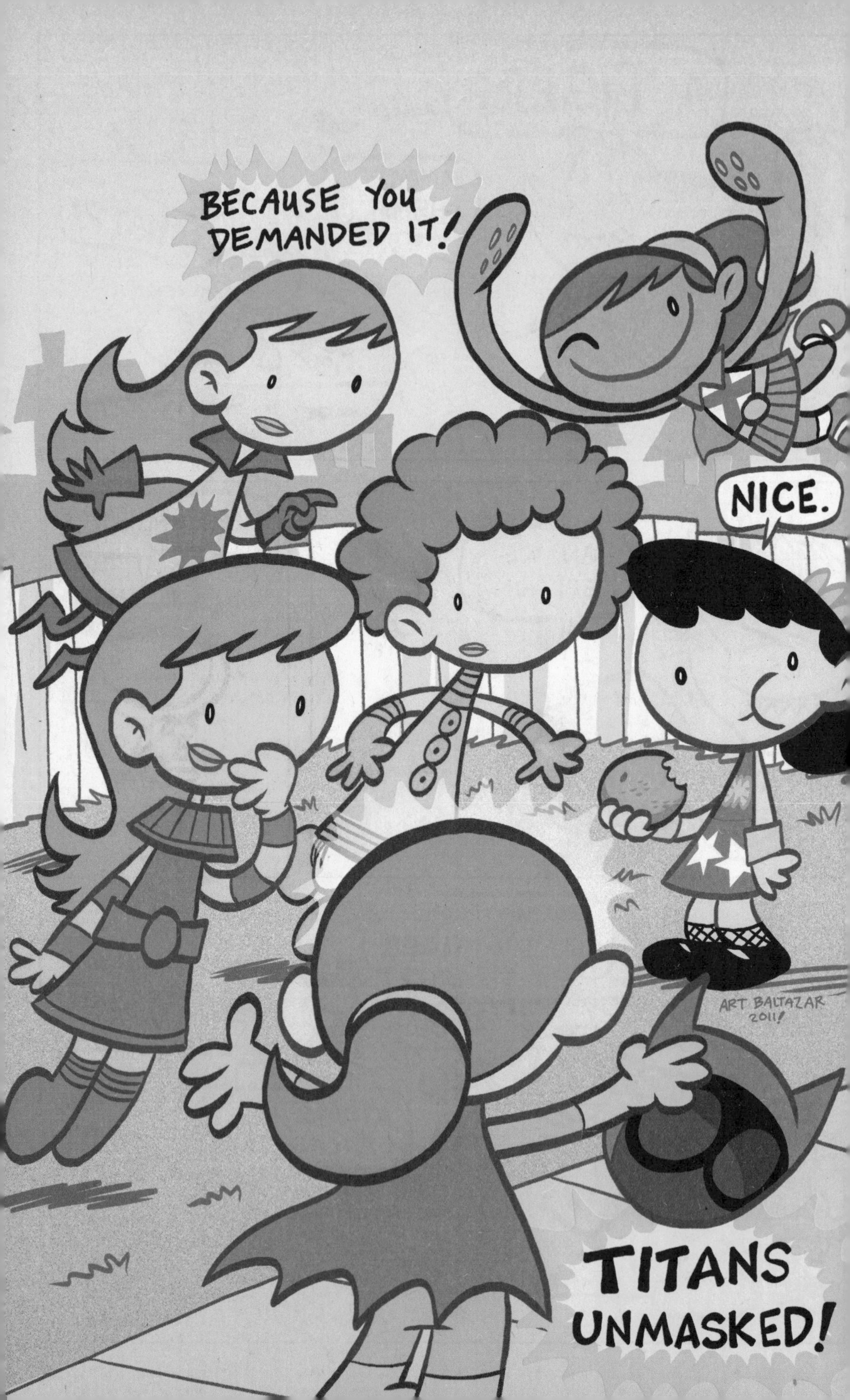
BECAUSE YOU DEMANDED IT!
NICE.
ART BALTAZAR 2011!
TITANS UNMASKED!

tiny titans

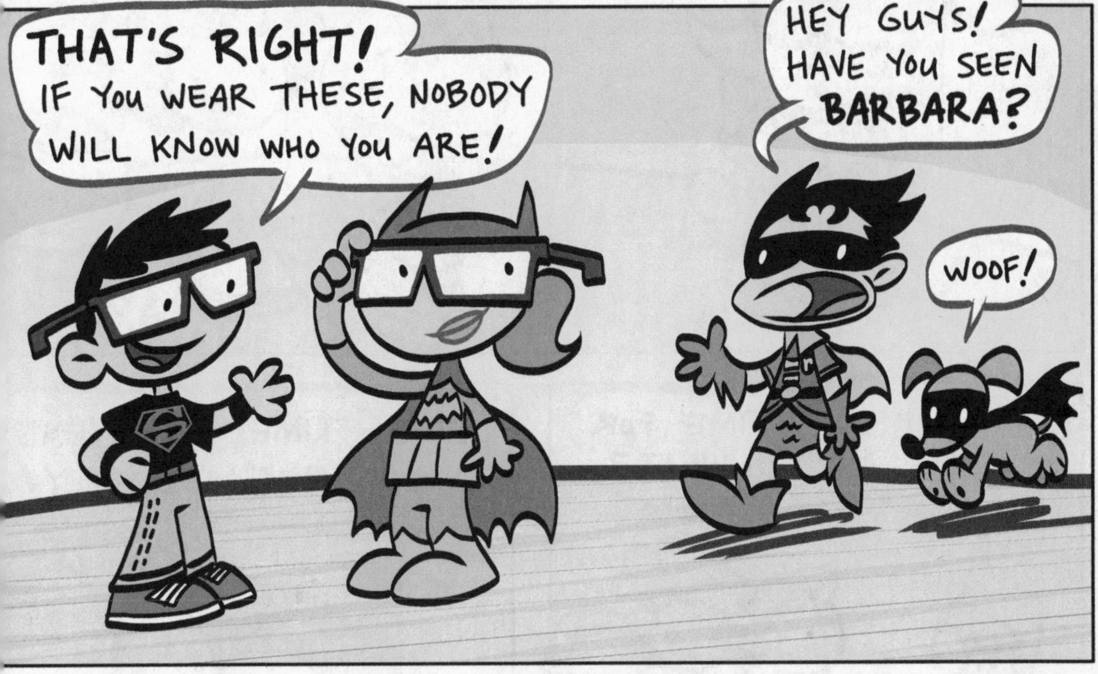
THAT'S RIGHT! IF YOU WEAR THESE, NOBODY WILL KNOW WHO YOU ARE!
HEY GUYS! HAVE YOU SEEN BARBARA?
WOOF!

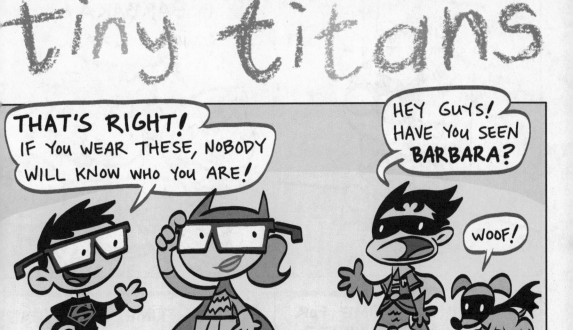

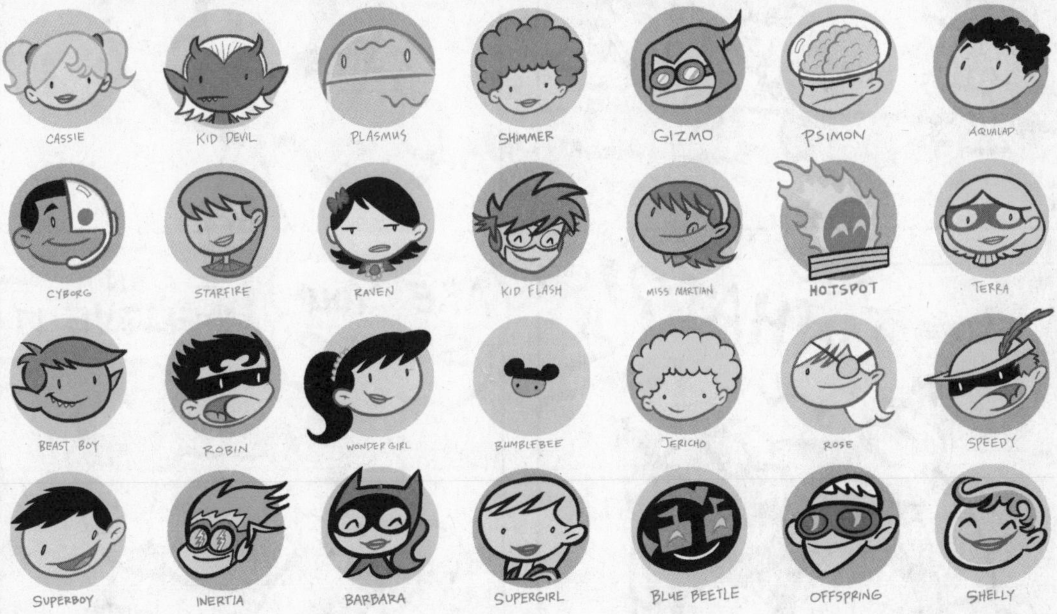
CASSIE
KID DEVIL
PLASMUS
SHIMMER
GIZMO
PSIMON
AQUALAD
CYBORG
STARFIRE
RAVEN
KID FLASH
MISS MARTIAN
HOTSPOT
TERRA
BEAST BOY
ROBIN
WONDER GIRL
BUMBLEBEE
JERICHO
ROSE
SPEEDY
SUPERBOY
INERTIA
BARBARA
SUPERGIRL
BLUE BEETLE
OFFSPRING
SHELLY

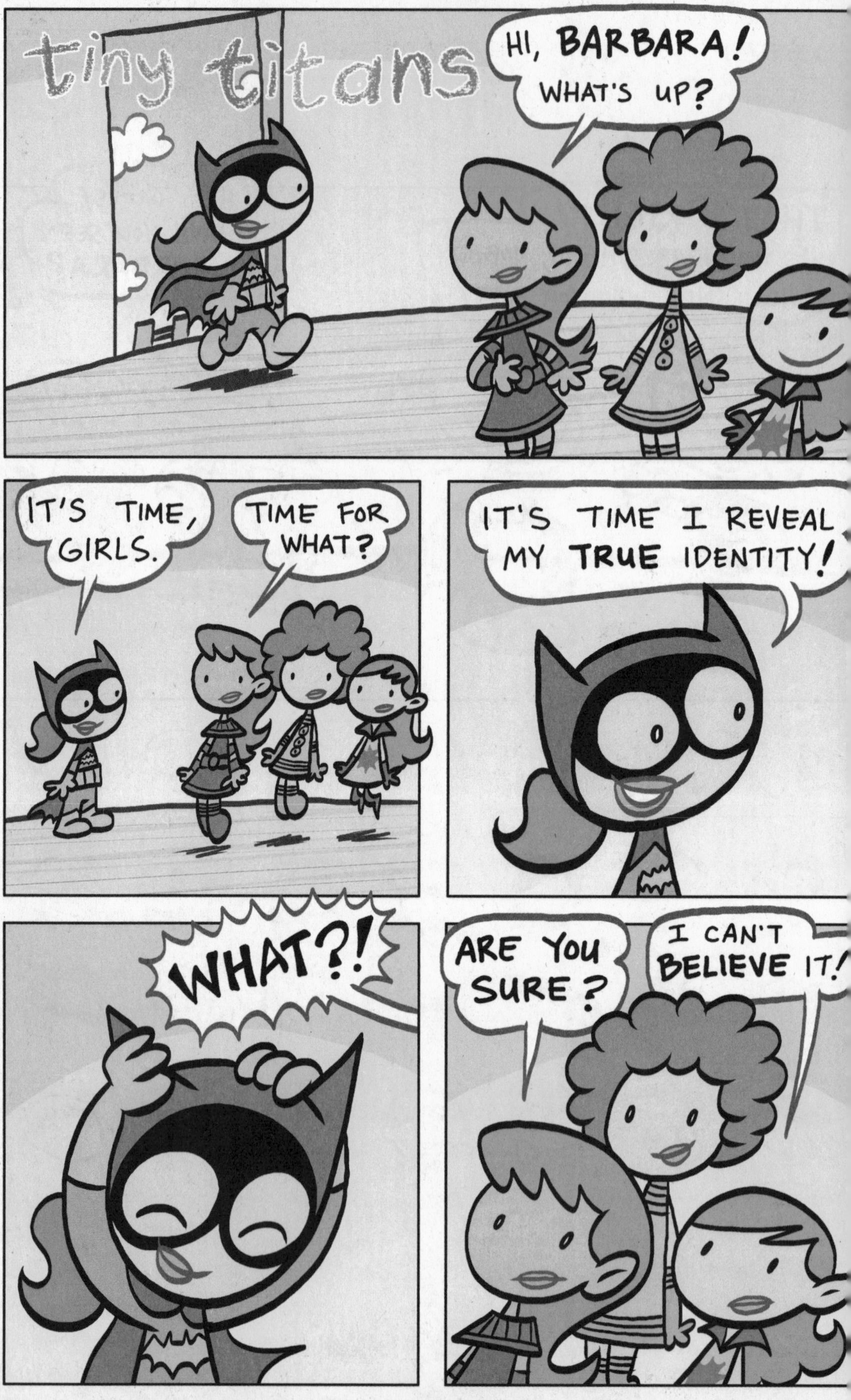
tiny titans
HI, BARBARA! WHAT'S UP?
IT'S TIME, GIRLS.
TIME FOR WHAT?
IT'S TIME I REVEAL MY TRUE IDENTITY!
WHAT?!
ARE YOU SURE?
I CAN'T BELIEVE IT!

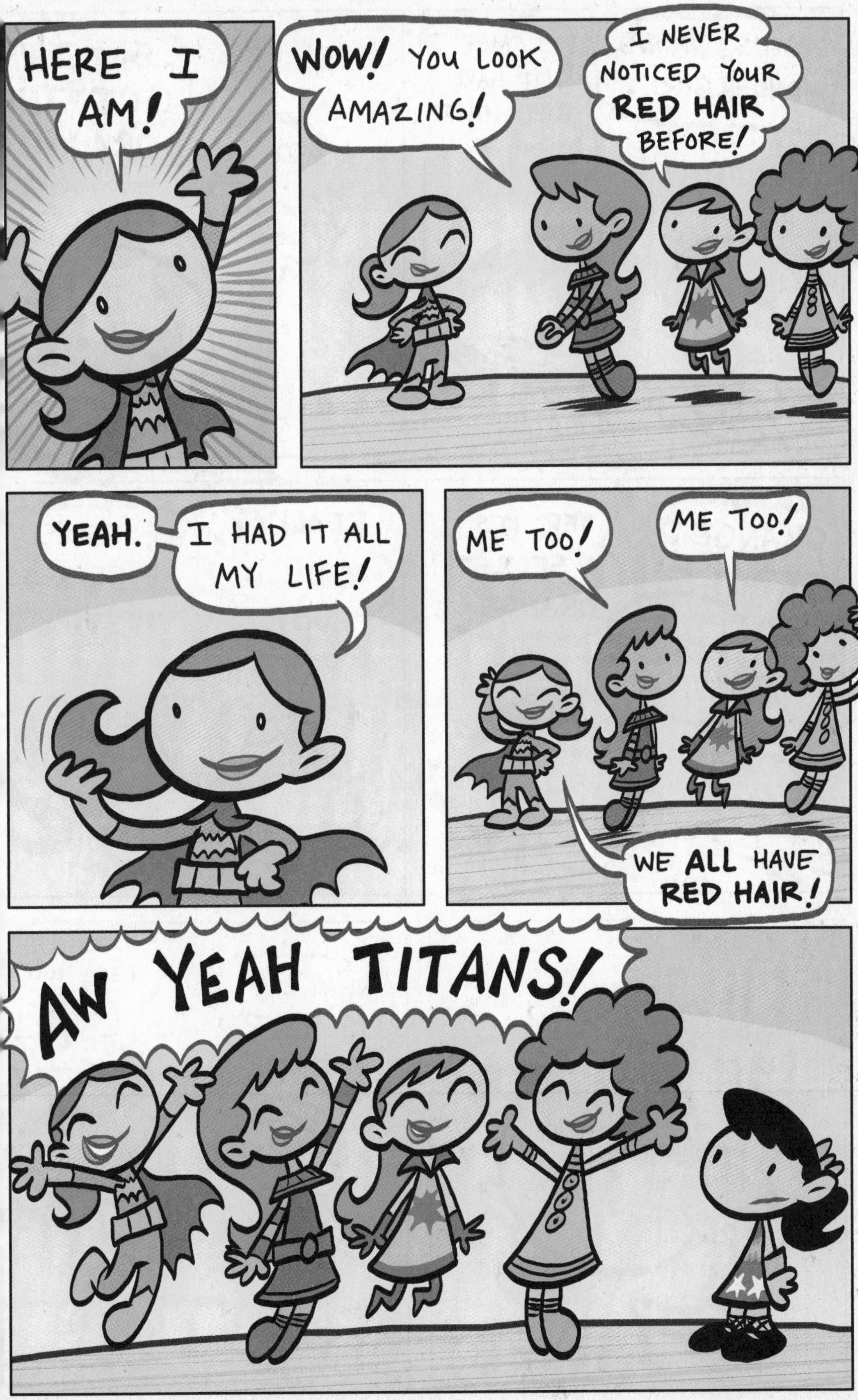
HERE I AM!
WOW! YOU LOOK AMAZING!
I NEVER NOTICED YOUR RED HAIR BEFORE!
YEAH.
I HAD IT ALL MY LIFE!
ME TOO!
ME TOO!
WE ALL HAVE RED HAIR!
AW YEAH TITANS!

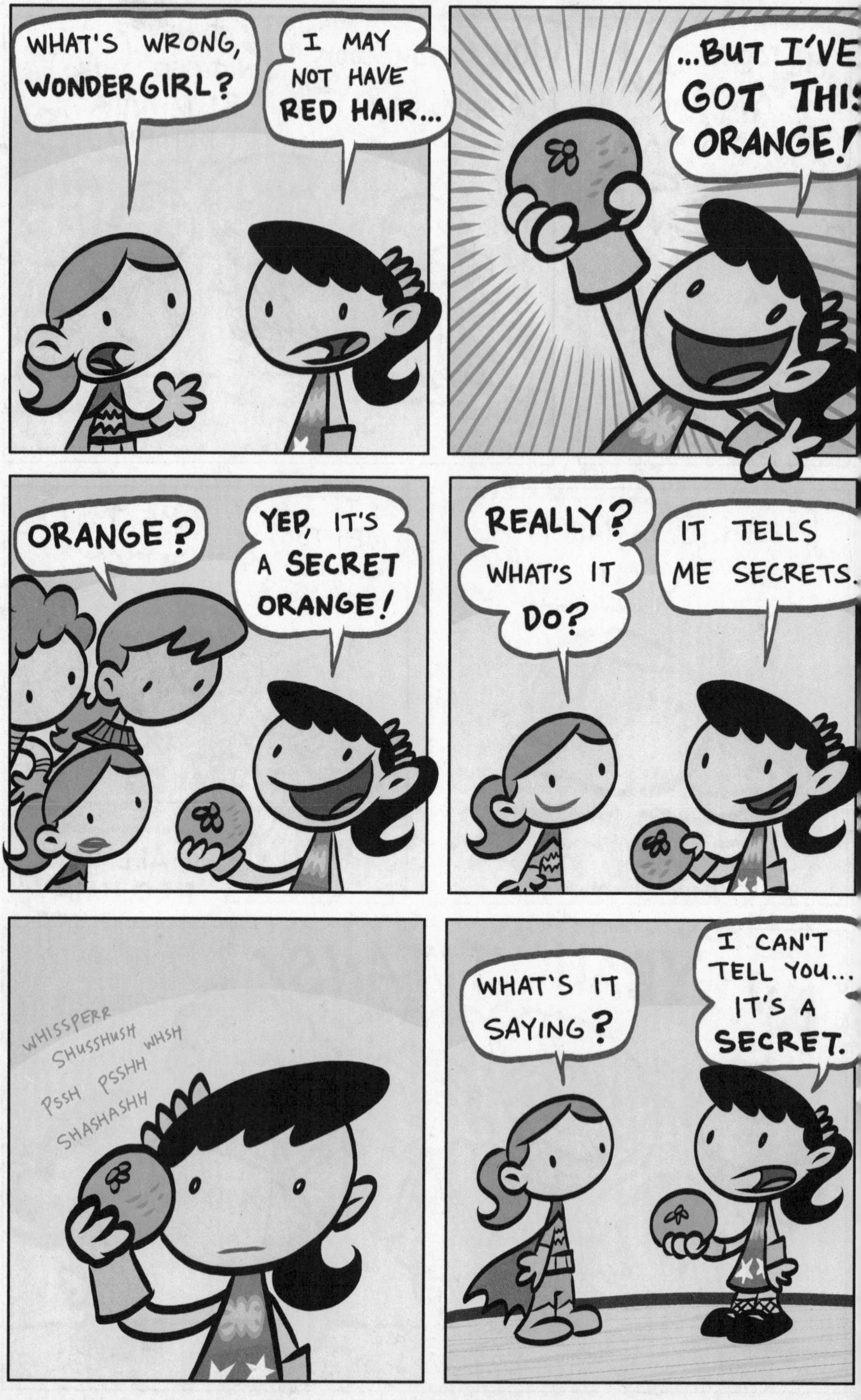
WHAT'S WRONG, WONDERGIRL?
I MAY NOT HAVE RED HAIR...
...BUT I'VE GOT THIS ORANGE!
ORANGE?
YEP, IT'S A SECRET ORANGE!
REALLY? WHAT'S IT DO?
IT TELLS ME SECRETS.
WHISSPERR
SHUSSHUSH
WHSH
PSSH PSSHH
SHASHASHH
WHAT'S IT SAYING?
I CAN'T TELL YOU... IT'S A SECRET.

—CITRUS!

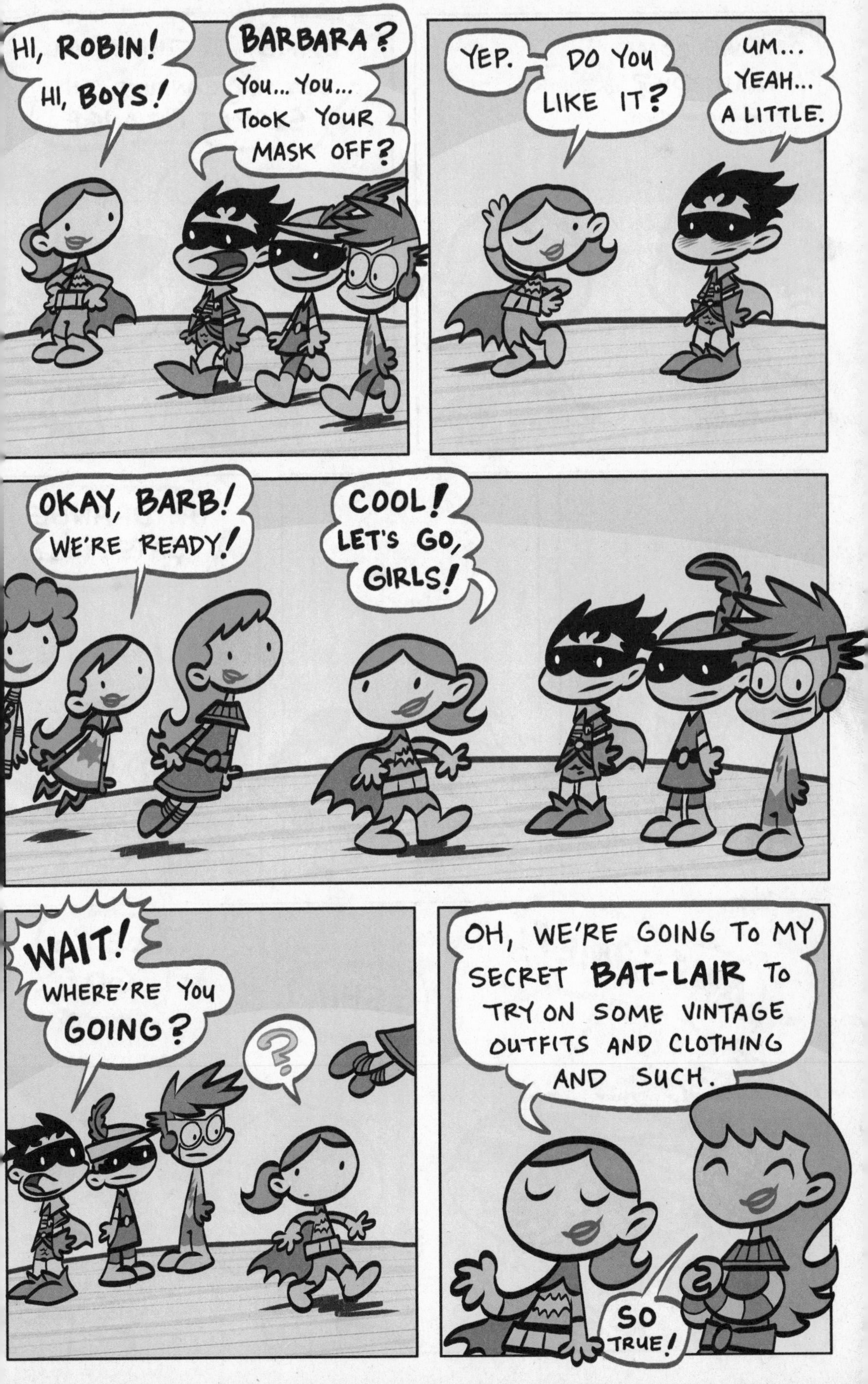

HI, ROBIN!
HI, BOYS!
BARBARA?
YOU... YOU... TOOK YOUR MASK OFF?
YEP.
DO YOU LIKE IT?
UM... YEAH... A LITTLE.
OKAY, BARB! WE'RE READY!
COOL! LET'S GO, GIRLS!
WAIT! WHERE'RE YOU GOING?
?
OH, WE'RE GOING TO MY SECRET BAT-LAIR TO TRY ON SOME VINTAGE OUTFITS AND CLOTHING AND SUCH.
SO TRUE!

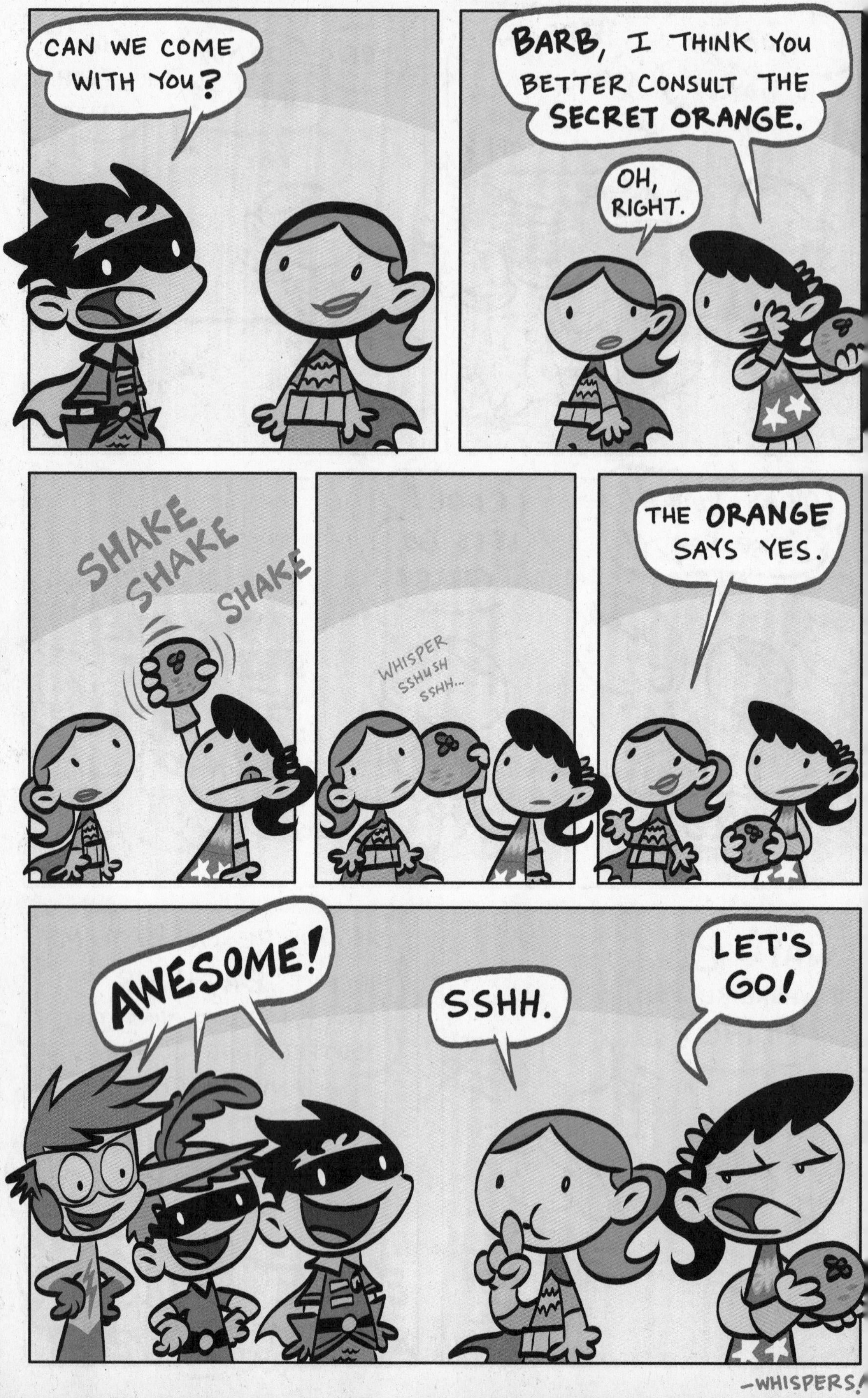
CAN WE COME WITH YOU?
BARB, I THINK YOU BETTER CONSULT THE SECRET ORANGE.
OH, RIGHT.
SHAKE SHAKE SHAKE
WHISPER SSHUSH SSHH...
THE ORANGE SAYS YES.
AWESOME!
SSHH.
LET'S GO!

-WHISPERS!

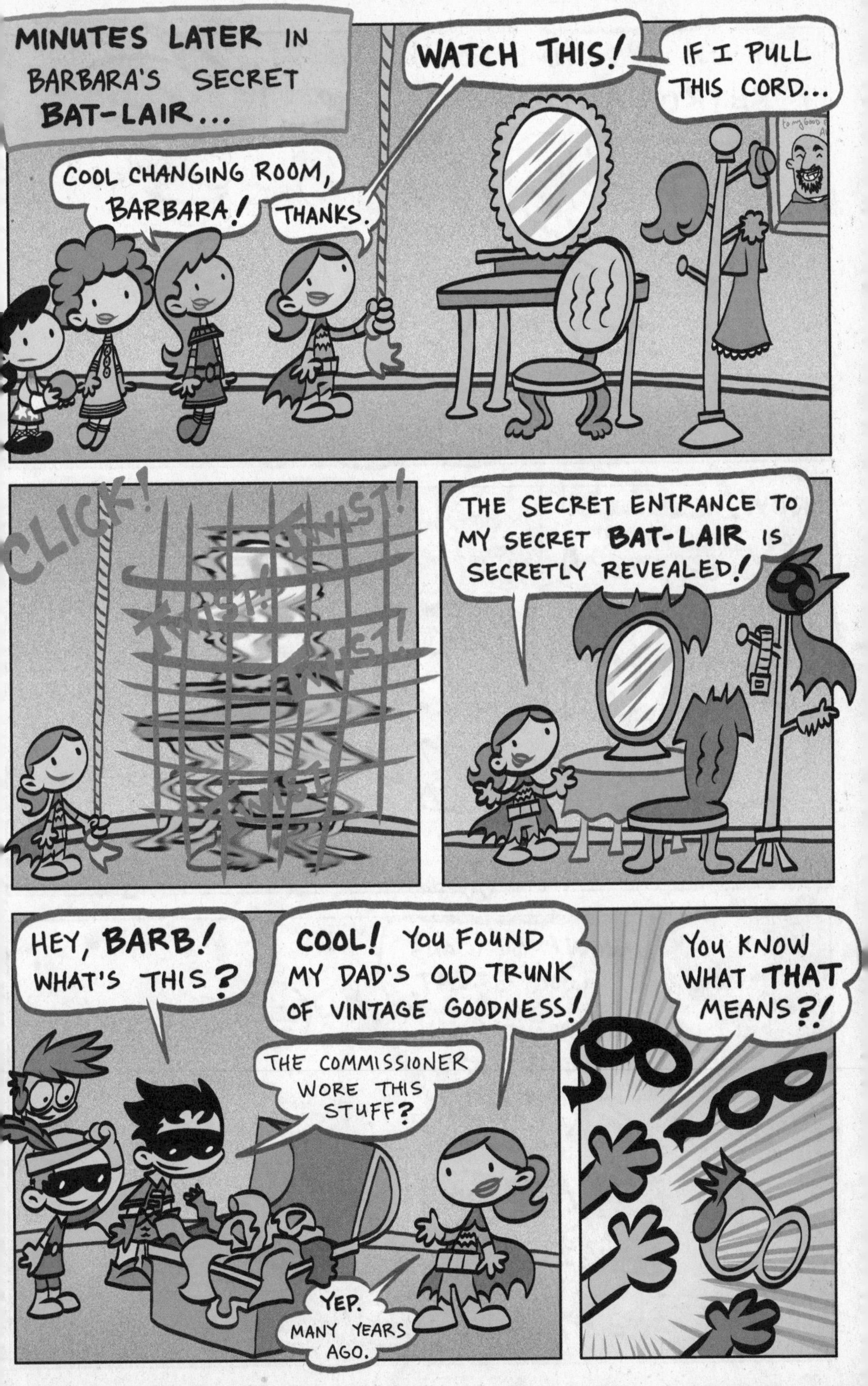
MINUTES LATER IN BARBARA'S SECRET BAT-LAIR...
COOL CHANGING ROOM, BARBARA!
THANKS.
WATCH THIS!
IF I PULL THIS CORD...
CLICK!
TWIST! TWIST!
TWIST!
TWIST!
TWIST!
THE SECRET ENTRANCE TO MY SECRET BAT-LAIR IS SECRETLY REVEALED!
HEY, BARB! WHAT'S THIS?
COOL! YOU FOUND MY DAD'S OLD TRUNK OF VINTAGE GOODNESS!
THE COMMISSIONER WORE THIS STUFF?
YEP. MANY YEARS AGO.
YOU KNOW WHAT THAT MEANS?!

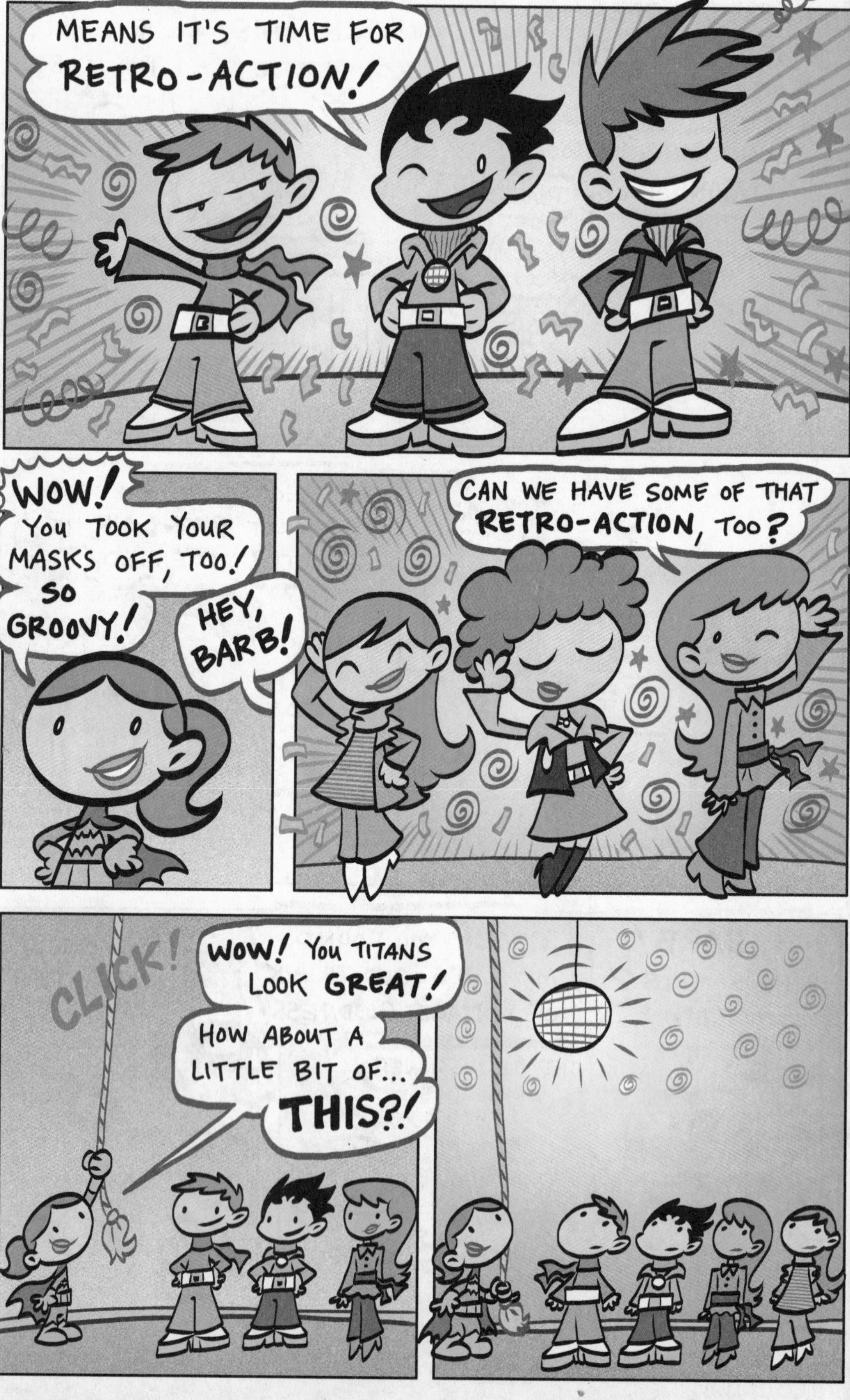
MEANS IT'S TIME FOR RETRO-ACTION!
WOW! YOU TOOK YOUR MASKS OFF, TOO! SO GROOVY!
HEY, BARB!
CAN WE HAVE SOME OF THAT RETRO-ACTION, TOO?
CLICK!
WOW! YOU TITANS LOOK GREAT!
HOW ABOUT A LITTLE BIT OF... THIS?!

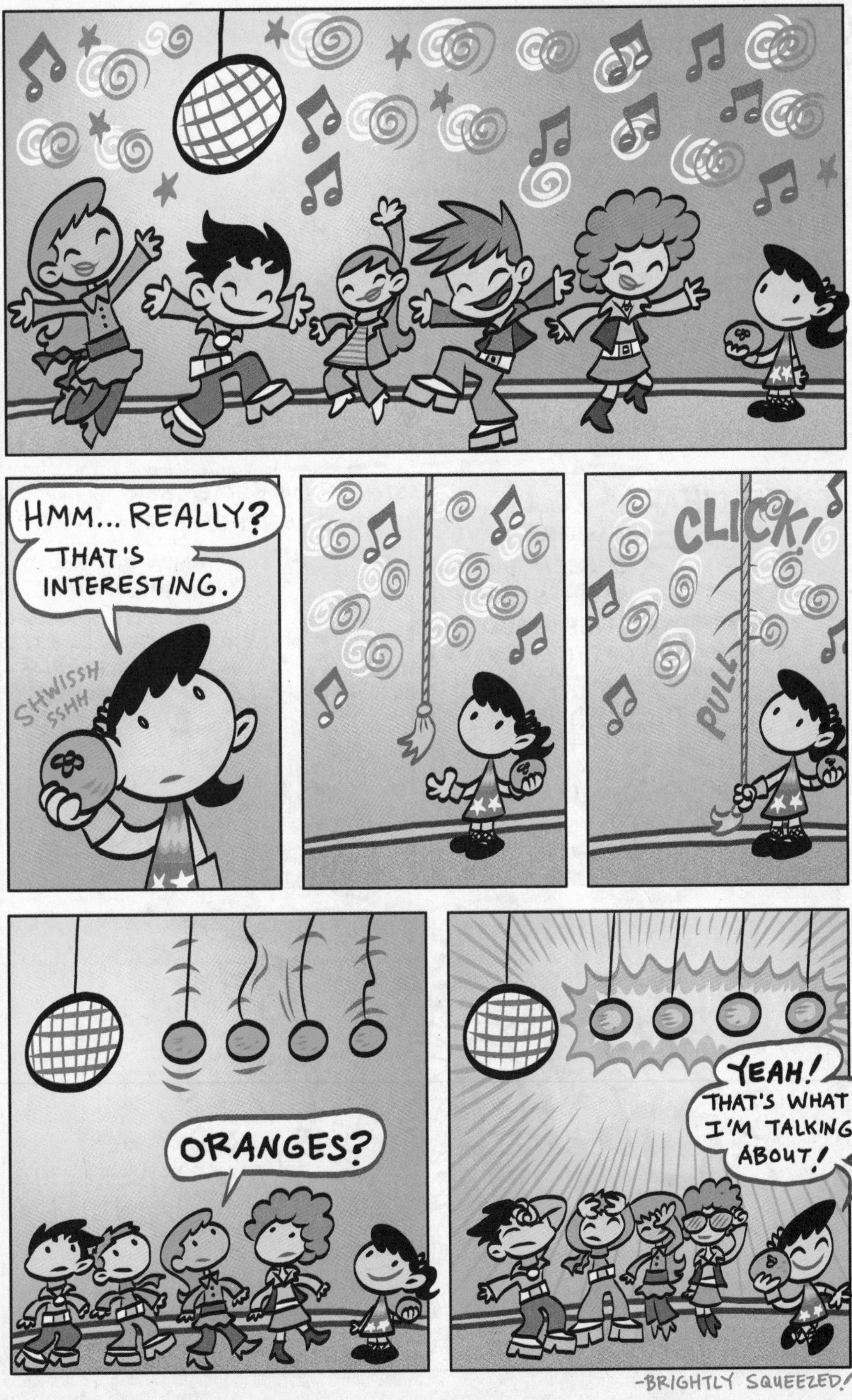
HMM... REALLY? THAT'S INTERESTING.
SHWISSH SSHH
CLICK!
PULL
ORANGES?
YEAH! THAT'S WHAT I'M TALKING ABOUT!
-BRIGHTLY SQUEEZED!

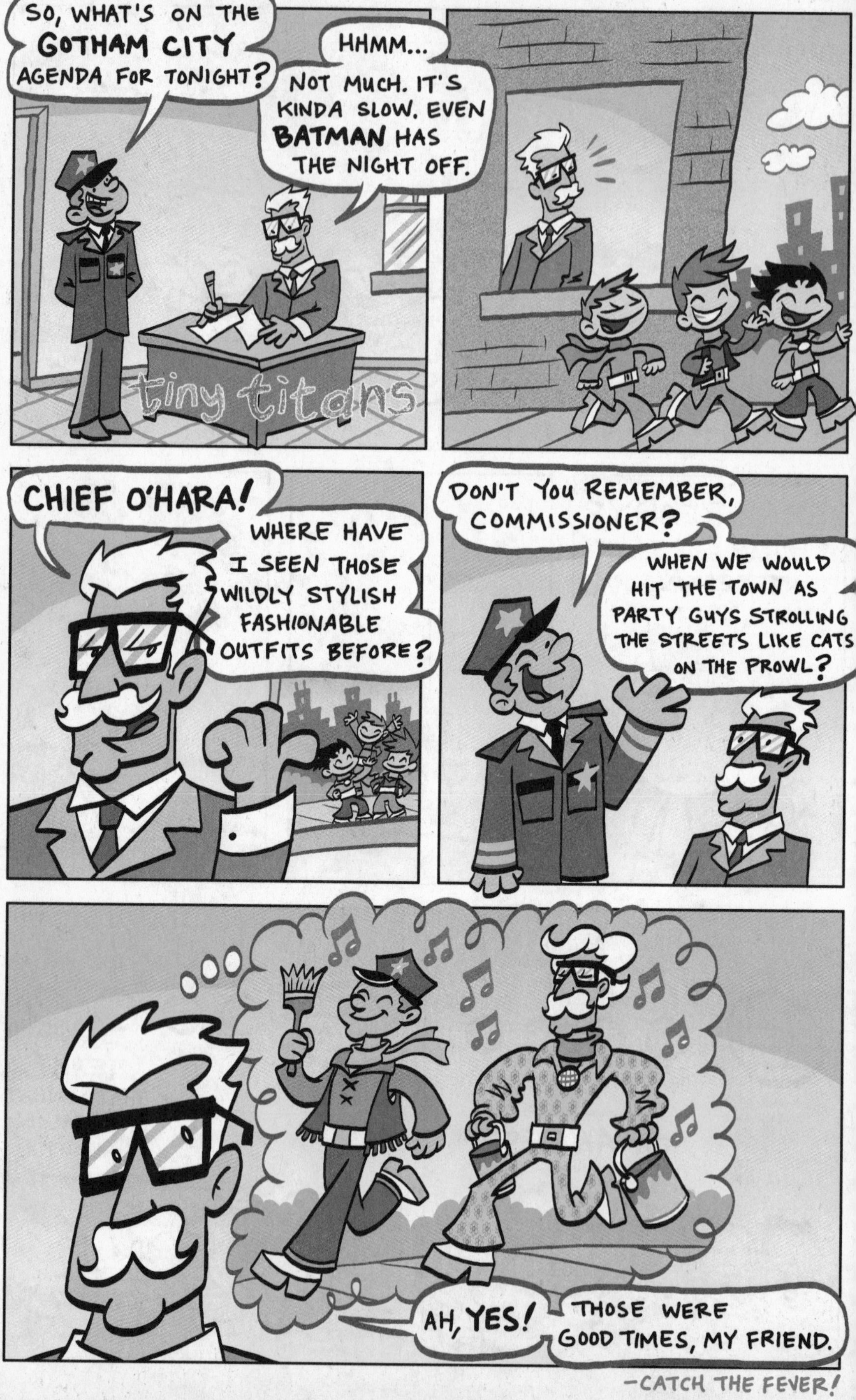
SO, WHAT'S ON THE GOTHAM CITY AGENDA FOR TONIGHT?
HHMM...
NOT MUCH. IT'S KINDA SLOW. EVEN BATMAN HAS THE NIGHT OFF.
tiny titans
CHIEF O'HARA!
WHERE HAVE I SEEN THOSE WILDLY STYLISH FASHIONABLE OUTFITS BEFORE?
DON'T YOU REMEMBER, COMMISSIONER?
WHEN WE WOULD HIT THE TOWN AS PARTY GUYS STROLLING THE STREETS LIKE CATS ON THE PROWL?
AH, YES!
THOSE WERE GOOD TIMES, MY FRIEND.
-CATCH THE FEVER!

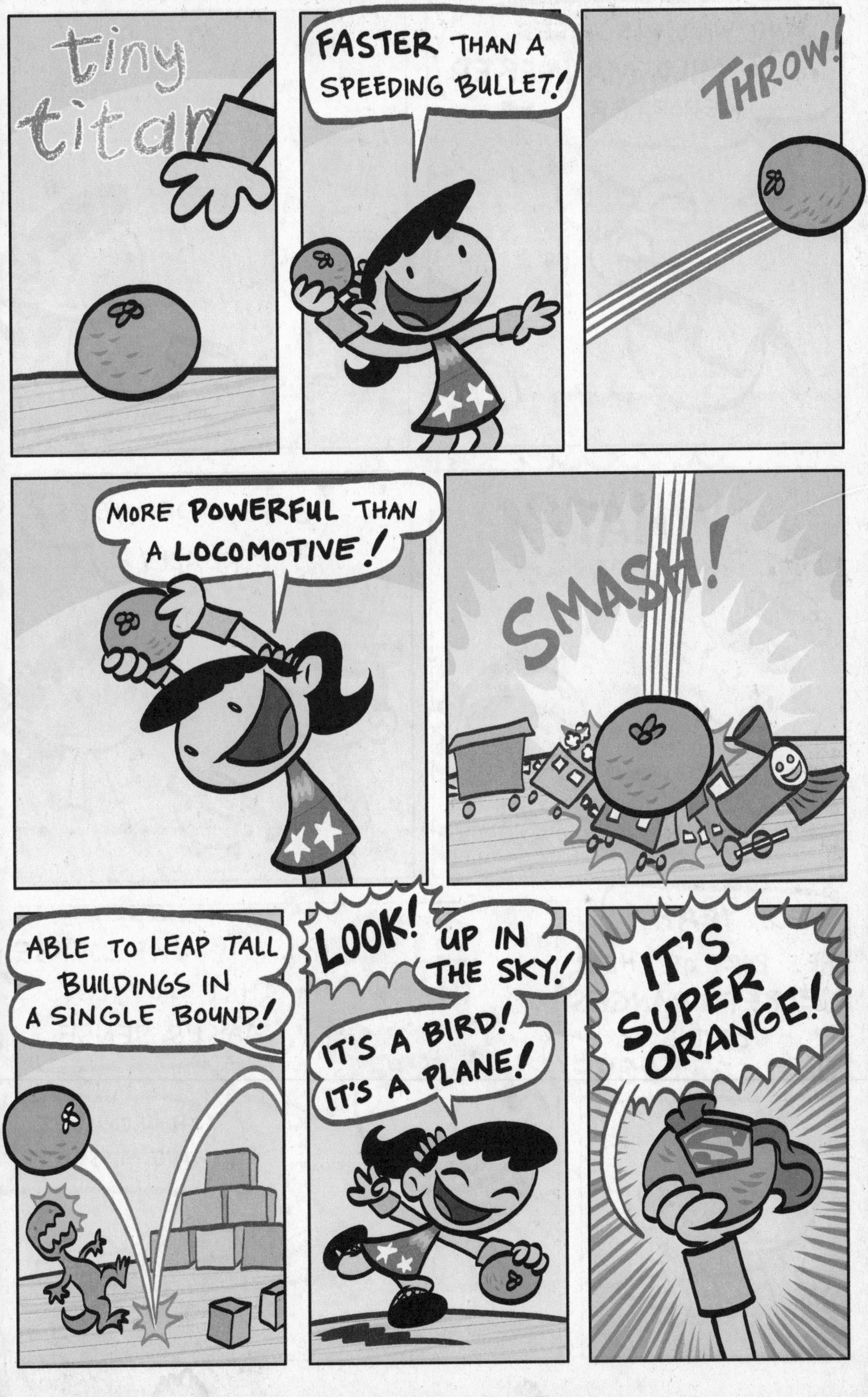
tiny titan
FASTER THAN A SPEEDING BULLET!
THROW!
MORE POWERFUL THAN A LOCOMOTIVE!
SMASH!
ABLE TO LEAP TALL BUILDINGS IN A SINGLE BOUND!
LOOK!
UP IN THE SKY!
IT'S A BIRD! IT'S A PLANE!
IT'S SUPER ORANGE!

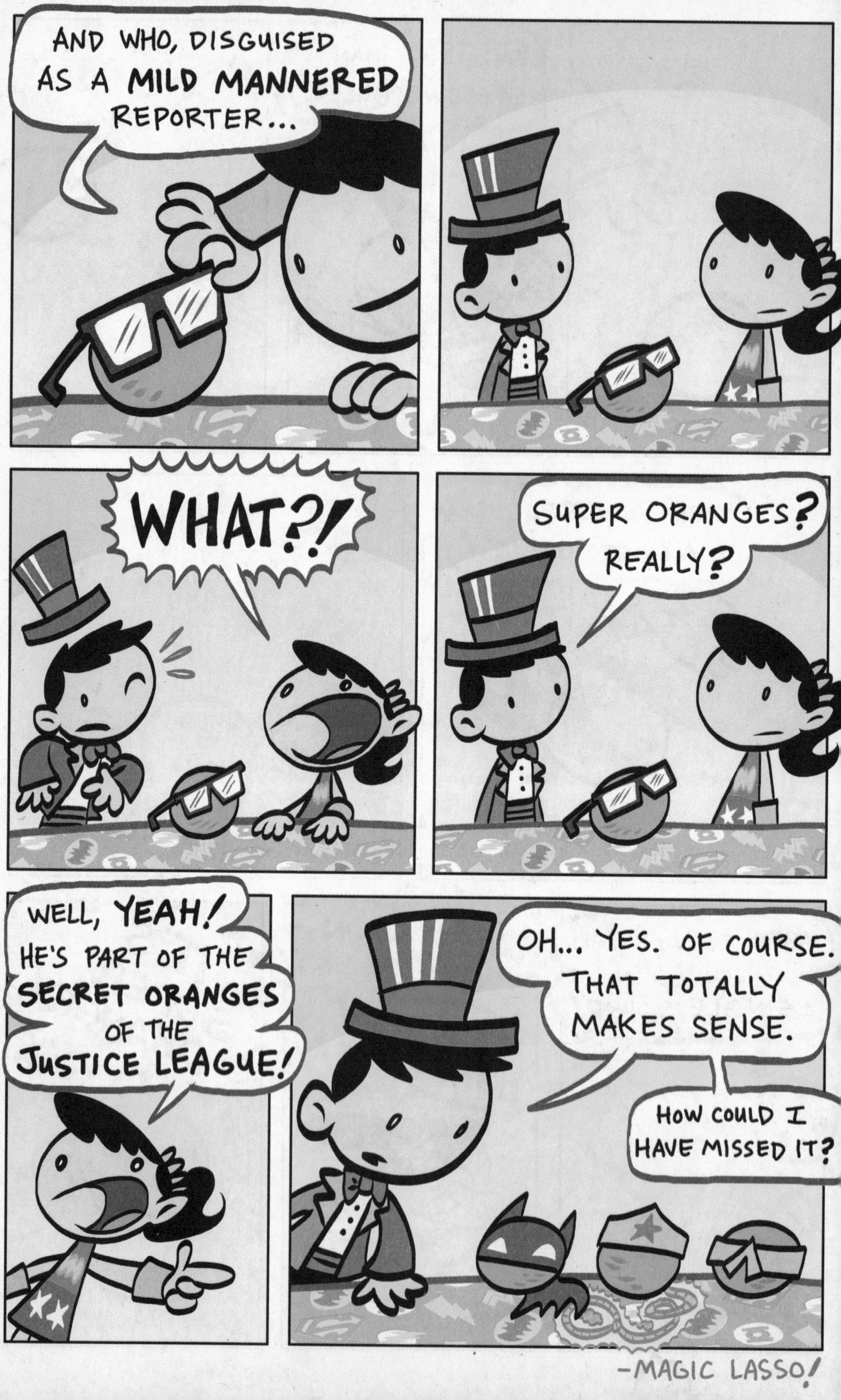
AND WHO, DISGUISED AS A MILD MANNERED REPORTER...
WHAT?!
SUPER ORANGES? REALLY?
WELL, YEAH! HE'S PART OF THE SECRET ORANGES OF THE JUSTICE LEAGUE!
OH... YES. OF COURSE. THAT TOTALLY MAKES SENSE.
HOW COULD I HAVE MISSED IT?
-MAGIC LASSO!

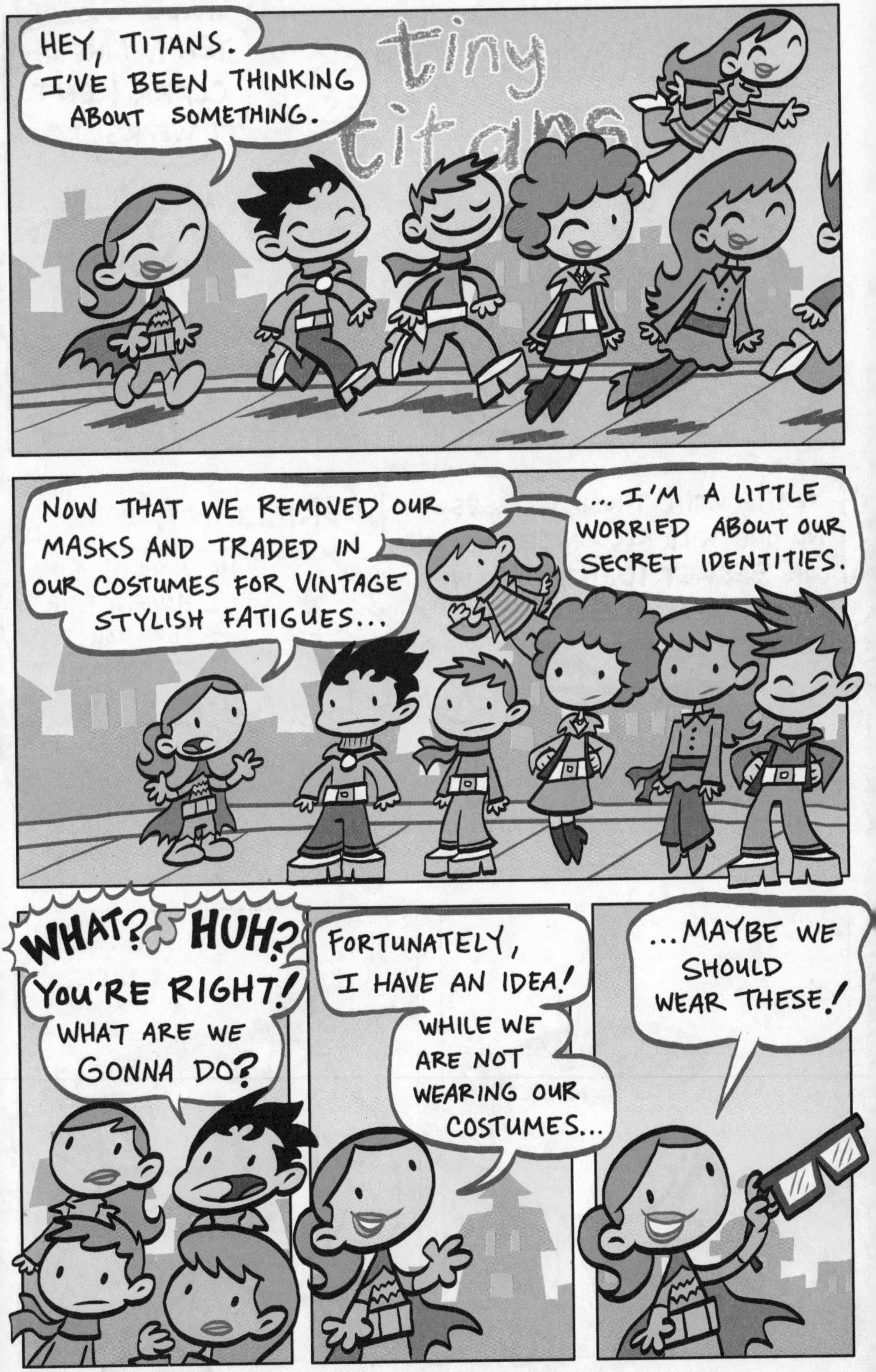
tiny titans
HEY, TITANS. I'VE BEEN THINKING ABOUT SOMETHING.
NOW THAT WE REMOVED OUR MASKS AND TRADED IN OUR COSTUMES FOR VINTAGE STYLISH FATIGUES...
...I'M A LITTLE WORRIED ABOUT OUR SECRET IDENTITIES.
WHAT?
HUH?
YOU'RE RIGHT! WHAT ARE WE GONNA DO?
FORTUNATELY, I HAVE AN IDEA!
WHILE WE ARE NOT WEARING OUR COSTUMES...
...MAYBE WE SHOULD WEAR THESE!

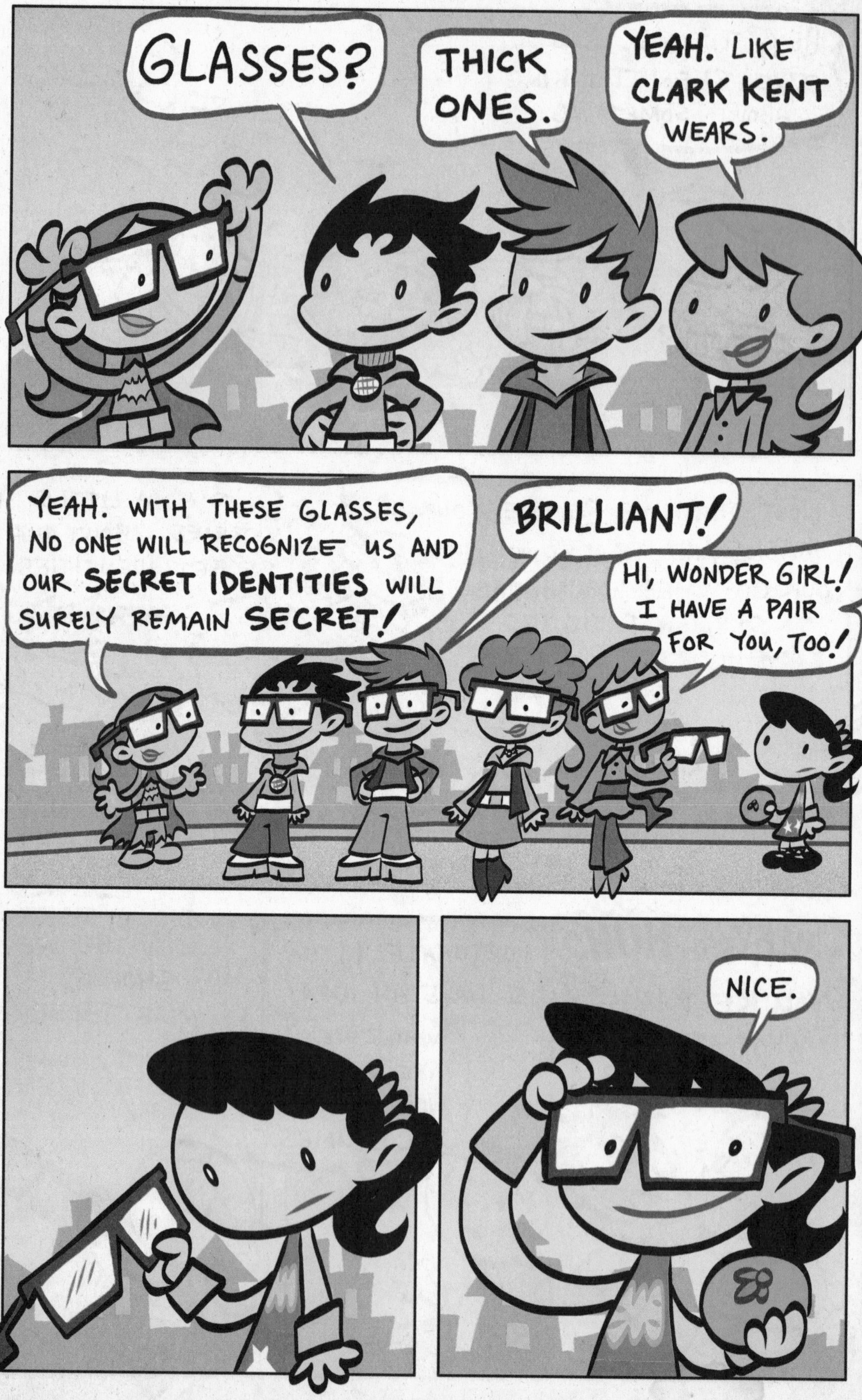
GLASSES?
THICK ONES.
YEAH. LIKE CLARK KENT WEARS.
YEAH. WITH THESE GLASSES, NO ONE WILL RECOGNIZE US AND OUR SECRET IDENTITIES WILL SURELY REMAIN SECRET!
BRILLIANT!
HI, WONDER GIRL! I HAVE A PAIR FOR YOU, TOO!
NICE.

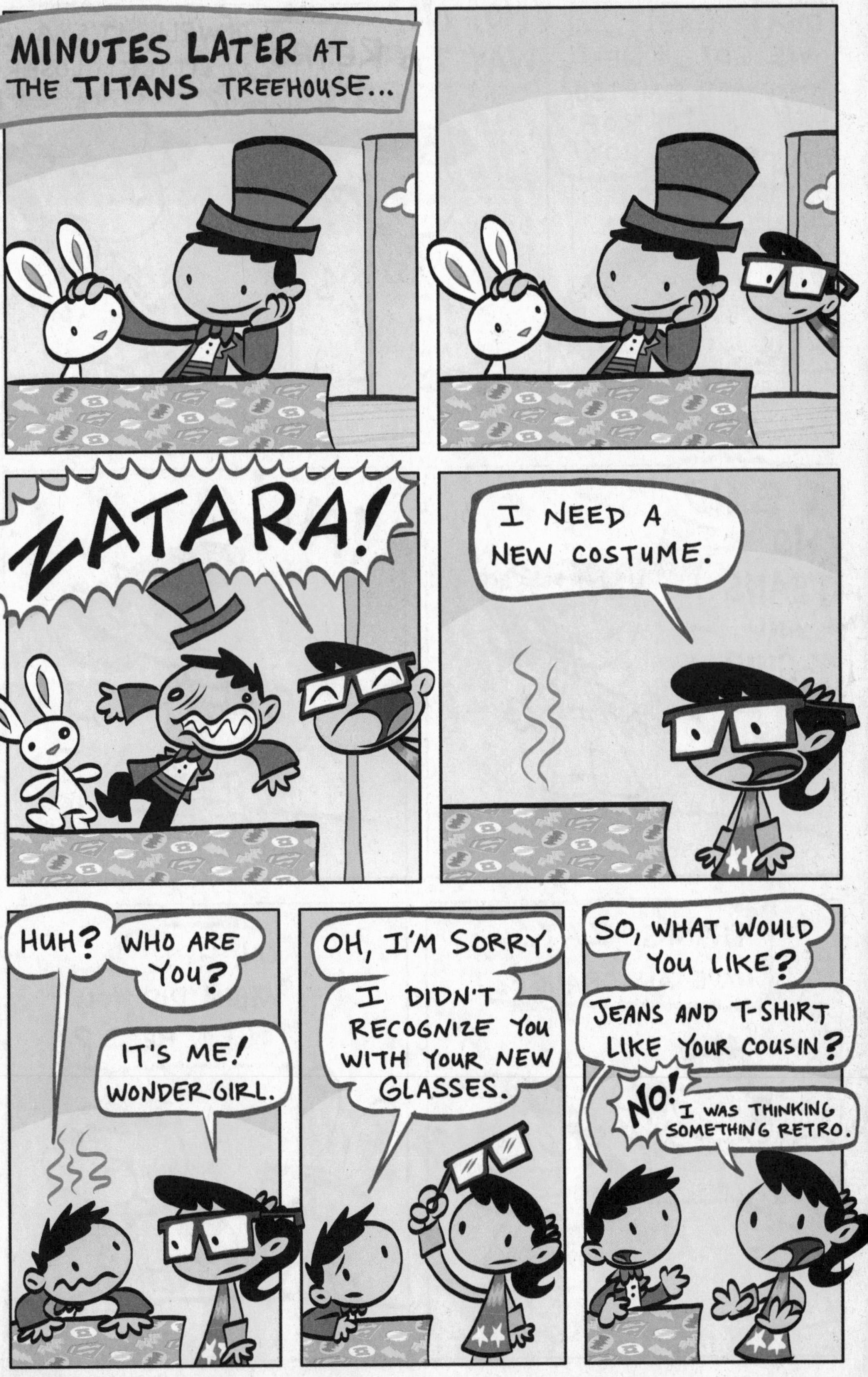
MINUTES LATER AT THE TITANS TREEHOUSE...
ZATARA!
I NEED A NEW COSTUME.
HUH?
WHO ARE YOU?
IT'S ME! WONDERGIRL.
OH, I'M SORRY.
I DIDN'T RECOGNIZE YOU WITH YOUR NEW GLASSES.
SO, WHAT WOULD YOU LIKE?
JEANS AND T-SHIRT LIKE YOUR COUSIN?
NO!
I WAS THINKING SOMETHING RETRO.

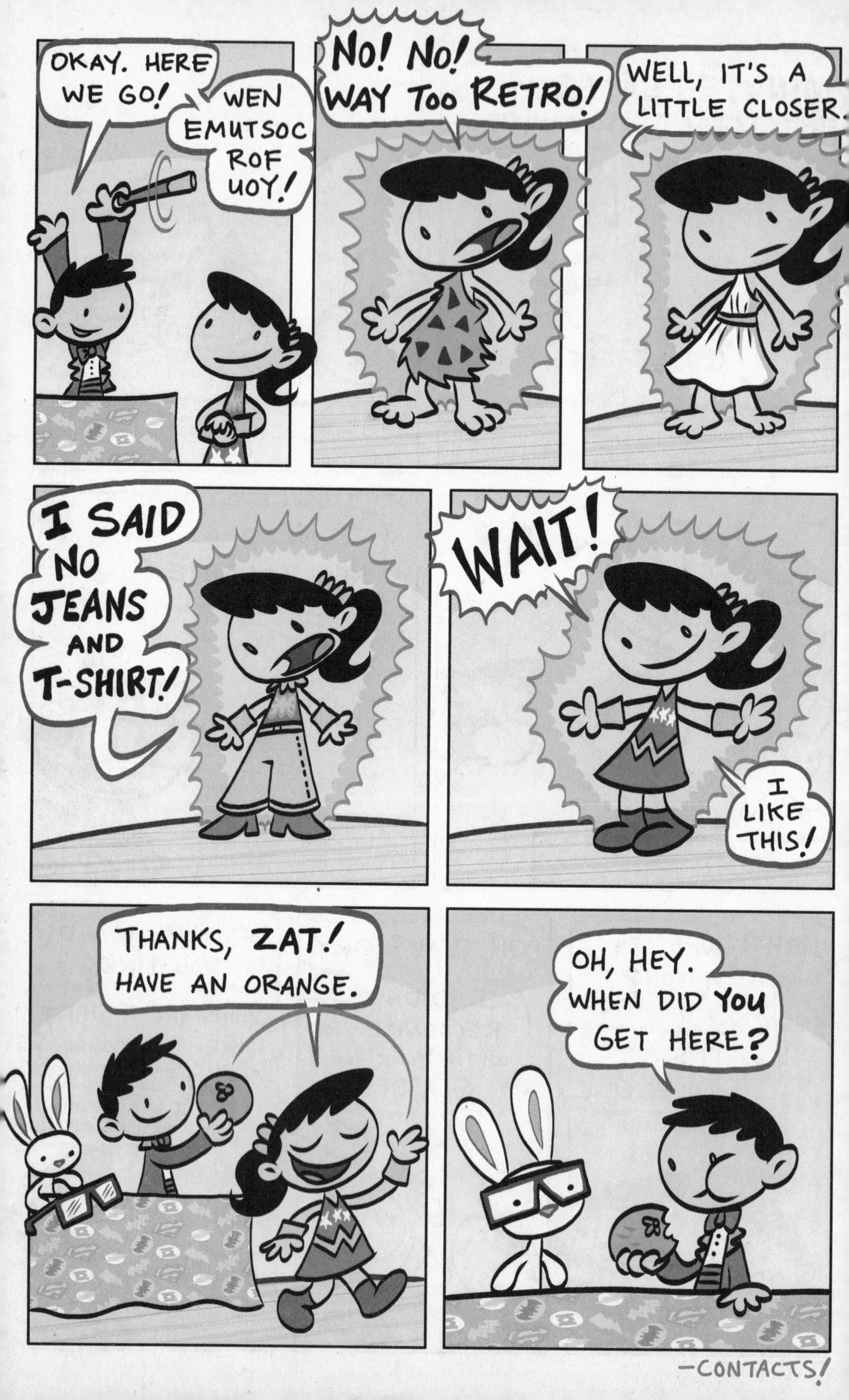
OKAY. HERE WE GO!
WEN EMUTSOC ROF UOY!
NO! NO! WAY TOO RETRO!
WELL, IT'S A LITTLE CLOSER.
I SAID NO JEANS AND T-SHIRT!
WAIT!
I LIKE THIS!
THANKS, ZAT! HAVE AN ORANGE.
OH, HEY. WHEN DID YOU GET HERE?
—CONTACTS!

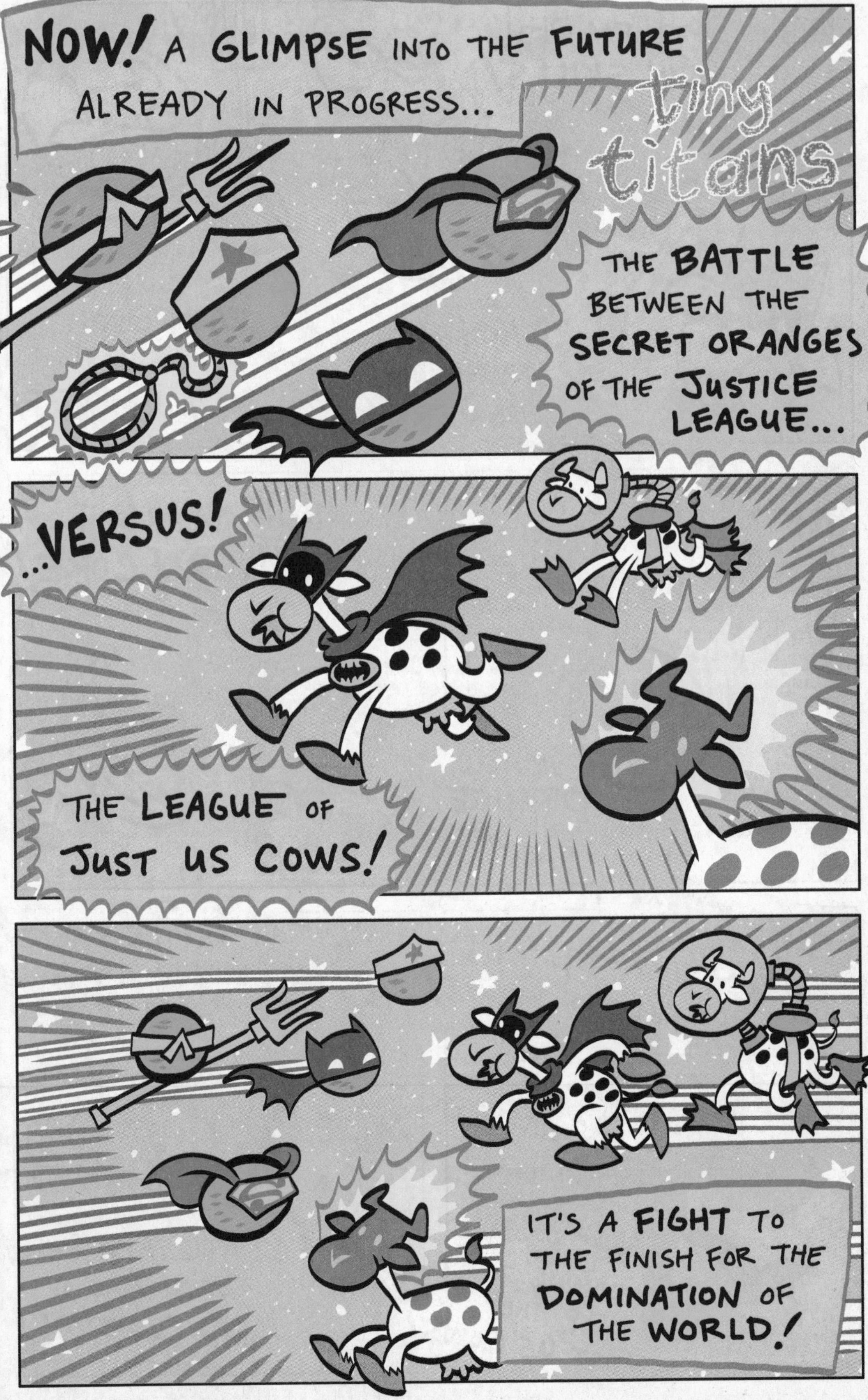
NOW! A GLIMPSE INTO THE FUTURE ALREADY IN PROGRESS...
tiny titans
THE BATTLE BETWEEN THE SECRET ORANGES OF THE JUSTICE LEAGUE...
...VERSUS!
THE LEAGUE OF JUST US COWS!
IT'S A FIGHT TO THE FINISH FOR THE DOMINATION OF THE WORLD!

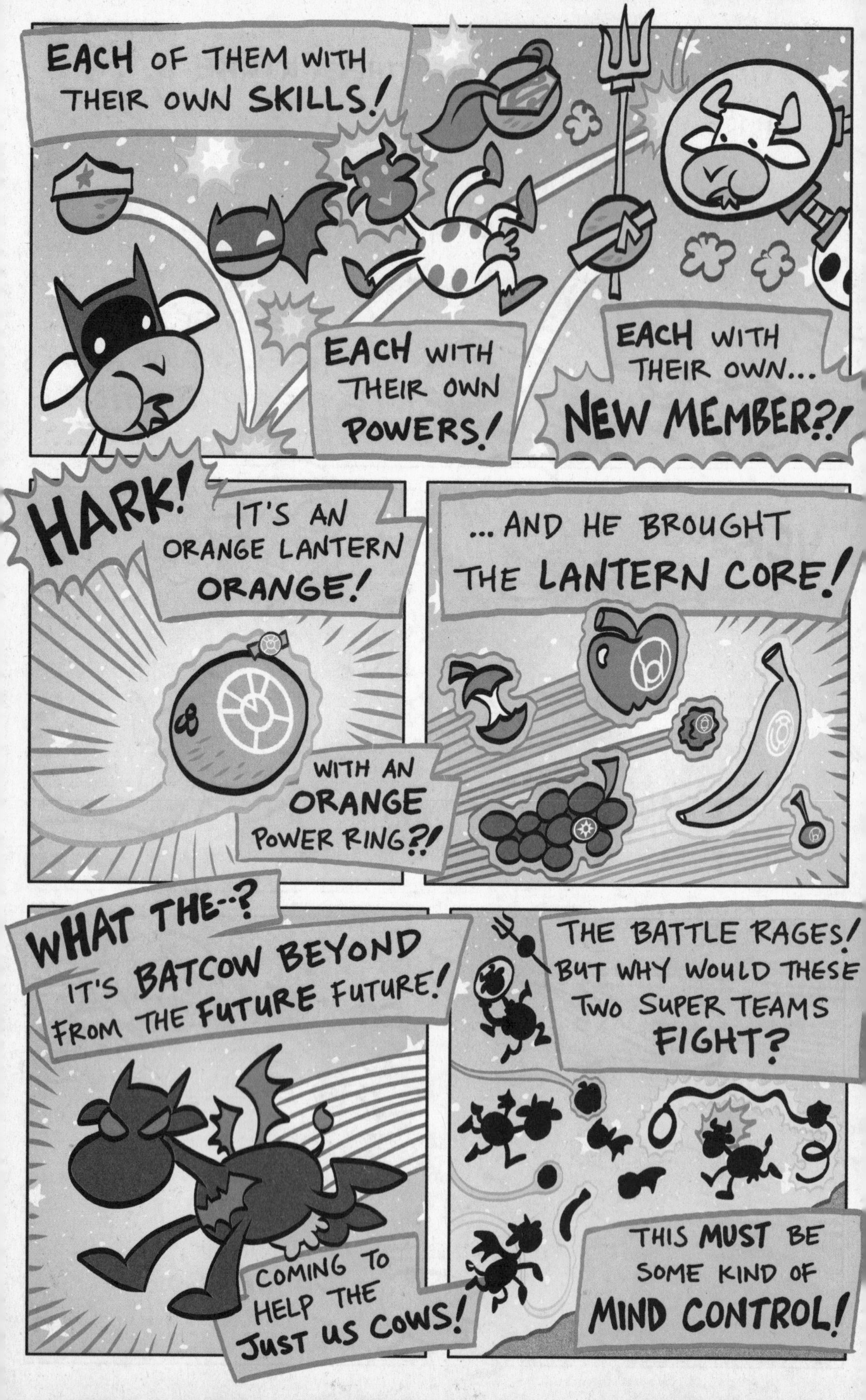
EACH OF THEM WITH THEIR OWN SKILLS!
EACH WITH THEIR OWN POWERS!
EACH WITH THEIR OWN... NEW MEMBER?!
HARK!
IT'S AN ORANGE LANTERN ORANGE!
WITH AN ORANGE POWER RING?!
... AND HE BROUGHT THE LANTERN CORE!
WHAT THE--?
IT'S BATCOW BEYOND FROM THE FUTURE FUTURE!
COMING TO HELP THE JUST US COWS!
THE BATTLE RAGES! BUT WHY WOULD THESE TWO SUPER TEAMS FIGHT?
THIS MUST BE SOME KIND OF MIND CONTROL!

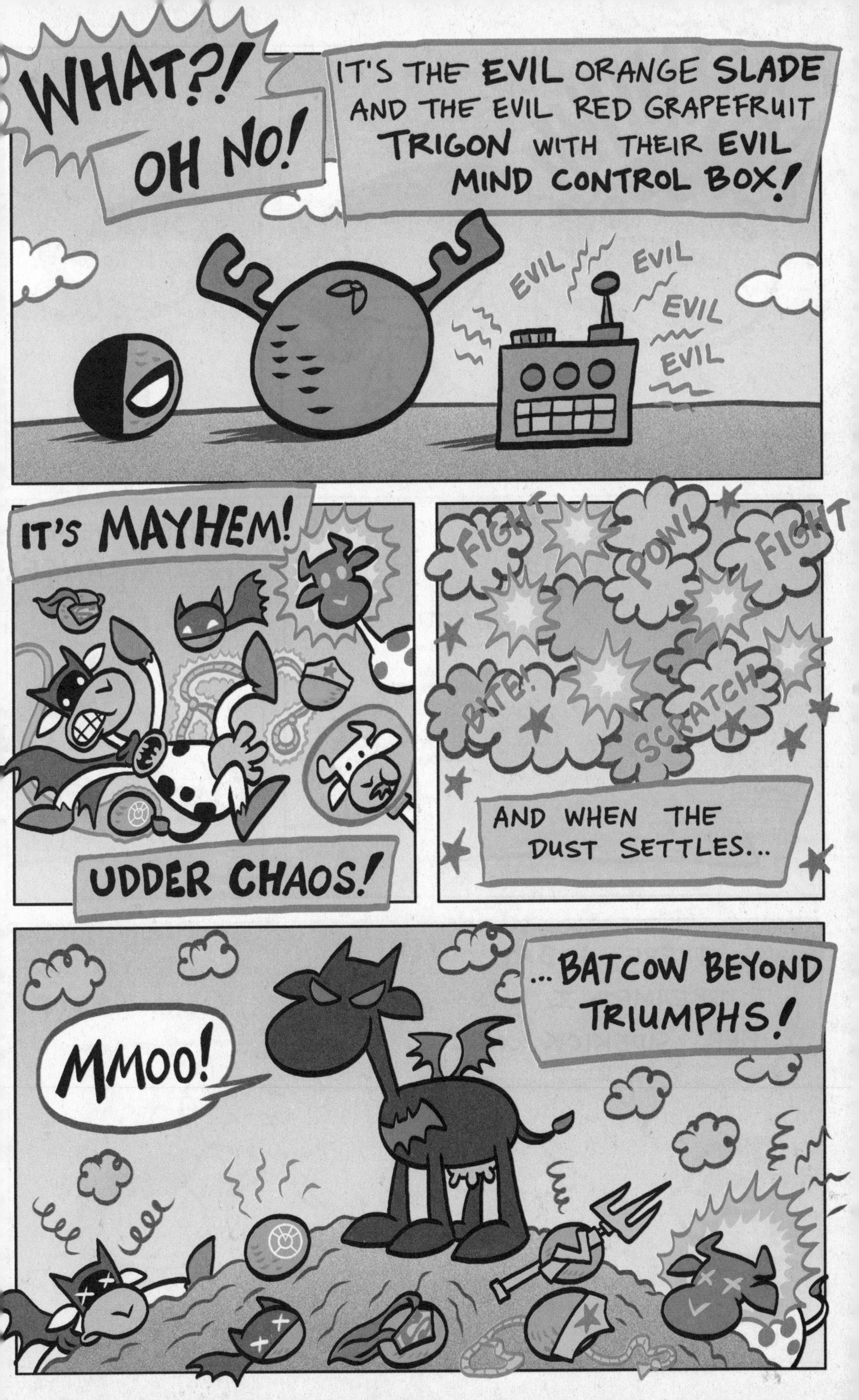
WHAT?!
OH NO!
IT'S THE EVIL ORANGE SLADE AND THE EVIL RED GRAPEFRUIT TRIGON WITH THEIR EVIL MIND CONTROL BOX!
EVIL
EVIL
EVIL
EVIL
IT'S MAYHEM!
UDDER CHAOS!
FIGHT
POW!
FIGHT
BITE!
SCRATCH
AND WHEN THE DUST SETTLES...
...BATCOW BEYOND TRIUMPHS!
MMOO!

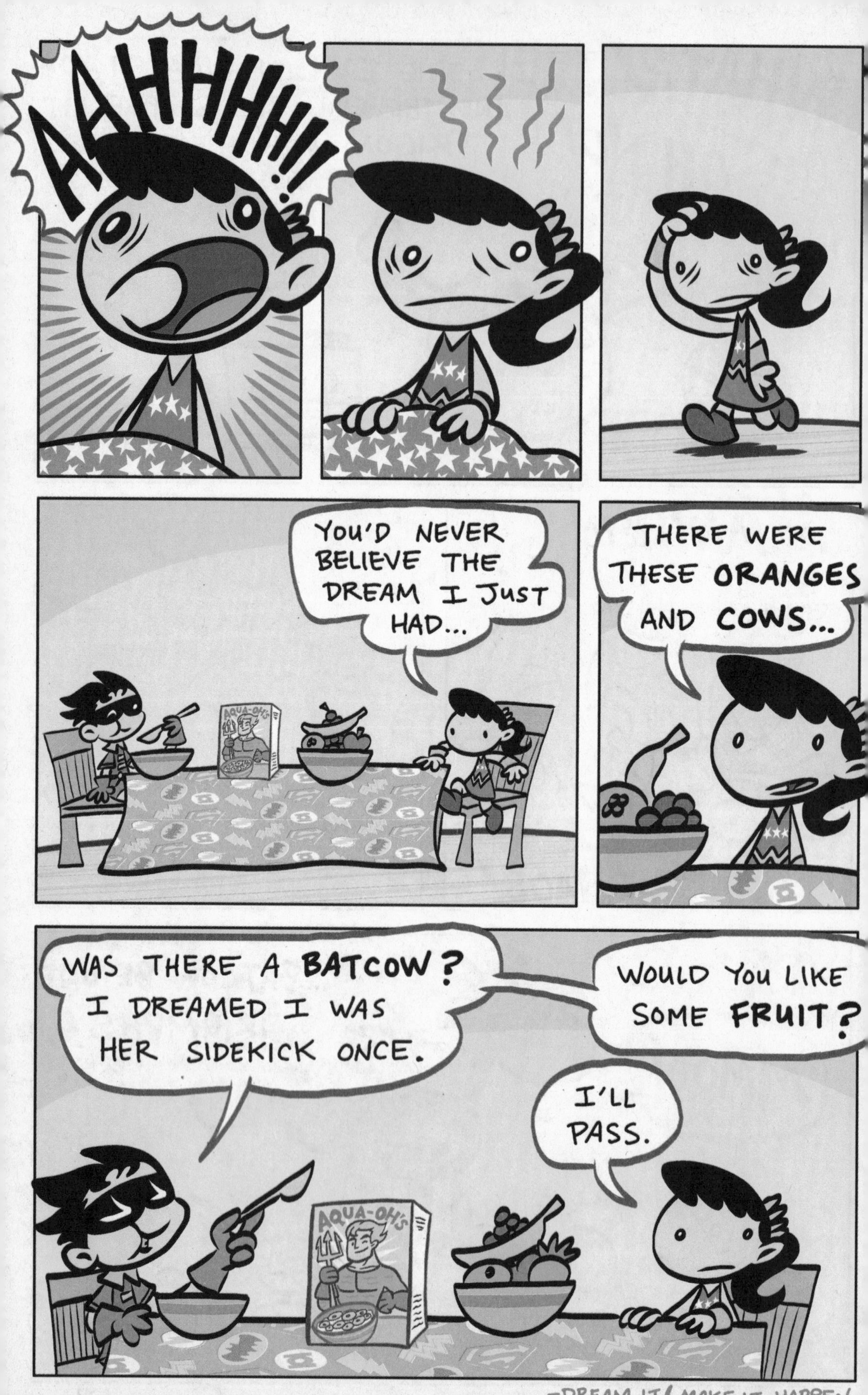
AAHHHH!!
YOU'D NEVER BELIEVE THE DREAM I JUST HAD...
THERE WERE THESE ORANGES AND COWS...
AQUA-OH'S
WAS THERE A BATCOW? I DREAMED I WAS HER SIDEKICK ONCE.
WOULD YOU LIKE SOME FRUIT?
I'LL PASS.
AQUA-OH'S

-DREAM IT! MAKE IT HAPPEN.

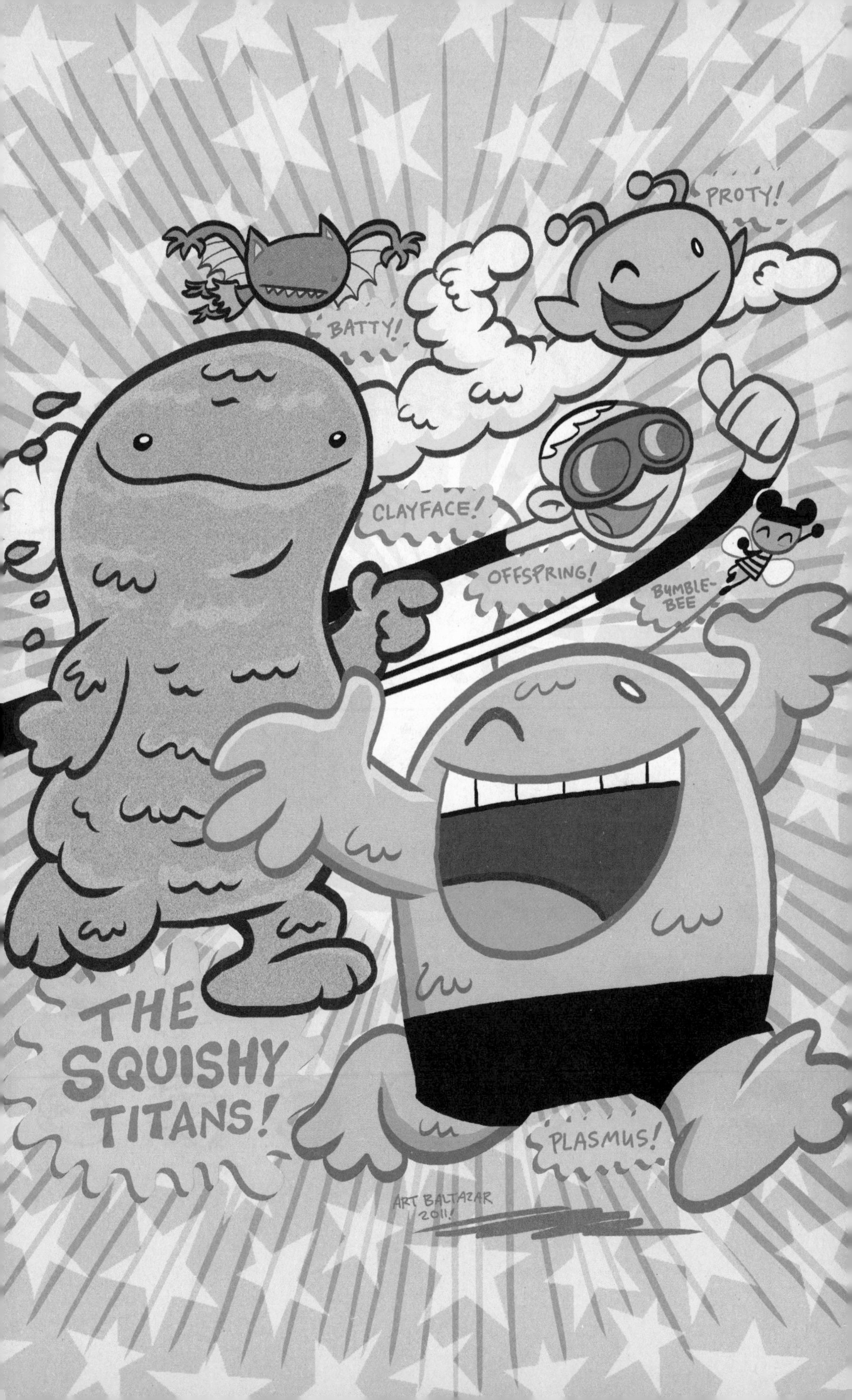
PROTY!
BATTY!
CLAYFACE!
OFFSPRING!
BUMBLE-BEE
THE SQUISHY TITANS!
PLASMUS!
ART BALTAZAR 2011!

tiny titans

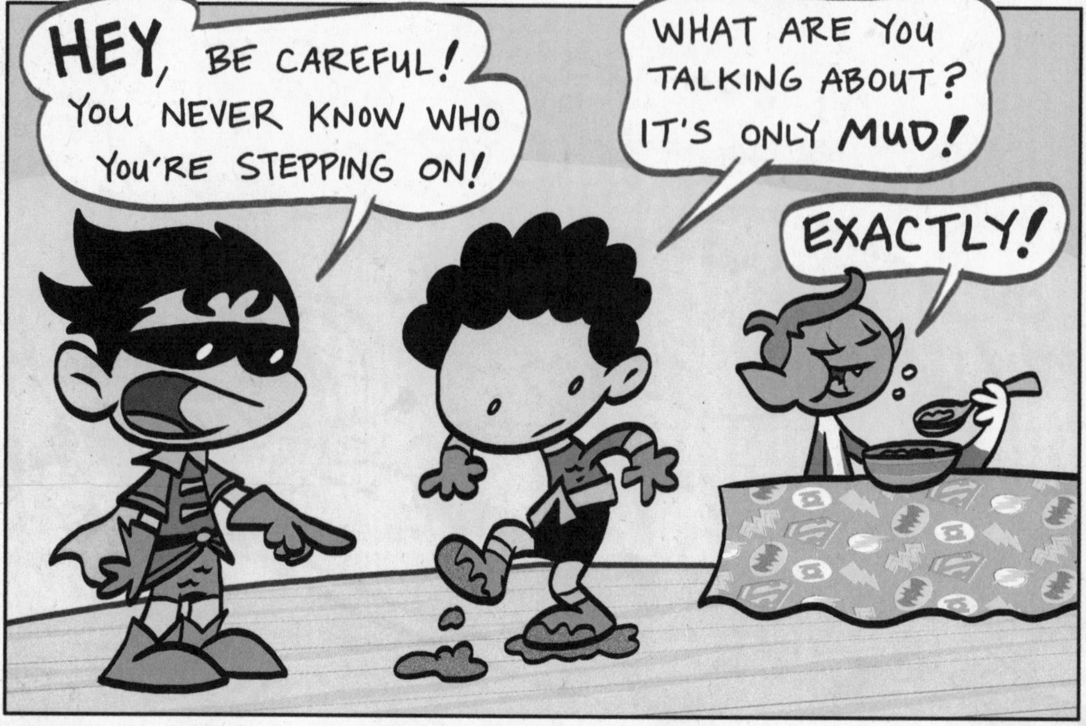
HEY, BE CAREFUL! YOU NEVER KNOW WHO YOU'RE STEPPING ON!
WHAT ARE YOU TALKING ABOUT? IT'S ONLY MUD!
EXACTLY!

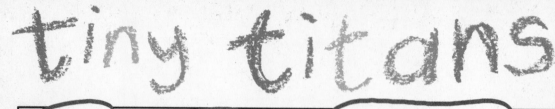

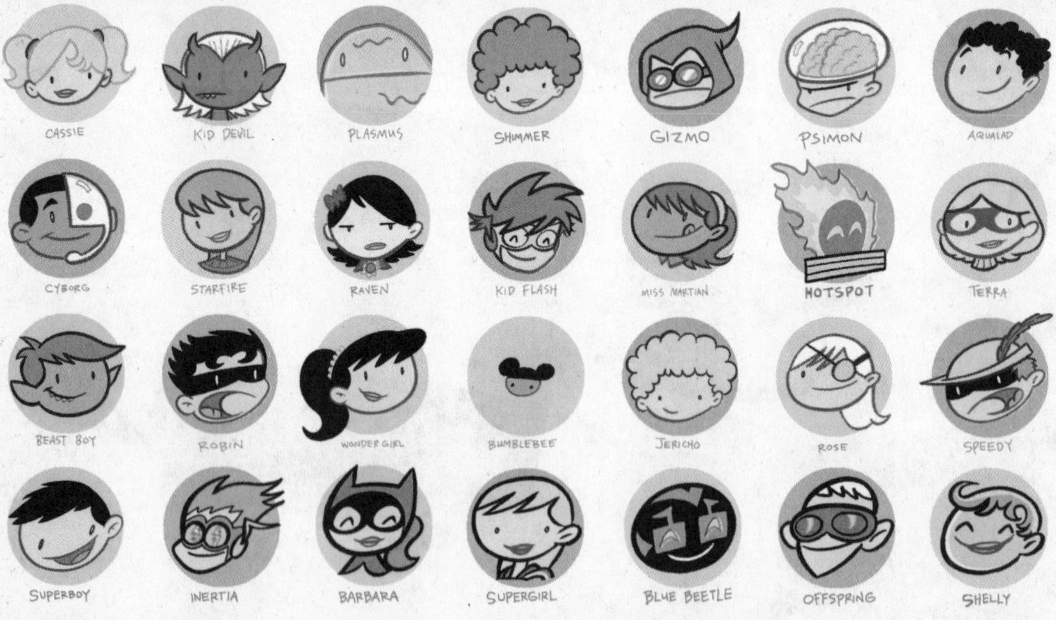
CASSIE
KID DEVIL
PLASMUS
SHIMMER
GIZMO
PSIMON
AQUALAD
CYBORG
STARFIRE
RAVEN
KID FLASH
MISS MARTIAN
HOTSPOT
TERRA
BEAST BOY
ROBIN
WONDER GIRL
BUMBLEBEE
JERICHO
ROSE
SPEEDY
SUPERBOY
INERTIA
BARBARA
SUPERGIRL
BLUE BEETLE
OFFSPRING
SHELLY

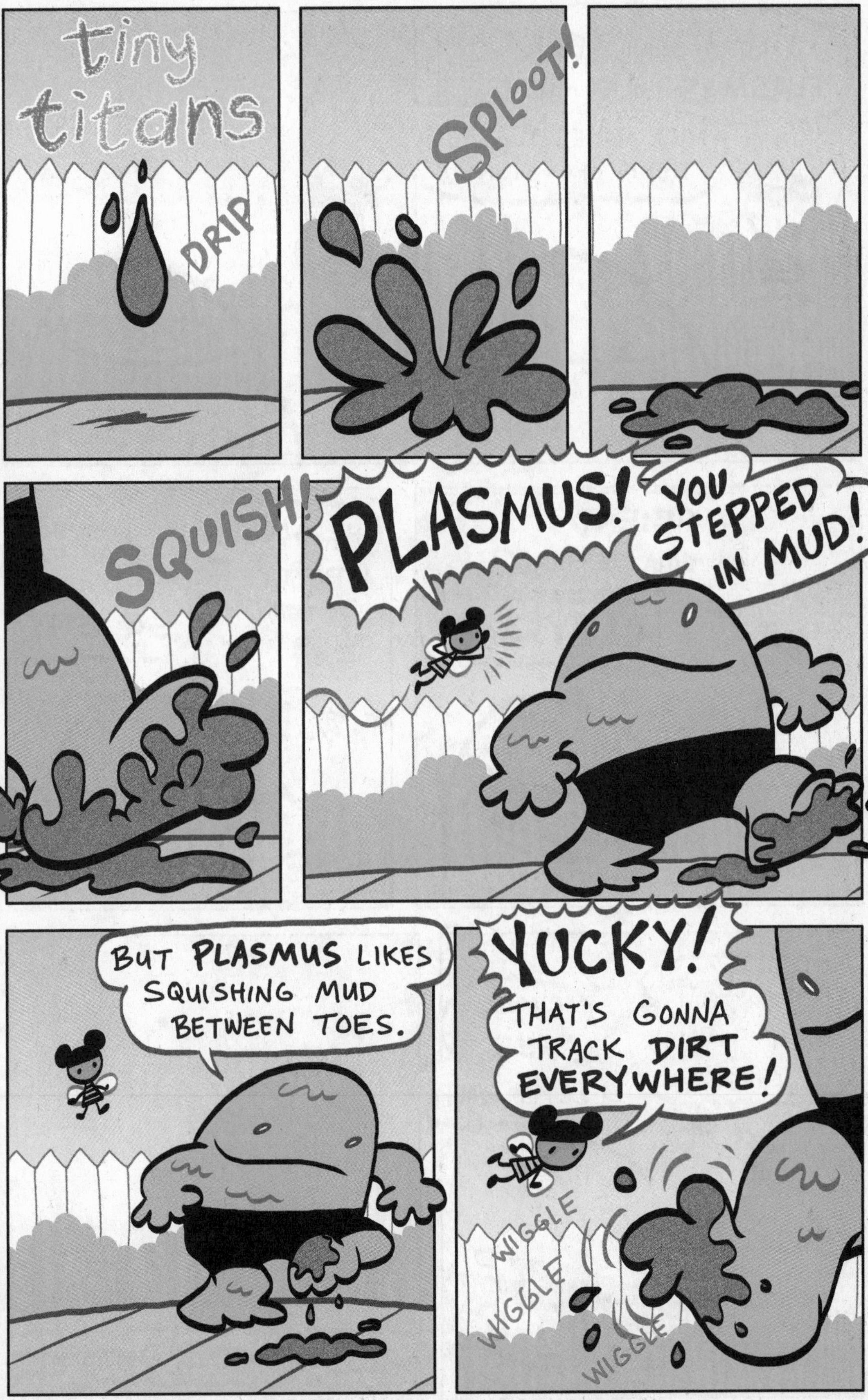
tiny titans
DRIP
SPLOOT!
SQUISH!
PLASMUS!
YOU STEPPED IN MUD!
BUT PLASMUS LIKES SQUISHING MUD BETWEEN TOES.
YUCKY!
THAT'S GONNA TRACK DIRT EVERYWHERE!
WIGGLE
WIGGLE
WIGGLE

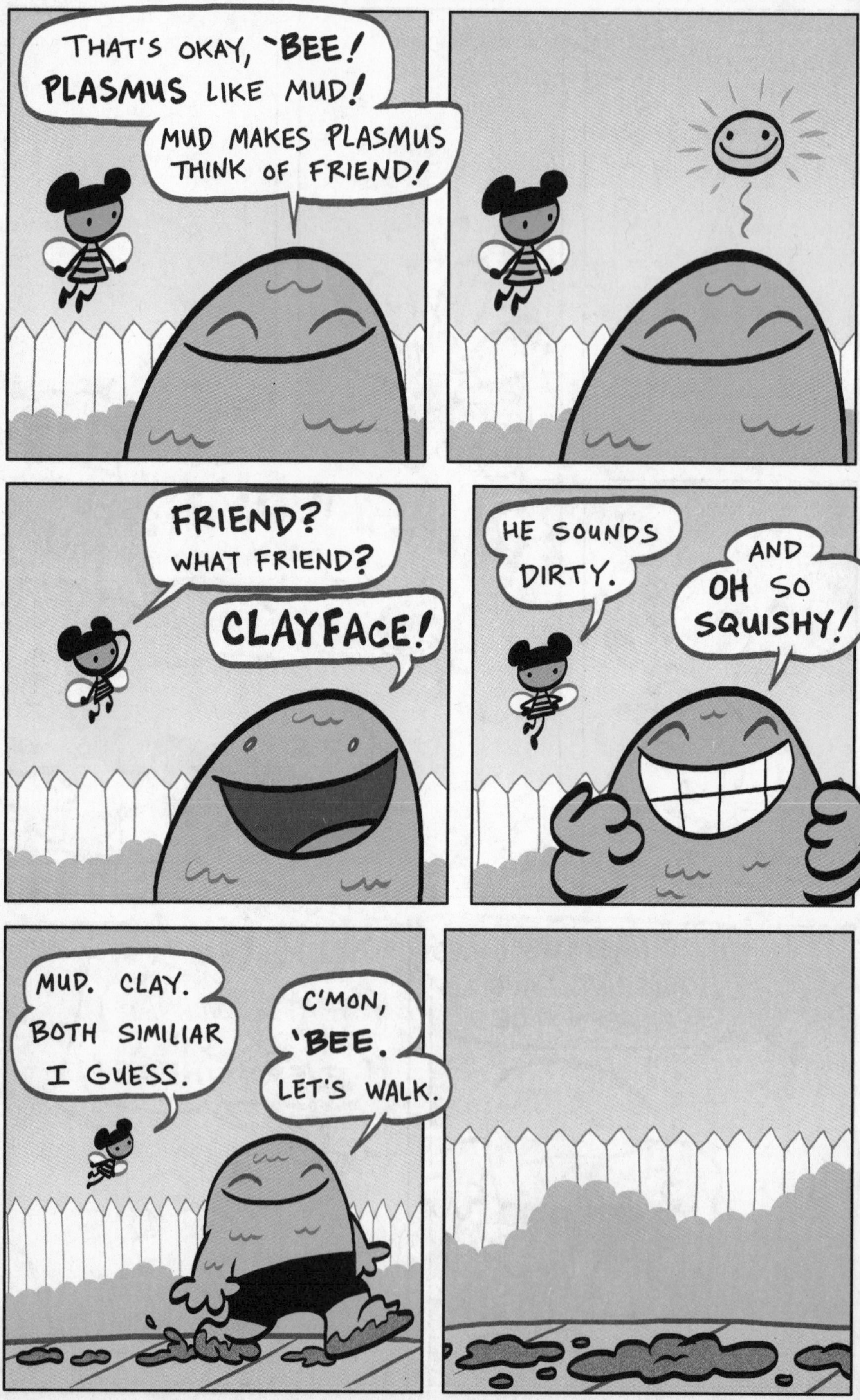
THAT'S OKAY, 'BEE! PLASMUS LIKE MUD!
MUD MAKES PLASMUS THINK OF FRIEND!
FRIEND? WHAT FRIEND?
CLAYFACE!
HE SOUNDS DIRTY.
AND OH SO SQUISHY!
MUD. CLAY. BOTH SIMILIAR I GUESS.
C'MON, 'BEE. LET'S WALK.

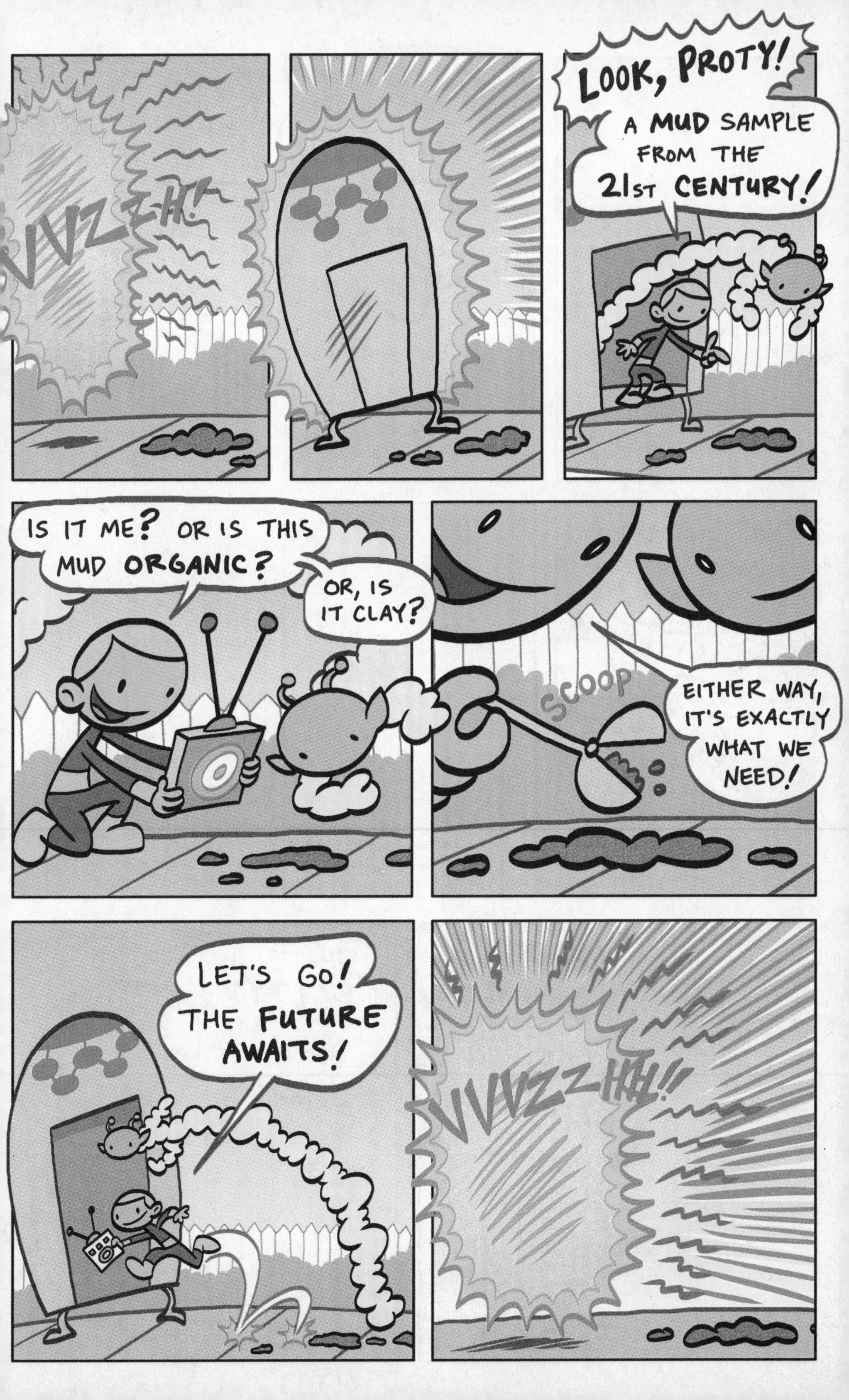
VVZZZH!
LOOK, PROTY!
A MUD SAMPLE FROM THE 21ST CENTURY!
IS IT ME? OR IS THIS MUD ORGANIC?
OR, IS IT CLAY?
SCOOP
EITHER WAY, IT'S EXACTLY WHAT WE NEED!
LET'S GO! THE FUTURE AWAITS!
VVVZZHH!!

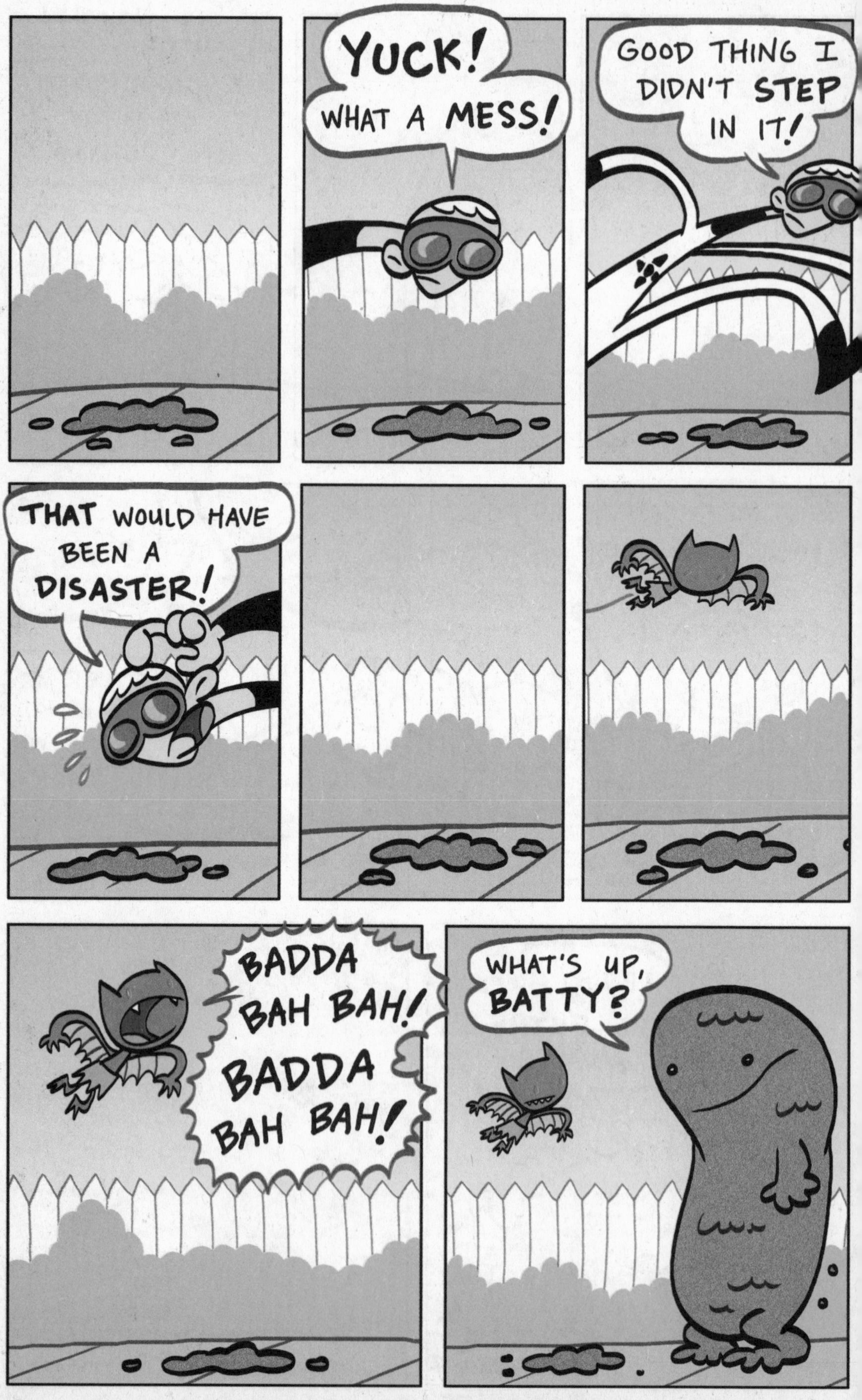
YUCK! WHAT A MESS!
GOOD THING I DIDN'T STEP IN IT!
THAT WOULD HAVE BEEN A DISASTER!
BADDA BAH BAH! BADDA BAH BAH!
WHAT'S UP, BATTY?

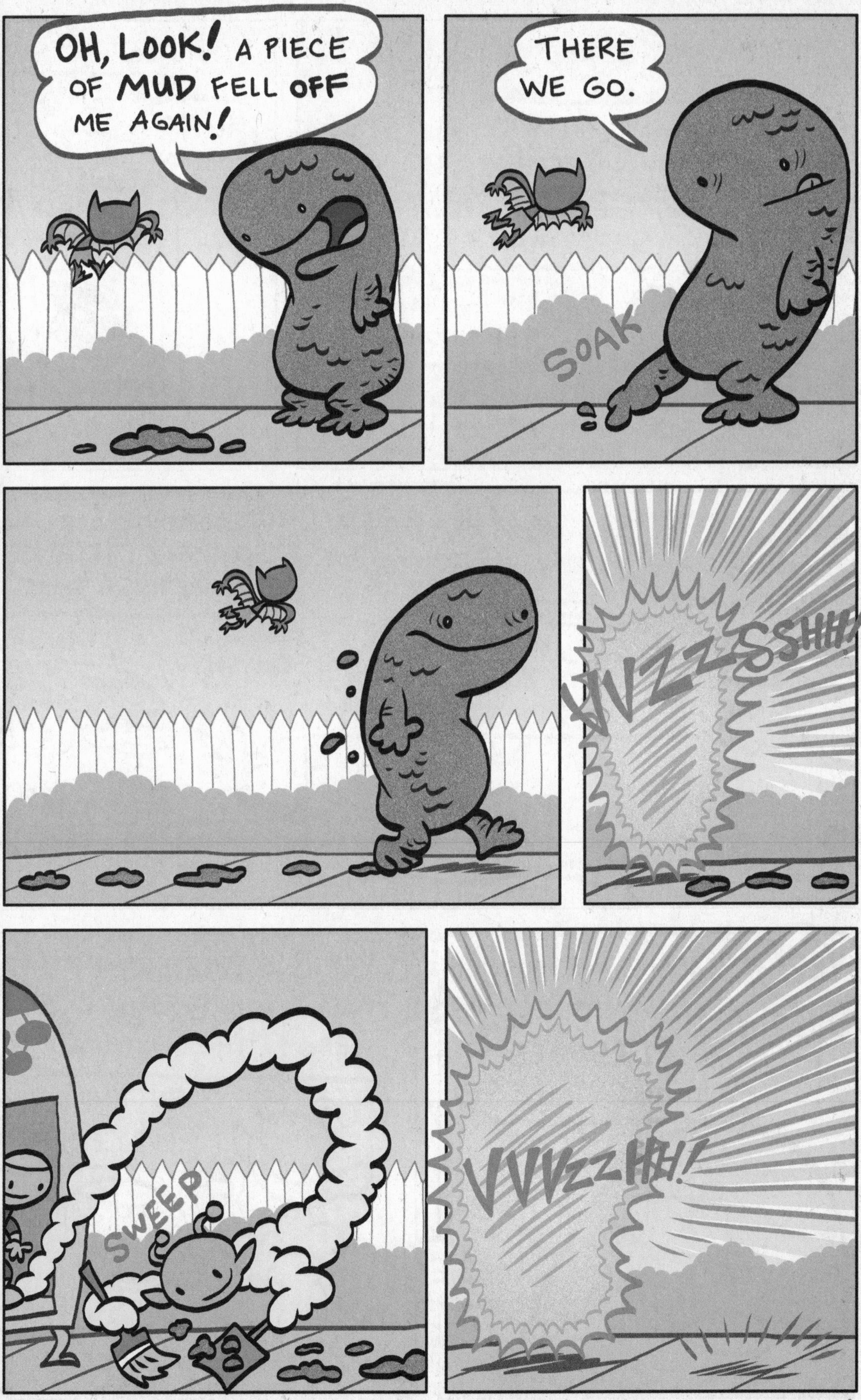
OH, LOOK! A PIECE OF MUD FELL OFF ME AGAIN!
THERE WE GO.
SOAK
VVZZZSSHH!
SWEEP
VVVZZHH!

-CLEAN!

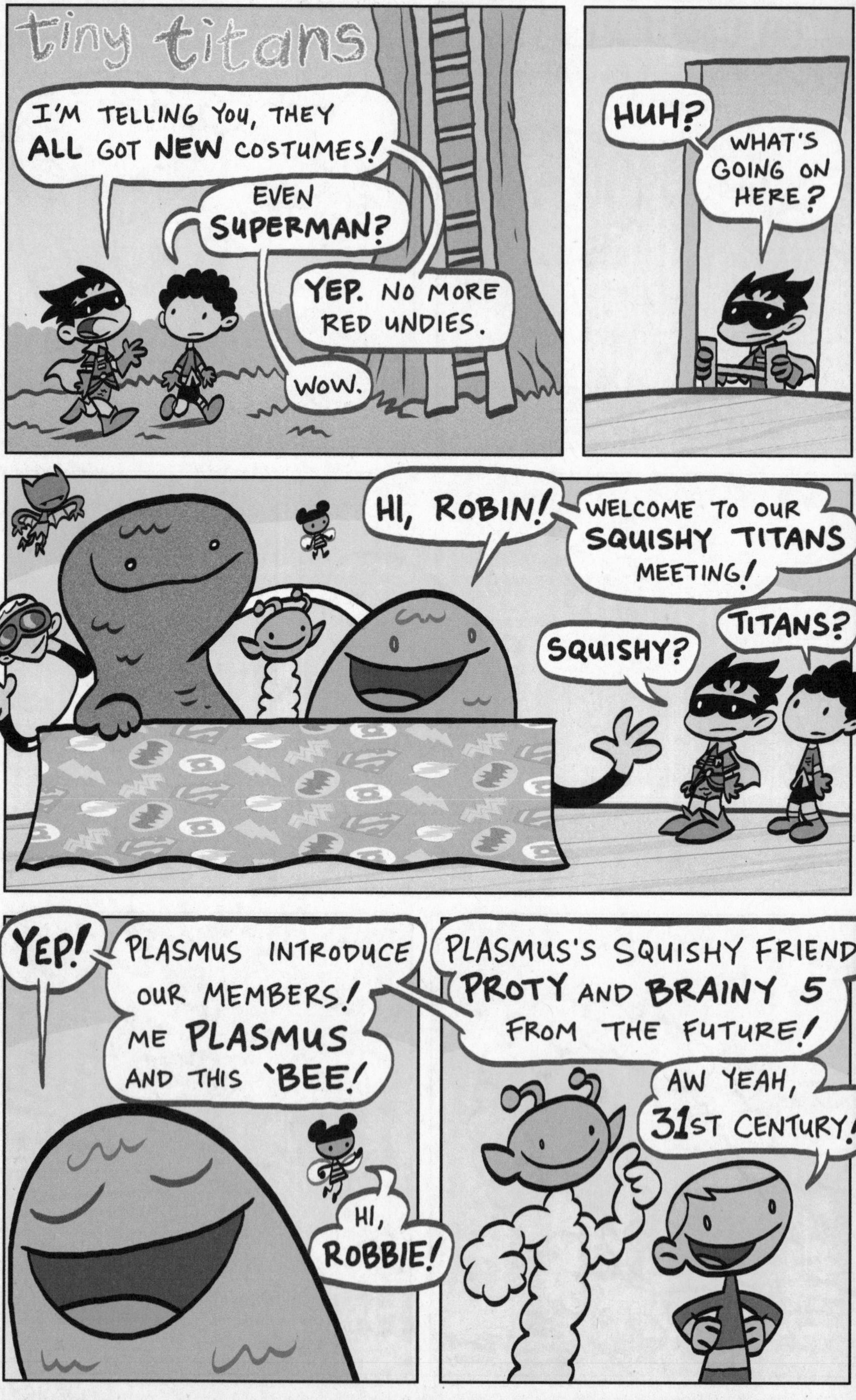
tiny titans
I'M TELLING YOU, THEY ALL GOT NEW COSTUMES!
EVEN SUPERMAN?
YEP. NO MORE RED UNDIES.
WOW.
HUH?
WHAT'S GOING ON HERE?
HI, ROBIN!
WELCOME TO OUR SQUISHY TITANS MEETING!
SQUISHY?
TITANS?
YEP!
PLASMUS INTRODUCE OUR MEMBERS! ME PLASMUS AND THIS 'BEE!
HI, ROBBIE!
PLASMUS'S SQUISHY FRIEND PROTY AND BRAINY 5 FROM THE FUTURE!
AW YEAH, 31ST CENTURY!

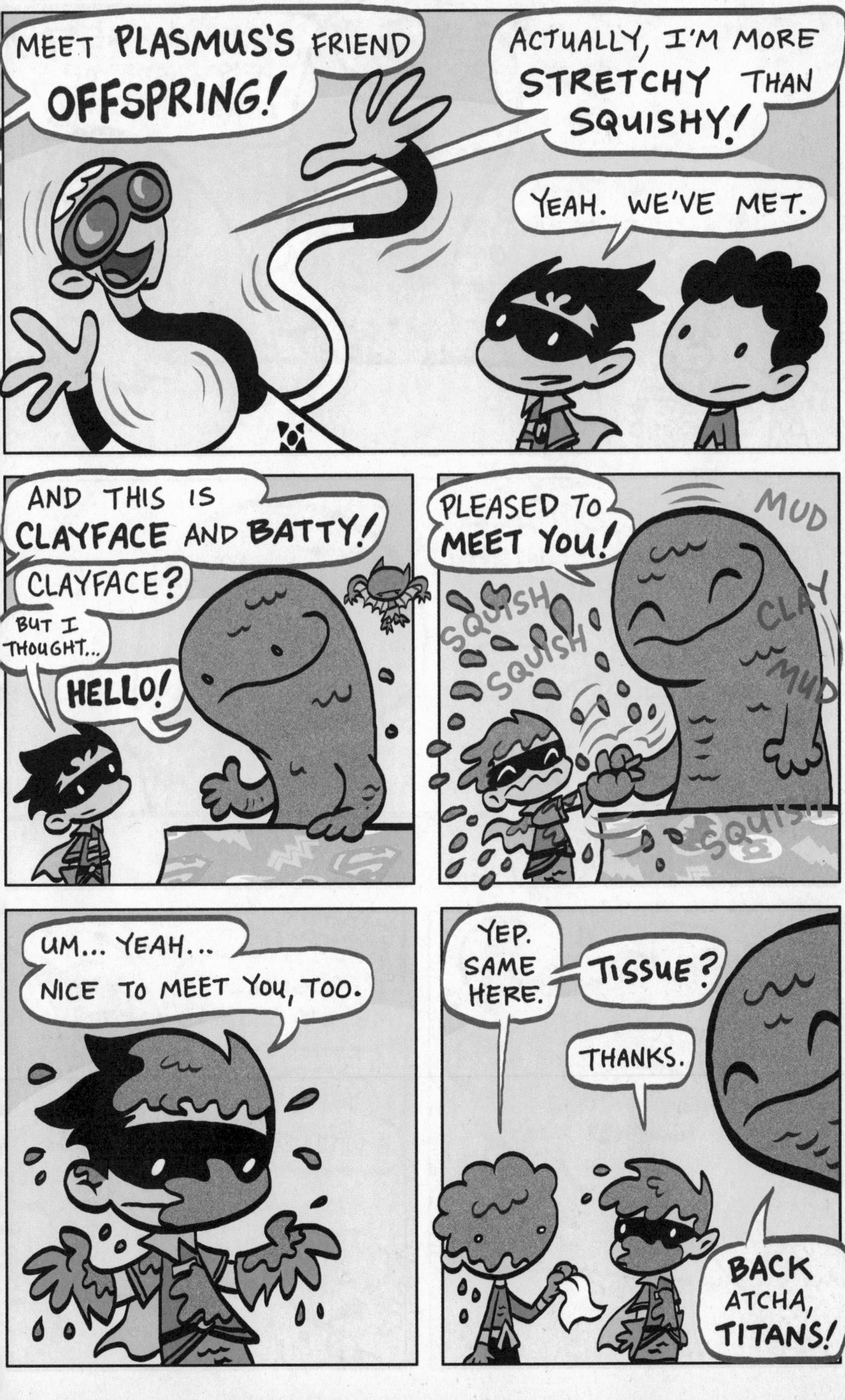
MEET PLASMUS'S FRIEND OFFSPRING!
ACTUALLY, I'M MORE STRETCHY THAN SQUISHY!
YEAH. WE'VE MET.
AND THIS IS CLAYFACE AND BATTY!
CLAYFACE?
BUT I THOUGHT...
HELLO!
PLEASED TO MEET YOU!
MUD
SQUISH
SQUISH
CLAY
MUD
SQUISH
UM... YEAH...
NICE TO MEET YOU, TOO.
YEP. SAME HERE.
TISSUE?
THANKS.
BACK ATCHA, TITANS!

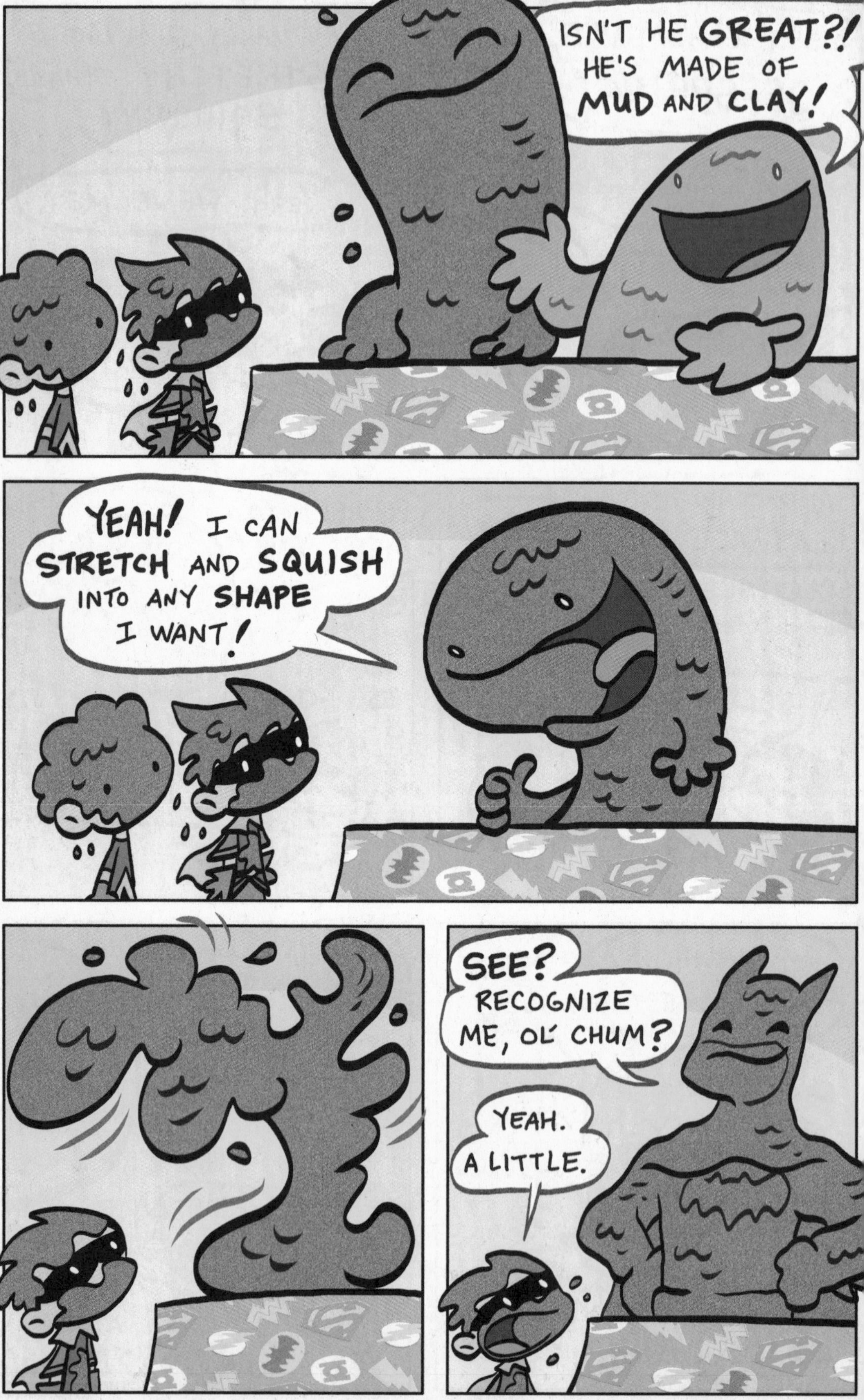
ISN'T HE GREAT?! HE'S MADE OF MUD AND CLAY!
YEAH! I CAN STRETCH AND SQUISH INTO ANY SHAPE I WANT!
SEE? RECOGNIZE ME, OL' CHUM?
YEAH. A LITTLE.

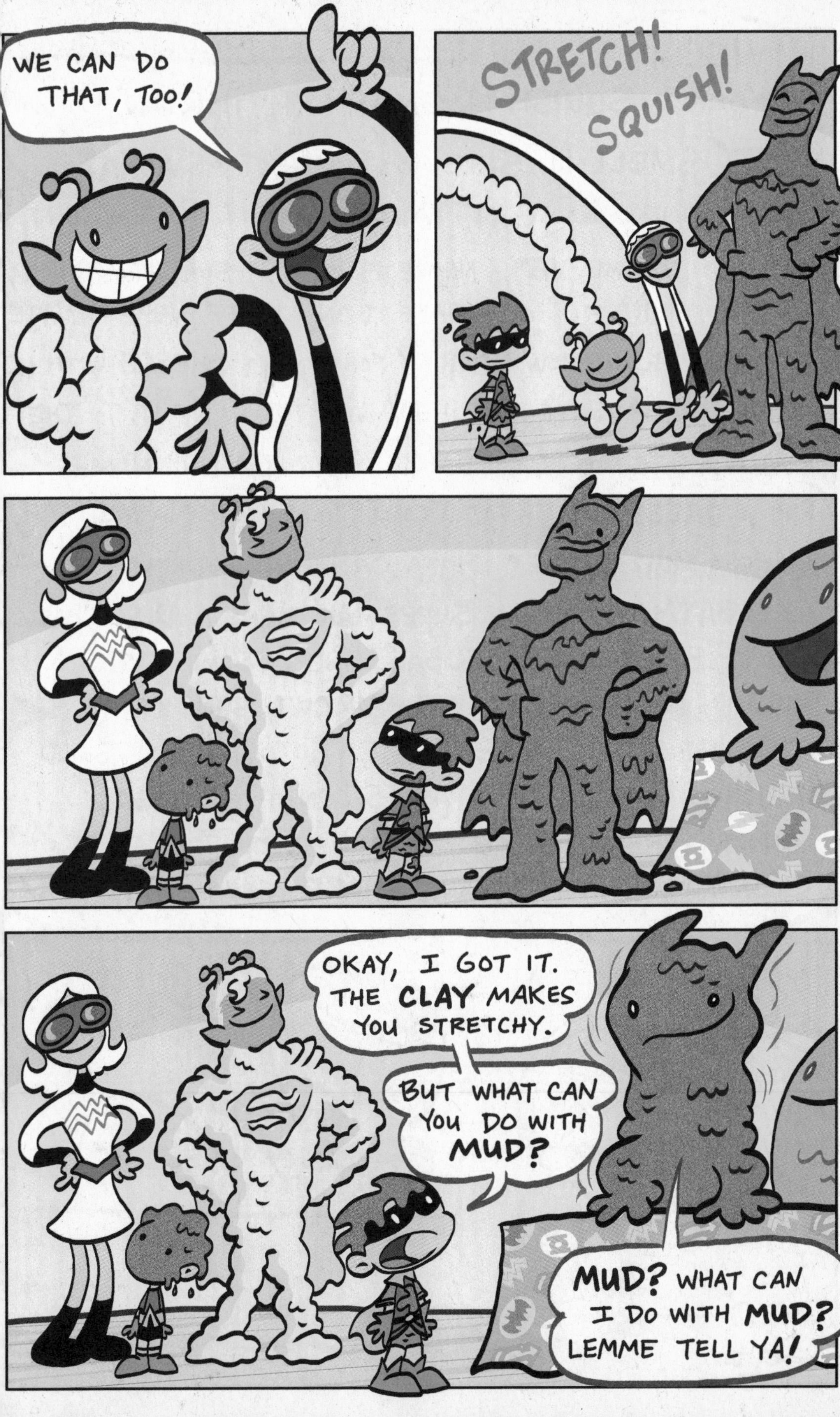
WE CAN DO THAT, TOO!
STRETCH!
SQUISH!
OKAY, I GOT IT. THE CLAY MAKES YOU STRETCHY.
BUT WHAT CAN YOU DO WITH MUD?
MUD? WHAT CAN I DO WITH MUD? LEMME TELL YA!

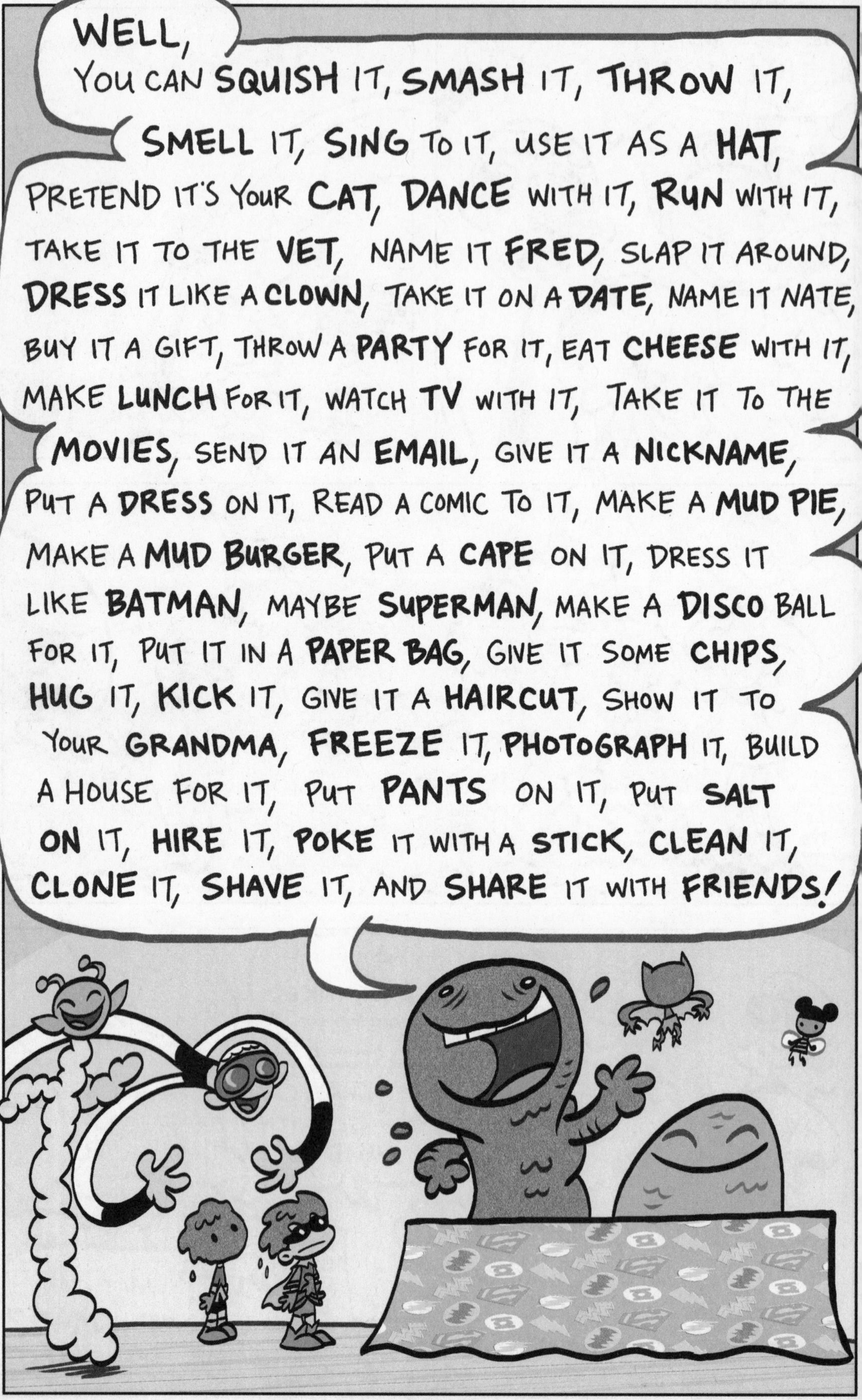
WELL, YOU CAN SQUISH IT, SMASH IT, THROW IT, SMELL IT, SING TO IT, USE IT AS A HAT, PRETEND IT'S YOUR CAT, DANCE WITH IT, RUN WITH IT, TAKE IT TO THE VET, NAME IT FRED, SLAP IT AROUND, DRESS IT LIKE A CLOWN, TAKE IT ON A DATE, NAME IT NATE, BUY IT A GIFT, THROW A PARTY FOR IT, EAT CHEESE WITH IT, MAKE LUNCH FOR IT, WATCH TV WITH IT, TAKE IT TO THE MOVIES, SEND IT AN EMAIL, GIVE IT A NICKNAME, PUT A DRESS ON IT, READ A COMIC TO IT, MAKE A MUD PIE, MAKE A MUD BURGER, PUT A CAPE ON IT, DRESS IT LIKE BATMAN, MAYBE SUPERMAN, MAKE A DISCO BALL FOR IT, PUT IT IN A PAPER BAG, GIVE IT SOME CHIPS, HUG IT, KICK IT, GIVE IT A HAIRCUT, SHOW IT TO YOUR GRANDMA, FREEZE IT, PHOTOGRAPH IT, BUILD A HOUSE FOR IT, PUT PANTS ON IT, PUT SALT ON IT, HIRE IT, POKE IT WITH A STICK, CLEAN IT, CLONE IT, SHAVE IT, AND SHARE IT WITH FRIENDS!

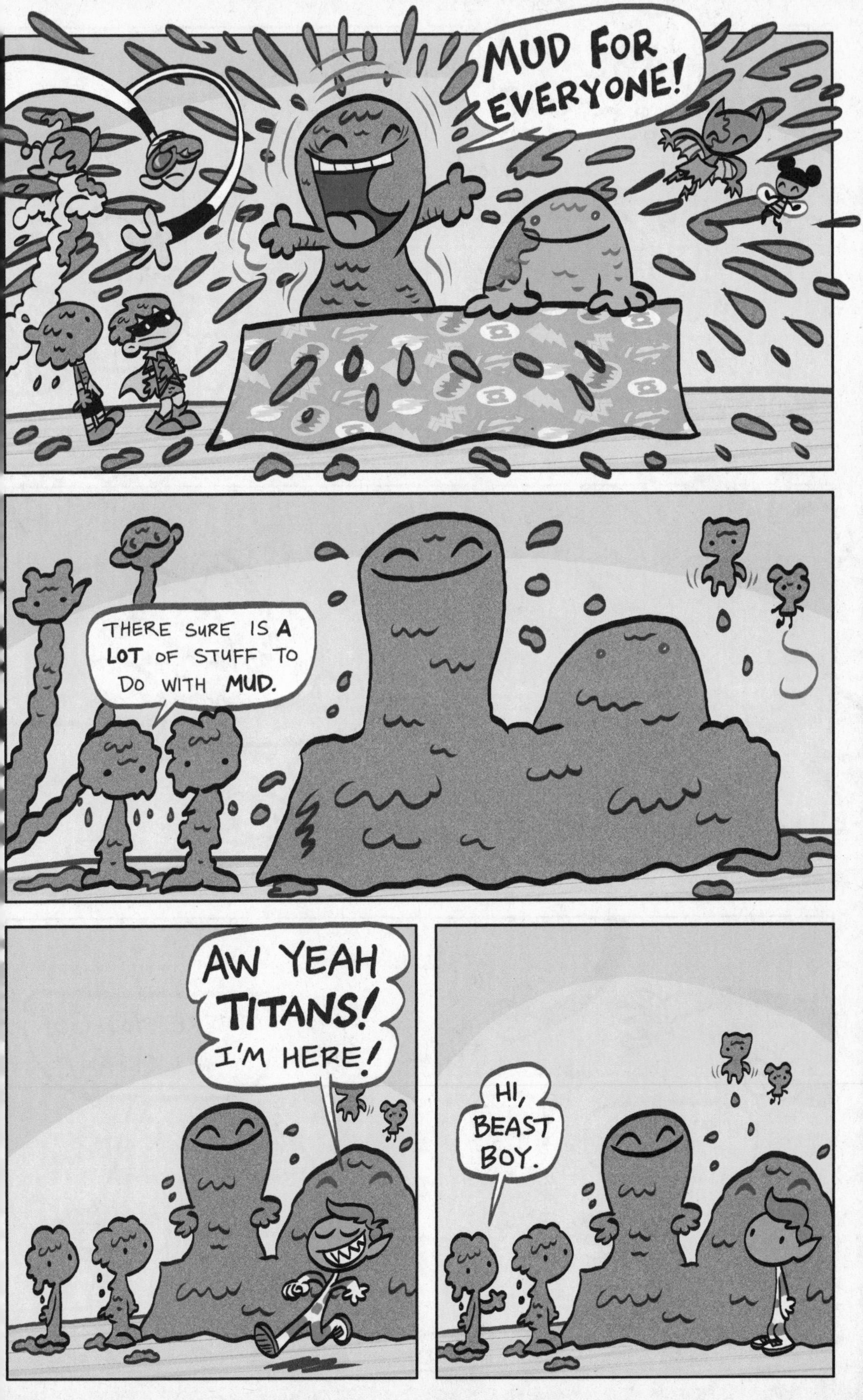
MUD FOR EVERYONE!
THERE SURE IS A LOT OF STUFF TO DO WITH MUD.
AW YEAH TITANS! I'M HERE!
HI, BEAST BOY.

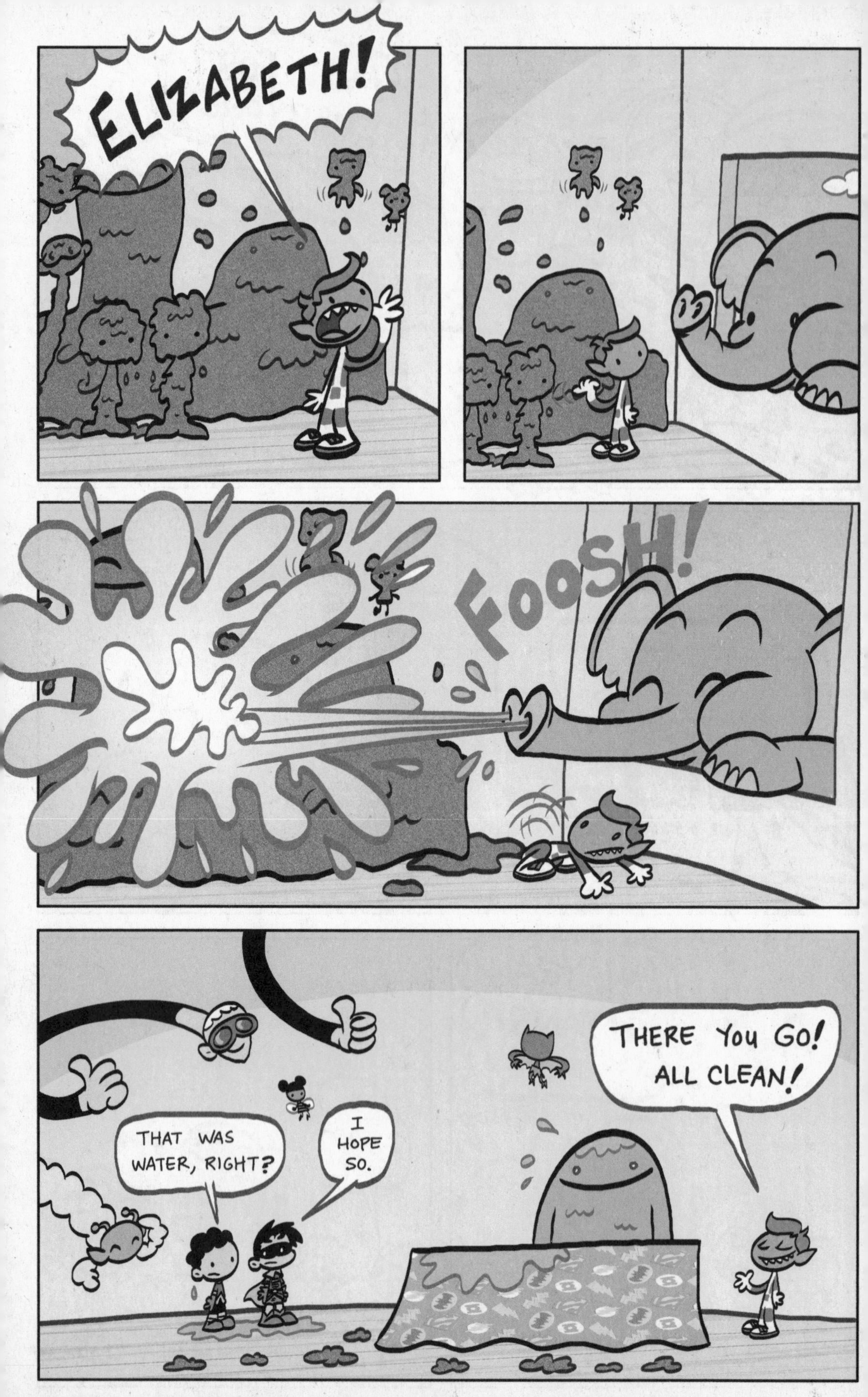
ELIZABETH!
FOOSH!
THAT WAS WATER, RIGHT?
I HOPE SO.
THERE YOU GO! ALL CLEAN!

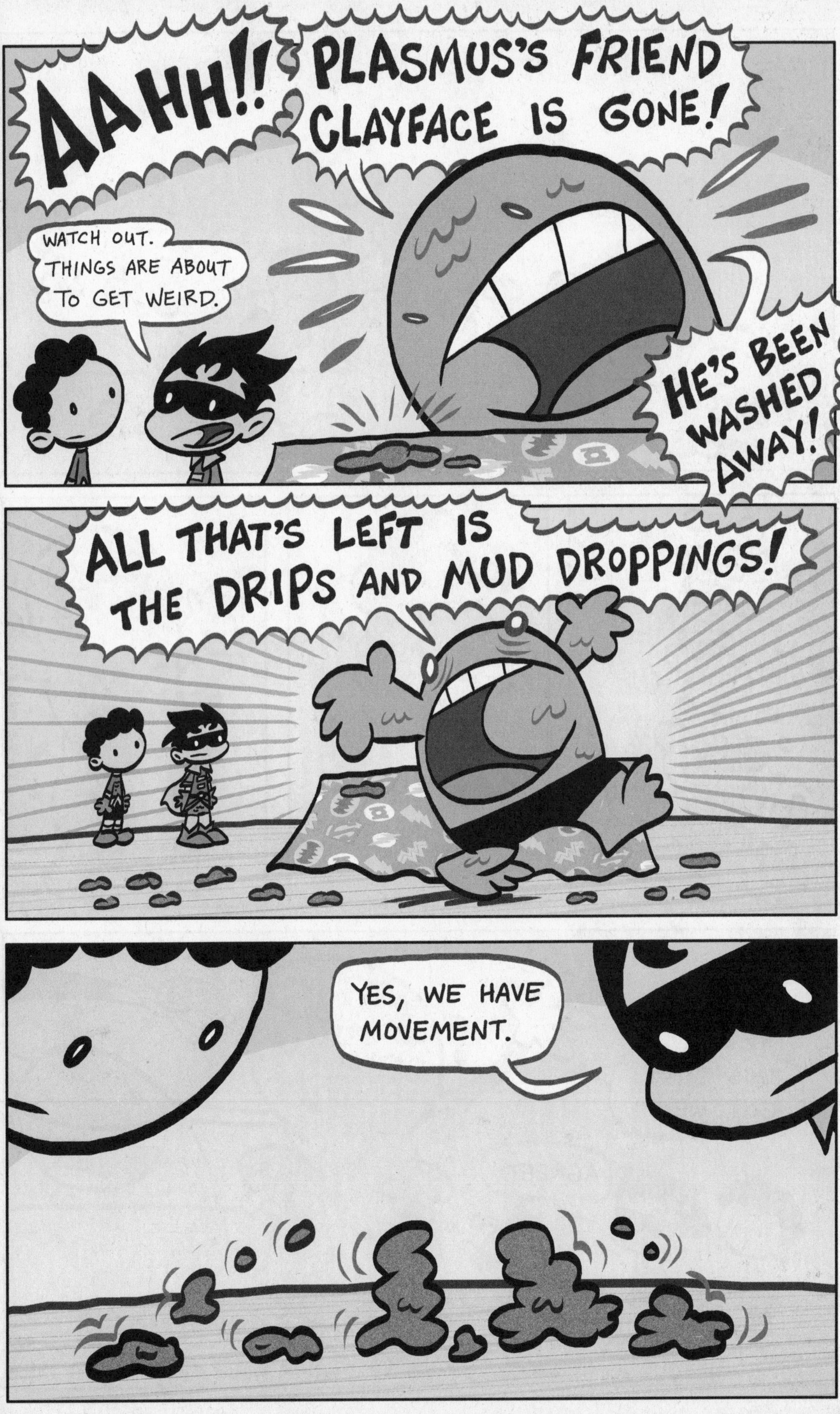
AAHH!!
PLASMUS'S FRIEND CLAYFACE IS GONE!
WATCH OUT. THINGS ARE ABOUT TO GET WEIRD.
HE'S BEEN WASHED AWAY!
ALL THAT'S LEFT IS THE DRIPS AND MUD DROPPINGS!
YES, WE HAVE MOVEMENT.

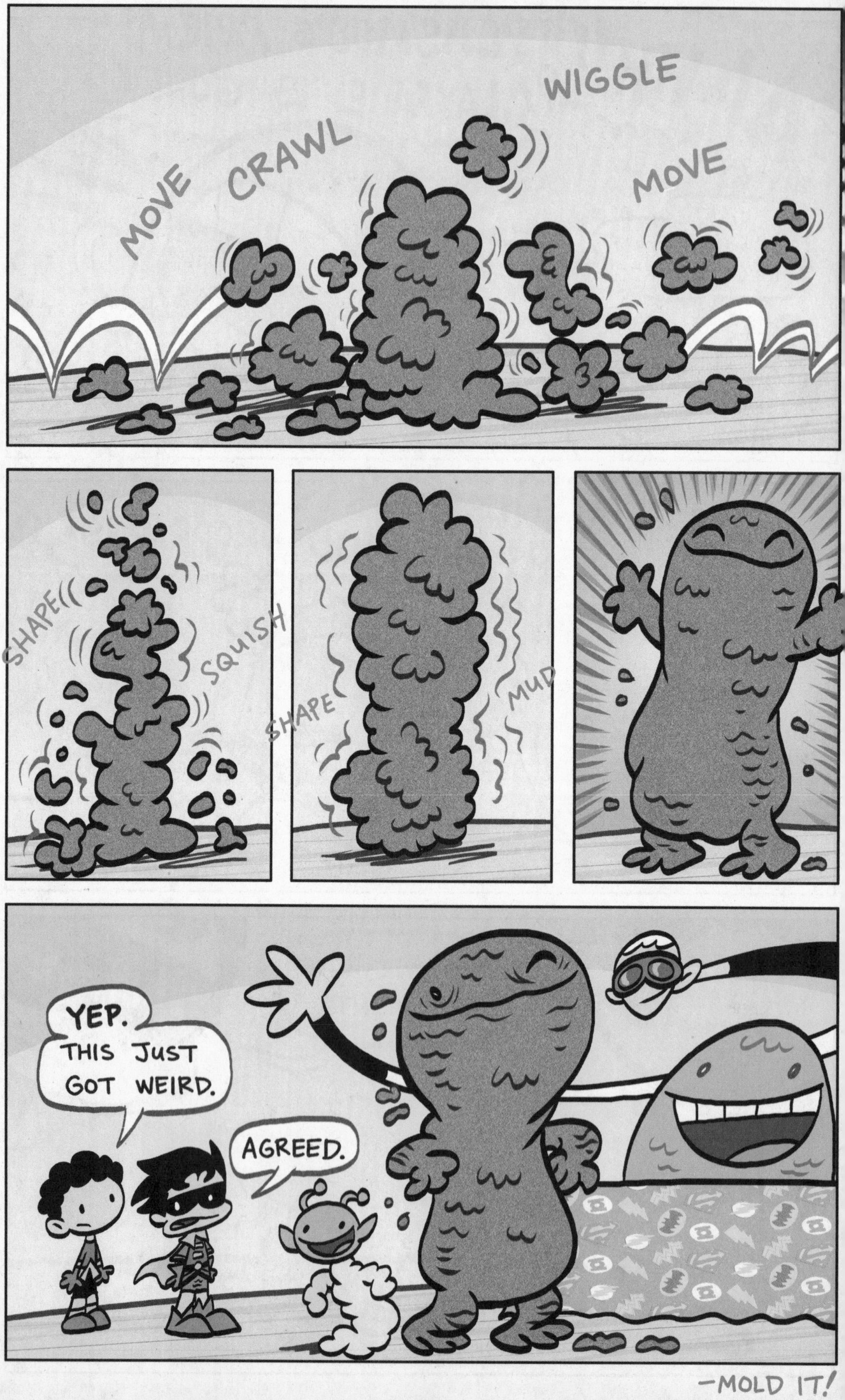
MOVE
CRAWL
WIGGLE
MOVE
SHAPE
SQUISH
SHAPE
MUD
YEP. THIS JUST GOT WEIRD.
AGREED.

—MOLD IT!

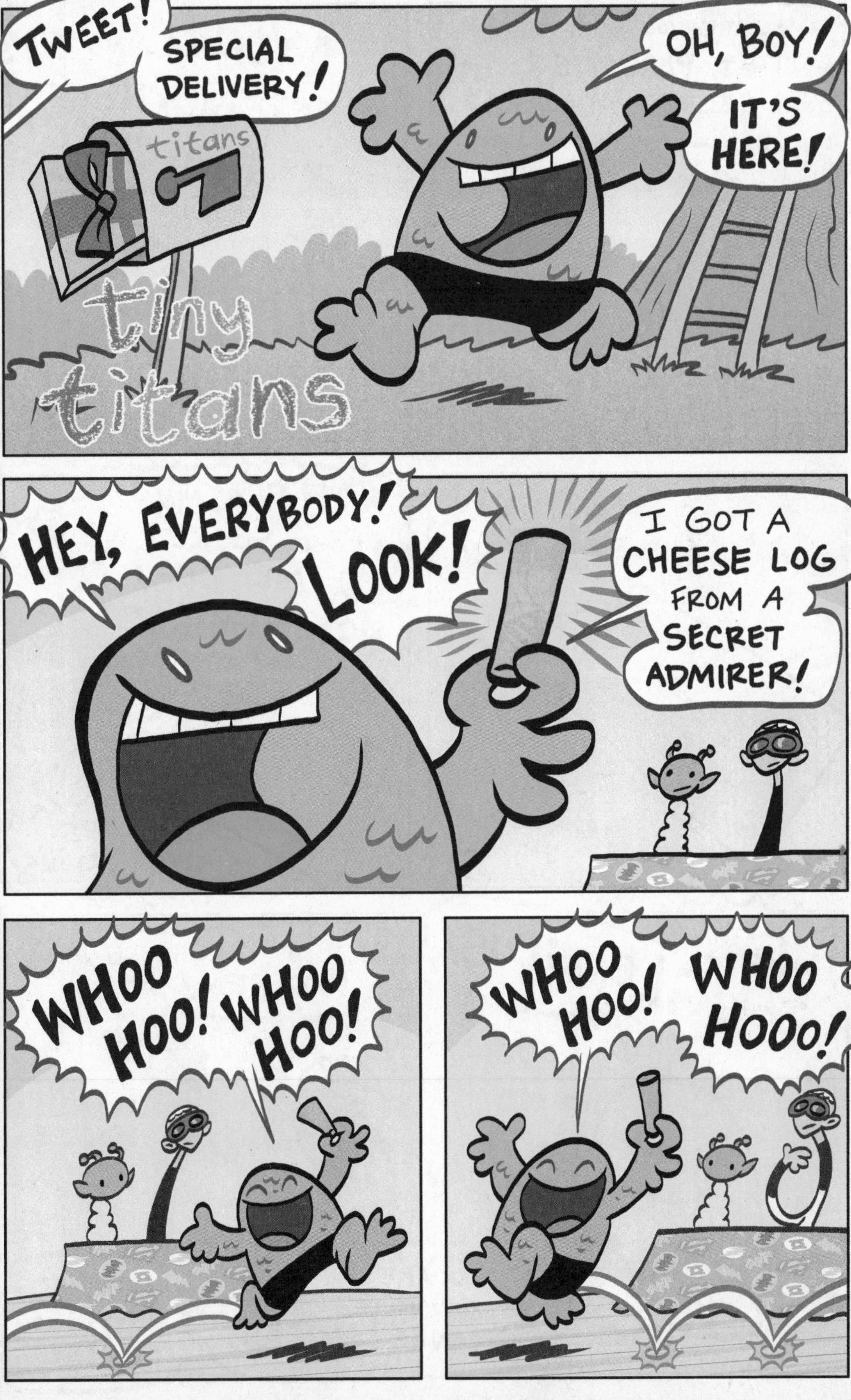
TWEET!
SPECIAL DELIVERY!
titans
tiny titans
OH, BOY!
IT'S HERE!
HEY, EVERYBODY!
LOOK!
I GOT A CHEESE LOG FROM A SECRET ADMIRER!
WHOO HOO! WHOO HOO!
WHOO HOO! WHOO HOOO!

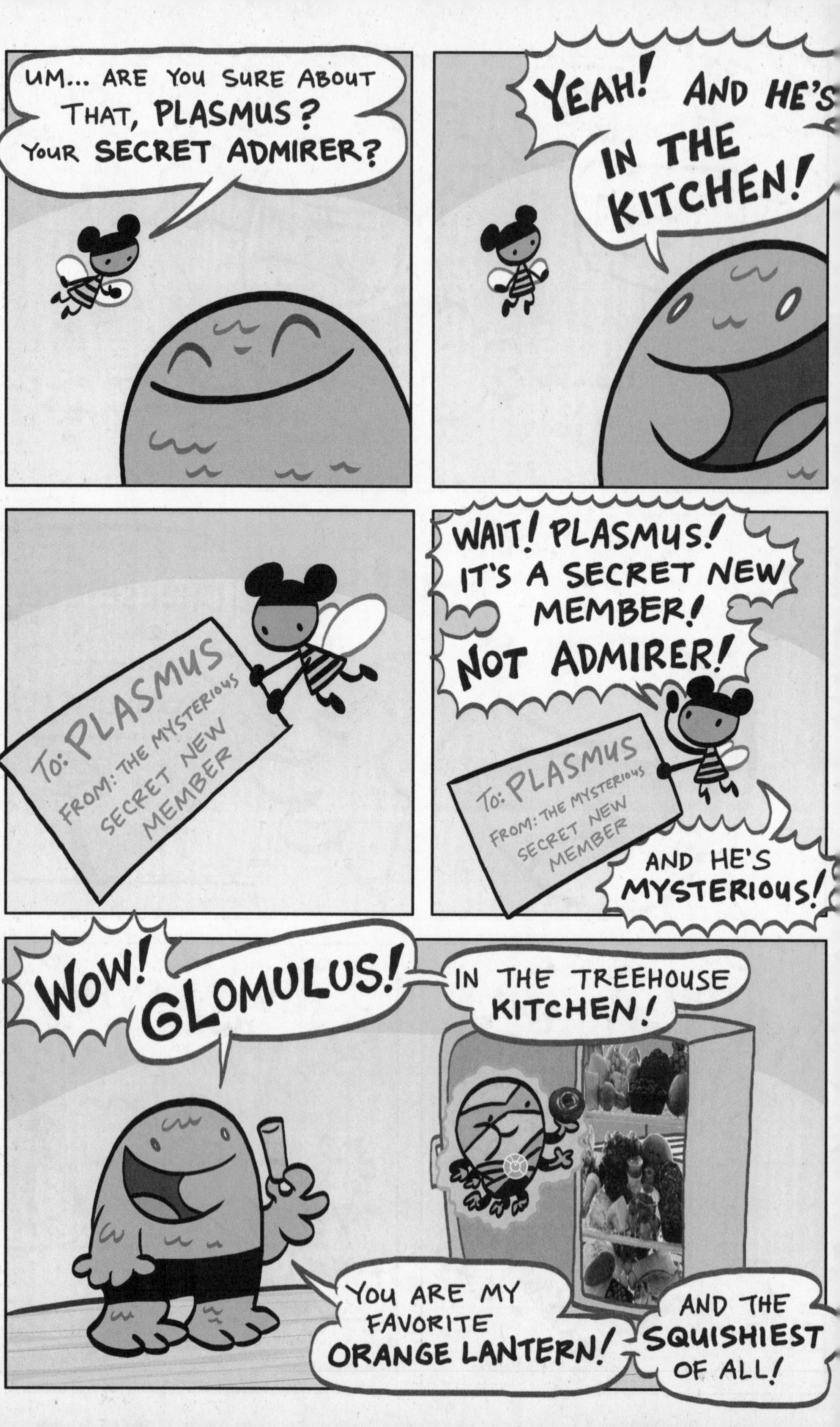
UM... ARE YOU SURE ABOUT THAT, PLASMUS? YOUR SECRET ADMIRER?
YEAH! AND HE'S IN THE KITCHEN!
To: PLASMUS
FROM: THE MYSTERIOUS SECRET NEW MEMBER
WAIT! PLASMUS! IT'S A SECRET NEW MEMBER! NOT ADMIRER!
To: PLASMUS
FROM: THE MYSTERIOUS SECRET NEW MEMBER
AND HE'S MYSTERIOUS!
WOW!
GLOMULUS!
IN THE TREEHOUSE KITCHEN!
YOU ARE MY FAVORITE ORANGE LANTERN!
AND THE SQUISHIEST OF ALL!

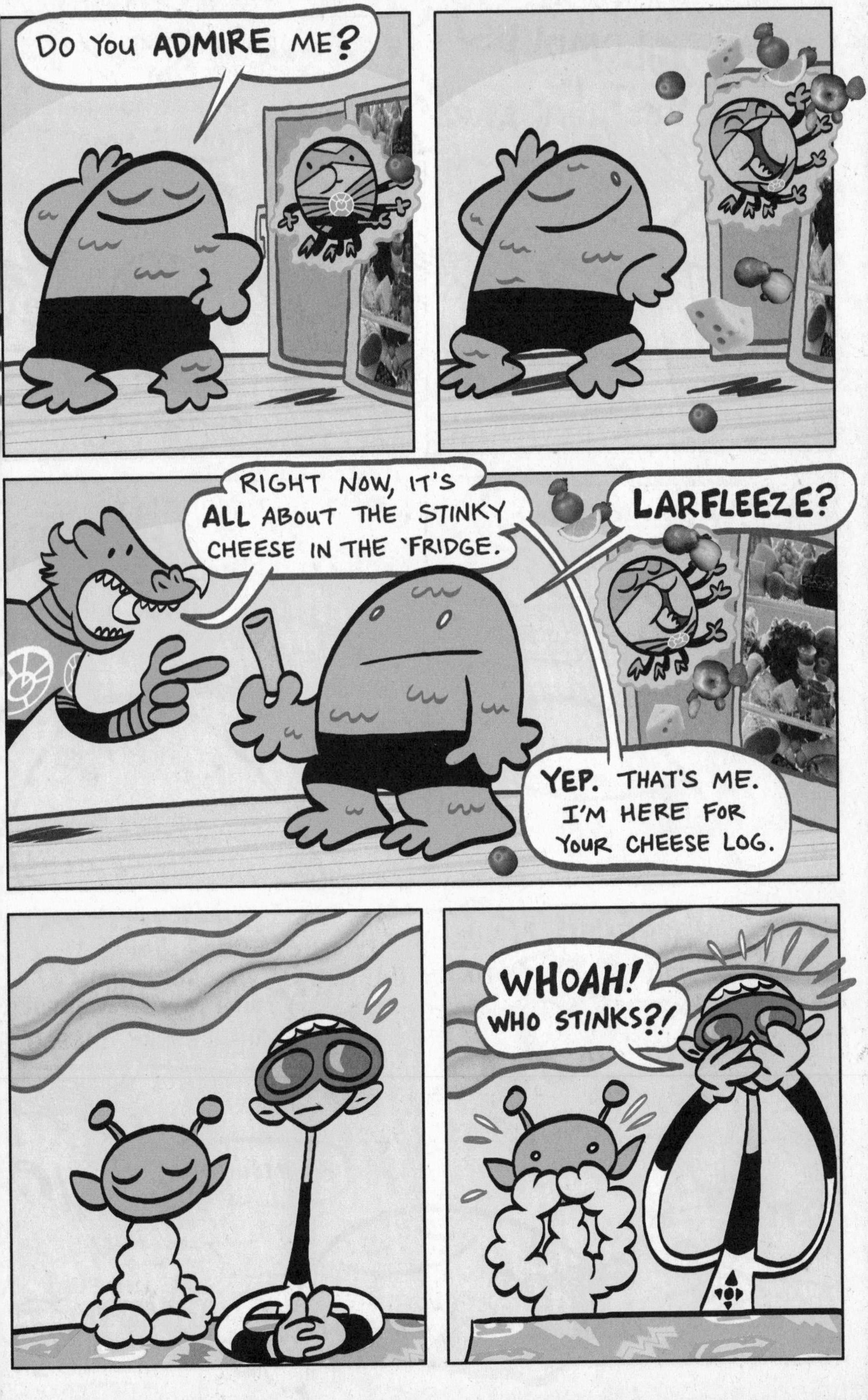
DO YOU ADMIRE ME?
RIGHT NOW, IT'S ALL ABOUT THE STINKY CHEESE IN THE 'FRIDGE.
LARFLEEZE?
YEP. THAT'S ME. I'M HERE FOR YOUR CHEESE LOG.
WHOAH! WHO STINKS?!

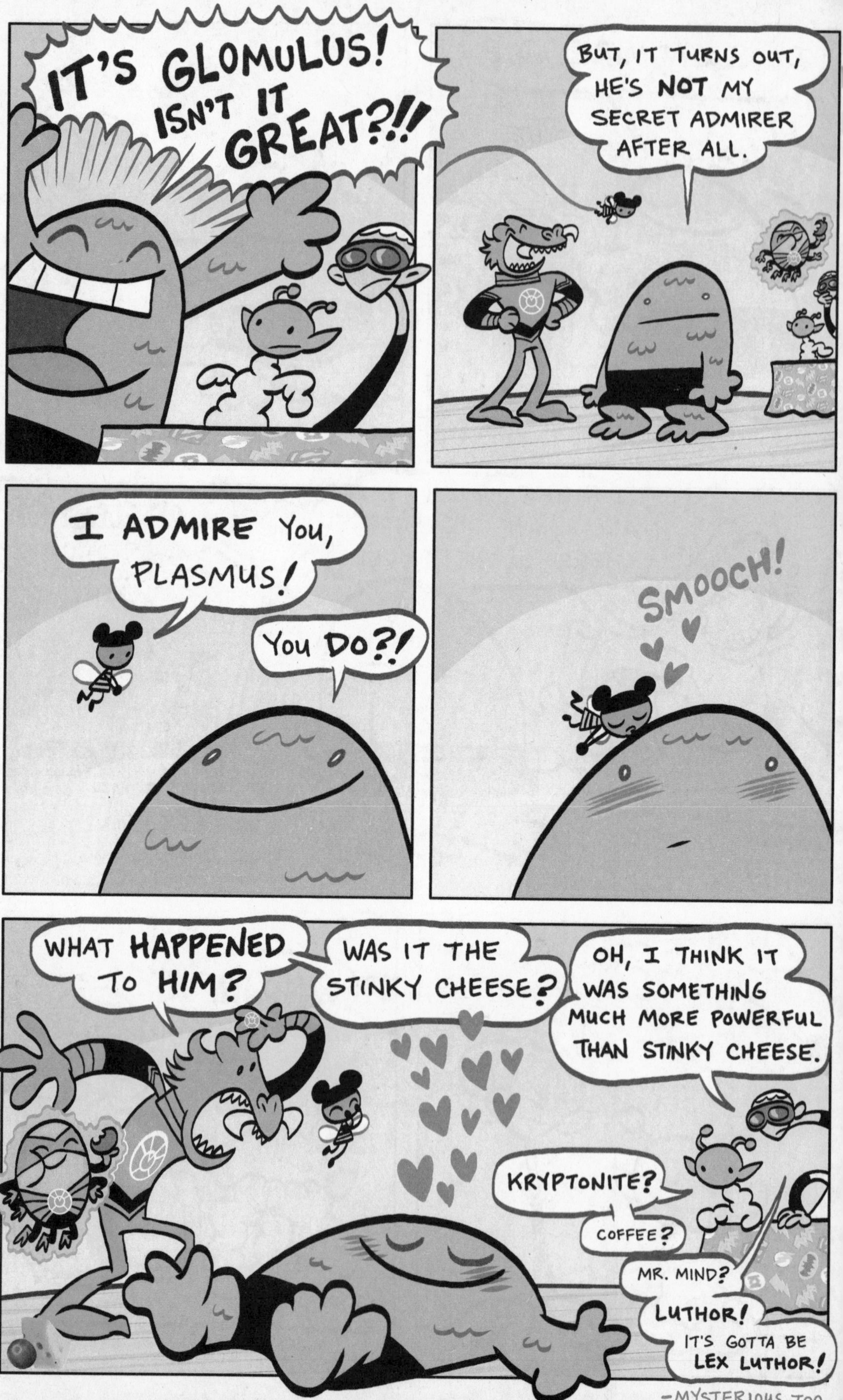
IT'S GLOMULUS! ISN'T IT GREAT?!!
BUT, IT TURNS OUT, HE'S NOT MY SECRET ADMIRER AFTER ALL.
I ADMIRE YOU, PLASMUS!
YOU DO?!
SMOOCH!
WHAT HAPPENED TO HIM?
WAS IT THE STINKY CHEESE?
OH, I THINK IT WAS SOMETHING MUCH MORE POWERFUL THAN STINKY CHEESE.
KRYPTONITE?
COFFEE?
MR. MIND?
LUTHOR!
IT'S GOTTA BE LEX LUTHOR!
-MYSTERIOUS, TOO.

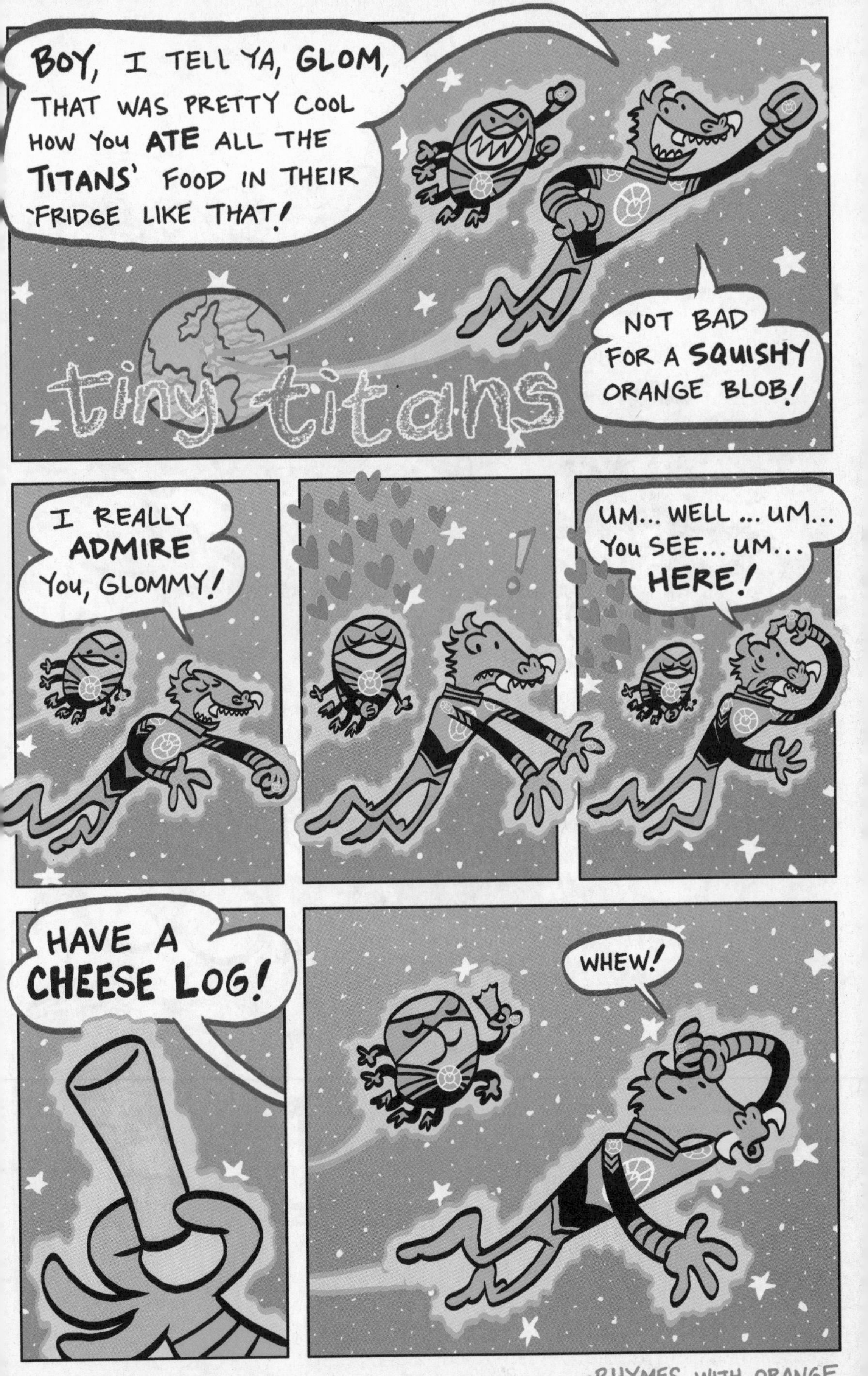
BOY, I TELL YA, GLOM, THAT WAS PRETTY COOL HOW YOU ATE ALL THE TITANS' FOOD IN THEIR FRIDGE LIKE THAT!
NOT BAD FOR A SQUISHY ORANGE BLOB!
tiny titans
I REALLY ADMIRE YOU, GLOMMY!
!
UM... WELL ... UM... YOU SEE... UM... HERE!
HAVE A CHEESE LOG!
WHEW!

-RHYMES WITH ORANGE.

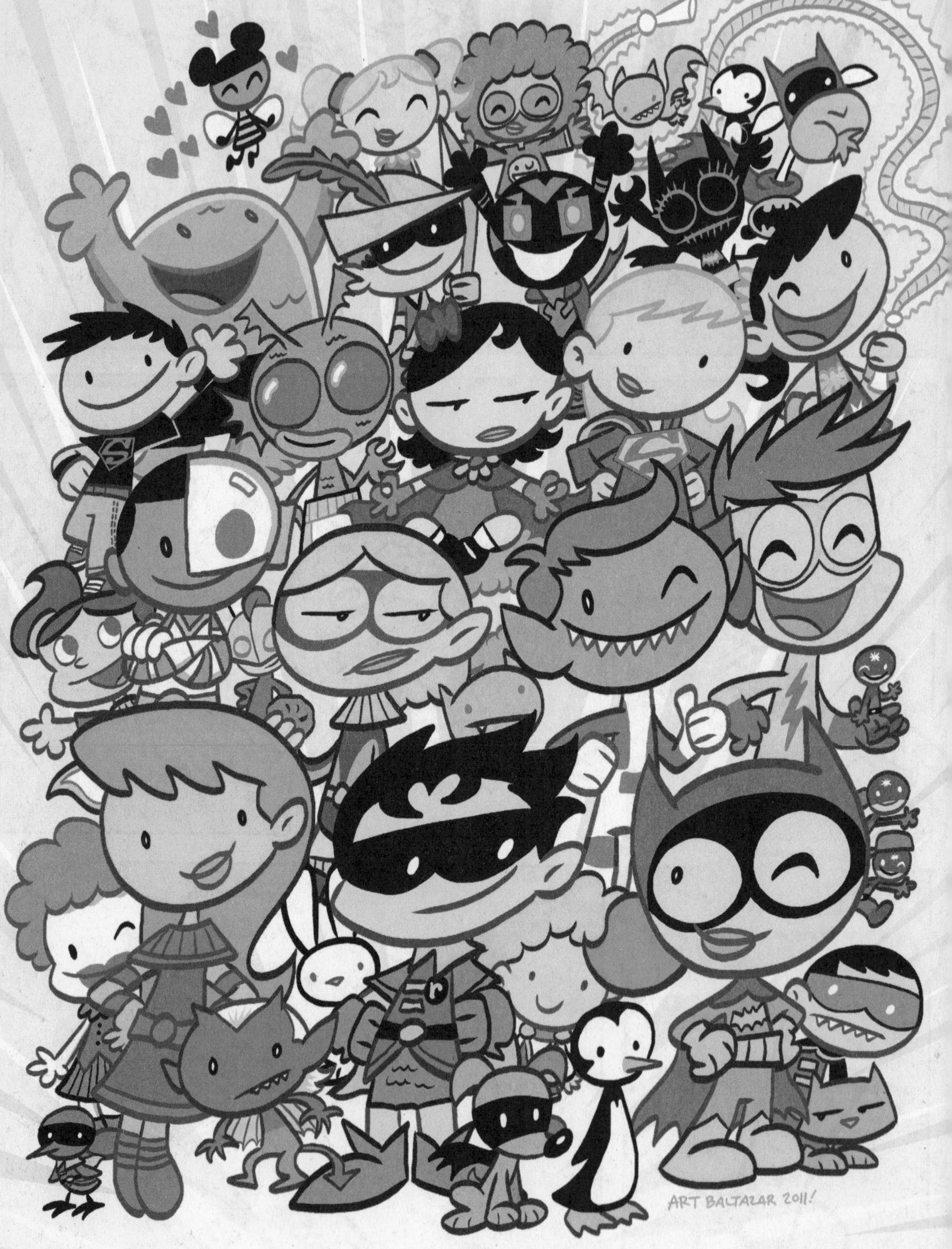
ART BALTAZAR 2011!

tiny titans

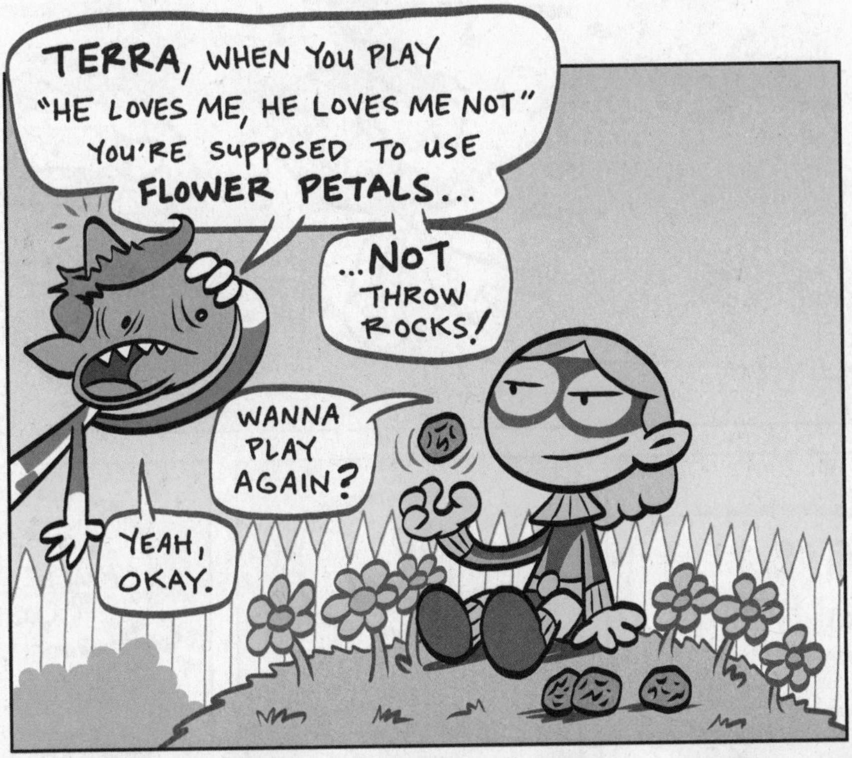
TERRA, WHEN YOU PLAY "HE LOVES ME, HE LOVES ME NOT" YOU'RE SUPPOSED TO USE FLOWER PETALS...
...NOT THROW ROCKS!
WANNA PLAY AGAIN?
YEAH, OKAY.

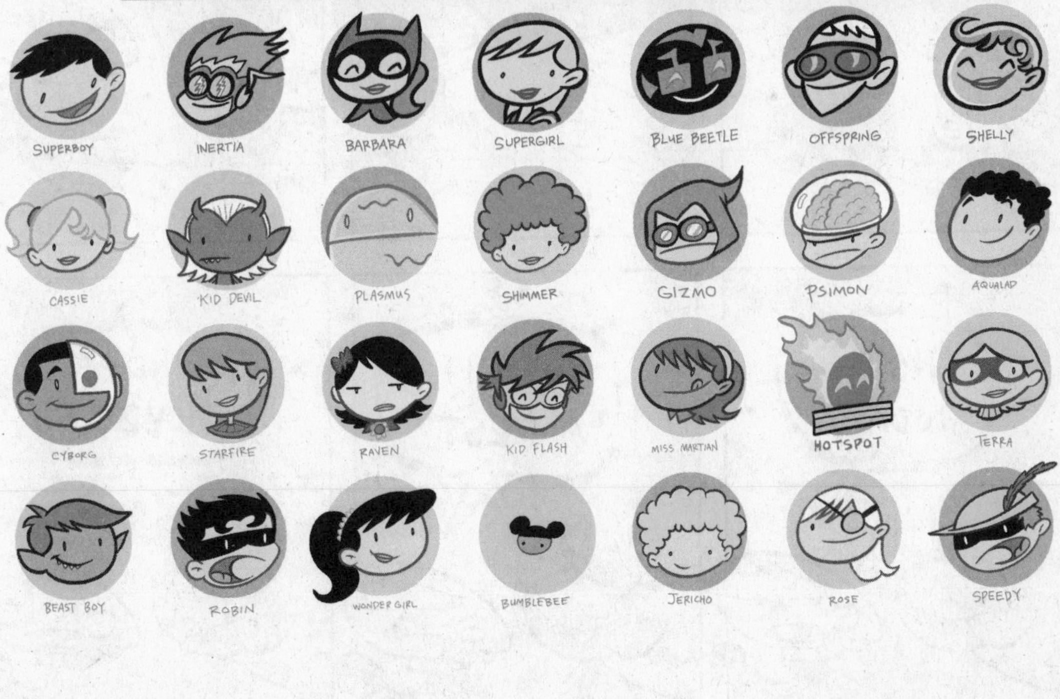
SUPERBOY
INERTIA
BARBARA
SUPERGIRL
BLUE BEETLE
OFFSPRING
SHELLY
CASSIE
KID DEVIL
PLASMUS
SHIMMER
GIZMO
PSIMON
AQUALAD
CYBORG
STARFIRE
RAVEN
KID FLASH
MISS MARTIAN
HOTSPOT
TERRA
BEAST BOY
ROBIN
WONDER GIRL
BUMBLEBEE
JERICHO
ROSE
SPEEDY

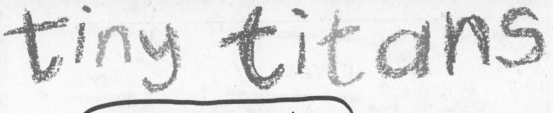

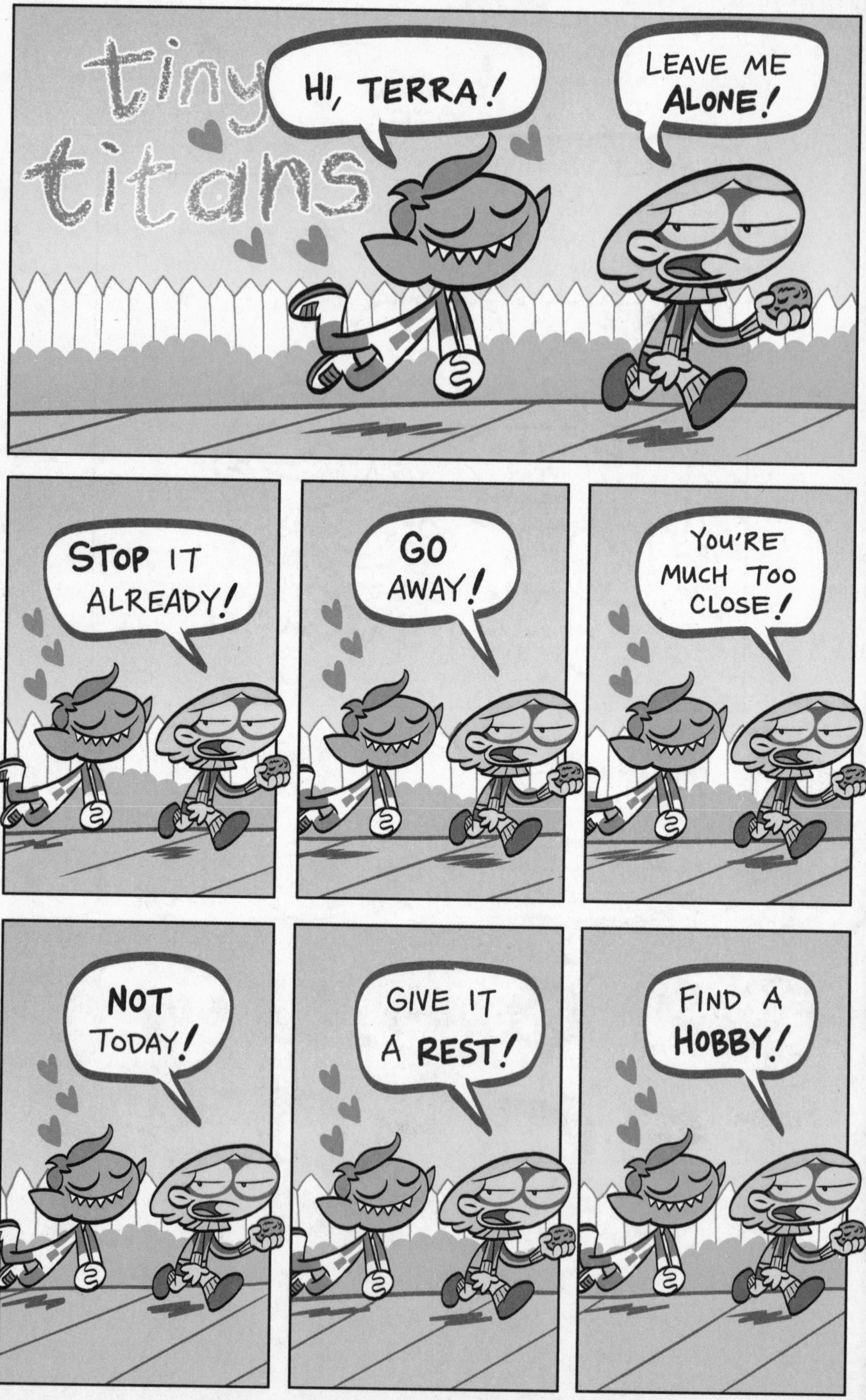
tiny titans
HI, TERRA!
LEAVE ME ALONE!
STOP IT ALREADY!
GO AWAY!
YOU'RE MUCH TOO CLOSE!
NOT TODAY!
GIVE IT A REST!
FIND A HOBBY!

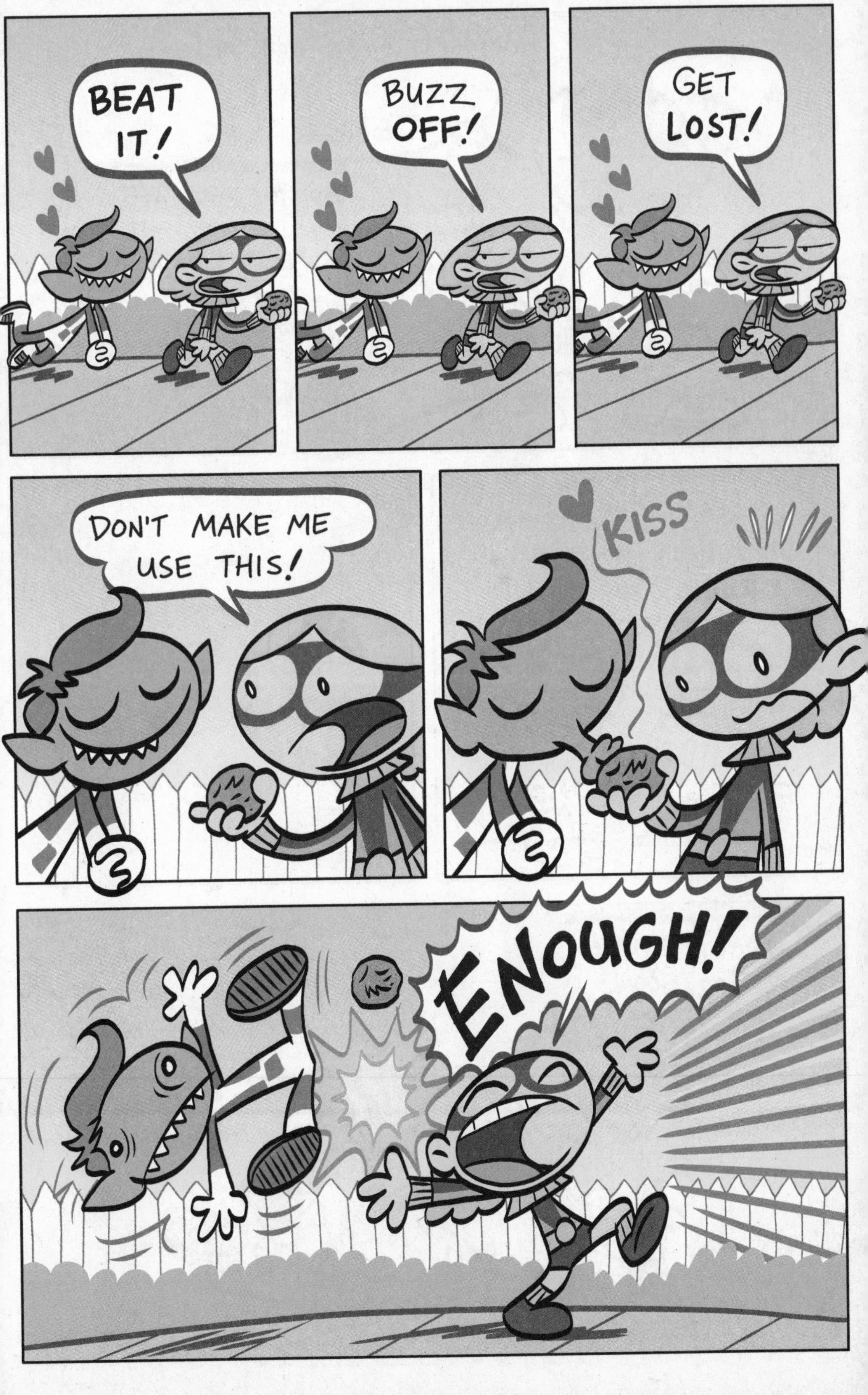
BEAT IT!
BUZZ OFF!
GET LOST!
DON'T MAKE ME USE THIS!
KISS
ENOUGH!

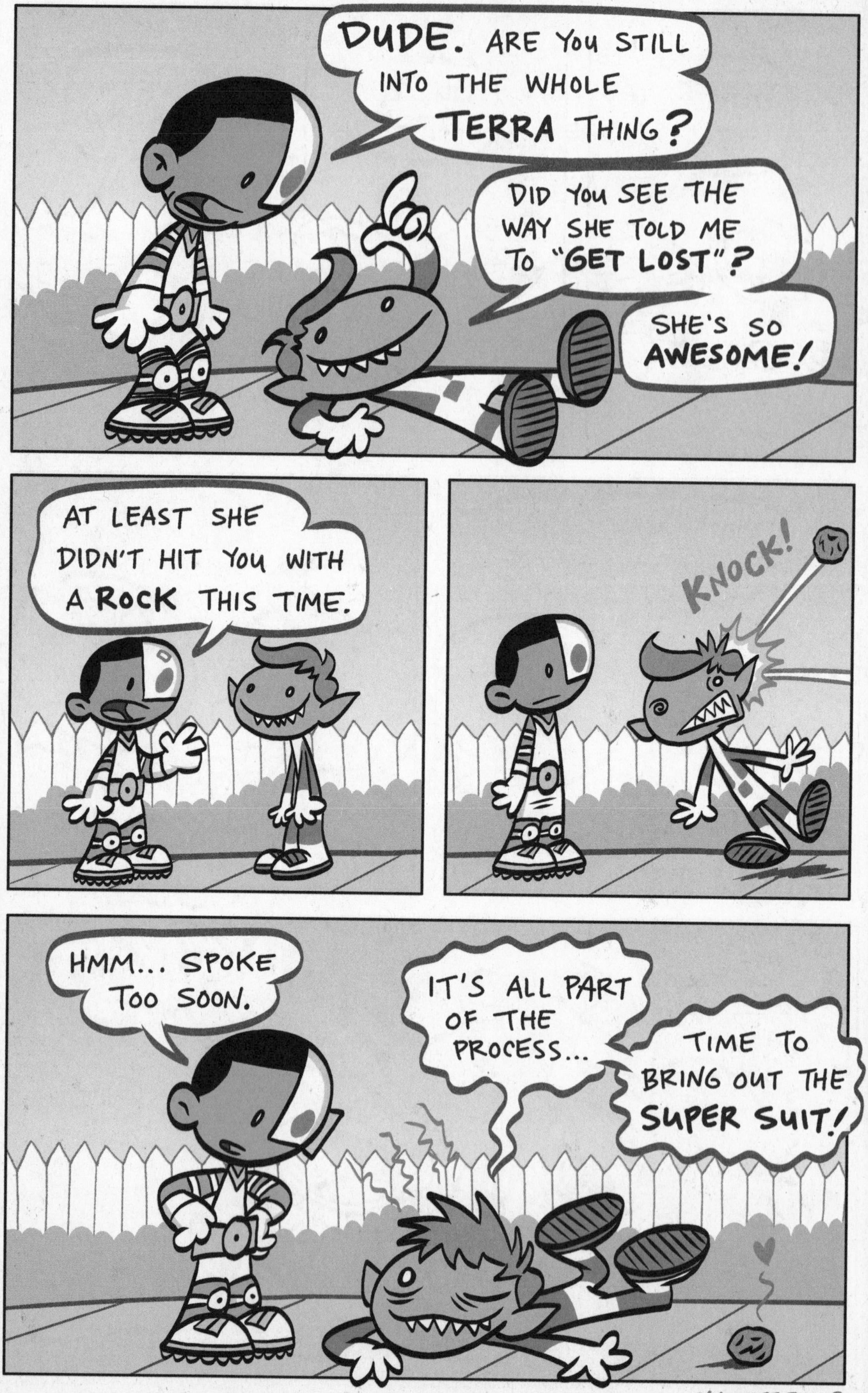
DUDE. ARE YOU STILL INTO THE WHOLE TERRA THING?
DID YOU SEE THE WAY SHE TOLD ME TO "GET LOST"?
SHE'S SO AWESOME!
AT LEAST SHE DIDN'T HIT YOU WITH A ROCK THIS TIME.
KNOCK!
HMM... SPOKE TOO SOON.
IT'S ALL PART OF THE PROCESS...
TIME TO BRING OUT THE SUPER SUIT!

-D'YOU SEE THAT?

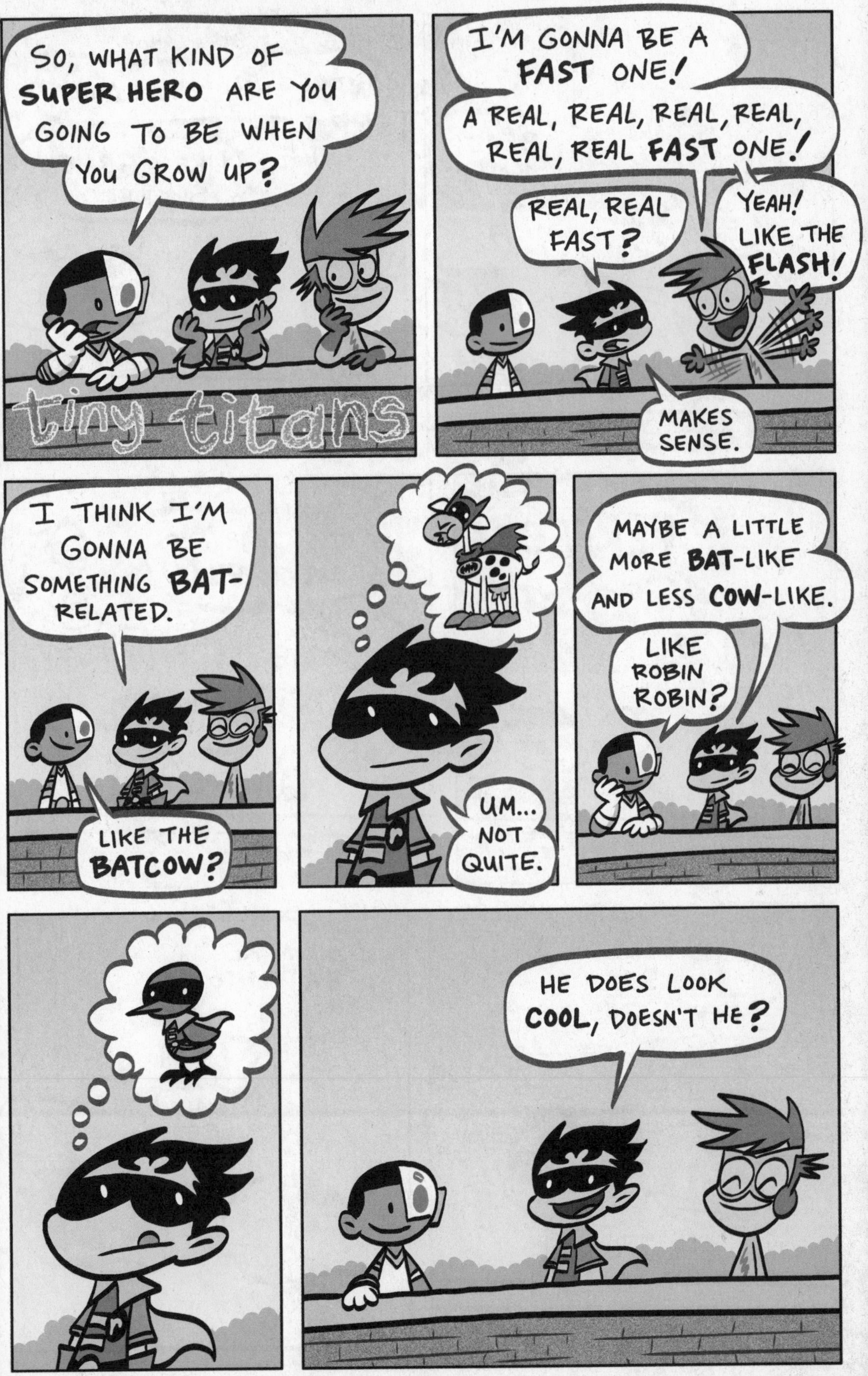

SO, WHAT KIND OF SUPER HERO ARE YOU GOING TO BE WHEN YOU GROW UP?
tiny titans
I'M GONNA BE A FAST ONE!
A REAL, REAL, REAL, REAL, REAL, REAL FAST ONE!
REAL, REAL FAST?
YEAH! LIKE THE FLASH!
MAKES SENSE.
I THINK I'M GONNA BE SOMETHING BAT-RELATED.
LIKE THE BATCOW?
UM... NOT QUITE.
MAYBE A LITTLE MORE BAT-LIKE AND LESS COW-LIKE.
LIKE ROBIN ROBIN?
HE DOES LOOK COOL, DOESN'T HE?

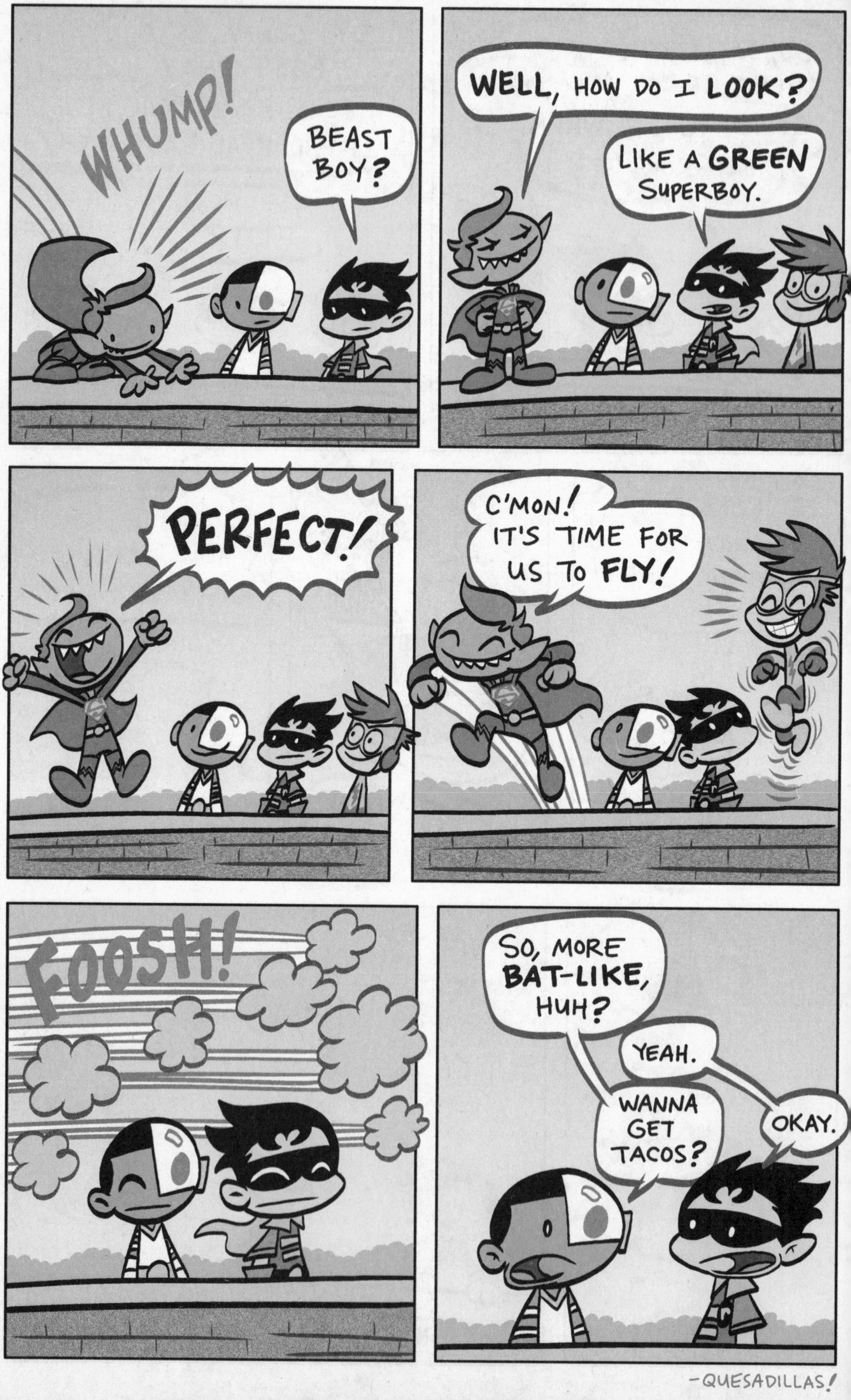
WHUMP!
BEAST BOY?
WELL, HOW DO I LOOK?
LIKE A GREEN SUPERBOY.
PERFECT!
C'MON! IT'S TIME FOR US TO FLY!
FOOSH!
SO, MORE BAT-LIKE, HUH?
YEAH.
WANNA GET TACOS?
OKAY.
-QUESADILLAS!

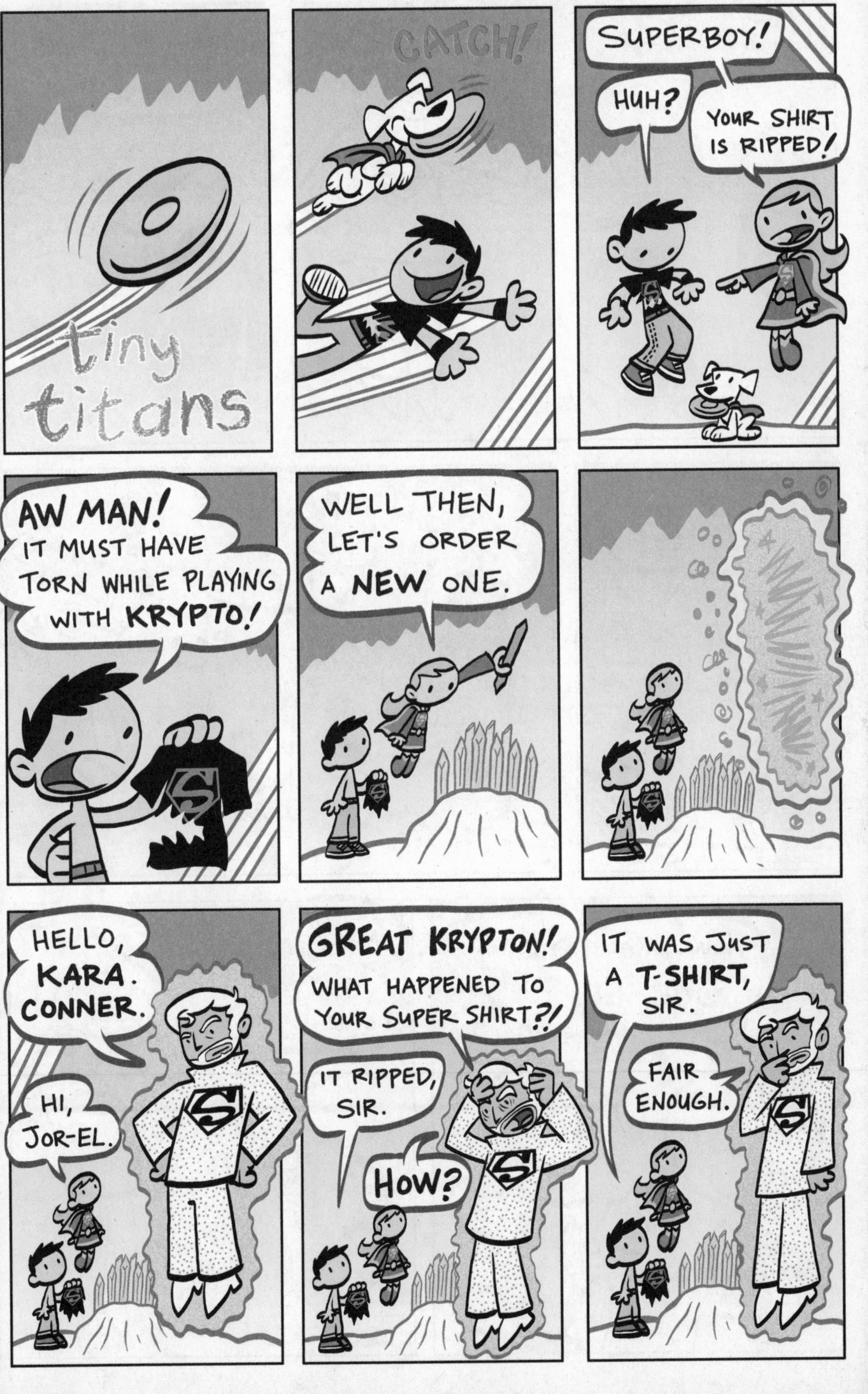
tiny titans
CATCH!
SUPERBOY!
HUH?
YOUR SHIRT IS RIPPED!
AW MAN! IT MUST HAVE TORN WHILE PLAYING WITH KRYPTO!
WELL THEN, LET'S ORDER A NEW ONE.
HELLO, KARA. CONNER.
HI, JOR-EL.
GREAT KRYPTON! WHAT HAPPENED TO YOUR SUPER SHIRT?!
IT RIPPED, SIR.
HOW?
IT WAS JUST A T-SHIRT, SIR.
FAIR ENOUGH.

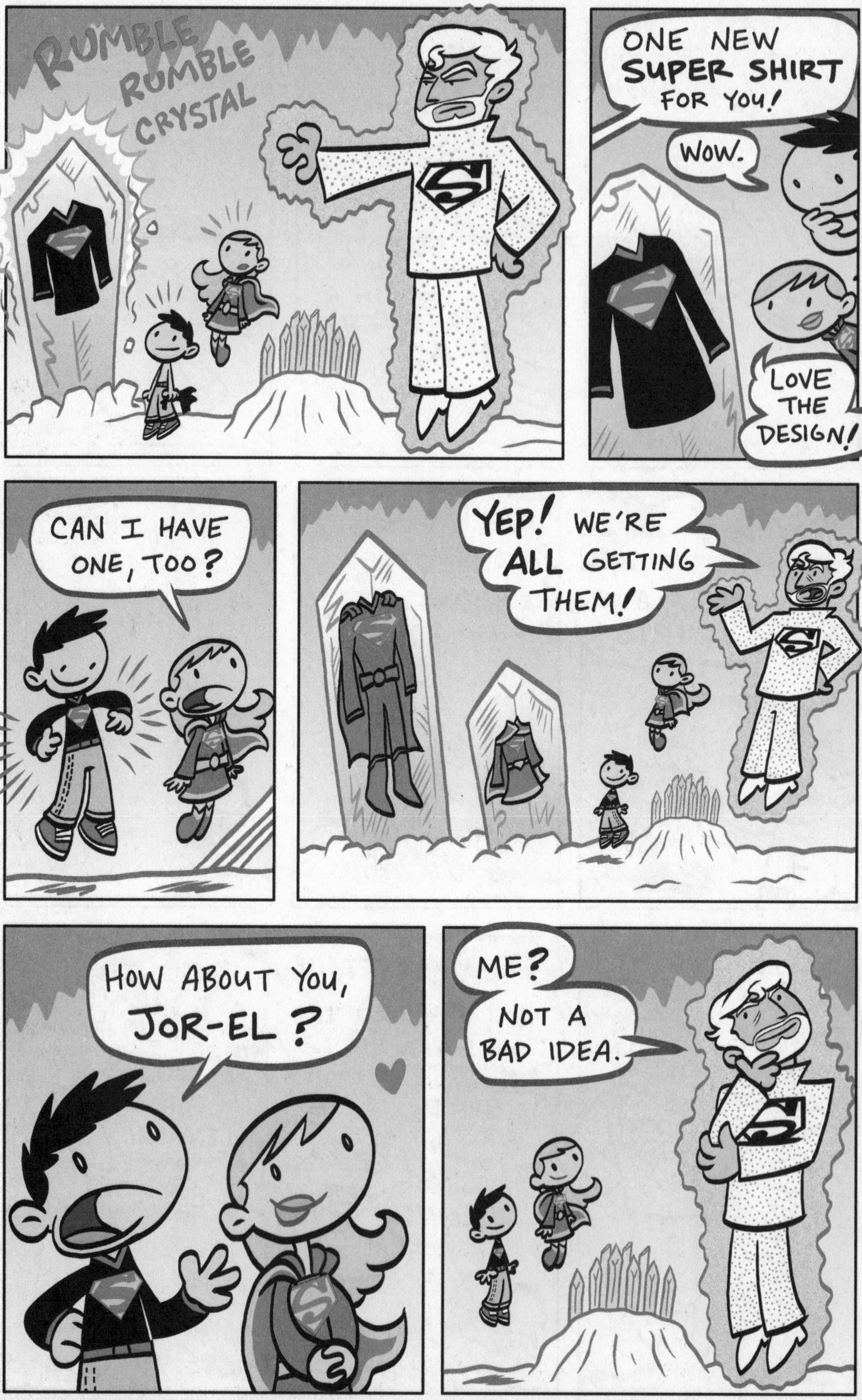
RUMBLE
RUMBLE
CRYSTAL
ONE NEW SUPER SHIRT FOR YOU!
WOW.
LOVE THE DESIGN!
CAN I HAVE ONE, TOO?
YEP! WE'RE ALL GETTING THEM!
HOW ABOUT YOU, JOR-EL?
ME?
NOT A BAD IDEA.

—NEW WARDROBE IT IS!

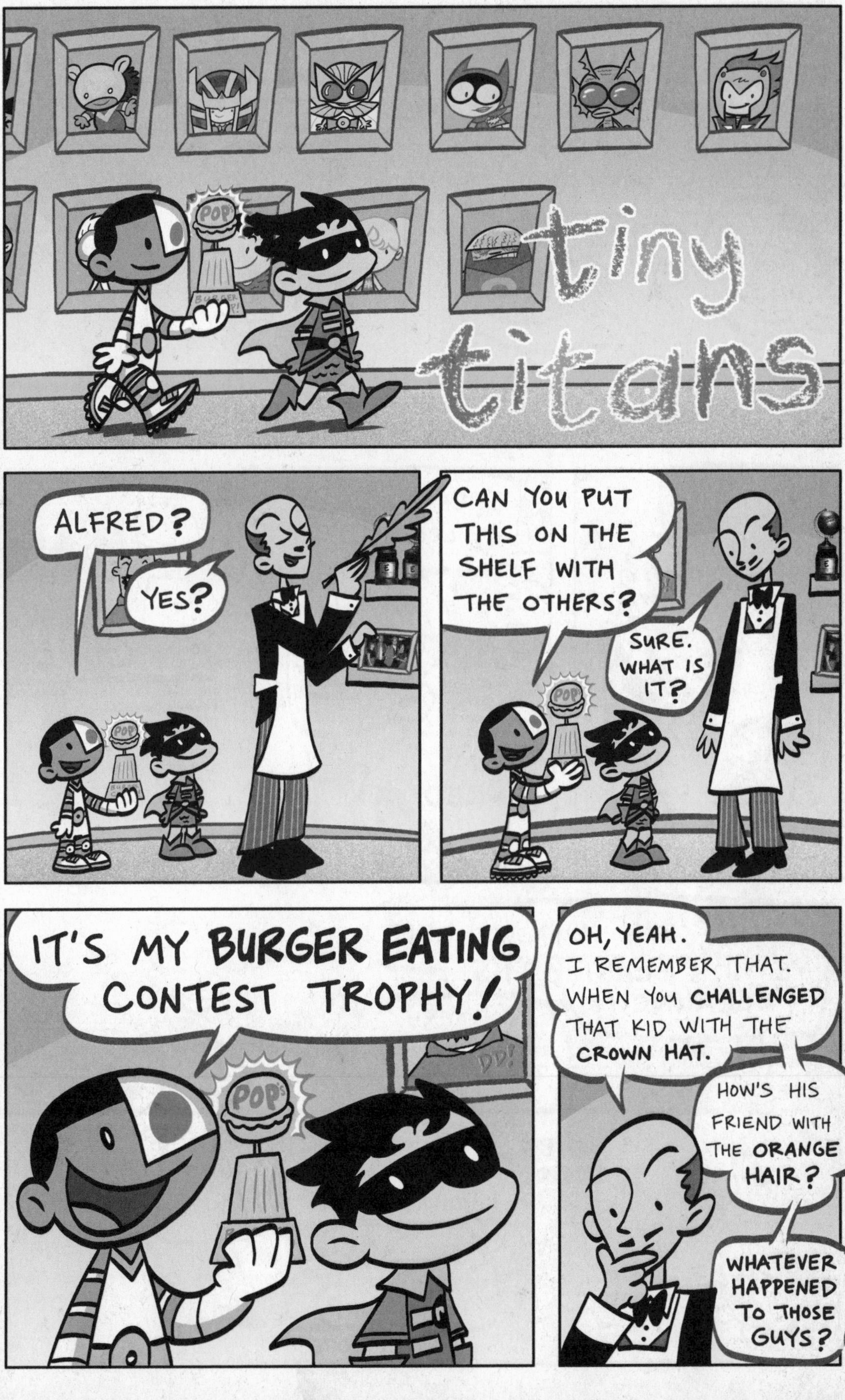
tiny titans
ALFRED?
YES?
CAN YOU PUT THIS ON THE SHELF WITH THE OTHERS?
SURE. WHAT IS IT?
IT'S MY **BURGER EATING** CONTEST TROPHY!
OH, YEAH. I REMEMBER THAT. WHEN YOU **CHALLENGED** THAT KID WITH THE **CROWN HAT.**
HOW'S HIS FRIEND WITH THE **ORANGE HAIR?**
WHATEVER HAPPENED TO THOSE GUYS?

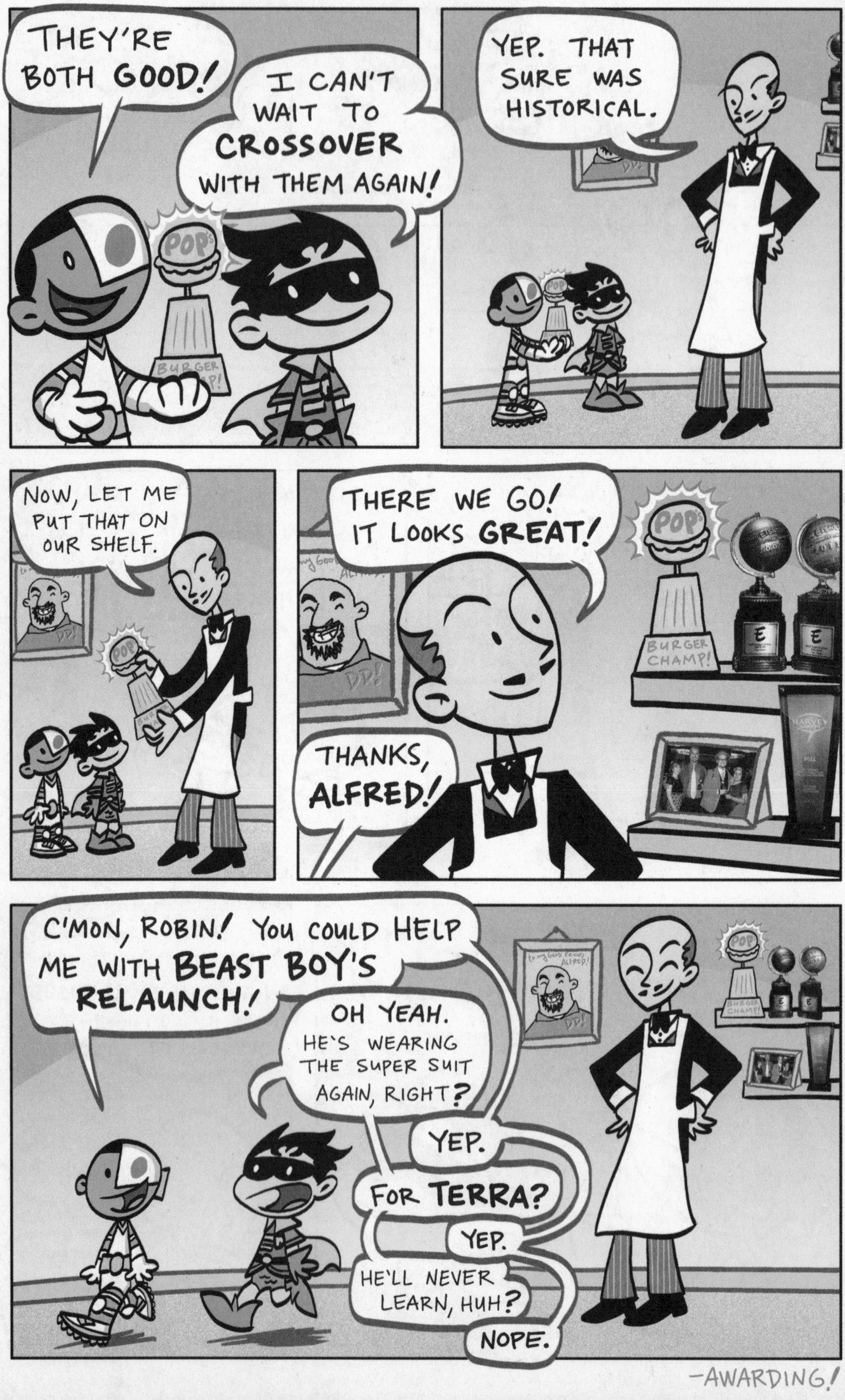
THEY'RE BOTH GOOD!
I CAN'T WAIT TO CROSSOVER WITH THEM AGAIN!
POP'S
YEP. THAT SURE WAS HISTORICAL.
NOW, LET ME PUT THAT ON OUR SHELF.
THERE WE GO! IT LOOKS GREAT!
POP'S
BURGER CHAMP!
THANKS, ALFRED!
C'MON, ROBIN! YOU COULD HELP ME WITH BEAST BOY'S RELAUNCH!
OH YEAH. HE'S WEARING THE SUPER SUIT AGAIN, RIGHT?
YEP.
FOR TERRA?
YEP.
HE'LL NEVER LEARN, HUH?
NOPE.
—AWARDING!

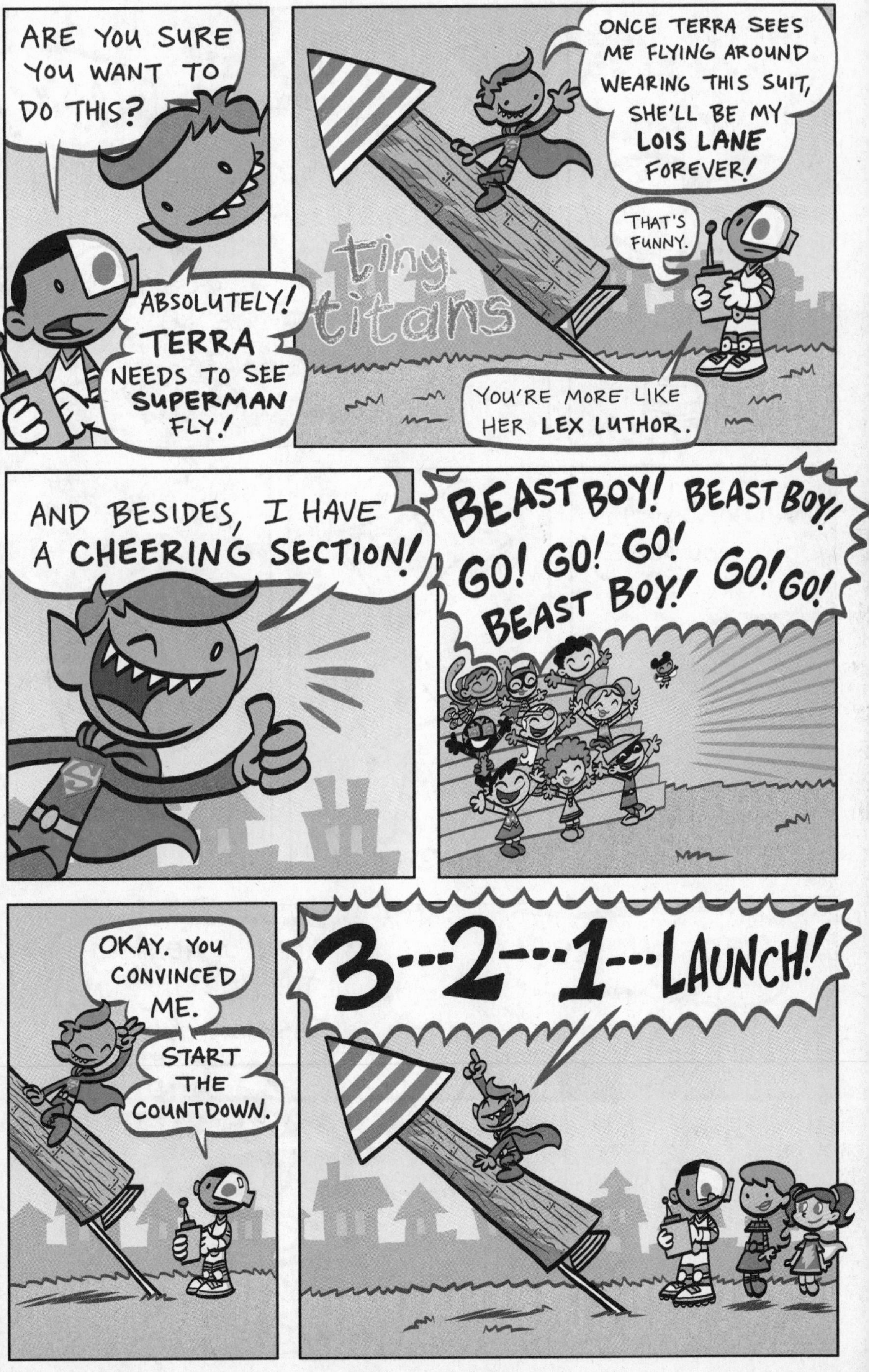
ARE YOU SURE YOU WANT TO DO THIS?
ABSOLUTELY! TERRA NEEDS TO SEE SUPERMAN FLY!
ONCE TERRA SEES ME FLYING AROUND WEARING THIS SUIT, SHE'LL BE MY LOIS LANE FOREVER!
THAT'S FUNNY.
YOU'RE MORE LIKE HER LEX LUTHOR.
tiny titans
AND BESIDES, I HAVE A CHEERING SECTION!
BEAST BOY! BEAST BOY! GO! GO! GO! BEAST BOY! GO! GO!
OKAY. YOU CONVINCED ME.
START THE COUNTDOWN.
3---2---1---LAUNCH!

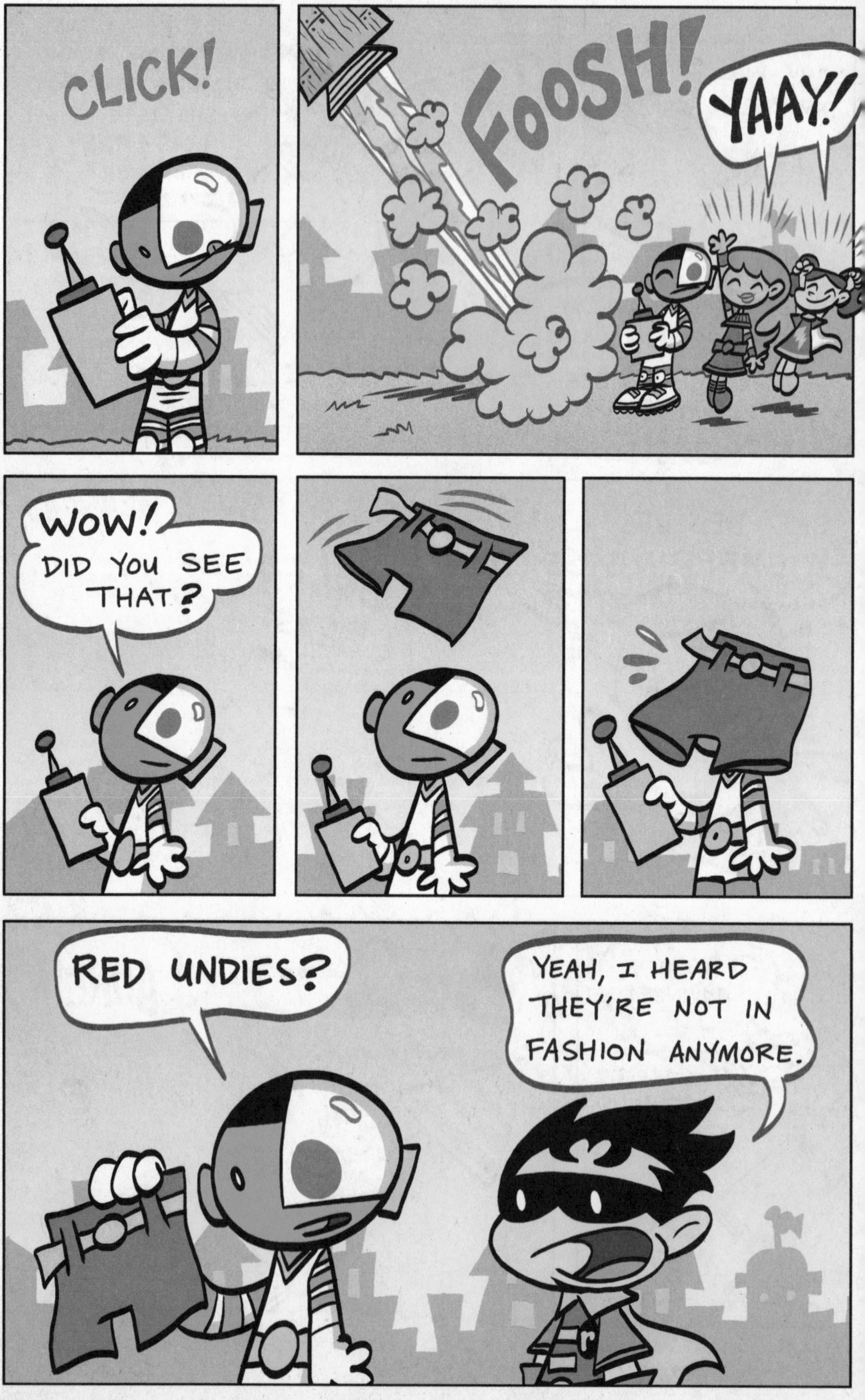
CLICK!
FOOSH!
YAAY!
WOW! DID YOU SEE THAT?
RED UNDIES?
YEAH, I HEARD THEY'RE NOT IN FASHION ANYMORE.

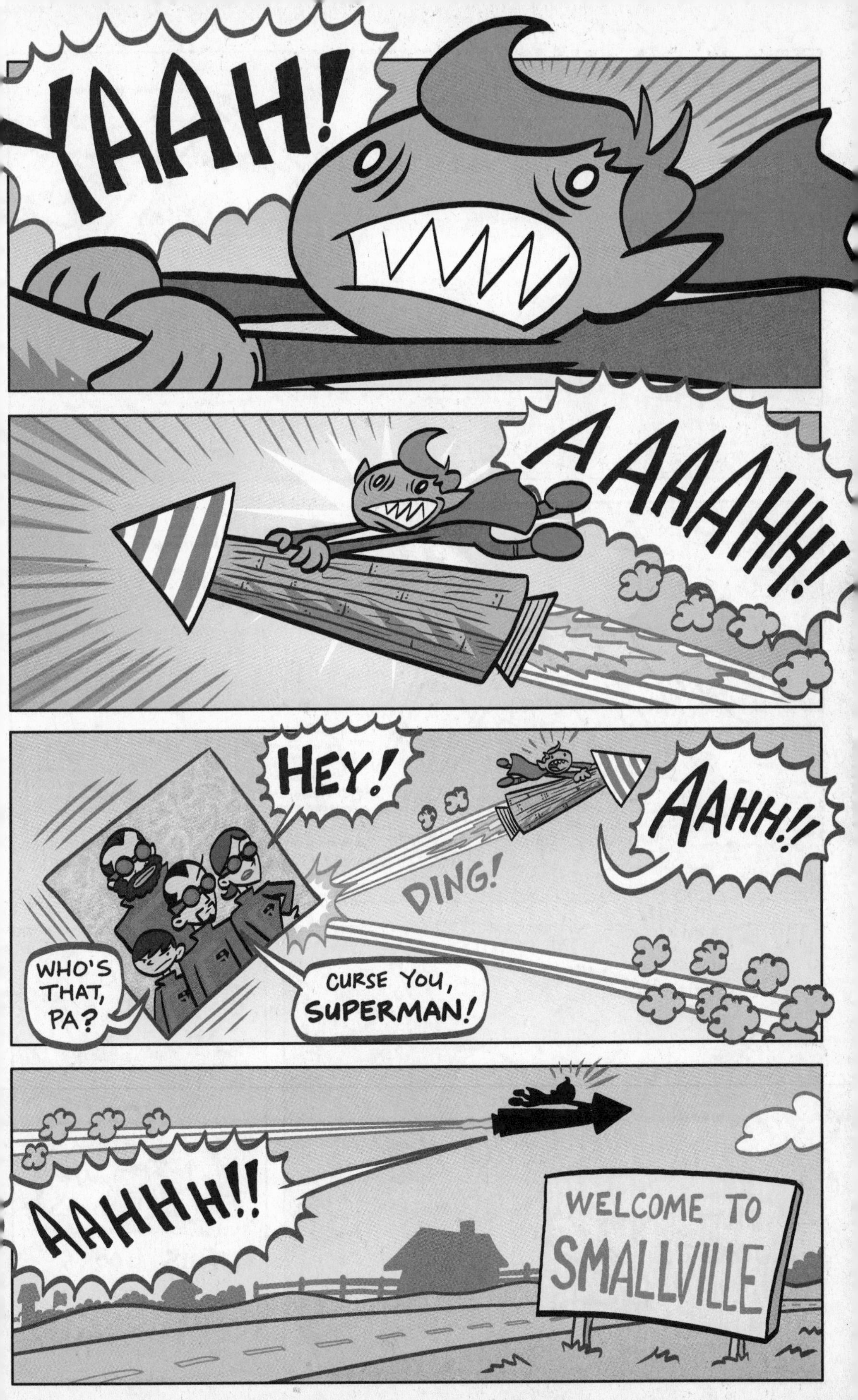
YAAH!
AAAAHH!
HEY!
AAHH!!
DING!
WHO'S THAT, PA?
CURSE YOU, SUPERMAN!
AAHHH!!
WELCOME TO SMALLVILLE

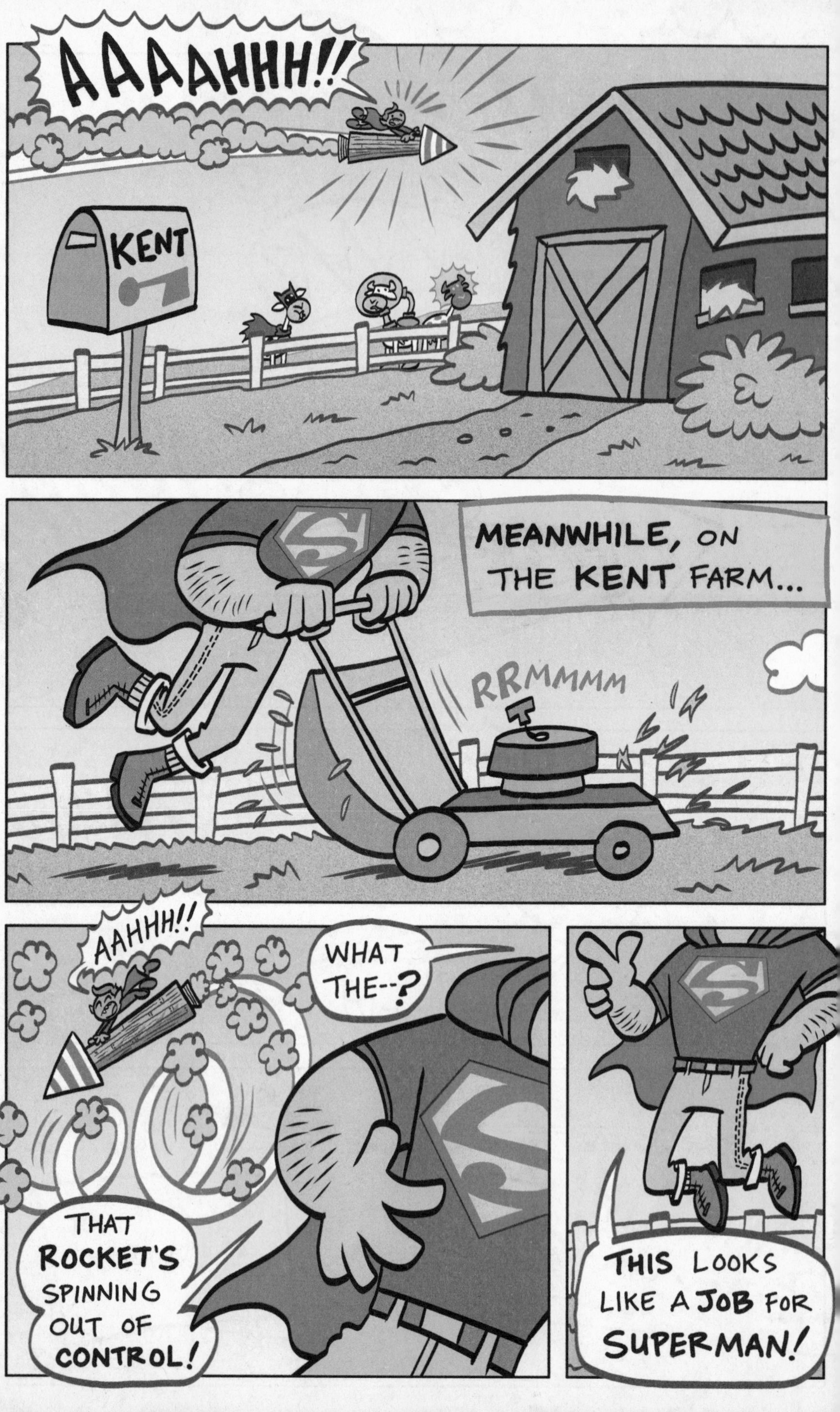
AAAAHHH!!
KENT
MEANWHILE, ON THE KENT FARM...
RRMMMMM
AAHHH!!
WHAT THE--?
THAT ROCKET'S SPINNING OUT OF CONTROL!
THIS LOOKS LIKE A JOB FOR SUPERMAN!

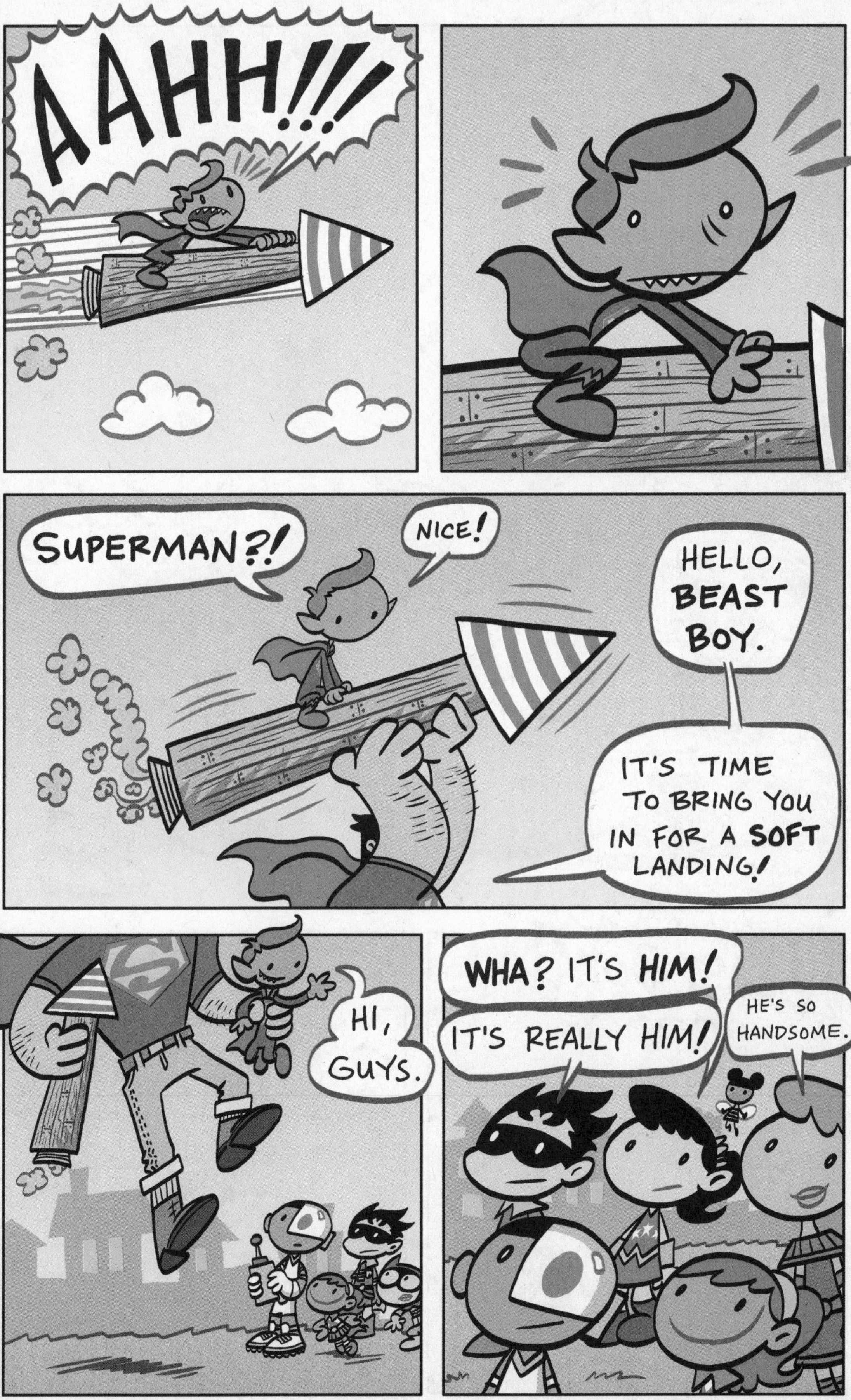
AAHH!!!
SUPERMAN?!
NICE!
HELLO, BEAST BOY.
IT'S TIME TO BRING YOU IN FOR A SOFT LANDING!
HI, GUYS.
WHA? IT'S HIM!
IT'S REALLY HIM!
HE'S SO HANDSOME.

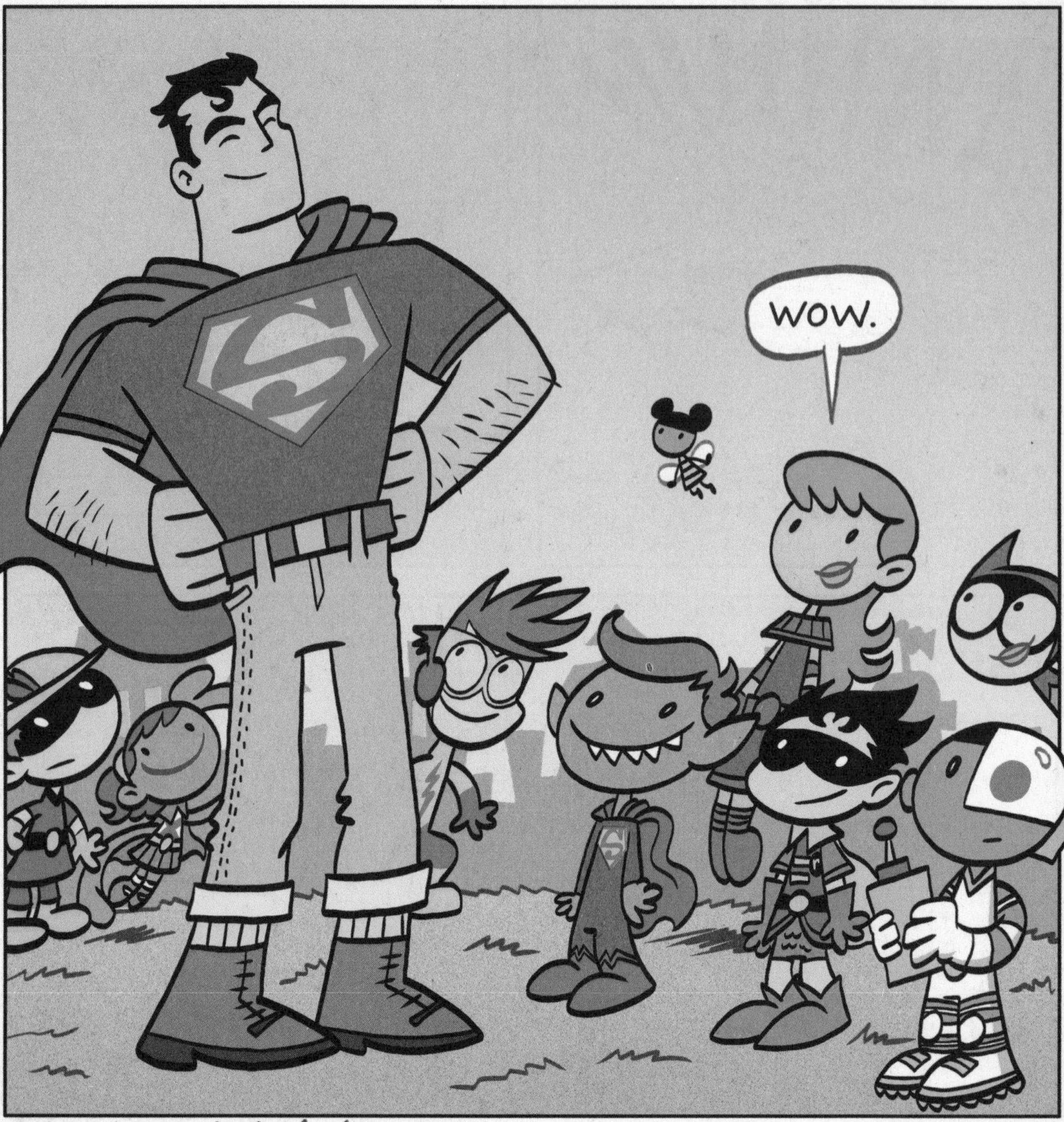
WOW.

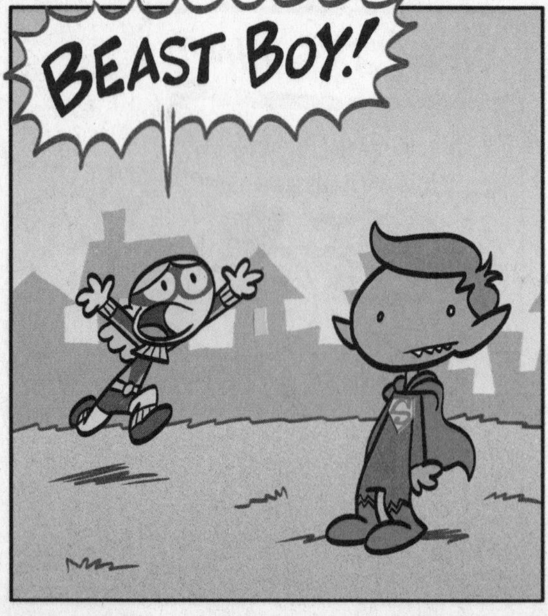
BEAST BOY!

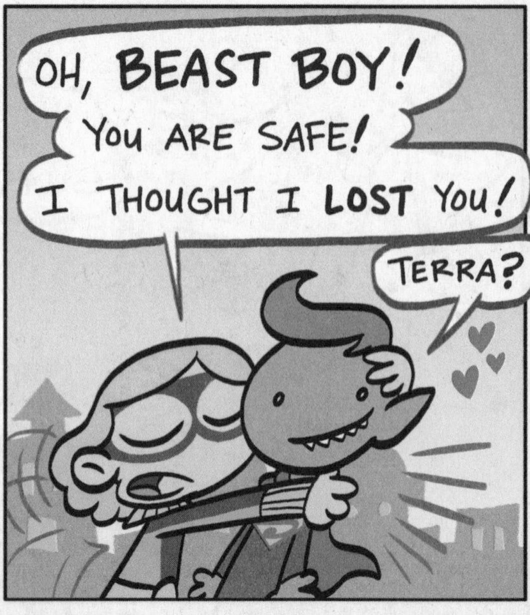
OH, BEAST BOY! YOU ARE SAFE! I THOUGHT I LOST YOU!
TERRA?

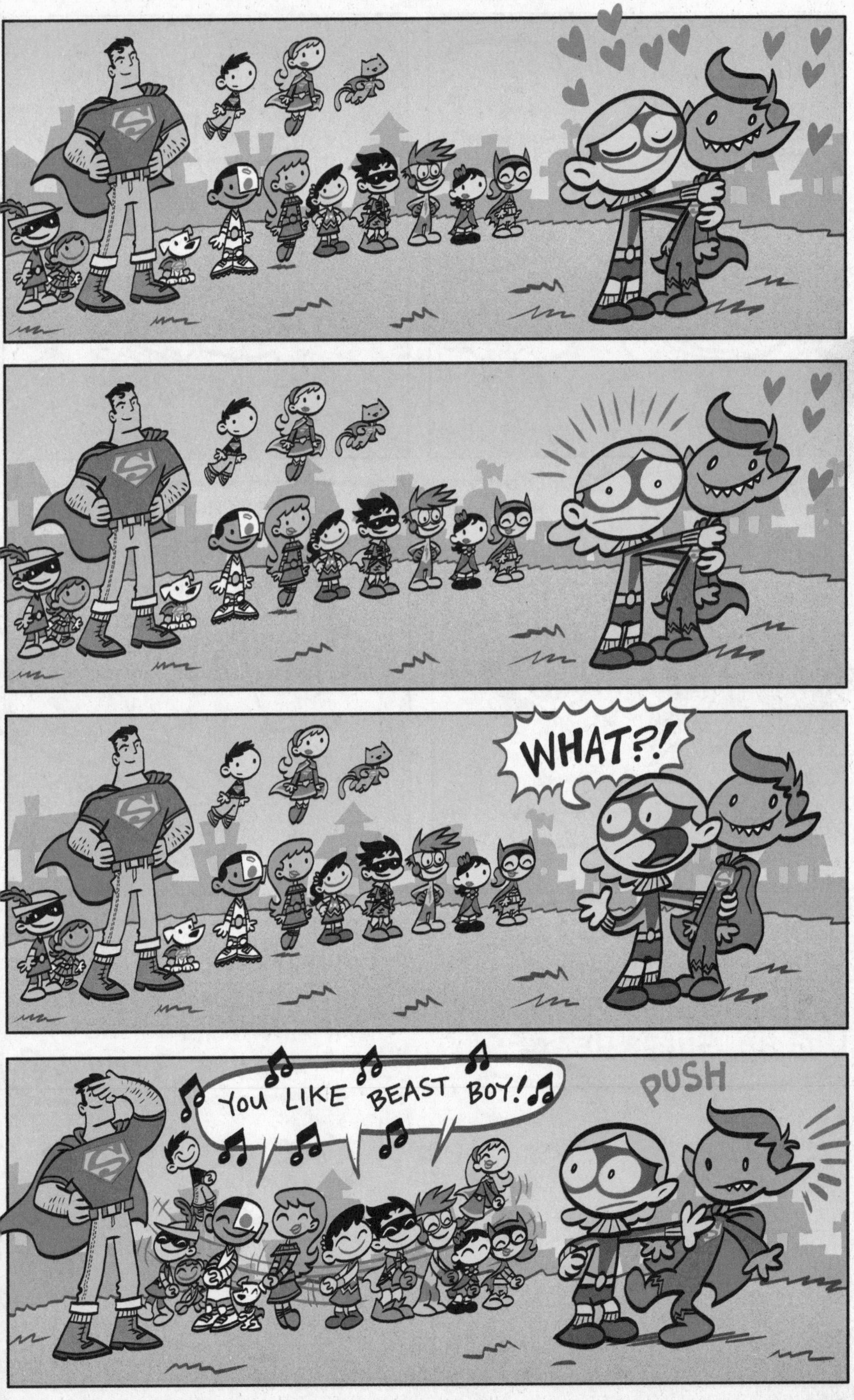
WHAT?!
YOU LIKE BEAST BOY!
PUSH

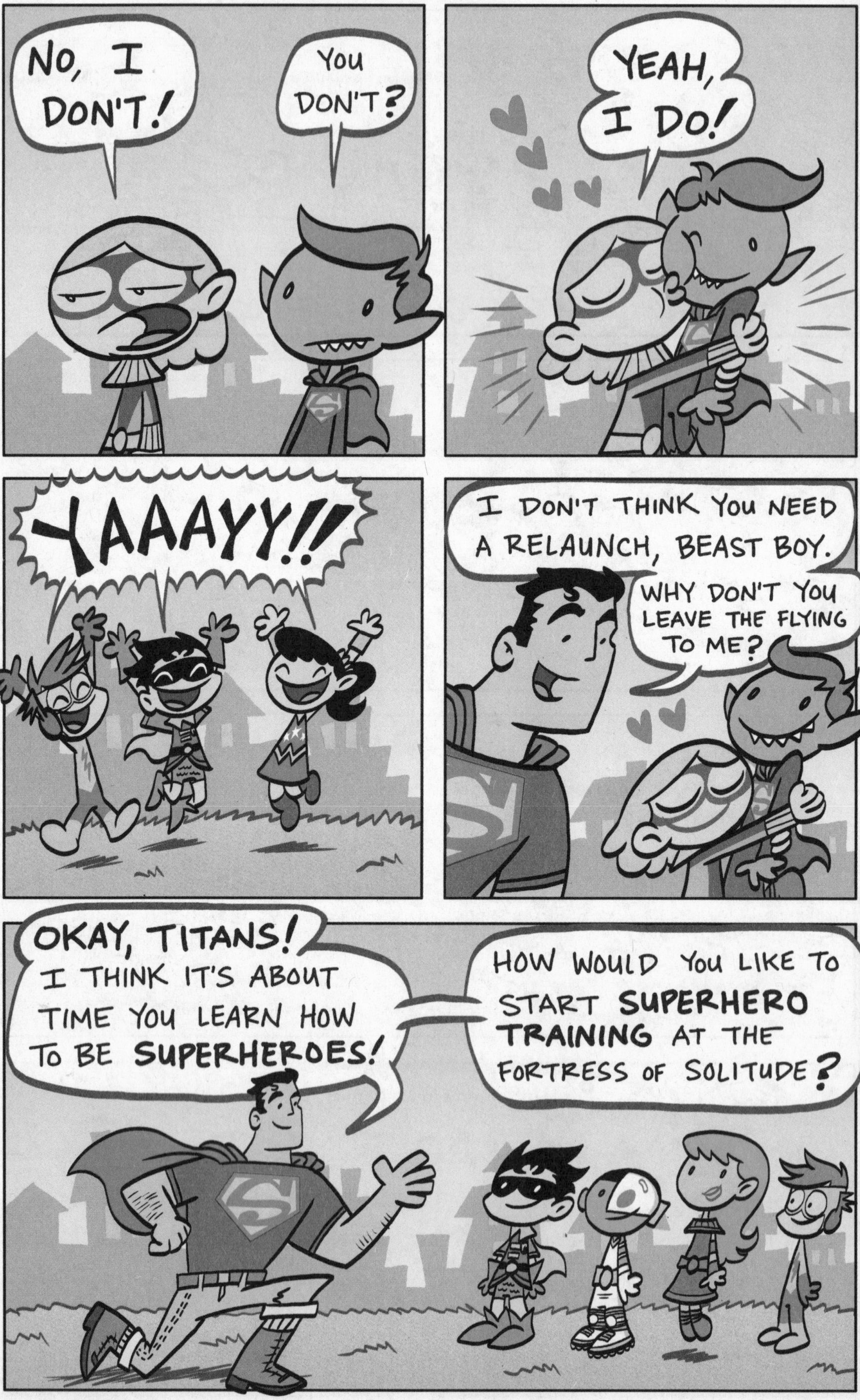

NO, I DON'T!
YOU DON'T?
YEAH, I DO!
YAAAYY!!
I DON'T THINK YOU NEED A RELAUNCH, BEAST BOY.
WHY DON'T YOU LEAVE THE FLYING TO ME?
OKAY, TITANS! I THINK IT'S ABOUT TIME YOU LEARN HOW TO BE SUPERHEROES!
HOW WOULD YOU LIKE TO START SUPERHERO TRAINING AT THE FORTRESS OF SOLITUDE?

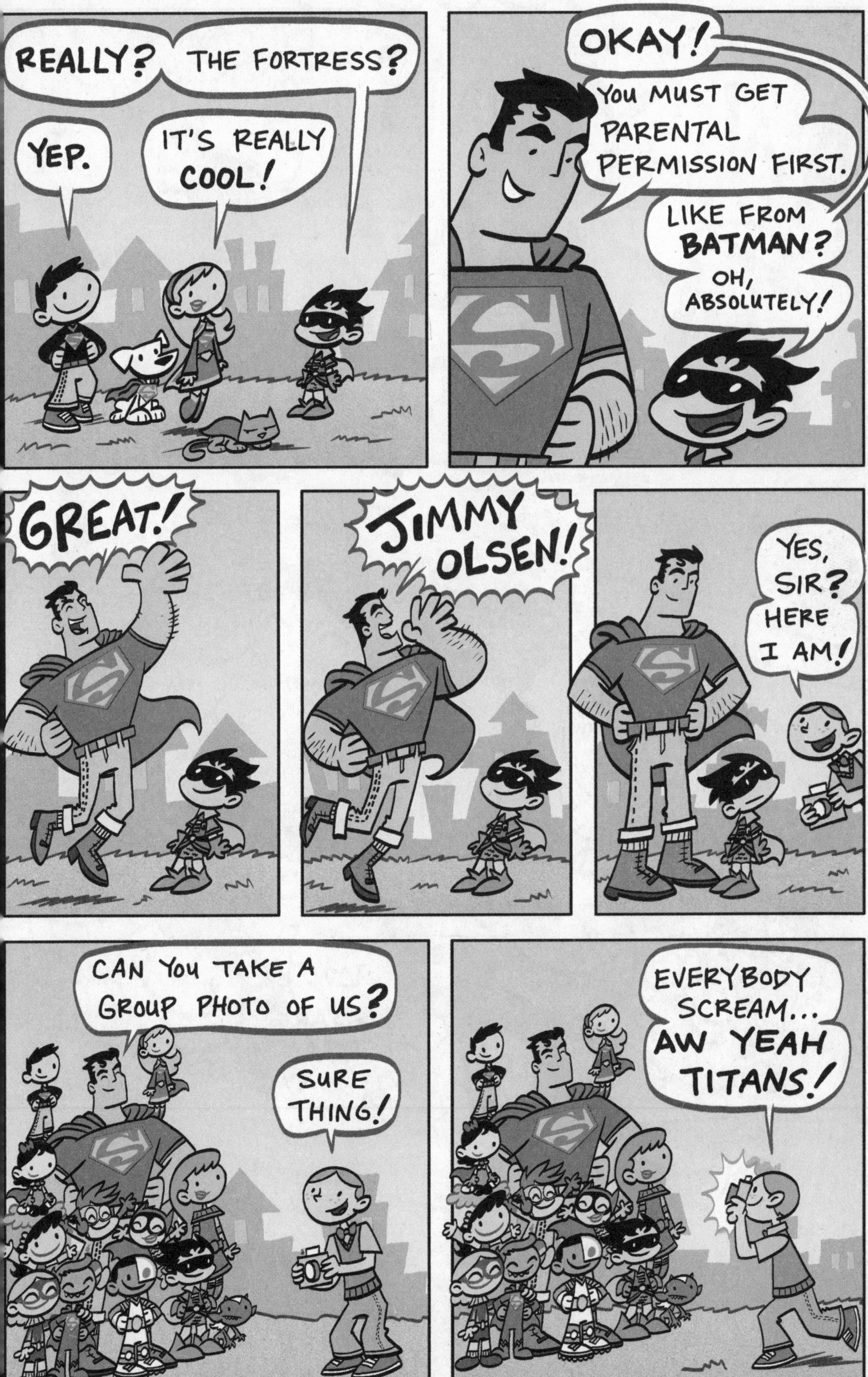
REALLY?
THE FORTRESS?
YEP.
IT'S REALLY COOL!
OKAY!
YOU MUST GET PARENTAL PERMISSION FIRST.
LIKE FROM BATMAN?
OH, ABSOLUTELY!
GREAT!
JIMMY OLSEN!
YES, SIR? HERE I AM!
CAN YOU TAKE A GROUP PHOTO OF US?
SURE THING!
EVERYBODY SCREAM... AW YEAH TITANS!

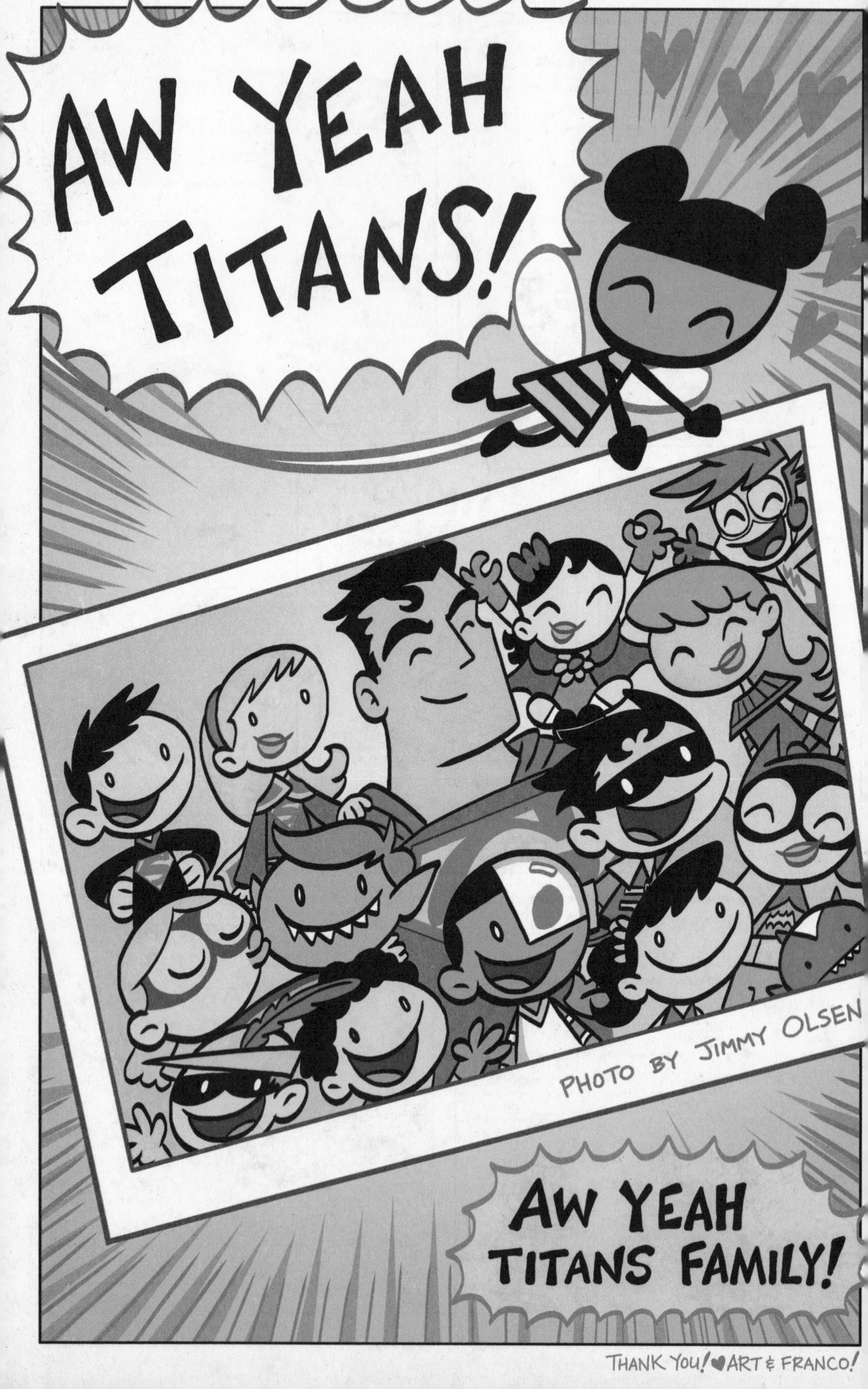

AW YEAH TITANS!
PHOTO BY JIMMY OLSEN
AW YEAH TITANS FAMILY!
THANK YOU! ART & FRANCO!